I0654358

# Sunshine and Shadows

## Another Modern Fairytale

# Books by Connie A. Walker

## Young Reader

*Timmy and the K'nick K'nocker Ring*

## Teen Fantasy

*Echoes: A Modern Fairytale*
*Dark in the Forest: Another Modern Fairytale*
*Sunshine and Shadows: Another Modern Fairytale*

## Fantasy

THE WOLKAREAN INSCRIPTION

*The Spire of Kylet*
*The Eyes of Landor*
*Triumph at Serpent's Head*

THE WOLKAREAN ENIGMA – Coming Soon

*Revelations of Riddles*
*Sorcerers in Shokareen*
*Temple of Rulianthabah*

# Sunshine and Shadows

## Another Modern Fairytale

Connie A. Walker

**Press Forward Press**
Fiction Division
5060 S 710 W
Salt Lake City, UT 84123

ISBN: 978-1-940802-21-3

LIBRARY OF CONGRESS CONTROL NUMBER:

2018959781

Cover Design by Bud Spencer, SUMO Graphics

First Edition: October 2021

Printed in the United States of America

This book is dedicated to
Marna Buffo, as promised.

# Chapter One

I'm at the head of the line.

My heart is thumping so hard I almost expect someone to tap me on the shoulder and tell me to quiet down.

When I gave my speech, I wasn't even a little bit jittery. But then I had to concentrate on remembering to smile, to speak clearly, and to pause for audience laughter at the right spots.

Now I feel as if I might faint. It's not like me to be nervous in the spotlight. Generally, I love it, but I've been on edge off and on all day.

"Angelica Prudence Powers."

That's my cue.

I calm myself by taking a deep breath before I step around the side curtain, which blocks the view of our line in the wings from the audience. I manufacture a smile and walk out onto the stage.

Although everyone was asked to save applause until the end, my boyfriend, Peter Bradley, whoops, "Way to go, Angel!"

A spontaneous burst of clapping and cheering erupts. Maybe it's just Peter and his friends, but there might be some of my friends too. I have always been popular.

I cross the wide expanse of hardwood flooring and accept my phony diploma. The official one will arrive in the mail in a couple of weeks.

While I'm shaking hands with the principal and the woman from the Board of Education, my twin sister's name comes over the loudspeaker.

"Hellenaura Dark Powers."

As always there are several audible reactions to her name, but they are not applause. They're questioning whispers and snide giggles, and I resent them all. Hellie is not responsible for her unfortunate name. That honor belongs to our well-meaning (but misguided) parents.

While I return to my seat, the students in the last row stand up and file out the door that leads backstage.

As they pass me, I am astonished to see several of my classmates sniffling, gulping, and wiping away tears.

Imagine!

Crying because they're graduating from high school.

What planet are they from?

The ceremony wraps up after Michael Vincent Zachery has accepted his rolled up piece of blank paper and has returned to his assigned seat.

There are a few more comments by the principal, and then the ceremony is over. According to tradition, we all jump up, shout, and throw our graduation caps into the air.

Turning to the side, I give Hellie a big hug. She's my identical twin, and even though we're not as close as we used to be, I love her.

"We did it!" I exclaim.

"Not a moment too soon," Hellie says. "I was about to go crazy these past few weeks."

"You're not the only one," I tell her.

We each grab a mortarboard from the floor. We have to turn in our caps and gowns. If we don't get our names crossed off the list, our diplomas will be withheld until we do.

When we get to the line backstage that's marked P - S, Hellie grumbles, "This feels like blackmail." Her voice drops into a melodramatic gangster imitation. "We've got your diploma, now hand over that cap and gown or you'll never see it alive."

I laugh.

Hellie grins.

"It is blackmail," says Courtney Bingham, my best friend, as she joins us. Apparently, she's already turned in her graduation garb. "It's the school's last chance to prove it has power and we don't." She smiles at Hellie and squeezes her hand. "Congrats, Grad!"

Then she turns and gives me a hug.

One of the things I like best about Courtney is that she's always aware of my sister and tries to include her. Most people don't.

Since Hellie and I look alike—we're both slender, 5' 7" tall, have long light brown hair, hazel eyes, and are equally attractive—I don't understand why people are drawn to me but not to her.

It's always been that way.

Hellie blames it on her unusual name, and maybe that's part of it.

More likely, though, it's because we have such different personalities.

I'm outgoing. Hellie's reserved.

I know and have interacted with over half the kids in the senior class. I got asked to all the dances, all the social gatherings, and all the holiday bashes. I dated dozens of guys. I went to almost all of the girls' slumber parties.

Hellie didn't.

That doesn't mean Hellie has been anonymous and devoid of fans. As the best female basketball player in our school district, lots of kids know and admire her. They just haven't become her friends.

Since junior high school, Hellie has only hung out with two girls: Karen Long and Nadine Middleton.

"Are you coming to the party at Jordy's house?" Courtney asks. She directs the question at both Hellie and me.

"Peter and I will probably swing by for a few minutes," I say.

"Jordy was nice enough to invite me," Hellie replies, "but I had already made plans with other friends."

"With whom?" I exclaim without thinking.

Hellie never mentioned this to me, and her friends, Karen and Nadine, are not the type of kids who throw parties.

Before Hellie can answer, though, I am literally swept off my feet by Peter Bradley.

"Hey, Gorgeous," he says, "I got tired of waiting."

Although Peter calls me Gorgeous, he's the gorgeous one.

He's not too much taller than I am, but he has a face, a physique, and a tan that would earn him millions if he decided to move to New York or California to become an actor or a model. His reddish-brown hair is thick and wavy, and he has the most amazing eyes. Sometimes they look blue, sometimes they look green, and sometimes they look gray. Tonight, he's wearing a short-sleeved sapphire-blue knit shirt, revealing that his muscles have muscles and bringing out the blue in his eyes.

Lucky for me, he likes living in Shawon, Colorado.

He's nearly four years older than I am and the best mechanic in town, specializing in motorcycles and vintage cars. He's had his own garage since he was nineteen.

"Your mom and dad are waiting out front," Peter says. "They want to congratulate you before we take off."

After Hellie and I turn in our caps and gowns, we pause long enough to make sure our names are crossed off the infamous list.

When we turn to leave, Peter links arms with me.

Then he pulls Hellie over and links arms with her too.

The first time he did that, Hellie pulled away.

Not anymore.

I think she realizes now that it's just his way. He comes from a very physically demonstrative family.

Courtney follows behind us.

"Your speech was great," Peter tells me as we walk. "It was much better than the valedictorian's remarks."

"You're such a flatterer," I say modestly. However, I agree with him.

Every year the graduating class votes for one person to represent them as a body to pay tribute to the faculty, to thank them for their guidance and support, and to say goodbye.

My class chose me.

My talk was clever, witty, and touching.

That's not conceit. That's just a fact.

I see Mom and Dad chatting with Mrs. Gilles, the choir director, over by the exit that leads from the floor of the auditorium to the parking lot.

I blink a few times as I adjust my sense of perspective.

Whenever I see my folks in a setting away from home, I always feel a bit startled. They're not like other kids' parents.

Mom is a tiny person, barely reaching 5' 2" tall and weighing less than a hundred pounds. She's beautiful and a real smart dresser. No one outside our family has seen her without makeup or with her hair mussed, EVER! As the mayor's public information officer, she's a power player in city politics. I've heard that the City Council members avoid her as much as possible, both fearing and respecting her.

Dad looks like a giant next to her. He played basketball in high school and college. He is probably a foot and a half taller than Mom. Next to his height, his most noticeable feature is his very full, very attractive moustache. He has a PhD and teaches English Literature at the state university here in Shawon.

As Peter, Hellie, and I work our way through crowds of parents, kids, and faculty, every other second, one of us mutters, "Excuse us, please."

We finally reach our folks.

Mrs. Gilles takes my hand. "Your speech was heart-warming and inspirational. You are so multitalented. I was just telling your parents how much we're going to miss your strong soprano in choir next year." She smiles warmly at me before turning back to Mom and Dad. "It was nice chatting with you, Mr. and Mrs. Powers."

She walks away without acknowledging Hellie at all. I don't care if she is a teacher. I want to kick her in the butt.

I'm the elder twin, having been born fifteen minutes before Hellie, and I feel a certain amount of responsibility and protectiveness. I don't like it when people insult her.

"You girls looked great up there," Dad says, disengaging us from Peter so he can hug us both at the same time. "I'm so proud of my girls."

"We have something for you," Mom says and hands us identically sized, identically wrapped, little gifts.

Hellie and I glance at each other.

In unison we say, "One, two, three, go!"

We rip the wrapping paper off, revealing black velveteen-covered boxes. We flip up the lids.

Inside my container is a gold heart-shaped locket with *Angel* and a rose

4

engraved on top. Hellie's locket is similar to mine, but hers is sterling silver with a butterfly above her name. (Hellie has always claimed to prefer silver jewelry. I don't know if it's true. Over the years, we've each found ways to assert our individuality. Hellie's favorite color is blue, so I tell everyone that mine is green.)

"Open them," Dad says, nodding his head at the lockets.

We do.

On the right side is my photograph and on the left is Hellie's. We're both in three-quarters profile with our faces angled toward each other. If we weren't wearing different colored dresses, you'd think we were mirror images of one person.

I don't know why the pictures touch me so deeply, but my eyes fill up with tears.

When I glance over at Hellie, I see she's reacting the same way.

We throw our arms around each other.

No matter what our differences are, no matter how much we diverge in the future, we started out together and nothing can ever change that.

Hellie and I help each other put on our new necklaces.

"They're beautiful," we tell our parents.

Peter and Courtney make appropriately complimentary remarks.

"You girls have a good time tonight," Dad says. "You only get to graduate from high school once."

"Be careful," Mom tells us, "and remember, absolutely no alcohol."

"Of course not," Hellie says.

"Naturally," I agree.

Our parents are very anti-drinking, not just anti-teenage-drinking, but anti-everyone-drinking.

They agreed to have an alcohol-free home before they got married. When they were kids, they both had traumatic experiences involving people who abused alcohol.

For Dad, it was his Uncle Norris. He was a heavy drinker and often became physically and verbally abusive when drunk. One night, he drank too much at an office Christmas party and tossed a coworker through a window. The man survived the two-story drop, but he died a few days later. Dad's uncle hardly remembered doing it. He went to prison anyway.

For Mom, it was a car accident that happened when she was eleven years old. On the way home from a picnic with her best friend's family, a drunk driver ran a red light and slammed his truck into their station wagon. Mom's best friend was killed, and Mom spent two weeks in the hospital.

If Peter Bradley had been a drinker, I'd never have dared go out with him. Many people consider him Shawon's "bad boy" even though he doesn't drink alcohol, doesn't smoke, doesn't do drugs, runs his own business, and has never been in trouble with the law. It's simply because he rides a motorcycle, wears a black leather jacket summer and winter, and chose to become a mechanic rather than a college graduate.

As the auditorium clears out, Peter and I tell my parents goodbye.

Our little group breaks up and drifts off in separate directions.

Mom and Dad head over to exchange a few words with the mayor, whose youngest daughter graduated with us tonight.

Courtney rushes off to meet the kids she promised to take over to Jordy's party in her parents' minivan.

Peter and I head for the parking lot.

And Hellie? She just disappears.

As Peter and I step outside, Hellie's friends, Nadine and Karen, drive past us. Hellie is not in the car with them.

Peter's buddies are waiting for us beside their motorcycles.

"We'll meet you at the midnight movie," Peter tells them. "We've got a couple of stops to make first."

After mumbles of "Okay" and "See you there," they peel off.

All the while, I keep my eyes moving, hoping to catch sight of Hellie.

I'm uncomfortable.

Hellie said she had made plans with friends, but I think that was just an excuse because she didn't want to go to Jordy's party. Hellie doesn't like big gatherings. She's not a party girl.

Peter hands me my pink motorcycle helmet. I put it on automatically, still looking for my sister. I can't just leave her behind if she really has nowhere to go.

It's graduation night!

She should be celebrating like the rest of us.

"Hop on, Gorgeous."

Peter is already straddling his bike, waiting for me to climb up behind him. I'm just about to do it when a red car pulls into the parking lot and stops at the curb in front of the auditorium.

I pay attention to it for two reasons.

First, it's the only car to enter the lot since Peter and I came outside. All of the other vehicles are crowded around the exits trying to leave.

Second, I've seen the car before. It belongs to an acquaintance of Hellie's. I can't remember his name right now, but this past summer he helped her find a job.

The back door of the red car opens, and a tall young man climbs out.

A moment later, Hellie emerges from one of the auditorium's side exits. When she sees the guy standing by the car, she rushes to him. At first, I think they're going to shake hands, but then he turns her hand over and kisses her palm.

Hellie looks up at him as if she's gazing into heaven.

Then they get into the car, and it eases away from the curb.

"Did that guy just kiss Hellie's palm?" Peter exclaims.

"Looked like it to me," I answer.

"Weird," Peter mumbles.

I'm having trouble processing what I've just seen.

Hellie has a secret boyfriend?

Where did he come from?

I'm sure he never went to our school. I haven't seen him around town either. I'd have noticed. He's a stunner.

"Come on, Babe," Peter says. "Let's get going."

Automatically I swing my leg over the back of the motorcycle.

Peter revs it up.

I wrap my arms around Peter's waist and rest my head on his back.

A second later, we're on our way.

# Chapter Two

Our first stop is at Peter's parents' house.

When Peter opens the front door for me and I enter, I'm showered with multi-colored confetti. Four voices start singing "Happy graduation to you" to the tune of "Happy Birthday." Peter's younger sister, Cindy, waves her arms back and forth, directing the music.

Cindy is eleven years old, developmentally delayed, and such a love. Her parents and Peter work together to pay for her to attend a special-needs program and to receive occupational and physical therapy through the university. Their medical insurance only goes so far, and the family has to come up with the rest.

Peter and Cindy look a lot alike.

They are almost male/female versions of one design.

It's not just that they both have thick reddish-brown hair and remarkable, changeable eye coloring. They also have the same angled jawline and square chin, the same straight noses with slightly flared nostrils, the same arched eyebrows, the same eyelashes that are so long they look artificial, and the same wide mouths and narrow lips.

When I look at them, I see Mrs. Bradley in the outline of their faces, the shape of their mouths, and their fair skin tones. But her brown hair doesn't have their reddish highlights and her hazel eyes don't switch colors. Although she's not as tiny as my mother, she's short, narrow, and very pretty. Peter and Cindy get their good looks from her.

Mr. Bradley, on the other hand, has a round face, a long body from shoulders to hips, and then relatively short legs. His graying black hair is receding, giving him a wide forehead, and his beetling eyebrows bush out over his dark brown eyes. He's a nice-looking man, but he's nowhere near as striking as his children.

"My present first," Cindy cries, grabbing my hand and pulling me into the living room.

When she reaches the end table between the sofa and the recliner, she picks up a flat, rectangular package that has been awkwardly wrapped in pink floral paper and covered with half a roll of cellophane tape. A bunch of red silk flowers and a big silver bow are stuck at one end.

Cindy grins as she hands it to me.

"It's almost too pretty to open," I tell her.

"I did it by myself," she boasts proudly.

I give her a big hug.

"Come on." She tows me to the couch, sits, and drags me down beside her. "Open it."

I look for a place to start. There's as much tape as paper.

Peter kneels on the floor between Cindy and me. "Do you mind if I help her?" he asks his sister.

She laughs. "She can't do it."

"No," Peter agrees. "I don't think she can, not alone."

Suddenly turning serious, Cindy looks at me and pats my hand. "It's okay to need help."

Peter pulls a pocketknife from his jeans' pocket. He slits through the tape at one end of the package.

"Thank you," I tell him.

I take hold of the object inside and slide it out of the wrapping.

It's an acrylic painting of a green and blue hummingbird hovering beside a scarlet daylily. Despite her other limitations, Cindy can paint, and she gets better with every picture she does.

"Oh, it's just beautiful," I exclaim, "and I adore hummingbirds."

"You told me," Cindy crows with delight.

"And you remembered." I give her another hug.

She loves hugs.

"Now Mom and Dad's," Cindy says. She picks up a package that's been professionally gift-wrapped in brown and gold striped paper. A one-inch-wide beige ribbon encircles the length and the width, and there is a big matching bow on top.

"You better help again," Cindy tells Peter. "Ribbons are tricky."

"You're right," Peter says. He retrieves his pocketknife and slices through the ribbon.

I peel the paper off, revealing a hardbound copy of *Agatha Christie: A Mysterious Life* by Laura Thompson.

"Thank you," I say with sincere enthusiasm. "Agatha Christie was one of my favorite authors in junior high school, and I've always been curious about her personal life." I grin. "The title says it all, doesn't it?"

"Peter told us you already have quite a collection of biographies," Mr. Bradley says. "You don't have this one, do you?"

"No. At least I didn't. I do now. Thank you. I've been looking for something new to read over the summer. This is just perfect."

# Sunshine and Shadows: Another Modern Fairytale

"Now Peter's," Cindy says impatiently. "His is biggest."

She's right about that. The package is about fourteen inches square and three inches thick.

Cindy has to use both hands to lift it.

As I take it from her, Peter sits down on the couch beside me, sandwiching me between him and his sister.

I glance at him quizzically.

Over the past few months, he's teased me about what he was going to give me for graduation. He's threatened me with a diamond ring, lacy lingerie, and a motorcycle.

I told him he couldn't give me anything that cost too much or that I'd be embarrassed to show my parents. The package weighs too much to be a ring or lingerie, and it's much too small to be a bike.

I rip off the paper and then lift the top off a cardboard box.

Inside is the most beautiful scrapbook I've ever seen.

It is cream-colored leather with gold vines and flowers in a band that goes all the way around the cover. My full name is stamped in the middle, but it's off center.

I measure it with my eyes.

I think I need to add "Bradley" after "Powers" to balance the printing.

I turn the first page, then the next, and then the next.

I can hardly believe my eyes.

Peter has made a pictorial record of our times together.

Besides many pictures of me by myself and nearly as many of us together, there are photos of places we've gone, things we've done, and people we've met. Every page has been scrapbooked beautifully, and several of them include things such as ticket stubs, pressed flowers, and printed programs.

The book is about half full.

As I flip through it, I become more and more impressed with the sense of design, the eye for color, and the general artistry exhibited. I'm certain Peter did every bit of the work himself. No one else could have included so much of his personality, his sensitivity, his values, and his sense of humor. I feel as if I'm holding a bit of his soul in my hands.

We don't have time for me to examine the entire book right now, but I have seen enough to know it is a treasure.

How Peter took so many pictures of me without my knowledge is a mystery, unless some of the calls he made on his cellphone were actually photo ops. And the pictures of us together? How did he get those? A few are selfies, but not the bulk of them. He must have arranged with his friends to take snapshots of us surreptitiously, which means he's been planning this for a long, long time.

"Do you like it?" he asks.

"Oh yes." My voice is barely a whisper.

How many guys would admit that they even know what scrapbooking is? Not very many.

Of those few, how many would take the time to learn how to do it? Probably just one, and I am dating him.

The first time I saw Peter in the woods behind our house, I knew there was something extraordinary about him, something that marked him as different from all the other guys I've ever dated.

When he said he was taking photographs of flowers for his little sister because she liked to paint, my heart just melted.

I think I fell in love with him at that very moment.

Glancing down at the book on my lap, I burst into tears.

Cindy reaches across me so she can pat Peter on the knee. "That means she likes it."

I sniffle and wipe my eyes with my fingertips.

"Thank you, Peter," I mumble. I cup his face with my hand and kiss him. I'm so lucky.

After learning the words to "Happy graduation to you" and making me a gift, Cindy somehow concluded that graduation is a special type of high school birthday.

As a result, Peter's mother comes into the living room carrying an angel food cake drizzled with dark chocolate, decorated with sliced strawberries, and topped with four lit candles.

"You have to blow them out," Cindy tells me, "but make a wish first."

Making a wish, I blow them out.

What I wish is that the knot in my stomach, which has plagued me sporadically all day, would go away.

Probably I should pass on the cake and ice cream, but Peter's mom makes the best desserts on this side of heaven, and all of them from scratch. Her angel food cake is divine and is my absolute favorite (and not because my name is Angel).

By the time I've finished indulging myself, it's Cindy's bedtime.

Peter and I each give her hugs.

While she scampers off, Peter arranges to borrow his parents' car. He doesn't like to do it, but since I have presents and leftover cake to take home, tonight he makes an exception.

"Where do you want to start?" Peter asks as we leave the house.

"I suppose we ought to stop by Jordy's first," I answer, "and at least put in an appearance. Then I'd like to walk down Main Street and check out the sales. After that, we need to swing by the all-night buffet at Sunset Diner."

"You can't possibly be hungry after downing all that cake and ice cream," Peter exclaims.

"I'm not." (Mr. Bradley was conservative when he scooped the ice

11

cream, but Cindy insisted on helping her mother cut the cake, and the pieces were HUGE.)

Still, I couldn't say no.

What's that quote by Oscar Wilde? *I can resist anything except temptation.* I know just what he means.

"My parents are volunteering at the diner until midnight," I explain to Peter after we're in the car. "I'd like to drop by and at least say *hi*."

"Whatever you want," he says. "Tonight's your night." He puts the car in gear and backs it cautiously out of the driveway and into the street. He's never completely comfortable behind the wheel. He says a car just isn't as responsive as a bike.

As we drive through town on the way to Jordy's house, the scene looks more like a busy Saturday afternoon than a Friday night. Many of the merchants have display racks and tables of merchandise set up in front of their stores, and nearly all of them offer graduation specials. Most of the restaurants, like the diner where my folks are helping out, provide a discounted menu and free soft drinks for the graduates. The movie complex in the mall runs free shows after midnight.

It's all part of a program that was initiated by the Chamber of Commerce and the school board several years ago after a tragic graduation party ended in a fire that took the lives of half a dozen kids.

Every year, about two months before school lets out, they begin a graduation night "zero accidents/zero fatalities" campaign.

At first there was some concern that the university students might think it was funny to crash the parties, sneak liquor to the teenagers, and generally tear up the town. So, the Chamber of Commerce solicited volunteers from the university student body to police the area.

There's never been a single problem.

It could only happen in a little town like Shawon, Colorado, where there is a strong sense of community.

We don't stay very long at Jordy's party. It's too crowded, and despite the parental presence and volunteer chaperones, there is still a bit of backroom drinking and smoking and doing drugs. Before we leave, we take a few minutes to walk through the entire house to see if Hellie and her unknown friends ended up here.

Wherever they are, it's not Jordy's house.

Next, Peter and I saunter down Main Street with our arms around each other's waists.

We get some strange looks from a few people who don't know us very well. All they know is "the angel" is out with "the bad boy."

Although we browse through Byrd's Gift Shop, the Main Street Drug Store, High Times Shoes, Fancy That Fashions, and the For Readers Only bookstore, we don't buy anything. The sales are nice and Peter offers to get me whatever I want, but the fact is I don't want anything.

I'm happy enough already.

When we swing by Sunset Diner, the place is a madhouse.

The volunteers rush back and forth between the kitchen and the dining room, bringing out fresh pots of coffee, getting soft drinks and glasses of water, carrying away dirty dishes, and wiping down tables while the regular staff takes orders, carries out trays of food, and keeps the buffet stocked. Mom and Dad are busy, so we just wave at them and leave.

We meet Peter's friends at the movie complex in the mall.

There are three different shows for us to choose from: a romantic comedy, a science fiction, and an action/drama. I decide on the action picture, assuming it will help keep me awake. Although it is full of gunfire, explosions, car crashes, and a blaring soundtrack, I still manage to doze through parts of it.

I am not a night person.

When it's all over, Peter takes me home.

"Good night," he tells me at the door.

We share one last, lingering kiss before I go inside.

There's a light on in the living room, but it's clear that Mom and Dad are not hovering and waiting to see what time their little girls come home and in what condition. Maybe graduating from high school marks a change in our parent/child relationships.

I take the cake into the kitchen and set it on the counter.

Then I tiptoe down the hall to the family room to see if the folks have crashed in front of the TV. They do that sometimes on the weekends. Towards daylight, they always awaken, stumble up the stairs to their room, and go to bed for a few hours of real sleep.

Not tonight.

The family room is empty.

I check the time. It's almost 3:00.

Obviously, my parents have gone to bed.

I should do the same.

I turn off the light in the living room before I head upstairs.

I assume Hellie is already home.

She and I shared a bedroom until we started junior high school, but even by then we were drifting apart. When Mom and Dad asked us if we wanted our own rooms, we jumped at the chance.

They had already planned to remodel our bathroom because the sink leaked and the bathtub was old and chipped.

Once they got started, however, they didn't seem to know when to quit. They ended up redoing the entire top floor. They enlarged the "master suite" by subsuming a small adjacent bedroom. Mom finally got the big walk-in closet she wanted, and Dad got the extra-long bathtub he wanted.

# Sunshine and Shadows: Another Modern Fairytale

They fixed up things for Hellie and me too. Now we each have a bedroom of our own with a bathroom in between that we share.

There is a door on each side of the bathroom so we can enter from our rooms, and they can be locked from either side. The knobs have a push button on the bathroom side, and the doors have a latch on the bedroom side. Hellie and I usually don't bother with either, but Mom and Dad said the locks were a precautionary measure so we couldn't burst in on each other if one of us needs a timeout and the other wants to pursue an argument.

When I get to the top of the stairs, I don't see a light at the bottom of Hellie's door, but I can hear one of David Garrett's albums playing softly in the background.

David Garrett is a German/American violinist that Hellie is absolutely obsessed with. She has all of his CDs and all of his DVDs that will play on American-made DVD players (and one that won't). When she's on her computer, she always opens two windows: one to work in and the other so she can listen to David Garrett on YouTube at the same time.

He's good-looking, I'll admit that, and he plays the violin with gusto, but obsession is obsession, and Hellie's got it bad.

At the top of her bucket list is to see David Garrett live in concert, even if she has to go to Europe to do it.

Myself, I prefer show tunes. A lot of great songs have been written for stage plays, movies, and animated features. I love to sing along.

I knock on Hellie's bedroom door.

"Hellie, are you awake?"

No answer.

I knock again.

"Hellie?"

I open the door and peer in.

Her CD player is going.

Her bed is turned down.

She's not here.

My first thought is that she must be in the bathroom, but the door is ajar and the light is off.

"Hellie?"

I push the bathroom door the rest of the way open, flip the light switch, and look around. I even check inside the shower.

She's not here.

In my mind I see her getting into the red car with that stranger.

Maybe he's some kind of psycho. Watching him kiss her palm gave me the creeps. Even though he got out of a familiar looking automobile, that doesn't automatically mean he's someone to be trusted.

Maybe the driver wasn't even the guy who helped Hellie get the job last summer.

Maybe crooks stole the car, and now they have Hellie at their mercy.

Maybe I've had premonitions that something bad was going to happen to her. It's been documented that some twins have that kind of connection.

Maybe that's why I've been jittery all day.

Maybe I should wake up Mom and Dad.

Still pondering, I go through the bathroom into my bedroom so I can put my purse and presents on my desk.

I hear a strange humming sound.

I turn to face the bathroom and see a brief flash of light.

I drop everything and run back into Hellie's room.

Her closet doors swing open.

Hellie walks out smiling and carrying a bouquet of flowers.

"What were you doing in the closet?" I ask her.

# Chapter Three

Hellie stops short and stares at me as if I just slapped her or something. "What are you doing in my room?" she demands.

"I heard a strange sound and saw a flash of light. I came to investigate. My turn: why were you in the closet?"

"I just got back from being with my friends Karissa Day and Neeve Maynard. They had a little get together for me to celebrate graduation. My turn: why are you spying on me?"

My mind is starting to function again. It sort of hiccupped when I saw Hellie step out of her closet.

Now that I can take in the whole picture, my stomach feels as if I'm on an elevator that has just lost its brakes and I'm plummeting to my death.

Hellie is not wearing the clothes she wore to graduation. She's in a pale peach, floor-length, ruffled prom dress. Her hair is in curls on top of her head, and she's wearing makeup—not just a little eye shadow and blush, but the works. She looks like she just came back from Cinderella's ball.

I'm so stunned I can't think.

The strange hum sounds again and a flash of light follows.

A girl I've never seen before steps out of nothingness and into the room. She looks like a princess straight out of a fairytale. She is delicate, fragile, and ephemeral. Her face is so lovely I have to concentrate to focus on individual features. She has big, pale green eyes, a small nose, and a Cupid's bow mouth. Her head is crowned with a mass of short, strawberry blond curls. Like Hellie, she is wearing a floor-length gown. Hers is butter-cream yellow.

"Hellie, you forgot your—." She cuts herself off. Her eyes bulge as she stares at me first, then at Hellie, and then at me again.

"Put her in a time bubble," the girl says in one quick gasp. "I'll go get Jerrin."

She disappears.

The next thing I know I'm somewhere else.

I'm sitting in a chair next to the door of a small office. Along the right side and across the back of the room are several bookcases that are crammed full of everything from skinny little pamphlets to six-inch-thick tomes. A desk faces the wall on the left, and in front of it is a leather swivel chair on casters.

Perched on the seat, facing me, is an old man with white hair, a neatly trimmed white moustache, and a face full of wrinkles. He is wearing a long black and purple robe (in design, it's much like our graduation gowns). On his head is a baggy black cap that hangs to one side like an oversized beret.

He points his finger at me.

"What is your name?" he snaps.

"Angelica Prudence Powers," I answer automatically.

"How old are you?"

"Eighteen," I say.

He stares at me, peering deeply into my eyes. As I stare back at him, I feel strange. I have weird sensations in my head, and I have trouble thinking.

*He's trying to hypnotize me!*

I am half afraid and half angry.

"What are your talents?" he asks.

Anger wins.

"None of your business," I retort, glaring at him. "Who are you? Where am I? Why am I here?"

"My name is Cushing. You are in the country of Auravale on the planet Panelda, and you are in my office to tell me what I want to know."

Something is wrong with his answer, but I don't know what.

My thoughts are fuzzy.

*He's not just hypnotizing me*, I tell myself. *He's trying to take control of my mind. But that's impossible!*

"What are your talents?" he demands again.

I glower at him.

He stares into my eyes. "Answer me!"

I try to turn away, but I'm mesmerized, frozen in place.

With great difficulty, I manage to push my eyelids closed.

Some of the wooziness disappears.

I hear his chair slide across the floor towards me.

"What are your talents?" he repeats.

"No!" I shriek while keeping my eyes tightly closed. "You tell me who you are, where I am, how I got here, and why you think you have the right to ask me anything."

The old man takes my face between gnarled hands.

That does it!

By touching me, he has crossed the line.

I open my eyes, glare at him, and start screaming.

"Help! I've been kidnapped. Please. Can anyone hear me! I've been kidnapped. My name is Angel Powers. Call the police. I don't know where I am. I don't know who has me. Call 911."

Cushing drops his hands as if he's been burned. He shoves with his feet and sends his chair rolling backwards until he slams into his desk.

I take advantage of the moment to grab a cane that's been leaning against the desk and to barricade myself behind a couple of chairs. I hold the cane in front of me like a sword.

I resume yelling. "Help! Can anyone hear me! I've been kidnapped."

Cushing presses back in his chair. The expression on his face is one of astonished horror.

He looks beyond me.

An accomplice?

I turn my head to see who or what he's gazing at.

A young man stands in the doorway.

"You'd better go ask His Majesty how aggressive he wants me to get," the old man says. "Tell him she's a resister."

"Yes, sir," the guy says. "I'll be right back."

Poof! He vanishes into thin air.

People can't do that.

Intellectually, I know I'm dreaming or hallucinating.

Emotionally, I'm terrified.

It's been a long day and night.

I was overly tired when Peter brought me home, and now I'm in an altered state, but I don't know if this is a nightmare or a delusion.

I concentrate on breathing.

Inhale. Exhale.

In. Out.

In. Out.

Relax.

Breathe.

I yawn.

My muscles go limp.

I hear a voice.

"Angel," Hellie calls. "Why are you asleep on my bed?"

"What?" I ask groggily.

"Why are you asleep on my bed?"

Shakily, I sit up and glance around.

What am I doing in Hellie's bedroom?

Then I remember seeing her walk out of her closet in a floor-length prom dress

That wasn't a dream.

But now she's wearing the slacks and shirt she had on under her graduation gown.

"You've changed your clothes again!" I say, pointing at her accusingly.

"What do you mean I've changed my clothes?"

"You know what I mean!"

I scramble up, lunge over to her closet, and throw open the double doors. If I confront her with the peach-colored gown, she won't be able to deny the truth and make me feel like I've gone crazy.

Where is it?

I shove hangers back and forth, looking for a new garment bag, but all I find are the three that are supposed to be there. I unzip the bags and check the contents.

The first one contains her nice black and gray herringbone dress coat. Behind it is the pink knee-length dress she wore to the Sweetheart Ball with Gary Butler last year.

In the next bag is the dainty green and yellow floral bridesmaid's gown from our cousin Jeanine's wedding (I have one just like it), plus two dry-clean-only church dresses.

The last bag holds the navy blue suit she wore to Grandma Powers' funeral four years ago. (Mine is the same style but in a bluish gray color. They don't fit anymore, but neither one of us can bear to give them away.)

"Angel, are you all right?" Hellie asks. She sits down on the edge of her bed and watches me. "What are you looking for?"

I stand with my fists on my hips and glare at her.

She gazes back with a puzzled expression on her face.

After a few minutes, I begin to feel a bit foolish.

When exactly did I fall asleep?

Was I dreaming when I saw Hellie come out of the closet?

I must have been.

I must have fallen asleep right after I entered her room.

I was tired enough.

Then Hellie called my name, and I woke up.

I sigh and sit down beside her.

I gaze off into the distance.

"When I got back from the midnight movie and you weren't here, I was worried. I must have sat down on your bed to wait for you and then fallen asleep. I thought I saw you walk out of your closet wearing a formal. A moment later, a fairytale girl materialized in the room and I was magically transported somewhere else."

Hellie grins at me. "You must have been exhausted if you had a fantasy dream."

"It's not funny, Hellie." I snap, near tears. "The dream might sound amusing to you, but it wasn't to me. I was really scared."

"I'm sorry, Angel. Why don't you tell me about it?"

"All right." I hardly ever have nightmares. I scrunch up my face as if it'll help me remember.

"It started with you coming out of your closet wearing a peach evening gown and looking like you just got home from Cinderella's ball. Then this really cute fairytale girl appeared out of nowhere. Suddenly I was in an unfamiliar room filled with lots of books. A weird old man kept asking me questions, but I didn't understand what he wanted me to tell him.

"Then I realized he must have kidnapped me, and I couldn't escape because I had no idea where I was. I was scared and angry. I started screaming for help. The old man asked some guy to find out how aggressive he should get with me. The guy disappeared, and then I was really terrified because I knew that was impossible." I sigh, and my lips start trembling. "It sounds crazy, doesn't it?"

"Most dreams do." Hellie puts her arms around me. "I've stopped having my recurring nightmares, but I remember how frightening they were. I wish I had a voice like yours, then I could sing you to sleep like you did for me."

I return her hug but then pull away as a new thought occurs to me.

"When I got home, you really weren't here, were you?"

"No," she answers. "I just got in a few minutes ago. My turn: did you intend to fall asleep in my room?"

"No," I say. "I could hear a David Garrett CD playing. I wanted to make sure you were home and to tell you good night. When I knocked and you didn't answer your door, I was worried, so I came inside. I must have dozed right off. My turn: who—?" I stop myself. I look at her suspiciously, "If I got home before you did, who turned on your CD player?"

She looks as puzzled as I feel.

David Garrett is still making music in the background.

Hellie reaches for the CD player on her nightstand. She pushes a button on top. When the little door slides open, there's no disc inside.

She shakes her head, gets to her feet, and crosses the room. Sitting down at her desk, she wakes up her computer.

When the screen comes on, it's clear that she left Spotify looping a David Garrett playlist. She quits Spotify and puts her computer back to sleep.

"Sorry," she says, still sitting at her desk. She leans back in the chair. "Go on. You were going to ask me something before we got distracted by the music."

"Oh, yeah. Who was the guy in the red car?"

For a moment I think she's flustered, but she sounds normal when she answers me.

"His name is Kaden Deke Katsenevas. He's a friend of Neeve Maynard's. You might remember Neeve from school. He's the violin soloist who played at the Spring Concerts. He helped me get my job at Quick Fix Repair Shop last summer. Kaden is visiting Neeve for a couple of weeks, and they suggested we double date as a way of celebrating graduation. My turn: you said you were worried about me. Why? You heard me tell Courtney that I was going out with friends."

Suddenly it hits me how truly far apart we've grown.

A few of years ago, we told each other everything. Back then she never would have gone out with people I didn't know without sharing every little detail about them with me first. I'll bet it never even occurred to her to confide in me tonight.

Maybe she thought I wouldn't be interested.

I want to cry.

I've lost something precious, and I didn't even notice it happening.

Keeping my voice steady, I answer her question. "I saw you get into a car with a stranger. I watched for you all evening, but you weren't at Jordy's party, or at Sunset Diner, or at the movie theater. When I got home and you weren't here, I was afraid something bad had happened to you."

Hellie leaves her desk, comes and sits beside me, and puts her arms around me again.

I lay my head on her shoulder.

"I'm sorry, Angel," she says. "I just didn't think. You can take as many turns as you want. Ask me anything you want to know."

# Chapter Four

I sniffle back the tears that want to flow.

"How long have you known this guy Kaden?" I ask.

"I met him last summer in the woods," Hellie answers. "He was looking for something a friend had misplaced. We got talking and he mentioned knowing Neeve Maynard. Of course, I remembered Neeve because it was his performance on the violin that got me interested in David Garrett's music. The four of us—Kaden, Neeve, Neeve's girlfriend, and I—had an impromptu picnic in the woods once. They showed up with food and invited me to join them."

"You never went on a real date with Kaden before tonight?" I ask.

"No," Hellie says a little sadly. "He doesn't live in Colorado. I saw him occasionally over the summer, and we talked about going out, but something always got in the way. Then school started again. He's studying medicine, and his schedule is grueling, plus he has complex family obligations. All we've been able to do is talk or text on the phone."

"What was that hand-kissing about?"

Hellie laughs. "You saw that? It's a custom where he's from. The first time he kissed my hand, I didn't know if I should slap him or kiss his hand in return."

"So," I ask, "where does he come from? I didn't think hand-kissing was a custom anywhere anymore."

"Somewhere over seas," Hellie answers with a shrug. "It's one of those little countries no one has ever heard of."

"Are you going to see him again?" I ask.

"Yes, tomorrow. We're going to get something to eat, and then we're going to a movie at the mall. He's coming over at 5:30 so he can meet Mom and Dad—and you, too, if you're here."

I exhale loudly through my mouth. "Why haven't you ever mentioned him before?" I'm working hard not to let the hurt sound in my voice.

"It was a little bit like you and Peter Bradley," Hellie says. "Kaden is older than I am, and I wasn't sure Mom and Dad would approve. Besides, he doesn't live here. Last fall, he said he'd keep in touch, but that's easier said than done. It didn't seem worth the trouble if I was never going to see him again."

I sense she's not telling me the whole story, but then, when she found out about Peter Bradley and me, I didn't tell her everything either.

Peter and I had been seeing each other secretly for months and would have continued on that way indefinitely if Courtney's little brother hadn't spied on us and forced us to go public.

Really, though, Hellie can't compare her situation with Kaden to my situation with Peter.

I love my parents, I truly do, but they are intellectual and educational snobs. Dad has his PhD in English literature. Mom has a BA in Media and Communications and is about halfway through her Masters of Public Administration degree, which she is taking online.

As soon as they learn Kaden is a medical student, all other questions about him will diminish in importance.

Not so with Peter. Peter dropped out of college before he completed his junior year. Even his own parents thought he had thrown away his future. They had cosigned on a loan for him to start a garage, but they thought he would do a little repair work on cars and motorcycles over the weekends so he could make his loan payment and save for his tuition and books. They didn't realize Peter had other plans.

I yawn and about crack my jaw bones.

"We probably ought to go to bed," Hellie says.

"I suppose you're right, but I want to finish talking about this tomorrow. Okay? I've still got questions."

"I'll answer them," Hellie says. "It's still your turn."

I go through the bathroom to my room and change out of my clothes and into my baby doll pajamas.

While I wash my face and brush my teeth, I think about Peter.

He has had to work very hard to win Mom and Dad's approval. Luckily, he's smart, well read, up on current events, and willing to discuss politics, literature, and philosophy with my folks. Also, he is not afraid to admit it when he doesn't know something.

Hellie comes into the bathroom to go through her nightly routine. We chat a while longer and then head for our rooms.

Before I turn out the light, I caress the cover of the amazing scrapbook Peter made for me. I just love it. I can hardly wait until I have time to sit down and go through the entire thing, page by page, studying and appreciating each masterpiece.

I love Peter. I can't imagine life without him, and to my immense relief, he can't imagine life without me.

Just as I'm about to nod off, a voice in the back of my mind says, *But Peter has secrets.* I try to rouse enough to question where that thought came from, but I can't.

I drift into an uneasy sleep.

When I wake up Saturday morning, the first thing I remember is thinking that Peter has secrets. I'm puzzled. Peter and I have been dating for a little over a year, and I can't recall a single interaction that made me question his sincerity, his honesty, or his openness.

Yet, I know enough about psychology to realize something planted that seed of doubt in my unconsciousness and something last night triggered my mind into recognizing it.

But what?

"Hey, sleepyhead," Hellie calls from the doorway of the bathroom, "it's going on 11:00. Get up. I've got money in my purse, and I want to go spend it."

I jump out of bed.

The last thing Hellie and I did before saying goodnight was to plan on going to the mall for lunch and then doing some shopping. We each got a graduation card and $50 from Grandma Dark. She lives in Pullman, Washington, and visits us at least once a year.

"Give me half an hour," I say.

"All right," Hellie says, "but I've got dibs on the car. If I have to go without you, I will."

"You'd better not," I tell her.

She holds out her keys and jangles them at me before she leaves, calling over her shoulder, "Thirty minutes."

Last year our folks got us a car to share. At first, we tried to set up some kind of schedule for using it, but things always seemed to change for one of us and we'd end up arguing about who needed the car the most.

Finally, Dad said, "Work something out, or I'll sell the damned thing."

Hellie and I decided that the rule had to be "first come, first served." So far, it's worked.

No time for a shower this morning!

I grab the first pair of jeans I see and my favorite red t-shirt. I don't bother making my bed. As soon as I'm dressed, I brush my teeth, do my hair and makeup, and dash down the stairs. It only took 26 minutes. Hellie is waiting in the kitchen beside the door to the garage, making a big deal of watching the time.

"Ready to go?" I ask.

"Ready and waiting," she says.

We have lunch in the food court, and then for the next couple of hours we wander around the mall looking in display windows but not seeing anything worth breaking a fifty-dollar bill for.

I don't ask her any more questions about Kaden. I'll meet him tonight. That might answer most of what I want to know.

As the afternoon progresses, my chest and my stomach feel tight and some of last night's tension returns. I wonder now if the discomfort I felt yesterday might have been caused by my unconsciousness trying to bring the question of Peter's secrets into my awareness.

I start replaying the evening in my mind, trying to isolate an incident that could have caused my doubts. Guilt gnaws at me. I feel disloyal just having these thoughts.

Nevertheless, I don't have anything else to be jittery about. Graduation is over, the choir isn't singing in church tomorrow, and I don't start work at *The Shawon Gazette* until Wednesday.

Yet, I feel as if I'm about to explode.

Suddenly Hellie stops. "I'm going to dash into the music store for just a minute. I want to check out a couple of CDs."

I try not to look too pleased, but a few minutes alone might be just what I need.

"All right," I say. "I'd like to see if Perry's has gotten their new bathing suits in yet."

Picking something up at Perry's Department Store is always calming, and I hate to go home empty-handed.

Hellie frowns at me. "If you start trying on bathing suits, you'll keep going until the store closes tonight."

"Ha, ha," I say without humor. Hellie is more likely to lose track of time looking through CDs than I am looking through the swimwear. There are dozens more albums to consider than there are bathing suits.

"I'm serious, Angel," Hellie says, jamming her fists on her hips. "I have a date at 5:30. I don't want to be late."

"Well, I don't want to stand around watching you look at CDs," I tell her.

Her expression changes, and I sense she's about to suggest that we forget it and leave now. However, since I've already mentioned Perry's, I feel like I simply can't go home yet.

"Let me just take a quick look," I tell her. "I can come back tomorrow if I see anything I want."

Hellie pulls her cellphone from the pocket of her jeans. "Let's set our alarms for half an hour. When they go off, we'll both head back to the car. Okay?"

"Fine."

We take off in separate directions.

As I walk away, I try not to feel resentful that Hellie has a date tonight and I don't.

Early this morning, just a few hours after telling me goodnight, Peter

# Sunshine and Shadows: Another Modern Fairytale

Bradley, his sister, and his parents left for Oskaloosa, Kansas, to attend a family reunion. A month ago, they invited me to go along.

I thought Peter and I had been going together long enough for it to be a reasonable suggestion and I was really excited about the possibility of going out of town for a few days. Besides, I thought it would ease the transition from school to workforce.

My folks said: *Absolutely not!*

Since I am eighteen years old and a high school graduate, I suppose I could have asserted my legal rights as an adult to make my own decision. The problem is that I want to start college in the fall, and I'm not ready to move out of the house and live on my own.

I figured it wasn't worth fighting over.

When I get to the Teen Shop in the corner of the women's clothing department at Perry's, I walk right past the bathing suits. There is no sense looking if there is no time to try anything on. Instead, I head for accessories so I can check out the jewelry, cosmetics, purses, hats, belts, umbrellas, and such.

The cash register for this section is in the middle of a "U" shaped glass counter. Inside the display cases are watches, bracelets, necklaces, and rings in either sterling silver or 24 carat gold.

The costume jewelry is hung on racks. I don't bother looking at it. I don't need any more fake jewelry and I can't afford the good stuff.

The same thing is true of the hats and purses—too expensive or too cheap looking.

On the left arm of the glass counter are a couple of interesting trays. When I get closer, I realize one tray holds vividly colored scarves and the other one is full of delicate, lacey handkerchiefs, all neatly folded and lined up in three overlapping rows.

Perfect.

They're small and pretty and portable.

I finger the hankies. I can picture a woman carrying one of these to a wedding or some other fancy affair, a place where she might need to dab at her eyes but not blow her nose. The cloth is way too flimsy for nose blowing. Personally, I prefer tissues to handkerchiefs, anyway, since you don't have to launder them.

For my purposes, the scarves are a better choice.

The one I pick out is silk with a geometric pattern in red, white, and blue. It makes me feel patriotic.

The sales clerk is busy waiting on another customer, so I take the scarf from the tray, refold it so the price tag is hidden on the inside, and tie it around my neck.

My movements are casual—nice and slow—so I don't draw attention to what I'm doing. Whoever is monitoring the security cameras probably doesn't spend much time focused on customers who are looking at items this inexpensive unless they do something conspicuous.

When the clerk glances my way, I'm holding a different scarf up to my face and looking at myself in a mirror that's standing on the counter. I smile at her, shake my head, and then refold the second scarf and return it to the tray.

The clerk smiles back.

As I start to leave, she greets a new customer without giving me a second thought.

When I walk out of the store, I'm still wearing the red, white, and blue patriotic scarf.

No one stops me.

During the time since I developed this entertaining little habit back in junior high school, no one has ever even given me a suspicious look.

I am not a kleptomaniac.

I know the difference between kleptomania and shoplifting.

Kleptomania is a psychological disorder.

People who have it simply can't resist the urge to steal. They know what they're doing is wrong, but they can't help themselves. If they try to ignore their impulses, they experience a sense of anxiety that doesn't go away until they take something. Then they go through a period of relief, followed later by feelings of guilt. They'll steal from stores, from family and friends, and even from churches. What they steal isn't important. Frequently they take things they don't even want and can't use.

Me?

I shoplift because it's fun.

I never take anything I don't want—like this scarf. It looks good with the red t-shirt, blue jeans, and white sneakers I'm wearing. In the future anytime I wear this combination, I'll probably include the scarf so I can re-experience the momentary thrill I got when I took it.

Stealing is an adventure, and the exhilaration has actually increased since I left the store.

No letdown, no sense of relief, and no guilt for me!

I suppose that means I'm a bad person.

*Angelica, the fallen angel!*

The thought makes me smile.

Of course, no one knows about my daring little hobby except for me—although sometimes I think Hellie suspects that I have a dark side. However, even though she might toy with the idea, I don't think she really believes it. She often calls me Miss Goodie Two Shoes (referring to some obscure fairytale that only she has ever read).

It's the name.

Because I'm called Angel (short for Angelica), everyone expects me to be perfect.

They expect me to be a loving person, to have a cheerful disposition, and to make good choices regardless of the circumstances.

They expect me to be kind and generous and thoughtful, disregarding my needs in favor of everyone else's.

They expect me to show compassion and forgiveness regardless of how others treat me, even when they are mean and hateful.

They expect me to engage in pious activities, to go to church regularly, and to smile until my jaws ache.

I hate it.

Most of the time I try to live up to the expectations, but sometimes I feel like buying some dynamite and blowing up a couple of buildings (and possibly a dozen or so people, but only if I get to select them in advance.)

However, instead of doing anything that damages people or property, I go window-shopping, and if the opportunity arises, I take home a souvenir with a five-finger discount.

I blame it all on my parents.

For two smart people, they have made some ridiculously stupid decisions—like naming their two defenseless baby daughters Angelica and Hellenaura.

I realize they were trying to save us from the overt, we're-joined-at-the-hip, rhyming names: Sandy and Randy, Jeri and Terri, Karen and Maren. (Or my personal favorites from the other end of the spectrum: Patty and Ratty, Pinky and Stinky, Kitty and Zitty.)

Mom and Dad's solution was to name us after our great-grandmothers, which wouldn't have been a bad idea if the women had been blessed with normal names.

Dad's grandmothers (for whom I'm named) were Angelica and Prudence. It would be hard to come up with a worse goody-goody combination than that.

Mom's grandmothers (for whom Hellie is named) were Helena and Aura. For some ridiculous reason, our folks combined the two names into one: Hellenaura (pronounced HEL LEN nor ah). Since they couldn't come up with a middle name to go with their four-syllable creation, they decided to use Mom's maiden name: Dark. Hellie says people think her name is actually *Hell and Her Dark Powers* (it kind of sounds like that if you say Hellenaura Dark Powers fast enough). Because of that, Hellie assumes everyone thinks she's evil. She resents it.

I think she's lucky.

She is free to make mistakes and to do questionable things, like getting into arguments when she's in a bad mood or hedging a little on her homework when she's tired.

If she's caught doing something wrong, she's held accountable.

Not me.

Even when I was young enough to throw tantrums, no one ever took me seriously. It didn't matter if I screamed or broke things or jumped up and down while I cried my heart out, everyone just said how cute I was.

If Hellie did the same things, our parents might yell at her and send her to her room, or they might take away certain privileges or ground her. Later, though, they would sit down with her and talk it over.

In the end, they'd comfort and reassure her, telling her that she was still lovable and loved even when she made poor decisions.

Many people would say that makes Hellie unfortunate and me lucky.

Even though it's true I could have participated in all kinds of mischief when I was little without ever getting into trouble for it, the fact is I never wanted to be naughty or disobedient.

What I wanted was to know my parents were paying attention to me, not just paying attention to the things I accomplished at school or at church or at home.

Getting praised all the time, regardless of how I behaved, made all the compliments, all the admiration, and all the approval meaningless.

If my parents didn't notice me when I was acting out, how could I believe they noticed me when I was being good?

I always felt like they loved Hellie more than they loved me.

If the clerk at Perry's had seen me pick up the scarf, rip off the price tag, refold the scarf, tie it around my neck, and walk out of the store with it, she wouldn't have said or done anything.

No one ever does.

Sometimes I think I might as well be invisible.

# Chapter Five

Since I beat Hellie to the car, I slide into the driver's seat. We each have a key. When Hellie jangled her keys at me while I was getting up, she was merely claiming the right to use the car.

I glance in the rearview mirror.

No sign of Hellie.

I knew she'd take longer in the music store than I did at Perry's.

About five minutes later, Hellie shows up. She automatically climbs into the passenger's seat.

"You find anything?" I ask her.

"No," she answers, "but it looks like you did. Did you break the fifty-dollar bill Grandma Dark sent you just to buy a scarf?"

"Of course not," I tell her. "You know I always keep a little money in my purse for impulse shopping."

"I don't know how you do it," Hellie says with an envious sigh. "You've always been able to make your money go farther than I can."

"It's a knack," I say.

When we get home, Dad has mowed the lawn and is trimming the edges. This is an unexpected additional graduation present.

Hellie and I assumed we'd have to do the yard work tomorrow morning before church. We have spent our summers mowing and trimming the grass every weekend since we were about ten years old.

We always take turns. I mow. She edges. Then the next weekend, she mows and I edge.

After I park the car, we both go over to give Dad a hug and a word of appreciation. He takes it like a man—with a bit of modest pride at having surprised and pleased his girls.

After giving Dad a kiss on the cheek, Hellie dashes for the house.

"What's the rush?" he calls after her.

I check the time on my cellphone.

"It's 3:45," I tell him. "The poor kid has less than two hours to get ready for her date."

Dad and I share a chuckle.

As 5:30 gets closer, I begin to feel as nervous about Hellie's date as she does. We're sitting in the family room trying to watch TV when the doorbell rings.

We both jump as if we'd been shot.

Glancing at each other, we start laughing.

When Hellie goes to answer the door, I trail behind her.

As we pass the living room, we see Mom and Dad doing their regular Saturday afternoon debriefing: sharing information they haven't had time to discuss yet and coordinating their schedules for the next few weeks.

"Come in," Hellie says.

When Kaden enters, I get a jab in the pit of my stomach.

I knew when I saw him get out of the red car after graduation that he was good looking, but I wasn't prepared for the impact of seeing him up close and personal. I mean no disloyalty to Peter Bradley, whom I absolutely adore, but this guy is Hollywood handsome. In fact, although everything about him shouts of masculinity, I think the only word that truly describes him is beautiful.

He's tall and lean. His hair, which is naturally dark brown at the roots, goes through several artificial (but artistic) shades of blond, ending with tips that are almost white. It is pulled loosely in a man bun at the back of his head. A few strands of hair dangle in front of his ears, emphasizing the graceful contours of his brow, cheeks, and jawline.

His facial features are impossibly perfect. His brown eyes are outlined with dark lashes. His smile is dazzling.

"Angel," Hellie says, "this is Kaden. Kaden, this is my sister Angel."

"I'm pleased to meet you, Angel. Hellie has told me a lot about you." He looks back and forth between us. "I can hardly believe how much you two look alike. When you dress the same, can anyone tell you apart?"

"It's not difficult when you really know them," Dad says as he joins us in the hall.

Dad's entrance saves me from having to reply to Kaden's comment.

I'm still in a state of stunned awe.

Dad extends his hand, and Kaden takes it.

"I'm Nathan Powers, Hellie and Angel's father. Won't you come in?" Dad leads the way into the living room.

"Thank you," Kaden says as he follows.

"Bethany," Dad says, gesturing at Mom, "this is Hellie's friend Kaden. Kaden, my wife Bethany."

"I'm happy to meet you, Mrs. Powers," Kaden says.

He takes Mom's hand and kisses it.

Mom blushes, but I can tell she's pleasantly surprised.

She invites him to sit on the sofa, and he and Hellie sit side by side.

I perch on a chair beside the picture window, out of the way but still with a good view of the two on the couch.

"Hellie said you're studying medicine," Dad says, "but you look a bit too young for medical school."

"I'm sure Hellie also told you that I'm not originally from the United States," Kaden says. "In my home country, primary and secondary education is more intense than it is here. Advanced studies can start as early as sixteen years old. Although we have some time off for national holidays, schooling is year round. Hellie had some difficulty trying to explain the concept of summer vacation to me."

"What is your home country?" Mom asks.

"It's called Auravale," Kaden answers. "I won't be offended if you say you've never heard of it."

"Maybe sometime you can point it out on a map for us," Mom says. "What does your father do?"

"He's a historian," Kaden tells her, "or maybe it would be more accurate to say he's a historic researcher."

"Your English is excellent," Dad comments. "I have a good ear, and I can catch only the slightest hint of an accent."

"Thank you. I take that as high praise. Hellie told me that you teach English at the local university—English literature, I believe."

"That's right," Dad answers with a smile. He knows that many people consider his size and his job as incompatible. They think if he's going to work at the University, he should be the basketball coach or nothing. He has often said that part of his mission in life is to demonstrate that large body doesn't mean small brain.

"I've often thought," continues Kaden, "that teaching literature in a country this large must be a difficult job. Do you deal with much diversity in ages, backgrounds, and educational preparation among your students?"

"Indeed, I do," Dad answers, "and it can be quite a challenge. I start each quarter with the assumption that no two students in my class have read the same material. On the first day I hand out a list of 100 significant literary works and have them check all of the ones they've read. The answers I get are fascinating."

"Are there many commonalities?" Kaden asks.

"A few. Most students have read *Tom Sawyer, To Kill a Mockingbird, Lord of the Flies,* and *Catcher in the Rye* by the time they've finished high school, as well as some poetry. Usually they've read a few Shakespearean plays, too. *Romeo and Juliet* and *Hamlet* are the frontrunners there. But when it comes to contemporary and genre fiction, there is no pattern at all."

"Contemporary and genre fiction?" Kaden asks.

"Contemporary fiction," Dad says, "means that the action takes place in the modern world, as opposed to happening during some other time period. Genre fiction refers to books or stories that follow a particular type of plot. For example mysteries, science fiction, romance, suspense, fantasy, intrigue, and historical narratives are all separate genres."

Dad stops to take a breath and Mom interrupts, preventing Dad from going into one of his standard lectures.

"Does your mother work?" Mom asks.

"Not outside the home," Kaden answers, "but I have an elder brother, two younger sisters, and two younger brothers. I'm afraid we make enough work to keep her busy for a century or two. But you! When I told my mother that you raised twins, she said she would never complain again. She said taking care of one baby at a time is difficult enough, but two? And you worked at an outside job also. How did you manage?"

Mom starts talking about the trials and tribulations of raising twins. She's always been a good speaker, and she has Kaden laughing within seconds. Then Dad adds his favorite twin anecdotes.

"The hardest part," Mom says, after Dad has finished embarrassing Hellie and me by recounting a series of bath-time mishaps, "is that they always cried in unison. When one fell down, they both cried. If the teacher at school scolded one of them, they both cried. When they got their immunizations, regardless of whose turn it was to get the shot, they both cried. It's not easy to comfort two children at the same time, especially when one is hurting and the other is sympathizing."

As I listen to my parents and Kaden, I wish Peter were here.

Something is wrong.

I feel it, but I don't know what it is.

Peter has an intuitive insight into people that is quite astonishing. I would like to hear his opinion of Kaden. I think this guy is way too slick and too polished to be real. Words just drip from his mouth like honey from a beehive.

Then it hits me!

I know what's jangling along my nerve endings.

Any time my parents ask Kaden a question, he gives them a simple answer and then somehow turns the conversation back to them.

He is actually revealing very little about himself.

Usually when I meet new people, after being introduced and having the opportunity to talk and get acquainted, I feel more comfortable with them, not less. But watching Kaden interact with my parents has made me more concerned for Hellie than I was before.

At 6:00, Kaden stands up and says they need to leave.

"Our ride will arrive shortly," Kaden says. "I don't have a car, but my friends have offered to drive us."

"Don't be out too late," Dad says as he walks Hellie and Kaden to the door.

"I'll have her home by midnight, Mr. Powers," Kaden says. He extends his hand, and they shake on it.

"What a nice boy," Mom comments as soon as Dad closes the door.

"He's got a good head on his shoulders," Dad says.

I knew they would react this way. They accepted everything he said without question. They didn't even ask where he attends school.

I go to the picture window in the living room and look out. The same red car I saw last night is now parked in our driveway, and I recognize the driver and his girlfriend. When Hellie mentioned their names, I didn't make the connection.

I do now.

For a couple of years, these two were the talk of the high school. He was in foster care, having been found behind the University Health Center injured and without any memories except for his name: Neeve Maynard. His girlfriend, Karissa Day, had been in a car accident and was in a wheelchair.

They made quite a couple.

I wonder how Neeve can afford a fancy new car that is obviously a recent model. He and Karissa were just one year ahead of Hellie and me. Maybe he got his memories back and was reunited with a wealthy family.

Right!

Like that could happen.

Hellie and Kaden climb into the back seat, and the car drives away.

Remembering Neeve Maynard and Karissa Day does nothing to relieve my anxieties for my sister.

How would someone like Kaden, who is from a small European country and is currently a medical student, meet and make friends with a former foster kid with no memories?

It doesn't make sense, and I don't like it.

# Chapter Six

It's a beautiful Tuesday evening.

The sun has dropped behind the western mountains, and the stars are blinking into existence. A cool breeze is gradually sweeping away the heat of the day.

Peter and I are holding hands and wandering through Centennial Park.

He and his family got home from Kansas last night, and Peter was at work in his garage early this morning.

He picked me up after dinner, fresh from his shower, and he smells wonderful. I love the scent of his aftershave. It has a spicy tang that makes me feel like keeling over. Or maybe it is just Peter, the whole package, that sets my heart thumping and my brain swooning.

It's late enough that most of the families with young children have left, and the park is quieting down for the night.

Peter and I stop at the playground and sit in the swings.

"I thought the one thing you said you never wanted was to go on a double date with Hellie."

"That's not exactly right," I respond. "I just didn't want you to fix her up with one of your friends to go double dating."

"My friends aren't good enough for her?" Peter says, pretending to take offense.

I stretch out my hand and give him a make-believe whack on the arm.

"You know that's not it," I say. "I like your friends. It's just that Hellie and I have to share so much I didn't want to have to share you and them with her, too."

"But now she has this boyfriend you don't trust, and that makes everything different. Right?"

He hops out of his swing, comes over, stands in front of me, and catches ahold of the cables with his hands just above mine, effectively stopping my movement.

"That's right." I give him my best pleading look. "Please say yes."

"You also want me to borrow my parents' car?"

"Well," I say, "he doesn't have one, and for all I know he might not even have a driver's license. But if borrowing your parents' car again makes you uncomfortable, we could do something that doesn't require transportation. We could barbeque in the backyard and then watch a DVD in the family room."

"If he's from Europe," Peter says, "he's probably ridden a motorcycle before or at least a motor scooter. Not many young people have their own cars over there. I've got that bike I just finished rebuilding. They could use that. I've even got a few extra helmets around somewhere."

I think he's teasing me, but I'm not sure. I answer him seriously. "You might be able to get Kaden on a motorcycle, but you'd never get Hellie on one. Besides, I want you to talk with him. You can't have a conversation if we're all on bikes."

"Wouldn't it just be easier if you or Hellie drove? You have a car, and if—" Peter holds up a finger in a *give-me-a-second* gesture.

After a brief pause, he continues. "How about this: you let Hellie drive and you wear a dress instead of slacks. You've mentioned how awkward it is for a girl in a skirt to climb into the backseat of a two-door car. I'll suggest that Kaden and I ride in the back so you can have the front passenger seat. Out of courtesy, he and I would start to talk to each other."

"You are brilliant," I say.

I lean forward and kiss him.

Like a gentleman, he kisses me back.

He lets go of the cables, moves around behind me, takes hold of my waist and then gives me a push forward.

"I do have one stipulation," Peter says.

"What?"

As I swing back, he grabs the seat and gives it another hard shove forward. As I fly up in the air, he ducks and runs under me, so when I swing down again, he's facing me.

"Before we go anywhere else," Peter continues, "I want you to agree to stop by my parents' house so Cindy can meet Hellie."

I smile at him.

He's not just a great boyfriend, but he's also a kind and thoughtful elder brother. Someday he'll make a wonderful father.

"Cindy's wanted to meet Hellie for a long time," I acknowledge. I drag my feet on the ground until the swing stops. "I guess I've been really selfish. I haven't wanted to share her either."

Peter takes my hands and pulls me off the plastic seat and into his arms. "So, can I tell Cindy you are both coming over?"

"Yes," I tell him, sliding my arms around his neck. "Anyway, I'll try to arrange it. I'm not sure how long Kaden's going to be in town, but I think

Hellie said it might be a week or two."

Peter gives me a long, passionate kiss.

I simply melt.

Whenever he kisses me, I experience the same rapid heartbeat and the same tingling inside. It's as if we're always sharing our very first kiss. I wonder if everyone who is in love reacts this way.

We head for his motorcycle with our arms around each other's waists.

"Why don't we invite them out for dinner and a movie on Friday evening?" Peter says. "My treat. Kaden might not have a lot of spending money if he's got tuition, fees, and books to pay for medical school again in the fall. If things go well Friday, maybe we can plan something for Saturday or Sunday too—maybe a picnic up one of the canyons. I can't promise to have any great insights, but I'll try."

"That's perfect," I tell him.

After Peter takes me home and we say good night, I start considering different ways of suggesting a double date to Hellie. I don't want her to suspect that what I really want is to know a heck of a lot more about this guy she's dating.

Hellie comes into the bathroom. We each have our own sink, towel racks, and toiletries shelves, so it's not unusual for us to get ready for bed or dressed for the day at the same time.

She leans against the vanity.

"Angel," she says, "do you think you and Peter would enjoy a double date with Kaden and me? He was disappointed that he didn't get a chance to say more than *hello* to you this evening. And, of course, he hasn't met Peter at all."

I'm pulling the scrunchie from my hair, letting down my ponytail, and I stop mid-movement. I'm taken aback for a moment, but I pull myself together quickly.

"Great minds must think alike," I say. "Peter and I were discussing that very possibility earlier tonight."

Since Hellie gave me a perfectly good rationale for suggesting a double date, now I have to give her one.

I've got it.

"We have a rather personal request, however."

I drop the scrunchie into a plastic container that holds half a dozen others, pick up my hairbrush, and start destroying all traces of my former ponytail.

Hellie raises her eyebrows in a questioning look.

"Peter's sister, Cindy, has never seen twins before," I say. "She's eager to meet you to see if we really look alike. Peter wanted me to invite you and Kaden out for dinner and a movie Friday night as his guests with the stipulation that we stop by his parents' house on the way. Do you think Kaden would mind?"

Hellie grins broadly. "I'm sure Kaden would be honored to meet Peter's family. I gather from what he's told me about life in his country that his people are very conservative and reserved. To be invited into someone's home is a privilege and a sign of trust."

I reach for the toothpaste. "After you've talked with Kaden, let me know what he says. Peter suggested we have dinner at the Villa, but they require reservations on the weekend."

Hellie glances at the clock on the wall.

"It's not even 10:30," she says. "Why don't I call him right now? The Villa closes at midnight on weekdays. Maybe Peter can make the reservations before he goes to bed. I love the food at the Villa."

"Who doesn't?" I say. "Go call." I make a little shooing motion with my hand.

I've barely finished brushing my teeth and rinsing out my mouth when Hellie comes back wearing a smile as big as the Cheshire Cat's.

"He said he'd be delighted."

"Wonderful," I say. "I'll go call Peter."

After I describe my conversation with Hellie, Peter is as impressed as I am that we were all thinking about a double date at the same time.

"But I guess that's why they're called coincidences," he remarks. "I'll ring the Villa right now. Good night, Gorgeous."

For the next couple of days I don't have time to think about anything other than my job at *The Shawon Gazette.*

I had an internship here last summer, which was part of my prize for winning their annual Future Journalists of Colorado contest. (I also got a very nice wall plaque and $50).

At first, I was disappointed to learn that, because I won last year, I wasn't eligible to enter again.

In the long run, however, it worked out just fine.

The judges decided that all of this year's entries were substandard, and they didn't choose a winner. As a result, the boss invited me back.

*The Gazette* is a small paper, but it has a substantial local circulation. Mr. Fenton—the owner, publisher, and editor—likes having a student intern over the summer because, in his words, "there is always more mischief afoot during hot weather." I understand he tried to get college students at first, but they all wanted too much money.

I'm not terribly worried about the amount of my paycheck. It's the experience I want. That I was invited back for a second summer will look really good on my resume when I start applying for fulltime employment at larger newspapers in the neighboring towns.

As soon as I walk into the office Wednesday morning, before I even have a chance to say hello to anyone, Mr. Fenton intercepts me.

"Parker is on vacation," he tells me, "and Vanessa went into labor last night, *six weeks early!*" He says it as if Vanessa was remiss in her planning and was, therefore, responsible for his inconvenience and bad mood.

He hands me half a dozen sheets of papers

"See what you can do with these," Mr. Fenton says. "I think a couple of them were written by an orangutan with a laptop and the rest of them by grade-schoolers." As he walks away, he points at Vanessa's desk. "You might as well use her desk. That way you can answer her phone."

I sit where I'm told and start reading.

Every week the newspaper receives dozens of press releases from various organizations and individuals. They all want to inform the public about their valuable services, grand achievements, or upcoming events. Most are either pleas for free advertising or someone's pet peeve that they want to turn into a cause. Only a few of them are newsworthy.

Press releases from the mayor's office (composed by my mother) and those from the university are generally well written and currently relevant, but those from smaller agencies, volunteer groups, and private citizens tend to be a mess.

Under normal circumstances, Vanessa screens them, tosses or deletes the worst, and then passes the rest on to Mr. Fenton so he can make the final decision about which ones to run.

Although we always get a few notices through regular snail-mail, most articles are submitted electronically. I'm surprised that Mr. Fenton took the time to print out hard copies for me, but he's old school and still prefers looking at a sheet of paper to looking at a computer screen.

However, as the staff here has told me, old school and old-fashioned are not the same things. Although Mr. Fenton likes to do his editing with a pencil, that doesn't mean he isn't good on a computer. He is, and he expects everyone in the newsroom to be even better.

I go to work.

The press releases aren't too bad for an orangutan with a laptop, but I would expect even grade-schoolers to know the difference between *your* and *you're* and *there* and *their* and *they're*.

When I shoot off the revisions to Mr. Fenton, I get an email back from him asking me to come to his office.

"Vanessa's husband called," Mr. Fenton says. "The doctors have stopped her contractions in hopes that she'll be able to hold onto the baby long enough for its lungs to develop properly. She's been admitted to the hospital and might spend the rest of her pregnancy there. I need you to take over some of her assignments."

My heart pounds with excitement. This might be my chance to do some real reporting.

Mr. Fenton continues, "Vanessa was gathering information about some of the local myths and legends to go in an article for the annual Founder's

Day issue of the paper. Most of what she found should be on her computer under the file name *Dark Doings*, but she also has a folder in her desk somewhere. I want you to go through everything and see what you can pull together. You give me a good enough story and you can have the byline."

"I'll get right on it," I say.

"You still need to do research and copy writing and—"

"Of course," I say as I start backing towards the door.

"All right," Mr. Fenton tells me. "Close the door on your way out."

It's almost lunchtime, but I'm anxious to get into Vanessa's files and see what her angle was. I wonder what kind of *dark doings* she dug up. I'll bet she was planning to make some kind of corollary between incidents in the present and happenings in the past. That's the approach I'd take.

Luckily, I happen to know a lot about Shawon's history since a lot of it concerns my family.

The town was officially established on August 26, 1861, after my great-great-great-grandfather Eugene Powers opened the town's first mercantile store, boarding house, and bank. He had purchased most of the valley and foothills with money he inherited when his father died. As the town grew, he sold off small parcels of land to make room for expansion.

Every year, we have a big Founder's Day celebration—almost as big as the 4th of July—and the newspaper runs a special edition, highlighting different aspects of the town's colorful past.

By combining whatever information Vanessa has found with what I can gather from decades of written family history, I should be able to do a superlative story.

I desperately want my byline to appear in a real newspaper. I have lots of them from the high school paper, but that's kid stuff. When I start looking for a regular job, I want an impressive portfolio to show prospective employers.

I go straight to Vanessa's computer and open up *Dark Doings*.

What I find dampens my enthusiasm.

She has copies of blogs and articles she's copied from the Internet, as well as pages of typed and handwritten notes that she's scanned. They all have titles like "Witches in the Woods," "Colorado's Haunted Hotspots," "Pagan Rituals among the Trees," "Local Black Magic," "Fact or Fiction: Witches, Warlocks, and Woodlands," and "Immortal Creatures and Eternal Enchantments."

I don't think any of the Powers' diaries cover these topics.

Nevertheless, she's collected quite a mass of information. I'll start going through it after I get back from lunch. I don't think I can face it on an empty stomach.

When Friday evening comes around, I am definitely ready to leave the journalistic world behind. The office has been frantic, frenzied, and frenetic with Bart, Penny, Leonard (the other reporters), and me trying to carry our own workloads as well as covering for Parker and Vanessa. Even April, the receptionist, has had to pitch in.

An evening with Peter ought to help me unwind and find inner peace. I kind of wish we weren't double dating with Hellie and Kaden, but it's too late to change plans now.

As usual, when Dad and I get home, Hellie is already here.

That's because she drives to and from work in our car and I have to ride with Dad. It would be nice if she and I could trade off now and then, but it's not practical.

Quick Fix Repairs, where Hellie works, is at the extreme northern edge of town. The newspaper office and the university are both at the southern end. There are only a couple of ways I'll ever get to drive: if Dad has a day off from work and lets me use his car or if Hellie gets sick, is fired, or decides to quit her job, leaving our car available.

Hellie follows me upstairs and into my bedroom.

I toss my purse onto my desk.

"Did you and Peter give any thought to transportation?" Hellie asks. "We can't all fit on his motorcycle."

I kick off my shoes and start changing out of my work clothes.

"Actually, we did," I say. "I suggested he borrow his parents' car, and he suggested that you and Kaden ride the motorcycle he just finished rebuilding. He said that if Kaden is from Europe he probably knows how to—."

"Why don't we make it simple?" Hellie says, interrupting me. "We have a car. One of us can drive. We can flip a coin to decide who."

"Great idea!" I say. "Peter really hates borrowing his parents' car. Should we ask the guys to meet us here, do you think, or should we pick them up?"

"We might as well go get them," Hellie says, "but you'll have to get ready in a hurry."

"What's the rush?" I ask. "Our dinner reservations aren't until 7:30."

I start sorting through the clothes in my closet, looking for a dress to wear.

"We have to allow enough time to pick up the guys," Hellie says.

"Right." I pause in my search. "Peter's duplex is on Pine Crest Drive nearly to Eighth Avenue. Where is Kaden staying?"

Hellie sits down on my bed before she answers. "He's staying with Neeve Maynard at the Americana Apartments."

"Where's that?"

"Over by the university on McKinley Street."

I step out of the closet and lean on the doorframe. "We're going to be driving all over town."

"I know," Hellie says. "How much time do you think we'll need to spend with Cindy?"

"The first time I met her," I say, "she insisted on showing me her bedroom, all the pictures she'd painted, and what she was working on for school. I don't know how much of that she'll want to do with you, but I doubt we'll be able to get out of there in less than half an hour."

"In that case," Hellie says, "we should probably plan on being at Peter's parents' house no later than 6:20. The Villa won't hold our reservations for long if we're late."

As I return to my closet, I start calculating times in my head, but before I've got things figured out, Hellie calls out to me.

"We'll need to pick up Peter by 5:50 and Kaden by 6:10," she says.

I turn around and take a quick glance at the alarm clock on my bed stand. "Holy cow! It's nearly 5:30."

I grab a dress. It's an aqua blue sleeveless shirtwaist, which brings out the blue-ish green in my hazel eyes.

I'm pulling it on as I step out of the closet.

"Why are you wearing a dress?" Hellie asks.

I turn around so she can zip me up.

"I don't get to wear dresses very often when I go out with Peter," I tell her, which is true enough. "I can't wear a skirt on the back of his motorcycle."

"While you touch up your makeup," Hellie says, "I'll go get a quarter so we can flip to see who drives."

"No," I say. "It was your idea. You drive."

We move into the bathroom.

The hassle at the Gazette shows in the frazzled mess of my hair. I grab a brush, bend over, and work the tangles out. Then I grab a scrunchie and pull my hair into a high ponytail. (This is the solution Hellie and I both use when we've had a bad hair day.)

I begin refreshing my makeup.

"Okay," Hellie answers, "I'll drive." Then she shakes a warning finger at my reflection in the mirror. "But I don't want any backseat driving or any backseat singing."

"I can promise the first but not the second," I tell her. "I never know when I might spontaneously burst into song."

Hellie laughs. "I'll bet that's why Peter always wants to ride his motorcycle. With his helmet on he can't hear you sing."

I take a pretend swat at her. She ducks.

"You'd better go call Kaden and let him know we'll pick him up," I say. "I'd better go call Peter too."

I set down my makeup brush and dash into my bedroom to get my cellphone. Hellie rushes back to her room for the same reason.

Peter answers on the first ring.

"Hellie's going to drive," I say. "We'll be at your place in twenty minutes and then we'll swing by to get Kaden. We should be at your parents' house by 6:20, which will give us about half an hour with Cindy."

"I'll be out front and waiting. Cindy is really excited about meeting Hellie, and I'm looking forward to checking out this Kaden dude for you."

"See you soon."

I run back into the bathroom to spritz a little hairspray around my face so I can smooth down any frizzy stragglers.

"I'm ready," I yell at Hellie as I dash into my bedroom to grab my purse.

We pick up Peter first, and he climbs into the backseat.

When we go get Kaden, Peter suggests, as planned, that they both ride in back because of the awkwardness and inconvenience caused by my skirt.

# Chapter Seven

Cindy's reaction to seeing Hellie and me side by side is wonderful. She runs over and puts her arms around both of us.

"Now I've got two sisters," she squeals.

"Can you tell which one is Angel?" Peter asks.

Cindy's lower lip starts to tremble. "Do I have to choose? Can't I keep them both?"

"You certainly can," Hellie and I say at the same time.

We glance at each other, surprised. When we were kids, we often unintentionally answered questions in unison. As we've grown up, however, we've done it less and less frequently. The last time it happened was probably two or three years ago.

"Even if you can keep them both," Peter says, "you can't call them both Angel. I think that would hurt Hellie's feelings."

"Why?" Cindy asks.

Peter takes her hand and leads her over to the couch. When Cindy sits, Peter crouches down in front of her. He holds both of her hands.

"You wouldn't like it if someone called you Peter, would you?" he asks her.

"That's silly," Cindy says. "Peter is a boy's name."

When Peter cocks his head to the side, Cindy looks down and makes scuffmarks in the carpet with her foot.

"Even if Peter was a girl's name," he says patiently, "you'd still want everyone to call you Cindy, wouldn't you? That's your name, and that's what people should call you. Right?"

She nods. Peter gives her a hug then sits down beside her.

"Take a good look at them," Peter tells her. "You've seen Angel dozens of times. I bet you can pick her out."

From the corner of my eye, I see Kaden watching this interaction with interest. I suppose he's studied developmental disorders in medical school and is happy to have an example to observe in real life. I want to throw my arms around Cindy so I can protect her. She is not some mad doctor's research subject.

Cindy stares at me, and then she stares at Hellie.

Grinning at Peter, she jumps to her feet.

She comes over and puts her arms around my waist. "I love you, Angel," she says. I hug her tight.

When I let go, she looks up at me. "Can I love Hellie too?"

"Of course," I tell her. "I love her myself."

Cindy smiles at me.

Then she steps to the side and stands in front of Hellie. The expression on her face turns serious, almost somber. Atypically, she doesn't reach out for Hellie's hand. She doesn't touch Hellie at all, but she does speak to her.

"At first," Cindy says, "I thought you looked just like Angel, but when I looked underneath, I could see how different you are. It's all harder for you, isn't it?"

Hellie shivers as if she's taken a sudden chill.

My heart almost stops. Hellie often says things are more difficult for her than they are for me. I've always assumed she meant my writing, my singing, and my talent for math and science. Now, for some reason, I suspect that neither Hellie nor Cindy is talking about Hellie's trouble with accomplishing things. I think maybe they're referring to emotions. Hellie has always been uncomfortable expressing her feelings. Maybe that's one reason I've always been more popular.

"Is it all right if I love you too?" Cindy asks Hellie.

I hold my breath. I can seldom predict how Hellie will answer an unexpected question, but I swear I'll never speak to her again if she says or does anything to hurt Peter's sister.

I should trust her more.

Hellie smiles at Cindy. "Only if I get to love you right back."

Cindy throws her arms around Hellie, and Hellie bends over and rubs her cheek against Cindy's hair.

I sort of expect Cindy to come back to me so she can hug Hellie and me together, the way she did when we first arrived. Instead, to my surprise, Cindy goes over to Kaden.

"I think I'm going to love you, too," Cindy tells him. "Is that okay with you?"

Kaden is very tall, and he sits on his heels so he and Cindy can see eye to eye. "I'd like that," Kaden says. "I can never have too many people who love me. Is it all right if I love you too?"

"Of course," Cindy answers.

"Hellie told me that you like to paint. Is that right?" Kaden asks.

"Oh, yes."

"I like to paint too," Kaden says. Lowering his voice almost to a whisper, he adds, "I'm not very good. Maybe you could give me a few tips."

Cindy runs over to a three-foot-square framed painting that hangs above the fireplace. It's a field of poppies rippling in a breeze, and it's one of her best. She painted it just this spring.

Kaden follows her over.

"Wow," Kaden says. "That is beautiful. Is there a secret to how you do it?"

Cindy motions for him to crouch down again. She cups one hand around her mouth and speaks into his ear. She thinks she's whispering, but she's not. She has never learned how. She only has two volumes: normal and shouting.

"When you paint," Cindy says, "you can't look from your eyes. You have to look from the inside."

She holds onto Kaden's hands and stares into his eyes as if she wants to check his brain and make sure he got the message.

He doesn't pull away. Instead, he stares right back at her.

They hold that position for at least a full minute, maybe two.

I start getting uncomfortable. I glance around the room, and everyone is watching Kaden and Cindy, but no one else seems to think the staring match is a little odd. They're all smiling stupidly.

Finally, Kaden breaks eye contact. "Thank you," he says. "I think I understand now."

"Me, too," Cindy says with a nod.

We stay another ten minutes to visit with Peter's parents. Then, after we give Cindy lots of hugs, we leave. When we get to the car, Peter and Kaden climb into the backseat again.

"The next car we get," Hellie says to me, "has got to have four doors."

"Amen to that."

As soon as the car is moving, Peter starts taking with Kaden. Hellie and I remain silent. It seems as if we're both content to listen.

"I've never seen her take to a complete stranger the way she did with you," Peter tells Kaden.

"She is remarkable," Kaden says. "How long has she been able to paint like that?"

"She's loved painting nearly all her life," Peter answers. "She started out with finger painting when she was only a few years old. She graduated to watercolors and a brush when she was about six. A couple of years after that, my parents started her on acrylics. But it's only been in the last year or two that her skills have developed to such a high level."

"How did your parents come up with the idea of starting her with finger-paint?" Kaden asks.

"When the doctors told my parents that Cindy wasn't meeting her developmental milestones, my mother went on a researching binge. She learned it was important to provide the proper environment. Every time she found a new suggestion on how to do that, she experimented. Finger painting was one of several dozen things my mother tried in order to stimulate Cindy's curiosity and to prolong her attention span. As it turned out, it was the activity Cindy responded to the quickest and with the most enthusiasm.

"Finger painting turned out to be a versatile tool, too. We used it to teach her colors and shapes and numbers. My parents and I set up a rotation to work with her every day. When she was accepted into the special-needs program at the university, we were ecstatic. She's made remarkable progress there."

"You're very good with her," Kaden says.

Peter chuckles softly. "To tell the truth, she's had me wrapped around her little finger ever since my parents brought her home from the hospital. The first time she gave me a gummy, drooling smile, I was all hers. She's eleven years old, just about half my age right now. I didn't realize how much I wanted a sibling until I saw her. She completes our family. How about you, Kaden? Do you have brothers and sisters?"

"I have an elder brother, two younger sisters, and two younger brothers," Kaden answers. "I'm afraid we're not as close as you and Cindy are. I was a bit envious when I saw how patiently you interact with her and how wise you are in your communications. Using Hellie and Angel's names as a tool to explain to Cindy about feelings, individuality, and selfhood was inspired. She is lucky to have you."

"You flatter me," Peter says. "Cindy is smarter than the doctors give her credit for. I try to explain things to her in terms she can understand, and I try to help her develop a vocabulary that she can use to express her thoughts and feelings. Cindy does the real work."

"I doubt she does as well when she's working with anyone else. You obviously see her potential more clearly than other people do."

"Is that your professional opinion?" Peter asks.

When Kaden doesn't answer right away, I turn around so I can see him. For just a few seconds he looks confused, but the moment passes.

"Please forgive me," he says, "but sometimes I am puzzled by American idioms. You mean to ask me if my observations about you and Cindy are a result of my medical studies. Is that correct?"

"Actually," Peter says, "I was just trying to lighten the mood. I was getting a little embarrassed by your compliments. It was a stupid thing for me to say."

"No question is stupid," Kaden replies, "and I will try to answer yours. I suppose part of my opinion was based on academics, but mostly I was reacting to the strength of the bond I sensed as I watched your interplay. Although much of a doctor's work is founded in science," Kaden continues, "there is a portion that is based on intuition, and its proper usage is an art."

"I've always suspected it," Peter says with a little laugh, "but I never thought I'd hear a doctor admit it."

"In my country," Kaden says, "the best doctors, the ones who are secure enough in their knowledge to trust their instincts, are referred to as healers. That's a step above a medical doctor, and that is what I am striving for."

"I think I understand," Peter tells him. "People wonder why I'm the best mechanic in town, but the answer is simple. I am in tune with the nature of motorized vehicles. I can usually sense what is wrong with one just by the sounds and vibrations it makes. Even when it won't run at all, it's telling me something.

"I don't mean to compare the complexity of the human body with the workings of a machine, but I believe there is an art to repairing and restoring vehicles. People who only focus on how the components go together might be able to reassemble an engine, but they can't make it hum the way I can."

"I like your analogy," Kaden says. "Bodies and machines have much in common, and they both respond best to the people who understand them."

When we arrive at the Villa and throughout dinner, it is much the same.

Peter and Kaden chat as easily as if they have been friends forever. They don't ignore Hellie and me. They include us in the conversations, listen to our comments, and respond appropriately, but if there's a lag, the two guys always find something they have in common that they can talk about.

While we finish with the main course, we begin debating the issue of dessert.

"They have a very nice dessert menu here," Hellie says.

"Or we could skip dessert," Peter says, "and get treats at the movie. Those huge cookies they have are great."

"I'm really full right now," I say. "Why don't we wait and go out for ice cream after the movie is over?"

We all look over at Kaden.

He ends the discussion by changing the subject.

"I've enjoyed this evening very much," Kaden says to Peter and me. "I would like to introduce you to my friends, Neeve and Karissa. A week from Sunday, they are having a little get-together at Neeve's apartment because his eldest two brothers will be visiting. I would be honored if you would come as my guests, and bring Cindy too."

"That's awfully nice of you," Peter says, "but I don't think we should intrude on a family gathering."

"It's not like that," Kaden says. "This is a party with a purpose. I don't suppose you know any of Neeve's history, do you?"

"Not really," I admit. "There were rumors about him at school."

"I don't doubt it," Kaden mutters. "What about you, Peter?"

Peter shakes his head. "I know nothing about him at all."

"Then let me explain," Kaden says. "Neeve is from a wealthy Auravalian family. His father comes from, what you call here, old money. He and my father work together. A few years ago, some people who were angry with Neeve's father kidnapped Neeve. They asked for no ransom. They did terrible things to Neeve and then dumped him here, far from his home and with no memories of his previous life.

"It took his parents a long time to find him. When they did, his wounds had healed, he had graduated from the local high school, and he had met and had fallen in love with Karissa Day.

"Although he was happy to be reunited with his family and to rediscover many of his memories, Neeve did not want to go home. He wanted to stay here and support Karissa in her rehabilitation. Her physical therapy was painful and often discouraging."

"Physical therapy?" Peter asks.

"Yes," Hellie answers. "She was in a car accident a couple of years ago and spent some time in a wheelchair. She had to relearn how to walk. For a while she was having physical therapy nearly every day."

"Brave girl," Peter mumbles. "I'm sorry I interrupted you, Kaden. Go on with your story."

"Thank you," Kaden says. He pauses for a few seconds before he continues.

"As I said before, Neeve didn't want to go back to Auravale. His father tried many different ways to entice him, but Neeve was stubborn. Neeve's father finally agreed to let Neeve stay here—he even offered to pay for Neeve's living expenses—as long as Neeve enrolled in college, maintained a high grade point average, and willingly allowed someone from the family to come and check on him every now and then. Neeve accepted his father's terms.

"But when Neeve's father sends someone to Colorado, it isn't just Neeve's welfare that he wants information about. Karissa is one of the few Americans he has met, and although he likes her, he wants to know if she is the exception or the rule in this country. He also wants to know about the environment Neeve is living in and about the other people he associates with.

"Whenever any of Neeve's brothers come to visit, Neeve has a little party so they can get to know his friends. They've met Hellie, and I'm sure they'd be delighted to meet her twin and her twin's boyfriend."

"Why do you want to include Cindy?" Peter asks defensively. "I refuse to have her presented as an example of one of Colorado's defectives."

"Holy stars!" Kaden exclaims. "I don't see Cindy as defective. She's remarkably talented and totally charming. I just thought she might enjoy dressing up and going to a party."

"Neeve's youngest sister, Shiane, will be there," Hellie inserts. "Shiane is fourteen years old, and she is one of the most loving, gentle, kindhearted girls you'll ever meet. Karissa's younger brothers will be there too. Jeremy is fifteen or sixteen, and Bennett is two years younger."

"There will be other adults as well," Kaden says, "friends of Neeve's and Karissa's from school. They are all good people. I promise no one will be unkind to Cindy."

Kaden's story about Neeve answers a lot of my questions, like how a former foster kid could afford an expensive new car and how he became friends with a medical student from a foreign country.

I'm still thinking about it, when Peter interrupts my thoughts.

"What do you think, Angel?" Peter asks me.

I consider for a moment. "I'd like to meet Karissa and Neeve, since they're Hellie's friends, and I'd just love to see Cindy all fancied up for a party. However, I see two problems."

"Which are?" Peter asks.

"First, next Friday night is the church social, and Cindy wants to come and watch the children's choir perform. If she goes to the social on Friday, a party on Sunday might be too much excitement for her. Your parents are pretty careful to make sure she doesn't get overstimulated."

"That's a good point," Peter says "What's the other problem?"

"Neeve might not welcome guests that he didn't invite himself."

Kaden pulls a cellphone from his pocket.

"Why don't I call Neeve right now and see what he says," Kaden suggests.

# Chapter Eight

After Kaden goes to the directory on his phone and taps Neeve's name, he punches the speaker button and sets the phone in the middle of the table.

"Hey, Kaden," Neeve's voice says when he answers. "What's up? I thought you were out on a date."

"I am," Kaden says. "I'm sitting in a restaurant with Hellie, her twin sister, and her sister's boyfriend. I invited them to come to next week's party, but they don't feel comfortable accepting without an invitation directly from you. I've got you on speaker phone."

"Please, come," Neeve says without a hint of hesitation. "I'd love to meet you, Angel, and your boyfriend. Peter, isn't it?"

"Yes," Peter and I answer at the same time.

"I hope you'll come," Neeve says. "I have plenty of room, and there will be enough food to feed an army."

"I also invited Peter's little sister," Kaden says.

"By all means, bring her too."

"She's never been to a party before," Peter tells Neeve. "She is only eleven years old and has special needs."

"Are you afraid she'll be uncomfortable in a crowd of strangers?" Neeve asks.

"No," Peter answers. "She is never uncomfortable around people. That's because my parents and I have showered her with affection and have sheltered her from the cruelties of others. She doesn't know anything except being loved and loving everyone in return. I don't want to risk having her hurt."

"You have nothing to fear for her from my family and friends," Neeve says. "There will be no cruelties in my home. Ever. I will not permit it."

I am taken aback by the harshness in Neeve's voice.

Then I remember Kaden saying Neeve's kidnappers did terrible things to him. At school there were rumors that he had been found naked, cut up, beaten, burned, and bleeding behind the campus infirmary. The very thought of what he might have suffered makes my skin crawl.

"I really would like you to come," Neeve says. "All of you."

He sounds sincere.

Peter looks at me and then at the cellphone and shrugs, meaning he is ambivalent and will leave the decision up to me.

I nod.

"Thank you," Peter says. "Angel and I accept your invitation. I will consult with my parents about Cindy."

"I look forward to meeting you."

Kaden retrieves his phone from the table. No one speaks for a moment.

Then Hellie points at the clock on the wall. "That solves the question of dessert. There is no time now. The movie starts in thirty minutes."

Peter signals the waitress.

She brings the bill in one of those leather folders.

Peter flips it open, takes out the customer's copy of the ticket, puts a stack of cash inside, pushes his chair away from the table, and says, "If we hurry, we should make it to the theater before the previews are over."

He's right. We make it with seconds to spare.

The movie is just so-so, but I enjoy it because Peter and Kaden have the same sense of humor. I don't know how the guys ended up sitting side by side with Hellie and me on the outside like a couple of bookends, but I'm glad it turned out that way. The show wouldn't have been half as entertaining without Peter and Kaden's interactions.

After the movie, we go to Thompson's Ice Cream Parlor and order root beer floats. Apparently, Kaden has never had one before.

Although Kaden comes across as a little stiff and pompous, I think it is probably the result of his culture and his upbringing rather than his personality and his character.

Sometimes he exhibits a childlike wonder.

When our root beer floats arrive, Kaden is puzzled by the carbonation. He puts his hand around the glass. "It's cold, but it looks like it's boiling. Ice cream isn't supposed to bubble like this, is it?" He asks the question with ingenuous sincerity.

Peter and I break out laughing.

Kaden, still with a straight face, asks, "Well, it isn't. Is it?"

Hellie pats his hand and says, "No. Usually ice cream is a very calm food."

Peter and I have to struggle to regain our composure.

"Good," Kaden says. "I don't want all of my ice cream to start bouncing around like this. Root beer floats are like milkshakes with bad manners."

He has us in stiches again.

I think Kaden is confused by our reaction, and maybe a little offended. I manage to stop laughing and so does Peter.

"I apologize," Peter says. "We weren't laughing at you. We were just enjoying how apt your description of a root beer float is. If they aren't constructed with care, they can make quite a mess."

When Kaden looks bewildered, Peter takes his spoon and stirs the ice cream around. Soon fizz is pouring over the side, and Peter is sucking hard on the straw to get it under control.

Kaden watches and then stirs his ice cream. He gives out a delighted burst of laughter when a lava flow of foam overspills the mug.

As the waitress delivers an order to the couple seated across the aisle from us, she eyes our table with dismay.

Giggling like idiots, all four of us start sopping up root beer puddles with napkins.

"I'll leave her an exceptionally large tip," Peter says with a grin. Then he asks Kaden, "Don't you have carbonated drinks in your country?"

"A few," Kaden answers, "but they've never been as popular there as they are here. Also, I don't think anyone has ever combined them with ice cream. I can hardly wait to show my younger siblings. I predict that, by this time next year, ice cream floats will be a popular new fad all over Auravale."

When we get back to the car, Kaden waits for Peter to climb into the backseat first. I think Kaden wants to sit behind me so he can watch Hellie in profile rather than just staring at the back of her head.

Taking the shortest route home from the ice cream parlor means we need to drop Peter off first and then Kaden.

As soon as we arrive at Peter's duplex, I climb out of the car and tip the seat forward. Kaden gets out, too, so Peter doesn't have to scramble over him.

It would have been easier for everyone if Hellie had let Peter exit on her side. The only problem is that the driver's seat is so difficult to adjust that, once Hellie and I got it into a good position for us, we agreed never to move it again.

I accompany Peter to the door, and we share a goodnight kiss.

When I turn around to return to the car, I see Kaden leaning on the back of the passenger's seat with his eyes closed. He looks as if he's in pain.

"Are you all right?" I ask.

He straightens up. "I'm fine," he says. "It's just—" He stops himself. "Never mind. I feel fine."

As I slide into place and close the car door, I glance at Hellie. She is staring at Kaden in the rearview mirror and biting her lip.

I don't understand.

Did they argue while I said goodbye to Peter?

If they did, they sure did it quietly.

I can't ask Hellie about it until after we take Kaden home.

I stomp on my curiosity.

# Sunshine and Shadows: Another Modern Fairytale

It's a tense ride.

No one says a word all the way from Peter's duplex to Neeve's apartment house.

When I get out of the car and slide my seat forward so Kaden can climb out, he avoids making eye contact with me. When he says goodnight, his voice is monotone. "Thank you for sharing your evening with us. I enjoyed it. I look forward to seeing you again next week."

Clearly his problem isn't with Hellie.

It's with me.

Somehow, I've unwittingly done something to offend him.

I can't imagine what.

As Hellie walks up the sidewalk with Kaden, they mumble a few words to each other. When they reach the door, he takes her hand, turns it over, and kisses her palm, and then goes inside.

As soon as Hellie is behind the wheel again, I ask her, "What did I do wrong? Kaden was having such a good time right up until Peter left. But when I returned to the car after telling Peter goodnight, Kaden wouldn't even look at me."

"Just let it go," Hellie says. "He'll be fine tomorrow."

"But if I don't know what I did to offend him," I persist, "how will I know what to avoid doing next week."

"Don't make a big deal out of it," Hellie snaps at me. "He's a foreigner. Give him a break. It was his problem, not yours. Let him work it through his way."

I feel as if I've been punched in the face.

I would never offend anyone on purpose, and now that I've done it unintentionally, Hellie won't even give me a chance to fix it.

Of course, I can't force her to explain, and that's really frustrating.

For a moment I consider grabbing her cellphone so I can call Kaden and ask him myself. Surely his number is in her directory.

But I can't do it.

I'm too big a coward.

Kaden might yell at me, or hang up on me, or tell me to go to hell.

However, regardless of how Kaden might react, if I tried snatching Hellie's phone, she would explode. She has quite a temper, and I don't want to risk making her mad.

Tonight, though, I'm more hurt than afraid. I thought—hoped—maybe this double date would draw us closer together.

Apparently not.

I don't say anything else. If I did, I'd start to cry.

When Hellie pulls into the driveway, I'm out of the car almost before she can put on the brake. I go straight to my room and lock both of my doors: the one to the hall and the one to the bathroom.

I feel tears dripping down my cheeks.

I undress in the dark and slip on a nightgown.

Soon I hear Hellie moving around in the bathroom, and rather than chance a confrontation, which would surely end in a huge argument followed by parental involvement, I get the travel case out of my overnight bag. It has an extra toothbrush, toothpaste, and other essential stuff in it. I take it with me and head for the guest bathroom on the ground floor.

I sleep on the couch in the family room.

Saturday morning, I am still feeling cold towards Hellie.

In addition, I am absolutely terrified about going to the party next week. What if I repeat the same mistake?

What if, right in the middle of the party, Kaden confronts me about whatever offensive thing I've done and makes a big scene?

I don't know what I'd do.

Even more importantly, I don't know what Peter would do.

He's as protective of me as he is of Cindy, and when Cindy was little, Peter's solution to the problem of people making fun of her was simply to pound them into the ground. Hardly anyone ever teased her a second time.

Despite his height, I don't think Kaden would stand a chance against an infuriated Peter.

I worry about it while I pull on my old jeans and a tank top.

It's Hellie's turn to mow the lawn and my turn to do the edging.

I grab a bowl of cereal for breakfast.

As I eat, I decide that after my Saturday morning chores are done and I've had a shower, today would be a good day to go to Perry's Department Store. I never got around to looking at the new swimming suits.

By the time I've trimmed the grass around the flowerbeds in front, down both sides of the driveway, and have started edging the sidewalk, I am hot and tired and grumpy.

Edging always takes longer than mowing.

I don't understand why.

Mowing requires going back and forth repeatedly across the whole length of the yard. Edging is a single tour around the perimeter and along the curbing surrounding the gardens and flowerbeds. To my way of thinking that means mowing should take more time than trimming, but it never does.

Whoever mows starts in the backyard, and whoever edges starts in the front. There are two reasons. First, we need to stay out of each other's way. Second, since the backyard is over twice as large as the front, we finish "round one" at about the same time.

Unfortunately, for "round two" whoever is edging still has the gigantic backyard to do while the mower has the smaller front. So, whoever mows has the additional tasks of deadheading the petunias, watering the planters on the patio, and blowing or sweeping the trimmings off the driveway and sidewalks.

It sounds unfair, but even so, whoever mows usually finishes first.

Today is no exception.

By the time I'm done, Hellie has already showered and is gone. I have no idea where or how.

Our car is still in the driveway.

In the past she probably would have taken off to wander through the woods behind our house, but last summer a fire burned down over half of it, taking a hunk of our family's history with it.

A hundred and fifty years ago, after our great-great-great-grandfather Eugene Powers settled here with his wife and began a family, he gradually sold off much of the land he had purchased. However, he set aside one huge section of forest that he said must never be sold, developed, or despoiled in any way. EVER!

To ensure this, his son, Michael, hired a very slick lawyer who was able to put Eugene's wishes into a legal document. The land was to be passed from eldest son to eldest son, unless one of them tried to sell or develop the protected property. In that case, the eldest son would lose ownership of the land and it would be passed on to the next son. There were all kinds of clauses about how things were to be handled if there were no sons and under what circumstances a daughter could inherit.

I don't understand how such a document could be legal, but apparently it was and still is. In the 1940s or 50s, Michael's eldest grandson tried to sell a portion of the protected land to a logging company. The next thing he knew the property had passed from him to his younger brother, my grandfather.

That's how our family came to live here.

After I've taken a shower and washed away all the bits of grass on my body and in my hair, I dress in cutoffs and a loose dark green t-shirt. I part my hair down the middle, comb it straight, and then use barrettes at my temples to keep the damp strands out of my eyes.

I grab my keys and my purse.

I go through the kitchen to get to the side door. I have my hand on the doorknob when I realize what my folks are doing.

Mom and Dad are leaning on the counter next to the sink looking through cookbooks, taking advantage of the natural light coming in through the window.

"Not another international night," I groan. "Can't we ever just eat American?"

"Don't complain," Mom says. "A lot of the foods that you consider to be the staples of life originated in other countries."

"Besides," Dad adds, "there are plenty of hungry people in the world who would be delighted to have a meal from any one of these books."

"Could you send them my portion? I'll just pick up a hamburger or a corn dog at the mall."

I'm only halfway joking.

Growing up, Hellie and I endured some awful mealtime disasters when our parents were feeling particularly adventuresome.

Mom chooses to change the subject.

"How long are you going to be at the mall?" she asks.

"Just a couple of hours," I answer. "Perry's has some new bathing suits I want to look at. If I try wearing my old one in public, I'll get arrested for indecent exposure."

"Are you and Peter going out tonight?" Dad asks, pushing aside the cookbook in front of him and reaching for another.

"Yes."

"How did it go with Hellie and Kaden last night?" he asks.

I hesitate.

I don't know what to say.

Dad pauses in the process of turning a page and looks over at me. "Did you and your sister quarrel?"

I sigh. I let go of the doorknob, cross the room, circle around the bar that separates the dining room from the kitchen and sit on a stool so I face my folks. The barstools swivel, and I twist back and forth in a semicircle for a few seconds.

I imagine one of them, or both, heard me in the guest bathroom last night or noticed me asleep in the family room this morning.

"It takes two people to have an argument," I say, "so, no, technically we didn't quarrel."

"What does that mean?" Mom asks. She turns around and leans back on the counter.

"It means Hellie won't talk to me."

Dad comes around and sits beside me at the bar. "Maybe you ought to start at the beginning."

So, I do.

I tell them about going to see Peter's family and how delighted Cindy was to meet Hellie and Kaden. I tell them about dinner, Kaden's inviting us to Neeve's party next week, and Neeve confirming the invitation. I tell them how well Peter and Kaden seemed to get along, especially sharing the same sense of humor during the movie. I describe the root beer float incident, which makes both of them laugh. Then I tell them about the cold shoulder I got from Kaden at the end of the evening and Hellie's refusal to explain to me what I did wrong.

"I know she knows. It's probably some cultural thing from Kaden's country, but now I'm afraid to see him again for fear I'll repeat the same mistake and offend him further."

I get tears in my eyes.
I'm more upset than I realized.
Dad gives my hand a squeeze.
"One of us will talk to her," Dad says.
"Go enjoy trying on swimming suits," Mom tells me. "We'll see what we can do."
"Thanks." I give them each a hug.
I feel much better.
Now shopping will be more fun.

# Chapter Nine

I get into the car and drive to the mall.

Perry's is as busy as it usually is on Saturdays.

That's good.

It's easier to get the clerks, security personnel, and the surveillance cameras confused when the store is crowded.

I know how to do this.

I start by looking through the two-piece bathing suits for one I like that's a size too small. Every now and then, I hold up the bottoms to my hips and the tops to my bust.

I finally select one and take it to the dressing room. There's a woman stationed at the entrance. I show her what I have. She nods, so I go in and select a stall. There are security cameras in the walkways but not in the individual changing compartments.

I strip, except for my panties, and try the suit on.

Lots of amateurs try to skip this step, and that's where they make their first—and usually their only—mistake. They don't realize that, although there are no cameras in the stalls, the ones in the hall can see your head, neck, calves, and feet. Depending on your height, they might also see your shoulders.

If the cameras don't pick up the right kind of activity going on in the observable areas, whoever is watching the monitors knows something isn't right. Once they single you out, they keep an eye on you until—BAM!— you're caught.

The suit I try on doesn't fit.

Surprise. Surprise.

When I'm ready to leave the changing area, the woman at the entrance says, "I'll put that back for you."

"Please," I say, "can't I take it with me. I need to compare it with some of the other bathing suits. I don't understand why it doesn't fit. I've worn the same size for the last three summers."

I give her my best *trust me* look.

"All right, honey," she says, "but then bring it back before you try on anything else."

"I will."

I smile brightly at her.

After that, it's just a matter of taking in two or three identical or similar suits in different sizes until she loses track.

What'll make you or break you, however, is the extra hanger. When you walk out of the changing area for the last time, there can't be an empty hanger in your stall. Either the staff will notice or the next customer will, and with a little backtracking on the video recording, they will know who you are. Then you'll have security people stopping you so they can check your handbag, your clothing, and your person.

I can hardly imagine how humiliating that kind of invasion of your privacy and your personal space must feel like.

Avoiding that outcome is paramount.

After I decide which style of swimming suit looks the best on me, I implement the solution.

I go back to the rack, and as I shift things around, apparently looking for new inspiration, I manage to get half a dozen hangers twisted together. It isn't hard to do since bathing suits are small and hangers are relatively big in comparison. While I am supposedly trying to untangle the mess, I carefully maneuver two swimming suits together on one hanger. One of them is the style and color I want to keep; the other is similar.

An empty hanger on the rack isn't particularly noticeable, but there's no sense in taking chances. While I maneuver two swimming suits onto one hanger, I slip the extra hanger under the straps of the suit next to it, so now there is one suit on two hangers. If or when it is noticed, the assumption will be that the hangers got tangled up and the extra suit slipped off and is caught on another piece of clothing.

I'll be long gone before anyone has the time to sort it all out.

I enter the dressing room with three hangers and four swimming suits.

Safely inside my stall, I take off my clothes (for about the $100^{th}$ time) and try on the three bathing suits I don't want.

When I'm finished, I dress carefully.

Here is another place where amateurs are likely to make a mistake. They put on a swimming suit and then pull their jeans or shorts or whatever up over it. Do they think the cameras miss that? If you put something on over your feet, you better make sure the camera shows you taking it off again. Same thing if you pull something on over your head.

These security people aren't stupid.

When I put my cutoffs back on, the bathing suit I want is tucked inside with the leg openings lined up. From the camera's point of view, I'm just getting dressed as I have a dozen times already.

I selected a one-piece suit so I don't have to worry about putting my bra on over a bikini top and risk having it bulge in the wrong places. That can be a real tip-off.

Instead, I fold the top over and smooth it across my lower abdomen before I zip up my cutoffs. I wore a baggy t-shirt specifically so any extra bulk around my midsection wouldn't show.

When I hand the last three hangers and bathing suits to the lady at the entrance, I laugh. "I surrender. I have absolutely lost the battle."

She laughs with me. "You gave it a good try."

"That I did. Well, you have a nice afternoon."

"You, too, honey. And better luck next time."

"Thanks."

I saunter away casually and leave the store.

I drive out of the parking lot feeling positively elated.

Of course, the next trick is to get the swimming suit into the house in such a way that it seems like I purchased it.

That's simple.

I keep a couple of Perry's Department Store bags and some tissue paper under the driver's seat. Since the seat is never repositioned, the chance of them being noticed and removed is slight.

When I enter the neighborhood, I pull over and fake a sneezing fit. (I have to have a reason for stopping). While I apparently fumble in my purse for something to blow my nose on, I slip a bag from under the seat, wad up a few pieces of tissue paper to represent the appropriate amount of bulk, put it inside, and then set the bag on the floor.

When that's done, I successfully find a wrinkled facial tissue in my purse, blow my nose, and drive the rest of the way home.

When I open the door to the kitchen, I discover my parents cutting up things and dropping them into a big pot. While I was at the mall, they must have discovered a recipe that they both considered promising.

"I see you found something," Mom says. "You can model it for us after we get this on the stove. All right?"

"Sure," I say and head for my room. If they had asked me to show them what was in the bag, I'd have told them I had to run to the bathroom first and would be right back.

This way is easier.

I lock both doors to my room and slip out of my cutoffs and the bathing suit. I take the tissue paper from the Perry's bag, smooth it out on my bed, fold the swimming suit into fourths, put it in the middle of the tissue paper, and fold the paper around it, making a nice little bundle, which is how Perry's handles lingerie, bathing suits, and other small intimates.

I put the packet into the Perry's bag and toss it onto my desk.

# Sunshine and Shadows: Another Modern Fairytale

My wall clock shows that it's not even 4:00 yet.

I lie down on my bed and reach for the book Peter's parents gave me for graduation: *Agatha Christie: A Mysterious Life.* I'm well into it when I hear a knock on my door.

"Who is it?" I call.

Hellie's voice answers, "It's me."

I mark my place with a lace bookmark that Cindy made at school and gave to me last year for my birthday. Then I get up and unlock the door.

Hellie comes in, sits on the chair at my desk, and swivels it around. I perch on the edge of my bed.

"I'm sorry about last night," she says. "Kaden said I should've told you what made him uncomfortable. He said he didn't feel right about doing it himself because he is essentially a stranger to you. But since you are going to meet other Auravalians next week at Neeve's party, he said it wasn't fair to let you go into that situation unawares."

I nod silently.

I knew it had to be a cultural thing.

"In Auravale," Hellie says, "the people have all kinds of rites and rules and rituals regarding relationships. I imagine most Americans wouldn't even believe this is possible, but not only do they not have sex before they're married, they don't even kiss on the lips."

I almost laugh.

That can't be true.

"Knowing that you and Peter aren't married, Kaden was shocked to see your goodnight kiss. He felt like a voyeur."

"What!"

"It's all very complicated. The hand kissing, on the back of the hand for courtesy and on the palm for intimacy, is kind of a substitute. Although there is nothing backward about Auravale's technology, in some ways the place is in the dark ages. They even still have arranged marriages where the bride and groom don't meet until the wedding ceremony starts."

"You've got to be kidding," I say.

She shakes her head. "I'm not. I think you'd better warn Peter. Maybe he'll decide he doesn't want to go to the party after all."

"What are you implying?" I demand, bristling at her tone. "You don't think Peter and I can go a whole evening without smooching in public?"

"I didn't mean it that way," Hellie says defensively.

"Of course, you did," I snap at her. "Ever since I started dating before you, you've hinted that boys only liked me because of what they could get." My voice grows louder. "But you're wrong. You don't know a thing about me." Suddenly I'm shouting. "Get out of my room. Get out!"

She stomps to the door, and when she's on the other side, she slams it.

I flop over on my stomach and bury my face in my quilted bedspread.

I hate arguing with Hellie.

No matter who says what, even when I'm right, I always end up feeling like I'm the loser.

I expect Mom or Dad to come and see what's causing the commotion, especially in light of what I told them earlier, but they don't. They must be making a clatter while cleaning up the kitchen, or maybe they've already turned on the dishwasher. It's pretty loud while it's filling up. Whatever the reason, they obviously didn't hear the ruckus.

It doesn't matter.

There's nothing they can do about it if Hellie thinks I have loose morals. I would try explaining the truth to her, but I know she wouldn't believe me. As unlikely as it might seem considering how many guys I've dated—it's true nonetheless—I never kissed a guy on the lips before Peter. It just didn't feel right.

When Mom calls me down to dinner, I sit at the table long enough to sample the spicy stew she and Dad concocted by combining a couple of different recipes.

Hellie and I ignore each other.

"When are you going to show us your new bathing suit?" Mom asks in an effort to get some dinner conversation going.

"Maybe after church tomorrow," I say. "The temperature is supposed to be in the 80s, so I'll probably work on my tan. Right now, I'd better go get ready for my date. Peter will be here in a few minutes. May I be excused?"

"Sure," Dad says.

Peter and I enjoy a nice quiet evening watching a DVD at his place.

Sunday afternoon I show off my purloined swimming suit.

Mom and Dad both compliment me on my choice.

"That's a great color and style," Mom says. "Don't you think so, Hellie?"

"Yes," she answers indifferently. "I've always liked that shade of turquoise."

Although Hellie and I are polite to each other, for the next few hours, we avoid speaking unless absolutely necessary.

That evening at dinner I ask her if she'll pass me the butter.

"Of course," she answers.

"Thank you," I tell her.

"You're welcome," she replies.

It's the longest conversation we've had since yesterday afternoon. I start trying to figure out how to avoid going to Neeve's party.

The weekend passes too quickly.

Monday comes out of nowhere.

When I get to work, Mr. Fenton is waiting for me.

"Vanessa called me at home last night," he tells me. "She wanted to know who was going to write the article for the Founder's Day issue. When

I said it was you and you were going to use her research, she was delighted. She said to tell you she's sending you a link to a website she just discovered. It's called *Witch's Wisdom*, and it claims to have historical ties to magical doings in Powers Forest."

I stare at him in stunned silence.

"I like it," Mr. Fenton says. "It's been a while since we featured your family's role in establishing the town. Many people believe Michael Powers fenced off that big section in your woods because it's haunted. If this *Witch's Wisdom* can connect supernatural forces with your family and Powers Forest, this'll be the most popular Founder's Day issue we've ever published."

I don't know what to say. I'm in shock. Mr. Fenton raises his eyebrows at me. I suppose he senses my incredulity.

"Remember," he points out, "if you do a good enough story, it'll be published under your byline."

He turns and walks away.

Thinking I might as well get the worst of it over, I turn on Vanessa's computer, open her mailbox, and look for the email addressed to me.

There's no message, just the link. I click on it.

The webpage is designed to look eerie.

The heading across the top is *Witch's Wisdom* written in red script, and centered below it are the words "by Miss Ellie." The illustration behind the title is done in sepia and depicts a typical forest floor. There's a patch of grass, a couple of rocks, some weeds, a few mushrooms, and the bottoms of several trees with protruding roots. On the right side, a spider's web (including spider) hangs between two low branches. On the left is a circular, colored photograph of a woman's face. If the picture is an accurate portrayal, then Miss Ellie is a middle-aged hippie.

Even though fine lines flow across her forehead and radiate from the corners of her dark eyes, she is still quite an attractive woman. Her long, dark hair is streaked with just enough white to make it look dramatic. The ends turn under where her hair drapes in front of her shoulders. A brightly patterned scarf encircles her head between her hairline and eyebrows and is tied in a big bow on the left side. Colorful beaded earrings shaped like arrowheads dangle from her earlobes and almost touch her collarbones. She is wearing a cream-colored peasant blouse with full sleeves.

Her website has three tabs.

The first is labeled "Witch's Brews: Homemade Health."

The second is "Witch's Strengths: Invaluable Intuition."

The third is "Witch's Magic: Power in Powers Forest."

She has over sixty thousand subscribers.

My stomach flips over.

It's as if someone—a stranger, no less—is holding our family and our family's history up to the world for ridicule.

I want my own byline, but I'm not sure I want it badly enough to write the story Mr. Fenton expects.

I leave Miss Ellie's site.

I need to talk to someone, someone I can show the website, someone who'll discuss it with me and maybe help me put it into perspective so I can go ahead and write the story for the paper.

I sure don't want anyone else on staff writing about us.

On the way home, I try to figure out how I can extend a white flag to Hellie, but she is so obviously rude to me during dinner that I give up.

If she wants to instigate a feud, that's fine with me. She can just explain to Kaden why Peter and I don't show up at Neeve's party.

When I go back to *The Gazette* the next day, I decide to pretend I'm an only child. I concentrate on tasks at work that don't require me to think about Hellie or to look at the material for the Founder's Day edition of the paper.

# Chapter Ten

Then on Wednesday, shortly after lunch, I get a phone call at work that puts the vendetta with Hellie to rest, at least for me.

"Guess what my mother is doing right now," Peter says to me.

"Baking a cake?" I ask hopefully.

"Sorry," Peter says, "no cake."

"Too bad," I tell him. "I give up. What's she doing?"

"She is taking Cindy to the mall to buy her first party dress and to have her hair styled. Cindy is almost beside herself with excitement. She keeps saying that on Sunday she's going on a date with us."

"Oh, Peter," I exclaim, "she is almost too adorable for words. Do you really think we should take her to Neeve's party?"

"I do," Peter says, "and my parents agree. They like the idea of her having the opportunity to meet a few young people away from her program at the university. She's almost twelve years old, and they still have hopes that she'll be able to attend public high school."

"So, you think it's worth the risk?"

"Even though I was nervous when Kaden first suggested taking Cindy with us, I believed Neeve when he said we had nothing to fear for her from his family and friends."

"I did too." As I say the words, I feel myself being caught in the trap of inevitability.

I can't disappoint Cindy.

Regardless of how I feel about Hellie right now or how I'll feel about her in a day or two or three, on Sunday, Peter, Cindy, and I are going to Neeve Maynard's party.

"Well, Gorgeous," Peter says, "I've got to get back to work. I'm having some problems with the Camaro, and I'll have to work late tonight and tomorrow if I'm going to have it done by Friday. If I don't, I'll have to come back after the church social to finish up. I promised the owner I'd have the car ready by noon on Saturday when I open up the shop, and you know how much I hate to break my word to a customer."

"I know," I say, carefully not letting any disappointment sound in my voice.

"I'll pick you up Friday evening at ten to six," he says. "I've got to go now. Bye."

"Bye," I echo the word, even though I know Peter has already ended the call.

I sit immobile with my mind a blank.

Then, gradually, my brain starts to work again.

Something doesn't feel right.

Last week, when Peter told me he had a 1967 Chevy Camaro coming in, he said he didn't expect the repairs and the detailing to take him very long. What's changed?

He hardly ever has problems with American-made cars. Occasionally a foreign job will give him a little trouble, but even that doesn't happen too often. I'm reminded of the thought that popped into my head after graduation: *Peter has secrets.*

Why do I think that?

I feel queasy.

I don't know if the uneasiness in my stomach is because something in Peter's voice didn't ring true or if I'm just reacting this way because I'm going to miss him. I hate it when circumstances keep us apart.

*Of course, I might not have the whole story*, I tell myself, trying to rationalize away my discomfort. *He could have additional obligations that I know nothing about that have slowed him down.*

It's a fact that he'll lose Friday afternoon getting presentable (making sure that there's no grease or grime under his fingernails and that he doesn't smell of gasoline and motor oil). He'll also lose Friday evening by taking me to the social.

Maybe giving me that chunk of time creates a hardship for him.

If so, he won't tell me.

He never wants to worry me about anything.

Does that mean he's being secretive or that he's being protective?

I shake my head in frustration.

I love Peter. Shouldn't that be enough?

I concentrate on all the positive things I know about Peter: how he helps his parents pay for Cindy's medical and developmental programs, how kind and patient he is with her, how hard he works taking care of the customers at his garage, how he spends so much of his free time finding interesting things for Cindy to paint, how he's there for me whenever I'm feeling lost and lonely, how he pays attention to me when I talk, how he acknowledges my feelings, how special he makes me feel, and how frequently he does unexpected things to make me happy, like putting together the beautiful scrapbook he gave me.

He is a good man, an exceptionally good man.

I am ashamed to have doubts about him.

If I were less selfish, I would tell Peter to forget the church social and just focus on getting the Camaro finished.

But I will be singing as part of the entertainment and I always do my best when he's in the audience. Actually, I'm going to perform twice, once as part of a trio and once by myself.

Peter has told me repeatedly that he loves my voice and loves to hear me sing, and I suppose he does. So far, he's never missed a single one of my performances.

In addition, the children's choir will be doing a number. For the past several months, I've been helping the church choir director work with the kids, and we are the last act, the finale.

I really want Peter to see the children's choir perform.

Hmm, I think slyly, if Peter goes back to the garage and works on the car Friday night after the social, and if he follows his regular routine on Saturday—doing household chores and grocery shopping in the morning and then opening his garage from noon until five—he might be too tired to go to Neeve's party on Sunday.

Then I wouldn't have to deal with Hellie.

I like the idea.

That would be a real bonus.

But I'm just daydreaming.

Peter would never risk hurting Cindy's feelings.

If necessary, in order to get adequate sleep for both the social and the party, he would call the Camaro's owner and tell him that he needed more time. Then he would do everything within his power to provide fair and reasonable compensation for the inconvenience—even if it meant renting the customer a car or offering him a discount on the labor.

Peter's integrity is one of the things I love about him.

Why on earth do I think he is keeping secrets from me?

I sigh loudly.

I need to let go of my doubts.

Instead, I ought to give some thought to Neeve's party.

Obviously, I have to go—if for no other reason than to support Peter's goal of giving Cindy some new life-enhancing experiences.

But that brings up another issue.

What am I going to wear?

I'm not sure I have anything good enough, and even if I do, Peter has seen me in everything I own.

Since Cindy will have a new dress and a new hairdo, maybe I should do the same for me.

Of course, that means a shopping trip.

Thursday evening, after I've had dinner with the family and have helped clean up the kitchen, I go to the mall to find something to wear that will dazzle Peter. In the Teen Dream Boutique, I find the perfect dress, and I take no chances.

I pay with cash.

For the church social, the pastor has reserved the large pavilion at Centennial Park. It has a stage at one end, and it has all the plugs and hookups necessary for a sound system.

Dad and I take off work early to help set up tables and chairs.

Mom and Hellie don't come with us because they're busy preparing our contribution to the meal. Mom is making her ever-popular sausage and veggie stir-fry while Hellie bakes a double batch of Grandma Powers' famous Ginger Cream Cookies.

Three tables are set up end-to-end in front of the stage for the potluck buffet. Filling the rest of the area under the pavilion are the collapsible tables and folding chairs that belong to the church.

If we have a good turnout, though, the pavilion won't hold us all.

While I'm helping some women tape down paper tablecloths, since there's a bit of a breeze building up, Dad, Pastor Keating, and two other men move half a dozen of the park's picnic tables into a semi-circle around the outside of the pavilion for the overflow.

"I don't like the looks of that sky," Dad says as we head home to change our clothes.

Glancing up, I can see what he means. Dark clouds are rolling down from the mountains. Generally, I enjoy summer storms, but if one is scheduled for tonight, I hope it will hold off until the social is over and the cleanup is finished.

At home, I change into jeans and a pale lavender t-shirt. Mrs. Michaels, the music director, told the kids in the choir that they could all wear jeans with any solid-colored t-shirt they wanted, as long as they didn't wear dark blue, brown, or black. When I told my friends in the trio what I was wearing for the choir, they agreed to wear jeans and t-shirts too so I don't have to worry about changing outfits.

Mom, Dad, and Hellie leave the house at 5:40 so they can pick up Kaden on the way to the park. Ordinarily Neeve would drop him off at our house, but Neeve is busy getting things ready for his party on Sunday.

Peter picks me up ten minutes later.

He gives me a quick kiss as soon as I open the front door.

It's not even 6:00 in the evening, but it is already getting dark. A storm is definitely on its way.

I glare at the clouds: *Don't you dare ruin our church social.*

"Cindy asked me to tell you that she's sorry she can't hear you sing tonight."

"So, your folks decided not to bring her after all," I say as I lock the deadbolt. We walk arm in arm down the sidewalk.

"As you predicted, our parents decided Cindy shouldn't be out late two nights so close together. They told her to choose."

"And she chose Neeve's party," I say. I put on my pink helmet, swing my leg over the back of the motorcycle, and climb up behind Peter. "I understand. She can hear me sing anytime, but being invited to an adult party given by a rich guy? That might be a once in a lifetime experience for her."

"For me too," Peter says with a laugh.

When we get to the park, Pastor Keating has already said a prayer and blessed the food. The pavilion is full of people holding paper plates and standing in lines on both sides of the serving tables.

Kids are running helter-skelter, throwing Frisbees, playing tag, or just chasing each other.

Music is blaring from somewhere, and several adolescents are dancing on the grass.

"Isn't it glorious," I say to Peter as I glance around.

There is something about a large crowd of happy people that fills me with so much joy that I can hardly breathe in and out.

"You are the glorious one," Peter whispers with his warm breath tickling my earlobe.

We hold hands and walk around, talking to people as we go.

Courtney intercepts us.

"Have you met James Patten, yet?" she asks.

"No," I say. "Who is he?"

Courtney points with her chin at a nice-looking young man about twenty years old who is talking to a girl our age.

"The guy with Linda Emmett?" I ask.

"Yes," Courtney says. "His mother is Mabel Goodwin's sister, and his family is here visiting her. Mabel asked me if I'd show James around town today, and I agreed, but Linda Emmett spotted him in Mabel's yard this morning while she was out jogging. She's latched onto him and hasn't let go. He's attending Colorado School of Mines. I was really looking forward to asking him about their engineering program."

"So," I say, "why don't you go over and tell Linda 'hello' and then ask her to introduce you?"

"You're joking," Courtney exclaims.

I grin at her and shrug. "What's the worst that can happen? If she tells you to get lost and if James Patten is worth knowing, he won't be impressed by her rudeness. If she introduces you, you'll have the opportunity to ask your questions. Knowing Linda, I'll bet she's been so busy telling him about herself that she hasn't asked him anything about his interests. He might appreciate talking to someone who wants to know about him, his education, and his college."

"I guess it can't hurt to try," Courtney says.

Peter and I watch.

I wonder what Courtney says when she gets over there, but it is clear Linda wasn't prepared for a rival to take a direct approach. James smiles. Linda frowns. Whatever Linda says next has a negative impact. James's words are unintelligible, but his facial expression tells volumes. After a few minutes, Courtney and James walk off together, chatting like long lost friends, and Linda looks as if she doesn't know what just happened.

I can't help grinning. I love it when the good guys win.

In the distance I hear thunder.

"No," I whisper under my breath. "Don't you dare rain until after the social is over."

"Come on," Peter says, "Let's go get something to eat. The lines are thinning out."

I take a few spoonsful of a couple of casseroles, just to taste, but that's all. I'll be singing soon. If I have a full stomach, it'll interfere with my breathing and I'll never be able to sustain the high notes.

There is another rumble of thunder.

People glance around, but no one leaves. Yet. *Please, please, please. Don't rain until the program is over.* It's part prayer, part entreaty, and part demand.

Peter and I are among the last people to go through the food line, and we sit down at a picnic table outside of the pavilion.

I glance around, looking to the west and then to the east. I tip back my head and gaze up at the sky. The cloud cover is thick enough now that I can't see the sunset, the rising moon, or any stars. Without a clock or a watch, you'd never guess it was still early evening.

Pastor Keating stands up and with a microphone in his hand announces the first act.

It's last year's high school cheerleading squad. They do a half-dance, half-gymnastics routine that ends with a cheer, getting the audience all fired up and ready to be entertained.

I suppose our church is like any other: we have some *excellent talent*, some *good talent*, and some *no talent*. Whenever we meet for a social, anyone who wants to put together an act has the opportunity to perform.

This year, the *excellent talent* is highlighted by a newly formed barbershop quartet that sounds as if they've been harmonizing with each other for all of their lives. Also included in the *excellent* category are a magician, two dueling guitarists, a tap-dancing class, and a comedian. Audience response is impassioned and prolonged after each act.

The *good talent* includes my trio, which we call "Singing in Thirds," some salsa dancers, two different garage bands, a seven-year-old who sings "All I Ask of You" from *Phantom of the Opera*, a string quartet, and a guy who plays classical music on his portable keyboard. Audience response is approving and supportive.

The *no talents* are comprised of a quintet of siblings who obviously hate singing with each other, a ten-year-old girl who is clearly being forced to take violin lessons, a couple of preschoolers jumping and gyrating to an old Chubby Checker tune, and a duet who couldn't decide what key to sing in. Audience response is polite and charitable.

My solo? I think it fits somewhere between *good* and *excellent*. Peter, his friends, and my parents lead the applause so it is biased from the start and can't be used to judge quality.

The pastor, knowing his flock, arranged the program so the four *no talent* acts are sandwiched between *excellent* and *good* ones. I'm sure he did that in hopes that people wouldn't start leaving before the finale.

His strategy works.

The last number is the children's choir.

After Pastor Keating announces us, the music director and I start gathering our kids (ages six to twelve) and arranging them in four staggered rows with the youngest in the front and the oldest in the back.

A flash of lightning is followed by a crash of thunder. I feel the first drops of rain being carried under the pavilion roof on a gust of wind.

*No,* I screech inside my head.

Since I don't dare throw a tantrum in public, I glare silently upward. *These kids have worked too hard to have a storm ruin their song. Go away. Rain somewhere else, somewhere that needs the water.*

There is another crash of thunder.

Irrationally, I get angry.

Mentally, I shout at the storm. *I said go away.*

As Mrs. Michaels gets the last of the children in place, I slip around the backdrop to collect our props.

Behind the stage, in the deep shadows of some trees, I hear a male voice that sounds even angrier than I feel. Although his voice isn't terribly loud, it is certainly enraged.

"What the hell did you do?"

"Nothing," I hear Hellie say. "Why did you pull us back here?"

"Did you want me to talk to you out there in the middle of the crowd?" the angry voice demands.

"I don't know," Hellie replies. "I don't understand why you're mad at me. What do you think I've done?"

"You don't notice anything strange?" the voice asks sarcastically. "Look around."

It isn't Hellie who responds. It's Kaden. "The storm is gone."

"That's right," the other voice says. "The weather has been altered. The storm has been magically translocated."

"I didn't do it," Hellie exclaims. "I wouldn't know how."

"Someone did it," the angry man says. "Someone right here."

I've gathered up the props, so I don't have time to listen to more.

But it doesn't make any sense.

Why would someone accuse Hellie of magically dissipating a storm? It would be nice if she could—if anyone could—control the weather. But, alas and alack, it's not going to happen in my lifetime, probably not even in the next century.

Quickly I pass out the props.

I sit on the floor at the front of the stage with my back to the audience. My job is to mark the tempo and keep the kids on beat. Mrs. Michaels is at the side to direct their movements and the use of the props.

She signals the sound technician to start our music.

The kids stand with their hands behind their back.

I stare at them with a somber expression, and then putting my fingers at the sides of my mouth, I push my lips up into a smile.

The kids respond by smiling back at me.

The music starts.

I count out four beats, give the kids their cue, and they take two steps right then two steps left in time with the music.

They start to sing.

*This little light of mine*
*I'm going to let it shine.*

When they sing the word *shine*, the kids in the first row give a little hop, produce a large cutout that they've been holding behind their backs, and then hold it with both hands at chest level. It's a picture of a lighted candle. They continue singing but they don't resume stepping to the sides like the other three rows do.

After the second repetition of the same two lines, at the word *shine*, the kids in the second row hop, stop moving, and hold up a picture of a light bulb.

At the third repetition, the kids in the third row hop, stop, and hold up a picture of a spotlight.

Then when they sing the last part—*Let it shine, let it shine, all the time*—the kids in the fourth row do the hop and stop on the word *time* and hold up a picture of the sun.

They all hold the pose while the music plays an interlude, and then they put their hands and the pictures behind their backs again.

As they start singing the verse, they start sidestepping again.

# Sunshine and Shadows: Another Modern Fairytale

They look and sound like little angels.

They are in tune, on tempo, and have remembered all of the words.

Then suddenly, as they begin to reprise the chorus, the music stops.

The kids stop.

Everything stops.

For a moment I can't move.

Then I jump up and run over to the nearest children. I touch them. They feel like warm-bodied statues. I rush over to Mrs. Michaels and give her a shake. Nothing.

I stare out over the audience.

No one is moving or speaking or laughing or crying.

I seem to be the only person capable of doing anything, and I think I'll start screaming soon.

# Chapter Eleven

Then Hellie and Kaden step out of the shadows and into the light.

Behind them are two men I've never seen before.

The strangers are nearly the same height, which is tall, and one is blond and the other is a brunette. They are both Handsome with a capital "H." They are strangely dressed, wearing poet shirts, tight pants tucked into mid-calf boots, and long vests.

The blond says, "Hellie, I'm sorry. I didn't realize how many people are out here. This is too large a group to hold in a time bubble for very long. We'll need to wait until the program ends to speak with Angel." He turns to me, "Angel, you need to get back into position so Hellie can restore time."

"Are you insane?" I blurt. "That's impossible! No one can stop and restart time."

"It hasn't stopped," the brunette says. "It's just going so slowly that movement is imperceptible to us."

"That's impossible too!"

"So, how do you explain what's going on?" he asks.

Taking in the scene with a glance, I shake my head. "I don't know. Maybe everyone's been dosed with some kind of paralytic drug. It could have been in the lemonade."

"And," the blond makes a big show of looking around, "other than us, you're the only person unaffected?"

"I didn't drink any," I tell him. "Or maybe there's a new virus going around and I'm immune."

"Hellie's already having difficulty holding on," the dark-haired man says. "You'll need to help her, Jerrin." He points his finger at me. "Angel, go back to your previous position."

Who the heck are these guys?

The blond, I realize, is the man with the angry voice.

I don't like him. I don't like his friend either.

What I'd like is to tell them where they can go, but my vocal cords aren't working.

"Angel," the dark-haired man snaps, "return to your position. Now!"

I don't like being bossed by a stranger.

I'm certainly not going to obey him.

Then, as if I'm a puppet, an inexorable force turns me around, walks me to the front of the stage, situates me so my back is to the audience, and sits me cross-legged on the floor.

The music comes up. The kids sing the chorus, the second verse, and the chorus again, making all of the appropriate movements.

After row four does its thing for the last time, the choir repeats the final line—*Let it shine, let it shine, all the time*—and on the last word, all of the kids drop their pictures, hop up, and land with their legs spread and their arms thrown out wide while they sustain the word *time* for four seconds.

The applause is loud and prolonged.

I count out four beats and then give the kids a cue.

In perfect unison, they drop their arms, take one step forward, and bow.

The clapping turns thunderous.

I'm so proud of the kids I could burst.

They stand there like pros and bask in their glory. When the applause starts to die down. I give them the final signal.

Like the kids they are, they start squealing and running to join their families.

I clamber to my feet.

Mrs. Michaels rushes over and hugs me. "Thank you, Angel. Thank you, thank you, thank you."

"They were great, weren't they?" I exclaim with a tear dripping down each cheek.

"The best children's choir we've ever had," she says. "I couldn't have done it without you. Please say you'll stay on as my assistant."

Before I can answer, she is swarmed over by admirers, including Pastor Keating, who are all competing for her attention.

My heart is full of happiness. I want to share it with Peter, and I look out over the crowd for him amid the chaos.

Before I can spot him, I am confronted by Hellie, Kaden, and the two men who were with them earlier.

"We need to speak with you, Angel," the blond says. "Tell Peter you're going to run an errand with Hellie and she'll take you home."

I shake my head. "Peter won't leave without me."

"Yes, he will," the brunette states flatly and indisputably.

From the corner of my eye, I see Peter approaching.

I pivot, walk down the three steps from the stage to the ground, and go to meet him.

"You were great, Gorgeous," Peter says, wrapping his arms around me.

"I videoed your numbers and the children's choir on my phone. Cindy is going to love them."

"Thanks," I say while returning his hug.

Hellie and Kaden come up beside us. The blond and the brunette are not with them.

"Angel?" Hellie asks. "Are you coming?"

I don't answer her.

I'm not going to answer her.

We haven't made up, not by a long shot.

I'm going to let Peter take me home.

Then the same inescapable power that forced me to resume my position on the stage earlier takes control of me again.

"Peter," I say. "Hellie needs me to run an errand with her. Afterwards we'll just go home together."

"All right, Babe," Peter says. "I need to spend a couple more hours on the Camaro. I think I'll go over to the garage and see if I can finish up tonight." He gives me a quick kiss on the cheek. (We agreed never to kiss on the lips in front of Kaden again, since he found it so offensive.) "Cindy and I will pick you up for Neeve's party on Sunday at 5:30."

As I watch him amble away, I'm swamped with shocked disbelief. He's going without me. He's leaving me behind.

I sense a slight movement at my back. I don't need to turn around to know that the blond and the brunette have returned.

"Where do you want to do this, Skyler?" the blond asks.

"I told Neeve and Shiane to meet us at the hunting lodge."

"Karissa, too?"

"I left that up to Neeve."

The next thing I know we're somewhere else.

*Oh, no,* I cry out silently to myself, *not again. I went through this on graduation night.*

We appear to be in a typical American ski lodge: vaulted, open beamed ceiling with a huge chandelier, log walls, spacious stone fireplace, fur rugs on the floor, overstuffed couches and chairs arranged in conversational groupings with end tables and standing lamps scattered about.

"Where are we?" I ask in a raspy, frightened voice.

"Auravale," one of the men answers.

*Auravale?* Where have I heard that word? It was just recently.

*Auravale?* Then I remember. *That's where Kaden said he's from, and it's where Neeve Maynard's rich family is from too. If I remember right, Kaden said his and Neeve's fathers work together.*

But this is crazy.

We did not just step out of Colorado's nighttime into some European country's daytime.

# Sunshine and Shadows: Another Modern Fairytale

Although, considering different time zones, I guess the night to day part is possible, but not that we did it instantaneously. By airplane, it should take between ten and twelve hours to get from Colorado to Europe, depending on what airport we left from and where we landed.

I glance around.

To my right, through a gigantic picture window, I see a valley thick with snow. In the middle of it is an icy lake surrounded by prickly looking shrubbery and oddly shaped trees. In the distance are craggy, white-capped mountains.

The cloudless sky is aqua blue and so is the center of the lake where it is free of ice. The trees are tall, skinny, and crooked. They have long rounded leaves that appear black in the shadows but are purplish green where they are touched by the sun.

Nothing in the scene is Earth-like.

I begin breathing in uneven gulps.

When I was little, my friends had all kinds of phobias. They were afraid of monsters under the bed and creatures in the closet. They were afraid their parents would move away while they were at school and not tell them. They were afraid of doctors and dentists and various people in authority. They were afraid of dogs and horses and snakes and other animals.

While my friends struggled with these relatively normal childhood fears, I had only one great big dread—and it has continued to this day.

I have been, am still, and always will be terrified of going insane, of losing my mind, of being unable to distinguish what's real from what's not. I have no idea how I developed this fear, but I can't remember a time when I didn't have it.

Right now, I'm petrified and heartbroken because it has finally happened. I'm wide-awake, and nothing is as it should be. In the blink of an eye, I've changed locations, seasons, and times of day.

All I need now is for the fairytale girl to appear out of nowhere, like she did on graduation night.

Then she does!

Coming right behind her are Neeve Maynard and Karissa Day.

I shriek.

My knees give out, and I land on the floor.

I burst into tears.

I've gone crazy.

My psychotic break must have happened on graduation night. That's why I was hallucinating.

I had such big plans for my future. Now I'm going to spend the rest of my life locked up in an institution somewhere.

I start crying harder.

I'll just sit here and wait for the men in white jackets to come haul me away and toss me into a padded cell.

"Angel," Hellie says, kneeling down beside me and giving my arm a rough shake. "You're not delusional. This is real."

Uh huh. If I'm nuts, what else would I tell myself?

The blond man crouches down beside my sister.

"Hellie is telling you the truth, Angel. There is nothing wrong with your mind. Your sanity is intact." He stands, reaches down with his hand, takes mine, and pulls me to my feet. "Let's go sit somewhere more comfortable."

He leads me over to a couch.

I sit, still crying with an occasional gulp and sniffle between sobs.

He sits beside me and hands me a box of tissues that he pulls out of nowhere.

I close my eyes. Not only am I delusional, but I'm also having visual hallucinations like I did after graduation. I can't handle much more. I want to fall down, scream, and pound on the floor.

If I did, I wonder if a psychiatrist would label it a seizure or a tantrum.

As my brain toys with the conundrum, I realize my crying is slowly subsiding. I guess I've resigned myself to taking up residency in the local loony bin.

I open my eyes so I can take a tissue from the hallucinatory box the blond man gave me. I wipe my eyes and blow my nose, using what I don't know. Maybe I've just made a mess on my fingers, or maybe mopping up my face was just another delusion. To be on the safe side, I wipe my hand on my jeans.

The brunette man says, "Hellie, why don't you introduce everyone? Start with those who are the most familiar to your sister."

Hellie nods at the two people who arrived last.

"Angel, you probably remember Neeve Maynard and Karissa Day from school. They were just a year ahead of us. It's their party we're all going to attend Sunday evening."

I give them a cursory nod. I don't know what the correct etiquette is for greeting make-believe people. My mind wants to shut down and drift off into madness and get it over with.

"This is Shiane," Hellie continues, "Neeve's youngest sister."

She's the fairytale girl. I smile at her, not because I believe she's real, but because she has an incredibly sweet expression on her face.

"These are Neeve's elder brothers," Hellie says. She gestures at the brunette. "This is Skyler. He's the eldest." She motions with her hand at the blond. "This is Jerrin. They've brought you here tonight because you have inadvertently used one of the great magics, and it puts your life in peril."

Magic?

Right.

If I believed in magic, that, all by itself, would prove I've lost my mind.

# Sunshine and Shadows: Another Modern Fairytale

Hellie starts to say something else, but Skyler puts up his palm to stop her. He addresses Jerrin. "Father is calling me. I'll be back as quickly as I can. In the meantime, tell her what you think she can handle."

Skyler vanishes.

It doesn't even make me blink.

"Angel," Jerrin says, "I'm going to tell you a story. It is a true story, although you might doubt it at first. If you can, please, try to open yourself up to the possibility of belief.

"In this world, what you call magic is a reality. Everyone who is from Auravale has at least one special and unique talent. Neeve can alter fabrics, especially the ones that are used to make clothing. Kaden can find anything whether it's been lost, stolen, or hidden. I can influence memory. Skyler can promote certain types of movements and behaviors. Shiane gets visions of the future.

"There are also some people who have more than one talent. They're called magic users and there are five levels.

"Your ancestor, Bree-Ella Dark, was a mage, which is the highest, most powerful level. She fled from our world to yours to escape from the sorcerer who seduced and impregnated her. His name is Maldon Darker, and he is the illegitimate son of our grandfather and thus the half-brother of our father. He is an evil man who wants only three things: as much power as he can get, to destroy our family, and to find Bree-Ella's child."

Somewhere in Jerrin's narrative I stop crying.

I'm not even aware when it happens, but it's probably when he first mentions Bree-Ella Dark. She is the greatest puzzle in my mother's ancestry.

One winter's morning, over a hundred and fifty years ago, Bree-Ella Dark walked out of Powers Forest carrying her baby daughter. No one knew where she came from or who the father of her child was. My mother's family has all kinds of eerie stories about her, some of which even imply that she had special powers.

The strangest thing about her, however, was that she said all of her female descendants had to keep the surname Dark, even after they married. If not, she insisted, a curse would ruin their lives. Although my mother wanted to follow the tradition, my father wouldn't allow it, so Hellie and I are the first girls in Bree-Ella's direct line who don't have the last name Dark.

I never believed in the curse before.

Tonight, I'm not so sure.

However, even though I am in the middle of a psychotic episode, I am alert enough to catch the flaw in Jerrin's story. It makes me feel better, knowing that at least part of my brain is still functioning rationally.

"You're wrong," I tell him. "Maybe I've gone crazy, and maybe I'm not as good at genealogy as Hellie is, but I know Bree-Ella Dark came to

Colorado while it was still wild and untamed territory, sometime in the mid 1800s. This Maldon person couldn't have seduced her and still be your uncle. They would have lived in different centuries."

"No," Hellie tells me. "It's complicated, but time doesn't move at the same pace on Panelda that it does on Earth. Time here is flexible."

"Right," I exclaim with a slightly hysterical laugh. "You probably ought to present that to a panel of scientists. They're dumb enough to think time runs laterally—yesterday, today, and tomorrow, occurring in a straight line—unless time is being influenced by something like a black hole." I make a sweeping gesture at the scenery outside the window. "That doesn't look like a black hole to me, but I could be wrong."

"It doesn't look like Colorado, either," Hellie says. "And there's more. We might as well get everything out in the open." She takes a deep breath before continuing. "Kaden and the others aren't precisely human." She looks over at Kaden, and her expression sort of melts into a gooey, adoring smile. "Do you mind?"

He looks at her with the same doting affection. "Not at all. Do you think you might need to move in a little closer to her? Just in case she needs you."

"Good idea."

Hellie pulls a chair over so she is sitting right next to me. She gently rests her hand on my forearm. I feel like shaking it off, but I don't. I suspect she means to prepare me or reassure me or support me.

Kaden turns around and holds his arms out to the sides, shoulder height. Two transparent lumps form on his upper back.

Seems to me things are getting weird even for a hallucination.

The lumps expand until they're beyond his trunk. Then they unfurl like two flags.

I don't understand what I'm seeing.

Even when they're fully extended, I don't believe it.

He has two sets of wings that overlap at his shoulder blades.

When he holds his arms up in the traditional "V is for Victory" stance, the central rib of the upper wing follows the line of his arms and extends about a foot and a half beyond his fingertips.

Next, he holds his arms pointed downward in a wide, upside down "V." The major rib of the lower wings follows the line of his arms again. The tips extend beyond his hands almost to the floor.

His wings are golden near his body, but the color lightens as it spreads out from his trunk until it becomes pale yellow at the farthest away points. Around the edges, outlining each wing, is a band of black that varies in width. Scattered randomly across the yellow are black dots that remind me a little of freckles.

I stand up and move closer.

How the heck are they attached?

# Sunshine and Shadows: Another Modern Fairytale

"They are a natural part of his body," Jerrin says, "as are mine." He turns around, and the same process unfolds (pardon the pun) on his back. His wings are red, fire engine red, with a white border that looks a lot like eyelet lace.

"How are you doing that?" I demand.

"They are part of our anatomy," Jerrin says. "Our wings come in when we're about eight or nine years old."

"You expect me to believe you can actually fly with them?"

Jerrin and Kaden barely twitch their shoulders, and they are both suspended in the air near the high ceiling.

A moment later Shiane is up there, too, fluttering wings that are incandescent pink.

My eyes well up again.

I am floridly psychotic.

Loony bin, here I come.

"Please, Angel," Hellie says. "Try to believe. We need your help."

"We?" I ask. "So, you're one of them? Do you have wings too?"

"I don't need wings to be one of them. We—."

Suddenly Skyler is back.

He glances up and then signals the fliers to land. Their wings disappear as soon as their feet touch the floor.

Skyler tells them, "Father insists that we break through her defenses. Master Cushing suggested that overkill might be the best method. Looks like you started without me."

"Desperate times," Jerrin responds, "require desperate measures."

"All right," Skyler says with a shrug, "since you've shown her our major anatomical difference, let's take her out for a ride." As soon as his royal purple wings form, he scoops me up in his arms and flies straight for the ceiling.

Even though I don't believe this is real, I cringe and brace myself for impact, but a panel opens up and we soar through.

# Chapter Twelve

The air is bitingly cold, and I'm dressed for a warm summer night.

But before I can even start to shiver, I am wearing a lavender parka with navy blue ski pants and boots.

Hellie, in Kaden's arms, is dressed similarly except her outfit is pastel blue like the matching t-shirt and slacks she wore to the social. Shiane is carrying Karissa, who is in green and white.

Everyone seems to be dressed in winter clothing that is similar in color to what they were wearing before—everyone except Shiane, that is.

Earlier, she had on a cherry red dress, but now she's all decked out in silver. In addition, her jacket and snow pants are covered with designs made of rhinestones.

Jerrin and Neeve are holding onto each other's wrists. Neeve's wings, which are gold and green, appear undersized, and he seems to be struggling to stay aloft.

For the first time, I notice that the Auravalians' wings go right through their clothing without any slits or tearing in the fabrics. I wonder how that works. I almost laugh at myself. I want a mundane explanation for the bizarre? I really must be crazy.

Although Karissa and Shiane are to the side and a little behind Skyler and me, I can hear them when they start to talk.

"Surely Neeve didn't concoct that outfit for you," Karissa says.

"No," Shiane answers, "I did it myself. I figured out how Neeve does it long ago."

All of a sudden Shiane's silver, rhinestone-studded snowsuit disappears. She is now wearing a mustard yellow fake fur jacket with seaweed green flannel pajama bottoms. Then in quick succession her clothes change so she's in a purple suede jacket with orange parachute pants, followed by a baby blue bunny suit, complete with floppy ears and a powder puff tail.

"Neeve," Shiane screeches, "you stop doing that right now."

"Sorry," Neeve calls. "I thought I heard you say you had figured out how

I do it."

The next moment, Shiane is dressed like a clown. She has on black baggy pants, bright red suspenders, a yellow polka dot shirt, a big green and blue plaid bowtie, a crumpled old brown hat, and humongous, clodhopper shoes. (Neeve must have insulated her outfit somehow because she doesn't seem bothered by the cold.)

"Skyler," Shiane shrieks, "make him stop!"

"You shouldn't have taunted him," Skyler says. "I'm sure he'll return your clothes to their original state before you have to go home."

"I can't go around like this all day," Shiane cries in alarm. "Jerrin, help me."

"I'm sorry, Shiane," Jerrin says, "but I agree with Skyler. You should know better than to rile Neeve. The way he can manipulate soft goods is almost mage-level. If I were you, the next time I felt like challenging him, I'd suggest a game of chess."

"Karissa?" Shiane whines.

"Perhaps," Karissa says, "if you apologized for making light of his talent, he might relent."

"Or maybe I should just turn him into a toad," Shiane grumbles.

"I heard that, Shiane," Jerrin snaps. Although I had detected a sense of good-natured teasing earlier, there is nothing lighthearted in Jerrin's tone now. "As your mentor, I have to warn you that was an unworthy and possibly dangerous thought for a mage."

I glance over at Shiane. She looks as if she's about to cry.

Skyler suddenly dips down and we are barely skimming above the lake.

I find I'm having trouble clinging to my belief that this is some kind of insane hallucination.

I'm afraid it might actually be happening.

For one thing, I'm freezing to death. Although I like the bite of cold air whipping around me when I'm riding behind Peter on his motorcycle, right now I'm colder than I've ever been before.

For another thing, there is so much detail. I'd have to be deaf, blind, and oblivious to ignore the high-pitched whistling of the wind, the stark whiteness of the snow, the pressing weight of the heavy winter clothing, and the sharp, distinctive smell of winter.

For still another thing, the exchange between Shiane and her brothers sounded too natural and too spontaneous to be anything other than what it appeared to be: the teasing and taunting of siblings. I don't have brothers, but Courtney Bingham has two, and I've heard her have similar squabbles with them. Besides, Hellie and I bicker and banter all the time.

My stomach turns over.

If I acknowledge that even one little bit of this experience is real then I have to acknowledge that magic is real.

But if magic is real, then everything I think I know is wrong.

"Skyler," I say, "can we go back now? I'm about frozen solid, and I have some questions."

"Of course," he answers.

Somehow Neeve manages to change our clothing back to normal, even Shiane's, the moment we land in the ski lodge.

I don't know about everyone else, but I'm chilled to the bone. I look at the fireplace and wish someone had thought ahead enough to light a fire before we left.

No sooner do I have the thought than the logs in the fireplace burst into flames. Not only that, but also the chill is taken off the room instantly.

"Whoever did that," I say, "thank you. I appreciate it." To myself I think, now if that person could only rustle up some hot chocolate and buttered toast.

Immediately a beautiful silver tea service appears on a low table that is sort of like a coffee table except it is round and has a diameter of about five feet. It's right in the middle of the room.

There are three different pots on the tray as well as a sugar bowl, a cream pitcher, a honey jar, a small plate of lemon slices, and an unmarked, red enameled box. I can smell cocoa and coffee. If the red box contains teabags, maybe the third pot contains hot water.

On a separate tray are delicately designed cups and saucers, napkins, dessert plates, and spoons.

Between the trays is a three-tiered server that has little cakes on the top layer, long, thin cookies dusted with powdered sugar on the middle one, and buttered toast without the crusts on the bottom.

"Where did that come from?" I ask. "I was just thinking about something like that."

"You called them to you," Jerrin says.

"What do you mean I called them to me?"

"You have the power to draw things to you, to attract them: people, objects, opportunities, and good luck, to name a few," Jerrin says. "You also have the power not to attract them. No, it's more than that. You have the ability to repel, to deter, and to fend off. I'll need a lot of time with you to understand the subtleties. You do these things automatically as the need arises."

I laugh right in his face.

"I promise you, if I had the power to pull or repel things at will, my life would be a lot different. For instance, I wouldn't let the hot chocolate and toast cool off before I had the opportunity to enjoy them."

"Well," Jerrin says with a smile, "we've made progress. You didn't start by telling me that no one has the power to control positive and negative attraction."

I don't know what to say to that, so I don't say anything.

"Shall I pour?" Shiane asks.

"Yes, please," Skyler responds.

"Besides hot chocolate," Shiane says, "we appear to have coffee and green tea. What is your preference, Skyler?"

"You should serve the ladies first," Skyler answers.

Shiane shakes her head.

"If you'll forgive me, Your Highness," she says, "I'd like to remind you that we're not in Colorado any longer. We're in Auravale. Angel is the only person here who doesn't know your true status, and she might as well learn it now."

Skyler scowls at his little sister. "You are becoming quite a bossy little hoyden, Shiane. You'd better start watching yourself. Even though I'm not king yet, I think I could convince Father to marry you off to some wasteland peasant if I really tried."

Shiane opens her mouth, probably to make a snappy comeback, but Jerrin points a finger at her and then brings the finger to his lips in a shushing gesture. She closes her mouth.

"In this case," Jerrin says to Skyler, "I think Shiane is right. It's been a terrible strain on Hellie, not being able to talk to her twin about all of this. We want Angel's help, but how is she going to learn to trust us if every time we interact, we parcel out another new bit of information? It'll seem like we're making it up as we go."

He pauses.

I assume he's giving Skyler the chance to comment.

When he doesn't, Jerrin continues.

"Angel, our father is the current king of Auravale, and Skyler isn't just a prince, he is the heir apparent. That means—"

"That means," I interrupt, "he has the most legitimate claim to the throne and unless something extraordinary happens—such as his death or abdication—he will become the next king."

"I'm impressed that you know that," Jerrin says.

"It's the same as with Earth monarchies," I respond. "His high status is why Shiane is determined to serve him first."

For a moment no one says anything, and Skyler takes the opportunity to tell Shiane, "Coffee."

Obviously Shiane knows how he takes it.

After she places a cup and a spoon on a saucer, she pours the coffee and then adds a splash of cream and two sugar cubes. She carries it to him, and he sets it on the end table at his elbow.

Before Shiane leaves, two of the long cookies (I think they're called ladyfingers) and two of the little cakes levitate and set themselves down on a dessert plate. It then drifts through the air until it lands on the end table beside Skyler's cup. A napkin flits through the air, unfolds, and spreads itself on his lap.

"Thank you, Shiane," Skyler says.

Shiane grins as she returns to her chair.

"Well done," Jerrin tells her, "but why did you levitate the dessert plate and not the cup and saucer?"

"I was afraid I'd spill the coffee," Shiane answers. "I didn't want to make a mess."

"Try again," Jerrin tells her. "Serve Angel next. I'll spot you."

Without assistance from visible hands, a pot pours steaming cocoa into a cup.

"Do you want either whipped cream or marshmallows with that?" Shiane asks me.

Neither one is present, but I decide to ask for whipped cream anyway.

Suddenly a white swirl appears out of nowhere and lands softly in my cup.

I watch, fascinated, as the cup on its matching saucer drifts toward me. Halfway here, the cup begins to jiggle. Shiane glares at it. It stabilizes and then successfully lands on the flat, wide surface of the sofa's arm. A plate of buttered toast arrives next to it without any trouble.

"Thank you," I say. I taste the hot chocolate. It's perfect. I try a piece of toast, and it's just the way I like it, slightly darker than most people probably prefer.

In turn, Shiane serves everyone in the room without ever using her hands. Twice she appears to be just about to drop the coffeepot or a cup, but then she gets control and continues.

I can't tell how much help Jerrin is giving her.

I startle myself.

When did I start believing that Shiane was actually using telekinesis— or magic—with or without Jerrin's assistance?

I answer myself.

When I decided earlier that the interactions among the siblings supported the hypothesis that this experience is real, I must have suspended my disbelief across the board.

When Shiane finishes serving Jerrin, he tells her, "We'll practice some more on Monday. Liquids are always a bit tricky since it doesn't take much to set them in motion. All in all, you did quite well."

Jerrin sips hot chocolate, and I notice it's still steaming. After he has eaten a piece of toast and a small cake, he turns to Hellie. "Skyler's cup is empty. Please refill it for him."

Hellie doesn't move, but suddenly the coffeepot, cream pitcher, and sugar bowl all sail gently across the room.

The liquids pour themselves, and two sugar cubes jump through the air and land without a splash in the cup. Then the coffeepot, cream pitcher, and sugar bowl float back to the silver tray.

"Showoff!" Shiane says, but she says it with a smile.

"Now, Hellie," Jerrin says, "please serve the rest of our guests with whatever they want. Start with Angel since she has—no matter how inadvertently—actually provided this afternoon's repast."

I put my hand over my cup to indicate I don't want more hot chocolate.

*More toast, then?* Hellie asks without moving her lips. *Or perhaps you'd like to try one of the cakes or the ladyfingers.*

"I'll try a ladyfinger," I say.

A moment later one appears on my plate.

It doesn't fly through the air.

One moment it's on the middle layer of the server, and the next moment it's on my plate.

I feel my eyes trying to pop out of their sockets, but I tell myself, *I've bought this much, I might as well buy the farm.*

I take a bite of the cookie. It is crisp with a slight lemony flavor. I try to use the newness of eating it to distract me from the discomfort caused by watching my twin defy the laws of physics.

Rather than providing a distraction, however, the cookie provokes a question I can't ignore.

"Jerrin," I say, "I've never eaten a ladyfinger before. You said I pulled all of this stuff here, so tell me, how was I able to call a cookie to me that I've never tasted?"

"When you have a strong wish," Jerrin answers, "but you don't identify the specifics, the magic will often fill in the blanks. I'm not sure why ladyfingers were included instead of something else. We can explore the possibilities on another occasion when we have more time."

"So," I go on, "if I can call all of this stuff to me, why haven't I done it at home? When I'm thirsty at night, why do I have to get out of bed and go downstairs to the kitchen to get a cold bottle of water? Why don't I have bottles appearing on my nightstand?"

"On Earth," Jerrin says, "magic is pretty much dormant. People don't believe in it, and they don't use it. It takes a fair amount of power to pull a physical object through space. Here you have access to a large readily available supply. If you gathered this much power at home when you were thirsty, you'd have water bottles popping up all over the place."

"Angel," Skyler says, "you and Jerrin can discuss this in more depth later. When we were flying, you said you had some questions. I'm afraid we've gotten caught up in other things. I apologize for not asking you sooner what you wanted to know. Do you remember?"

"Of course," I state.

"Go ahead and ask," Skyler says.

In my mind I try to prioritize my questions, but I have so many I don't know where to start.

I decide to just plunge in and see what comes out.

"All right," I say. "Tell me how all of this is possible. I've studied a lot of science, and I thought I knew how the universe works. I can prove mathematically why it is impossible for your wings to support your weight, let alone allow you to fly around carrying my weight too. Explain to me how your magic makes my math wrong.

"After that, please tell me how we went from my world to yours without taking a single step, even though we know other solar systems are light-years away. Explain how instantaneous travel across the universe is possible.

"Tell me—"

Skyler holds up his hand to stop me. "The answers to these questions are as complex as the ones you've already asked Jerrin. I'd like to make a suggestion if I might."

I nod. As the crown prince of his country, I imagine Skyler gives more orders than he makes suggestions, especially when dealing with foreign peons. I suppose I should feel flattered.

"You've already had a full day," he says, "and you've had to deal with several new concepts tonight. I suggest that we send you home, let you get a good night's sleep, and then get together again sometime tomorrow. Hellie can let us know when it's convenient for you."

The moment Skyler says I've had a full day, I feel a yawn developing in my throat. I swallow it down.

"That's probably a good idea," I admit.

The next thing I know Hellie and I are both standing in my bedroom.

I look at my sister. "Jerrin said Skyler could promote certain types of movements. This is what he meant, isn't it? He can move people around at will—like pawns on a chess board."

Hellie nods. "Basically, yes."

I get angry. I don't like being picked up and plopped down somewhere without even being consulted.

"What's the penalty in Auravale for slapping a member of the royal family?" I ask.

Laughing, Hellie answers. "I don't know, but I'd advise you against trying it. These people are more powerful than you can imagine. I don't think you could even reach the 'taking aim' stage before Skyler knew what you were planning and had taken steps to prevent it."

"You believe in all this stuff, don't you?"

"I have to," Hellie answers, giving my hand a squeeze. "I've seen too much, and I've experienced too much, to doubt it. But I know what you're going through. I wasn't a believer at first either."

She heads for the bathroom but pauses in the doorway.

"If you think of anything I can say or do to help you get through this, let me know. Good night, Angel."

"Good night, Hellie."

As I get undressed, I realize that somehow over the course of the evening Hellie and I have made up.

I go to bed thinking about the powerful Auravalians.

Sleep is slow in coming.

When I wake up Saturday, I feel jittery.

Now that I'm not dreading Neeve's party because of hostilities between Hellie and me, I've got to make some preparations.

I rush through my morning chores so I can move on to more important things, like figuring out how I'm going to wear my hair with my new dress.

After I take a shower, I put on some old cutoffs and a loose tank top. I stand in front of the bathroom mirror and glare at the mess on my head.

Spread out on the vanity I have three magazines opened up to articles about ways to wear your long hair up. I have my curling iron plugged in and an assortment of elastic bands, scrunchies, clips, barrettes, and hairpins dumped in the sink.

I start with hairstyles that are variations of the ponytail because they look the simplest, but my creations don't bear the slightest resemblance to the sleek, sophisticated styles pictured in the magazines. I look like an escapee from a 1980s teen movie—just bring on the shoulder pads and the sequins.

I move on to some half-up, half-down styles. I do no better with them. I'm about ready to consider shaving my head when Hellie comes into the bathroom.

"What are you trying to do?" she asks.

"The impossible, it seems." Dejectedly I plop my butt down on the side of the bathtub. "I bought the cutest dress to wear to Neeve's party, but I can't make my hair do anything except droop."

Shoving the magazines onto the floor, Hellie perches on the vanity between the two sinks. She stares at me for a few seconds and then smiles.

"When you saw me step out of my closet wearing that floor-length gown, did you notice anything special about me?" she asks.

I gape at her.

"You mean that really happened? It wasn't a dream?"

"It really happened," Hellie says. "I wanted to tell you, but I knew you wouldn't believe me if I said I attended a dance on another world and I came home by stepping through a portal into my closet."

I don't know to react. I'm too stunned.

"Does that mean it was all real?" I ask. "The old man in the office full of books, was that real too?"

"Yep."

"So why don't I remember? It's all a hazy blur."

Hellie's eyes drift upward, and she appears to focus on the upper right corner of the ceiling. I seem to remember reading somewhere that people often do that when they're preparing to tell a lie. Or maybe they focus on the left-hand corner. I can't recall which.

She looks back at me. "I don't know if I should tell you this, but Jerrin mentioned it himself, so I hope it'll be all right." She drums her fingers on the inside of her sink for a few seconds. "Jerrin told you that one of his abilities is affecting memories. Do you remember?"

"Yes," I say.

"Well, he did something to scramble yours."

My mouth drops open.

"Of all the mean, highhanded, imperious tricks!" I exclaim. "Maybe I need to smack him too."

Hellie begins laughing.

"Welcome to my world," she says.

# Chapter Thirteen

"Dealing with Auravalian royalty is generally a pain in the neck," Hellie tells me. "I don't know how Karissa stands it, except maybe Neeve is different from the others since he's been living in Colorado for the past couple of years. You'll get used to it."

"I'm not sure I want to," I say.

The expression on Hellie's face turns somber. "I'm afraid you don't have a choice. They know you've inherited powers from Bree-Ella, and you've already performed one of the great magics instinctively. They'll never leave you alone now."

"You mentioned before that I did some kind of super magic. What did I do?"

Hellie shakes her head at me. "I've probably already told you more than I should. Jerrin will contact me pretty soon to find out when we're going to meet with him and Skyler today. Let's take advantage of the time we have and get back to the question of your hair. Do you remember what I looked like when I stepped out of my closet all dressed up in the peach formal?"

"Sure," I answer. "I thought you looked like you just came home from Cinderella's ball. Your hair was done up in curls, and your makeup looked as if it had been applied by a professional."

"It had been." Hellie leans so far forward that I fear she might slip off the counter and hit the floor. She lowers her voice to a whisper. "Last summer I went to Auravale and met the king."

"What—?" I start to exclaim, but she puts a finger up to her lips.

"Shh," she says. "I don't want to draw Mom and Dad's attention. Right now, they're rushing all over the house trying to find Mom's golf bag and shoes. They've got a 2:15 tee time with Marv and Betty Berkley. Let's not distract them."

I nod silently, and Hellie resumes.

"How and why I ended up in the king's court is a long story, and I'll tell it to you sometime, but the significant thing is that I wasn't dressed appropriately. So, His Majesty assigned a young woman to help me find something to wear and to make me presentable for dinner.

"Her name is Jacie. She dressed me and did my hair and makeup for the king. She's helped me a few other times, too, including for the dance Neeve and Karissa held in my honor on graduation night.

"When I told Jacie I was going to attend a party tomorrow evening and Skyler and Jerrin would both be there, she offered to fix me up again. I'm sure she'd be happy to do your hair and makeup at the same time."

"What makes you think so?" I ask.

"We're twins. Although a few Paneldan creatures have twin or even triplet births, the humanoids don't—not ever, not even once. Jacie will be thunderstruck to see us together. Do you want to come with me?"

"You're absolutely sure she won't mind?" I ask, trying not to sound too eager. "I don't want to presume—"

"Shall I call and ask her?"

"Call her? How?"

"Same as on Earth," Hellie says, pulling her cellphone out of her jeans' pocket.

"Jacie has a cellphone?" I exclaim in disbelief. "Are our technologies that closely related?"

"Not at all," Hellie says. "The Auravalians copied cellphones from us. Kaden told me that Neeve went home a couple of years ago and had his cellphone with him. Jerrin was so impressed with it that he took it to the Guild of Artificers and had them make an Auravalian equivalent.

"It only took them about a month to come up with a prototype that worked both on Panelda and on Earth. Then they took the prototype to the Magicians Guild. There, the mages modified the design so the phones could work between our worlds too."

Magic and technology?

Functioning together?

I don't think I want to know.

"Although the entire royal family is telepathic," Hellie continues, "not all Auravalians are. In fact, those who work in the palace are selected specifically because they can't read minds. The cellphone has been a boon for them. It saves the servants a lot of running from floor to floor, from wing to wing, and from outside to inside when they need to communicate with each other. Last year, I bought Jacie her first cellphone as a way of thanking her for being so kind to me."

As Hellie dials, I count the number of taps she makes. She has to do an extra three to reach Auravale.

The conversation is short. After just a brief explanation from Hellie, Jacie readily agrees to do my hair and makeup for Neeve's party. They negotiate a time, and Hellie hangs up.

I'm just about to make a comment, but Hellie holds up her hand to stop me. Her face goes blank for a couple of seconds.

"That was Jerrin," she says.

Obviously, being a royal, he doesn't need to use a cellphone.

"He'd like us to meet with him and Skyler right now. What do you think? Shall we go and get it over with?"

"Might as well," I say. "Procrastinating won't improve it any."

Then I glance down at what I'm wearing. My raggedy cutoffs and baggy tank top are not appropriate attire. It's not just because I don't want a couple of princes to see me looking so grungy, but it's also because it's winter in Auravale.

"Wait!" I exclaim as I jump to my feet. "I need a few minutes to change my clothes and brush out my hair."

"Right," Hellie says. "I probably ought to change too. I'll tell Jerrin we'll be there in half an hour."

I'm just about to take a step.

I stop and glance over my shoulder.

"Doesn't someone need to come get us?" I ask.

Hellie blushes. "Actually, no," she says. "I can open a doorway between our worlds. Jerrin taught me how."

My mind floods with questions.

I turn all the way around so I can look at my sister face-to-face.

"I hate to keep repeating this," Hellie says, "but you'll get used to it. Now, hurry. I told Jerrin half an hour, but our times don't run at the same rate, so it's hard to predict how soon he'll start getting impatient."

I hurry.

When Hellie and I arrive at the lodge, only Skyler and Jerrin are present.

"Thank you both for coming," Skyler says. He motions for us to take seats near the fireplace. "I'd like to start by having Jerrin answer a few of your questions, Angel. As a mage mentor, he has been trained to teach and is much better at explaining theoretical concepts than I am.

"However, you need to realize that in-depth understanding will only come through education, training, and experience. We're not here to answer all of your questions. It can't be done in a day. We just want you to know there are answers, and you'll have the opportunity to learn them over time. Jerrin?"

Jerrin nods and leans back in his chair, shifting around a little as if he wants to get as comfortable as possible before attacking the problem.

He starts by asking me a question. "Angel, how would you define energy?"

"That's simple," I answer. "Energy is the property that is transferred from one object to another in order to perform work or to produce heat."

"Good," Jerrin says, sounding a bit surprised.

I think he's been underestimating my intelligence.

"What else do you know about energy?" he asks.

"It exists in various forms," I answer as if I were still in school, "such as hydro, electrical, mechanical, chemical, thermal, and nuclear, among others." Trying to impress him, I add, "The Conservation of Energy law states that energy can be converted in form, but it cannot be created or destroyed."

"Good, again," Jerrin says with a smile.

"It's just basic physics," I say with false modesty. "At least it is on Earth."

"It's basic physics here on Panelda, too. Magic doesn't change that. Now, how would you define power?"

"That's a little more complicated," I admit. "Some people use the terms power and energy interchangeably, especially when referring to electricity. But power is actually the ability of a person or a force to directly influence things outside of itself, such as influencing people, objects, or events."

"Excellent," Jerrin says. "People here sometimes use energy and power interchangeably, too, especially when trying to describe magic. Scholars like to debate whether magic is a form of energy or a psychic power. Maybe it's both.

"The important thing is that magic, like energy, cannot create or destroy. Instead, it manipulates. By using our thoughts and our will, we can reshape the mechanics, the functioning, and the physical properties of items within the world around us."

"How?" I ask. "How do you do it?"

Instead of answering me, Jerrin makes an offhanded request. "Will you pick up the pillow next to you and toss it to me?"

I try to be tolerant.

"Sure." I throw him the pillow.

"How did you do that?" he asks me.

"I don't know what you mean," I say, puzzled by the question.

"How did you pick up the pillow and throw it to me?"

I frown. "I don't understand."

"I simply want you to detail the process you went through in order to throw the pillow to me."

"I still don't get it." I glare at him. "What do you want me to say?"

"I'll explain," he says patiently. "Before you tossed me the pillow, you thought about it, you possibly even envisioned it, and then you decided to do it, all within a split second. Once you made the decision, your brain instructed your body to reach over, pick up the pillow, and throw it, again within half a moment's time.

"Because of those instantaneous and subconscious steps, you influenced the position of the pillow. It was there, and now it's here. That is all that magic does, except it doesn't necessarily involve using the body, although it might. If you have the ability and if you focus properly, you can make your desires become realities."

Uh huh.

I know I'm smart.

My high school GPA was 3.97. I graduated third in my class.

Still, I can't wrap my head around what Jerrin is saying.

He doesn't get flustered or angry.

He simply tries a different tack.

"When we came in from flying yesterday," Jerrin says, "you were very cold. You wanted heat, and you wanted it fast. Your desire was so strong, I actually felt you call the energy you fed into the logs to make them combust."

I make a sweeping gesture with my hand at the now empty coffee table. "And I called all of the food, the drinks, the tea set, the cups, and the dishes that appeared too. Right?"

"Yes," Jerrin says. "Every bit of it."

"From where?" I practically shriek. "You said magic doesn't create anything, it only manipulates. So where did all of that stuff come from? Did I call the cakes and the ladyfingers and the toast right out of someone's bakery or restaurant?"

"It's possible," Jerrin says. "It's one of the things we'll explore when we start your training. I'd like to know where you call things from too. However, not all of it is a mystery. The tea set, the china, the napkins, and the silverware came from the kitchen here at the lodge, probably the coffee and the tea as well. I don't know where the hot chocolate came from. It's better than the mixture I'm used to. Perhaps—"

"Jerrin," Skyler interrupts him. "You're getting ahead of yourself. Angel hasn't agreed to accept training yet." He looks at me with a probing gaze. "Maybe we'd better take care of that right now. Angel, do you agree to let Jerrin train you in the use of magic? Are you ready to accept him as your teacher?"

Something in his tone cautions me not to make a quick response.

I turn to the only person in the room I know I can trust.

"Hellie?"

I'm on a sofa, and Hellie is sitting in a chair at a ninety-degree angle from me. I twist to the side so we have eye contact.

"Hellie?"

"If you let Jerrin train you," my twin tells me, "he'll teach you how to recognize the magical powers within you. Once you can identify them, he'll teach you how to use them responsibly. Our ancestor, Bree-Ella Dark, was a powerful mage, and we inherited the ability to use magic from her. Jerrin has been training me since last summer."

Hmm.

Hellie has been learning magic for a year?

That explains her ability to bring us here, I guess.

Still, I feel a little hurt that she didn't tell me before.

Even if I wouldn't have believed her, she could have tried.

We really have grown apart.

Now what?

Could I learn to do magic too?

The thought scares me.

"Before you answer Skyler," Hellie says, "I think it's only fair to warn you of two things."

"What?" I ask nervously.

"First, if you tell Skyler you accept Jerrin as your teacher, you will have just entered into a legal agreement. He's the crown prince. Telling him you'll do something is the same as telling the king, and when you tell the king you'll do something, you are in fact taking an oath of service. Be sure you know what you want before you commit yourself."

My mind starts spinning around.

I have so many questions that I'm getting dizzy.

I look at the people in the room and try to formulate a thought.

"Second," Hellie continues, "we are distantly related to the royal family. Like I told you yesterday, they are all telepathic. They can read our minds—plus almost everyone else's—with or without our consent. In turn, because of the family relationship, we can learn to communicate with them telepathically, but only when they allow us to. You need to decide if that will bother you."

Skyler turns to me. "There is much more that you need to understand if you're going to handle magic, and if you choose to proceed, Jerrin will be your teacher. But you don't have to commit yourself to accepting training right now. You and Hellie can discuss it at home, and you can give me your answer at the party tomorrow evening. Hellie, you have permission to explain anything to Angel that you think she's ready to understand."

Hellie nods. "I'll do my best."

"Now, Angel," Skyler continues, "I want to talk with you about Peter and Cindy."

"What about them?" I ask defensively. I'm flustered because I can't imagine how he knows their names, let alone enough about them to need to discuss them with me.

"The king wants us to talk with them and to ask them some questions. We'll bring them here tomorrow sometime during the party at Neeve's apartment. We—"

"What!" I yelp. "No. You can't do that."

I seldom express my feelings verbally. I'm too passive-aggressive. I'm more likely to write poison-pen letters, or put peanut butter in someone's coat pocket, or badmouth people behind their backs, than I am to confront them. But this is my boyfriend and his little sister we're talking about.

"You can't just swoop over to my world and drag Peter and Cindy here," I snap.

"Yes, we can," Jerrin asserts, sounding as if I'd just told him they can't breathe oxygen.

"No," I repeat, letting my anger out by emphatically slapping the arm of the couch. "I don't care who you are or what kind of mystical powers you have, you do not have the right to bring Peter and Cindy here without their consent."

"Why?" Jerrin asks. His lips have the hint of a smile, and his tone verges on the sarcastic.

I expect him to smirk.

If he does, I swear I'll pick up the nearest heavy object and beat him over the head with it until he's black and blue and bloody.

Lucky for him, he doesn't.

Instead, he merely repeats, "Why?"

"Because you'll scare them," I answer. "Or at least you'll scare Cindy. Right now, she feels safe about going to Neeve's party because she knows Peter and I will be with her. But if you just pick her up and plop her down here, she'll recognize that she's not where she should be, and she'll be afraid.

"Automatically, she'll turn to Peter for clarification and reassurance, but he won't have any idea what's going on either. Since Peter is adaptable, he'll look around, ask questions, try to make sense of the situation, and wait for information. He won't panic, but if he can't find a way to reassure Cindy, she will."

"What do you suggest?" Jerrin asks.

"There's got to be a way to prepare them, or at least to prepare Peter."

"All right," Skyler says, "we'll give it some thought."

"Promise you'll talk to me before you do anything," I say. "Promise you won't just snatch them away."

Skyler gets the same almost-smirky expression on his face that Jerrin had a moment ago.

I boil inside.

I've never wanted to pound on someone with my fists so badly before.

I don't like Skyler and Jerrin's imperialistic attitudes.

Maybe Americans aren't cut out to deal with foreign royals. Anyway, I don't suppose I am.

"I promise," Skyler says condescendingly, "we won't bring Peter or Cindy to Auravale without discussing the situation with you first. Does that satisfy you?"

"Yes," I manage to say between clenched teeth.
"Good. Hellie, I assume you'll take her home."
Hellie nods.
"Then I bid you both a good afternoon."
He and Jerrin disappear.

# Chapter Fourteen

Saturday evening is awful.

Hellie leaves with Kaden right after dinner.

Mom and Dad go next door to play Bridge.

I stay home alone.

It's the first time in ages that Peter and I haven't spent a Saturday evening together. He didn't even mention it to me. I try to convince myself that he's just exhausted after working so many hours on the Camaro, doing his chores this morning, and then working all afternoon in his garage.

But if that was it, why didn't he just tell me?

I don't want to be one of those whiney, clinging, insecure, demanding girlfriends.

I won't call him and ask for an explanation.

I refuse to feel hurt or jealous or suspicious.

Thumbing through my DVDs, I look for something that'll distract me. I don't find anything that grabs my attention.

I glance over the spines of my books.

Usually reading is one of my favorite activities, but I'm not in the mood to read about people who are happy (since I'm not), and I don't want to read about characters who are struggling with problems (since right now I have my own).

In desperation, I turn on my computer and watch some dumb cat and dog videos on YouTube.

This is one of my guilty pleasures.

Not that I ever want the responsibility of taking care of a pet. When I see people on the videos joking about the messes their animals make, I know it's not for me. If my cat climbed up the Christmas tree, knocked it over, and shattered all of my ornaments, or if my dog dug into the couch and ripped all of the stuffing out of the cushions, I wouldn't find it funny in the least. I certainly wouldn't laugh about it and post it on YouTube.

Just not a pet person, I guess.

Frustrated and bored, I go to bed early.

I have a fitful night, but I wake up so excited about going to Neeve's party that I can hardly sit through church services.

As soon as I change out of my good clothes, I go through the bathroom into Hellie's room.

"When do we leave to get our hair and makeup done?" I ask.

"As soon as the Berkleys pick up Mom and Dad," she answers.

Since we told our folks that we were going to spend the afternoon getting ready for Neeve's party and wouldn't be eating with them, they arranged to go out with their best friends. I'll bet they try to fit in a round of golf between lunch and coming home to see us off.

I hear a horn honk.

A moment later, Mom sticks her head into the room.

"We're leaving now," she says. "We'll be back by 5:00."

"Have fun," I say.

"Tell Marv and Betty hello for us," Hellie adds.

"Come on, Bethany," Dad says impatiently. "They're waiting."

"I'm coming," Mom tells him.

"Bye, girls." Dad takes Mom by the arm and steers her out into the hallway and down the stairs.

Hellie and I watch out the window until we see them get into the Berkleys' car and drive away.

"Ready?" Hellie asks.

"Absolutely," I answer.

A moment later, we're standing in a beautiful white and pink bedroom.

I'm still gawking at the room's splendor when we're joined by a young woman who's not more than a couple of years older than we are.

She is carrying a tray full of ribbons, bows, combs, barrettes, silk flowers, and who knows what else?

"Hellie," she exclaims.

When she notices me, her eyes bulge. She drops the tray, steps back, and presses herself flat against the wall. She covers her mouth with both hands.

"Jacie." Hellie rushes over and guides the young woman to a white velvet chair that is one of a pair situated beside a fireplace.

"I'm sorry it was such a shock," Hellie says. "I tried to warn you. This is my twin sister, Angel."

Watching Jacie tremble, I'm not sure she'll be able to do anything for us that requires the use of her hands.

"Is she real?" Jacie asks.

"Of course, she's real," Hellie says. "She's my sister. I know twin births don't happen in Auravale, but they do on Earth."

"Stand together," Jacie says.

When we comply, she walks around us slowly, looking us up and down, as if measuring us with her eyes. Finally, she takes a deep breath and sighs.

"At least you're not exact copies of each other. I don't think I could've coped with that."

She crouches down and scoops up the items she spilled on the floor.

"Well, which one of you wants to be first?" she asks.

"You go ahead," I tell Hellie. "I'd like to watch."

Before Jacie begins, she has us each describe in detail what we will be wearing.

She selects a variety of hair ornaments from the tray and sets them on a vanity that also holds her combs, brushes, clips, and pins. She has Hellie sit down in front of a mirror and goes to work.

She does Hellie's hair in a kind of French braid that follows her hairline and encircles her head. Then poking flowers in among the plaits, Jacie decorates the braid so it looks as if Hellie's hair is part of a floral wreath.

When she's finished, Jacie has us switch places.

"I'll do your makeup after I've done Angel's hair," Jacie says to Hellie. "I'll need to put away all of this," she gestures at the things on the vanity, "to make enough room for the cosmetics."

Jacie brushes my hair and then pulls it up into a ponytail high on the back of my head. She divides it into sections and curls them, making my hair into a crown of ringlets. She fastens down the coils in front with hairpins adorned with tiny white and black bows and lets the curls in the back dangle freely.

After she clears the vanity of her hair grooming tools, she sets out a variety of skinny bottles, delicate crystal jars, and squat little golden pots with glass lids, each of which contains a colored substance: creams, powders, foundation makeups, blush, eye shadow, and lip dyes would be my guess.

With a touch of color here and a highlight there, Jacie transforms my attractive twin into a beauty.

Just a few moments later, she does the same thing for me.

When Hellie and I stand side by side and look in the mirror, I think what Jacie has done might be the first true magic I've seen. Hellie and I still look like twins, but we also look like individuals.

Jacie has created a separate style for each of us.

We look stunning.

It's impossible to thank her enough.

Before we leave, Jacie takes her cellphone from a pocket in her dress and snaps a couple of photos of us.

Then Hellie takes us home.

We spend the rest of the afternoon sitting around and talking, taking care not to mess up our hair or smudge our makeup.

At 5:00 we put on our dresses. The hairstyles and makeup that Jacie did for us complement our outfits perfectly.

Mom and Dad make it home just a few minutes after five. When we come downstairs, they *ooh* and *ah* all over us.

"See you soon," Hellie tells me right before Kaden pulls up in Neeve's car. I guess he knows how to drive after all.

At 5:30, Peter and Cindy arrive. They come to the front door together.

Cindy looks so grown up.

Her new dress is pale pink taffeta. It has a fitted bodice, a full skirt, and short puffy sleeves. She is wearing hose (probably her first ever pantyhose) instead of anklets with her Sunday shoes, which are white leather flats.

Her reddish-brown hair has been trimmed so the natural curl falls in gentle waves around her face. Her fingernails have been shaped by a professional and polished a shade of pink that's slightly darker than her dress. Although she's not wearing any makeup, she has on some clear lip-gloss.

"Cindy," I say, "you're lovely."

She twirls around. "I am, aren't I?"

"Absolutely."

She grins at me, and I put my arm around her.

Next, I turn my attention to Peter.

I am used to seeing him in jeans and a t-shirt.

For special occasions, he puts on a dress shirt with his jeans.

Not tonight.

Tonight, he is wearing black slacks, a black silk shirt that's open at the neck, and a white linen sports coat.

I seldom get to see him all dressed up.

He takes my breath away.

I guess he thinks I look pretty good too.

He puts his arms around me and whispers in my ear, "Angel, you're beautiful. What on earth are you doing with a grease monkey like me?"

I answer him simply and honestly. I whisper back, "I love you."

Although we didn't plan it, my outfit looks great next to Peter's.

My new dress is a lightweight, sleeveless sundress with a knee-length flared skirt and a scooped neckline. It is white with a narrow black stripe and has red piping outlining the neck and armholes.

A wide red belt encircles my waist, I have on red, low-heeled sandals, and I carry a small red clutch. Around my neck I'm wearing the gold locket my parents gave me for graduation.

I look at us in the hall mirror.

We look like we belong on the cover of a magazine.

My parents join us a few minutes later, giving me the opportunity to introduce them to Cindy.

When they tell her hello, Cindy holds her skirt out at the sides and curtseys. I imagine she learned that from a TV show or a movie.

It is an endearing gesture, and my father (who is a die-hard romantic) bows from the waist.

Cindy beams.

Dad takes half a dozen pictures of us, and then my parents wish us a pleasant evening.

After we're outside, Peter hooks arms with me on one side and with Cindy on the other.

We've taken a couple of steps before I realize that the car in the driveway doesn't belong to Peter's parents. It's a classy black vehicle that's something between a sedan and a sports car.

"Where did you get it?" I ask as I glide my hand across a sleek black fender.

"I rented it," Peter says. "When I am escorting two lovely ladies to a party, I can't expect one of them to ride in the back. This car has a front bench instead of bucket seats."

"What is it?" I ask.

"2013 Chevy Impala," Peter answers. "It's the last regular car you could buy with the option of a bench seat in front. You can order a bench for some minivans and some trucks, but cars went to bucket seats years ago."

He opens the car door and has Cindy slide in first.

"The seat has a 40:20:40 ratio," Peter says. "That means the bench is really 2 ½ seats wide, with the half part being in the middle. That's why Cindy needs to sit between us. She's the smallest."

"Besides," I say, "since she's on a date with both of us, she shouldn't be shunted to the side."

"You're right." Peter gives me a quick kiss before I slip in next to Cindy. Then he circles around the car and climbs into the driver's seat.

The Americana Apartments is one of those buildings that have security doors that lock automatically after anyone passes in or out. Peter taps Neeve's apartment number on a keypad that's beside an intercom.

"Peter," Neeve's voice says without waiting for Peter to identify himself. "I'm glad you came. I'll buzz you in."

Glancing up, I spot a camera above the door.

Nice.

When someone taps in an apartment number, the camera must send a picture of the visitors to the appropriate unit. Of course, Neeve would know right away who the guy is who's standing beside Hellie's twin.

Although useful, that kind of technology sounds awfully pricey to me.

Since Neeve is rich, maybe the CCTV is his property, used for his personal safety, with everyone else just having access to the intercom.

Or, maybe, the camera is part of the building's security system and Neeve has hacked into it to monitor his callers.

Neeve is a prince and he has been kidnapped and tortured once already.

An experience like that would certainly make me feel a little paranoid.

A buzzer sounds, and Peter pulls the door open.

We take the elevator to the 8ᵗʰ floor and find Neeve standing in the doorway of his apartment ready to welcome us.

He is tall and thin. His long blond hair is parted down the middle and hooked behind his ears. His facial features are attractive and he has a great smile, but it's his eyes that dominate. They are green: bright green, true green, emerald green. There's none of that almost green or brownish green or golden green.

He is dressed much like Peter except his slacks are brown, his silk shirt is cream, and his lightweight sports coat is tan.

"Angel, Peter, thank you for coming." Then glancing down, he says, "You must be Cindy. My name is Neeve."

Repeating the gesture that she made for my father, Cindy curtsies. Neeve bows, takes her hand, and kisses it.

Cindy practically dislocates her jaws from the size of her grin.

Then Neeve offers Cindy his arm. "May I escort you inside and introduce you to my other guests?"

"Yes, please," Cindy says as she places her hand in the crook of his elbow.

Peter and I follow them in.

I have heard of palatial apartments before, but I never expected to see one, especially not in Shawon, Colorado. I think the flat must cover over half of the building's top floor.

No wonder Neeve said he had plenty of space. There must be at least thirty people present, and the room doesn't even begin to look crowded.

When I glance over at the buffet table, I think Neeve underestimated when he said he had enough food to feed an army. More likely he has enough to feed a small country. No, I tell myself, that's an exaggeration, but he might be able to accommodate a moderately sized city.

Neeve leads Cindy over to the two men who are standing beside a huge aquarium full of exotic fish.

"Cindy," Neeve says, "I'd like you to meet my brothers. This is Skyler. He's the eldest. And this is Jerrin."

Seeing the three brothers standing so close together, I recognize qualities I didn't notice Friday.

Skyler is a bit shorter than the other two, his brown hair is beginning to show a little gray, and his dark brown eyes look menacing.

Jerrin resembles their younger brother more than Skyler does. His hair is just a shade or two darker than Neeve's, and his eyes are as brilliantly blue as Neeve's are green.

Cindy repeats her curtsy, and Skyler and Jerrin both bow to her. When she extends her hand, they each kiss it.

Then Neeve tells his brothers, "I'd also like to introduce you to Angel, Hellie's sister, and Peter, Angel's fiancé."

I wondered how Neeve was going to handle the situation since, from Peter's point of view, I've never met these men before. Simple. Just pretend Friday night never happened.

But fiancé? Where did that come from?

Peter and I have been dating for over a year, but he has never asked me to marry him.

Before I can challenge the choice of words, however, Skyler says, "I am pleased to meet you, Angel." We shake hands. "You and Hellie certainly look alike. It's quite remarkable."

"Thank you."

Then I shake hands with Jerrin.

I'm standing there, trying to figure out how to make small talk with two men that I know are royalty from another world, when Hellie approaches.

"Excuse me, guys," she says casually, "while you get acquainted with Peter, I'd like to take Angel and Cindy over to meet Karissa and Shiane if that's okay."

"Of course," Skyler tells her.

As we walk away, Hellie squeezes my hand. "Did you and Peter coordinate your outfits?"

"No," I say, "pure coincidence."

"Or maybe your tastes are just that similar." Then Hellie bends down and says, "Cindy, your dress is lovely, and your new haircut is just darling. You look beautiful."

"I know," she says. Then she catches herself.

She motions for Hellie to bend down lower so she can do her version of a whisper. She cups a hand around her mouth and speaks into Hellie's ear. "Mama says the only right answer to a compliment is *thank you*. Can we try again?"

Cindy drops her hand.

Hellie repeats her comment, ending with, "You look beautiful."

Cindy assumes a highbrow expression.

"Thank you for thinking it," she says in a fairly good British accent, "and thank you again for saying it."

My mouth almost falls open.

Cindy made a joke!

Not only a joke, but also one that has attitude and accent!

I want to clap and make a big fuss, praising her, the way parents do when a baby starts toddling around or when a preschooler can finally recite the alphabet.

I don't do it of course.

Cindy is old enough to resent that type of condescending attention.

However, I make a mental note to tell Peter about it later.

As we approach Karissa Day, I'm reminded of the evening she and Neeve graduated from high school. She was in her wheelchair right up until her name was called. Then Neeve helped her stand, and leaning on him for support, she walked across the stage to receive her diploma. People in the audience stood up and cheered.

Looking at her tonight, as she stands and moves with perfect ease, I can hardly believe it's the same girl.

She's not very tall and is cute rather than pretty or beautiful. When she graduated, her curly golden hair was so short that it barely covered her earlobes, but she has obviously been letting it grow out. Now it brushes the tops of her shoulders.

She is dressed almost entirely in green: green slacks, white tank top covered with small green shamrocks, green sandals, and a little green shoulder bag. I don't think it's a coincidence that the shade of green matches Neeve's eyes.

"I'm so happy to see you, Angel," Karissa tells me. "Hellie talks about you all the time. I hope we have the chance to get to know each other."

Then she smiles at Cindy. "I'm very happy to meet you, too. Let me introduce you to Neeve's little sister." She calls out, "Shiane."

When Shiane turns around and starts walking towards us, Cindy smiles broadly and claps her hands. "She's a fairy princess."

I remember thinking the same thing the first time I saw Shiane. She has an elongated physique, tiny bones, a delicate beauty, and short curly strawberry blond hair. She looks like a beam of sunlight in her lemon-yellow sundress.

Two young guys accompany her.

"And these are my brothers," Karissa continues, "Jeremy and Bennett."

Jeremy, the elder brother, looks as if he's old enough to drive, but just barely. He is tallish (not as tall as Neeve and Kaden, but taller than Peter) and really skinny. His hair is that washed out color that used to be blond but is in the process of turning brown. Other than that, he's not bad looking. I can tell just by the expression in his eyes that he's smart, he knows it, and he'd love to demonstrate it.

Bennett, on the other hand, looks like a sweetheart. He probably doesn't stand out too much in a crowd. His only outstanding physical characteristic is that he has no outstanding physical characteristics. He probably has an average IQ, but there is something immensely kind and gentle in his expression. A person has to look for it, though, because his eyes are fairly well hidden behind dark-rimmed glasses.

"We were just going to watch a DVD," Bennett says to Cindy. "Want to come with us?"

Cindy glances up for Peter, but since he isn't immediately available, she turns to me. "Angel?"

"What are you going to watch?" I ask, knowing that certain types of shows are prohibited, specifically horror and violent crimes.

"The animated *Beauty and the Beast,*" Bennett answers.

"I've never watched it all the way through," Jeremy says. "Next year, the orchestra is going to do a concert that features music from the film. I thought it might help if I knew how the tunes fit into the story." He adds proudly, "I play clarinet."

I smile and nod in acknowledgement.

"I know the fairytale," Shiane says, "but I've never seen the movie."

"Can I go with them, Angel?" Cindy asks.

"I think we'd better check with Peter," I tell her. "It has some pretty scary scenes."

"I've seen it once already," Cindy asserts.

"If it gets too scary," Shiane says, "Cindy and I can hold on to each other, can't we, Cindy."

"Yes," Cindy answers. She reaches over and takes Shiane's hand in her own. "I'll warn you when the scary parts are coming."

"Nonetheless," I say, "I'd like to clear it with Peter just to be sure."

As if on cue, Peter comes over to join us.

I introduce Peter to Shiane, Karissa, and Karissa's brothers.

"We're going to watch *Beauty and the Beast,*" Cindy says. "Shiane and I are going to hold on to each other during the scary parts. Is that okay, Peter?"

"I suppose so," Peter says. He glances around the room. "Where exactly will you be?"

Jeremy points to a door about halfway down the interior wall. "TV room is in there."

"All right," Peter says. "I'll come check on you a little later."

Skyler approaches.

"I'll be right with you, Cindy," Shiane says. "I had better wait and see what my eldest brother wants first."

"I'll take care of her," Bennett says.

Cindy lets go of Shiane's hand and takes Bennett's. They turn and head for the TV room.

"Hellie," Skyler says when he reaches us, "now, please. Just you, Kaden, Karissa, Angel, and the family."

Before I can even finish opening my mouth to ask "Now what?" the room goes silent.

Except for the few of us who are grouped around Karissa and who were named by Skyler, there appear to be only three other people who can move. Everyone else looks frozen solid.

I watch Kaden, Neeve, and Jerrin approach.

Cindy, Peter, and Karissa's brothers are frozen like the others.

"Hellie, what did you do to them?" I whisper.

Tears trickle down my cheeks.

"Hellie," I repeat. "What have you done to Peter and Cindy?"

# Chapter Fifteen

"They are not injured or drugged," Skyler answers before Hellie can. "They are like the people at your church social Friday night. Hellie has significantly slowed down time for them. We need—"

"But," I interrupt him, "you said the king wanted you to meet with Peter and Cindy. You didn't say anything about immobilizing them."

"We need to talk with you for a few minutes first. When we have completed our discussion, we'll bring them through."

"Excuse me, Skyler," Jerrin says, "but I think this would be easier on all of us if we went somewhere else. I'm not very comfortable looking at these vacant faces myself, and I'm sure it's even harder on Angel."

Skyler nods. "All right, go ahead."

"Anywhere in particular?" Jerrin asks.

After a moment's thought, Skyler answers. "We might as well go back to the hunting lodge."

Suddenly, we're there.

This time I don't have to do whatever it is that I did last time to get the place warm. A fire is already burning in the fireplace, and it has taken the chill off the room.

I plop down in a chair and watch the flames.

I have never felt so helpless before.

These people think they can do whatever they want with us poor, defenseless humans—they move us around like puppets.

What powers do we have to fight back with?

An image flashes through my mind, and I prop my elbow on the chair's arm, dip my head, and cover my mouth with my hand to keep from laughing.

Jerrin said I can call things to me.

I picture conjuring a bakery's worth of cakes and cream pies and pelting Skyler and Jerrin with them. If they don't have food fights in Auravale (and the elder two brothers seem way too stuffy to have ever participated in such childishness), maybe I could catch them off-guard and get them both right in the face before they stopped me.

Imagining Skyler and Jerrin covered in cake crumbs, fractured piecrusts, fruit fillings, and whipped cream does a great deal toward lightening my mood.

I have to struggle to get my amusement under control.

When I deem it safe, I lift up my head.

Hellie and Kaden are sitting in a love seat. His arm is around her, and her head is resting on his shoulder. I have never seen Hellie in so intimate a position before. Regardless of when they had their first date, this is not a casual relationship.

My sister is in love.

It will take me a while to get used to that.

My sister is in love.

"Angel," Skyler says, "yesterday we never got around to explaining to you why it is so important for you to understand that you have magical powers and why you must learn to control them."

With a nod of his regal head, he turns the stage over to Jerrin.

"You might remember," Jerrin says, "I started to tell you about our uncle, Maldon Darker. He is an evil man who wants to gather enough power either to dethrone or to assassinate our father. We believe, when he sired a child with your ancestor Bree-Ella Dark, he was trying to force her into a position that would allow him to use her powers. By combining them with his own, he would have been strong enough to attack us.

"However, she fled. Since then, Maldon and his kin have been trying to locate her or her child. Luckily the Darkers don't have finders or farseers in their genetic line. However, they have enough magical talent in the family to assign a rotation of magic users to listen for the echoes of Bree-Ella's power.

"When you were just influencing people to like you or to gain advantages for yourself, you were in no danger. Those are small magics without any far-reaching consequences.

"But Friday night you used one of the great powers. If the Darkers felt it, they will assume it was either Bree-Ella or the child. Last year, the same thing happened to Hellie, and Maldon Darker came for her. She managed to elude him, and since then, we've taught her how to mask her talents. So far, she has kept herself hidden.

"However, the feel of your magic and Hellie's is so similar, if you don't learn how to control and mask yours, you'll draw their attention back to your world. That puts you and Hellie in extreme danger, and Peter and Cindy as well because of their association with you."

I feel as if I've been stabbed in the heart.

"Are you saying Peter and Cindy are in danger because I love them?"

"Not exactly," Jerrin says, "but they can be used as tools against you, and that puts all of you at risk."

"Then tell me what I have to do to keep them safe," I say with a quiver in my voice. "I'd rather die than expose them to harm. Having them in my life is the best, the most positive experience I've ever had. Before I met Peter, I didn't think I'd ever know what true happiness was."

"Right," I hear Hellie mumble. "As if you haven't gotten everything you ever wanted."

I glance to the side.

Hellie has an incredulous, almost bitter, expression on her face.

"I know you think my life has been perfect," I tell her, "but you're wrong. Do you think it's been easy, always having to be the angel—not being allowed to get angry, not being allowed to feel hurt, not being allowed to be sad? I've had lots of acquaintances who pretended to be my friends, but they weren't, not really. They wanted too much. They wanted me to be upbeat and cheerful and self-sacrificing all the time. They didn't want to support me. They wanted me to support them. As soon as I was feeling needy, they were gone. They had no idea who I was or what I wanted."

Tears drip down my face.

"How do you think I felt in high school, knowing I didn't dare have a boyfriend? I didn't even dare date a boy more than once or twice. Why? Because the guys ran a locker-room lottery, taking bets on who would finally seduce—not their word—the angel. They made me feel cheap and dirty, but I was the angel, and I had to smile and be happy anyway.

"Then I met Peter. As soon as I saw him, I knew I wanted to spend the rest of my life with him. When I'm angry or discouraged or lonely, Peter is the only person who understands. He listens to me, he takes me seriously, and he cares. I try to do the same things for him. It's not easy for Peter to accomplish everything he does for his family and still find time to have a life of his own. Together we are so much more than either of us is alone."

No longer just dripping, my tears become a deluge.

I try swallowing my sobs, but I'm not successful.

If I pose a danger to Peter, there is only one thing I can do.

I turn away from my sister and gaze at Jerrin, trying to swipe my cheeks dry with my hands. But I can't quit crying.

"Tell me how to stop doing whatever I'm doing. I promise I'll follow your instructions precisely. I don't understand anything about magic or greater powers and lesser powers. All I know is that I can't bear the thought of being a threat to Peter. If I am, I'll let him go. I'll have to.

"I want him safe and secure and alive, even if it means we can never be together." I have to fight to force the words out. "I love him. If anything happened to him through me, I'd die of a broken heart. Please, please, don't let me hurt him."

"This gets more and more complicated by the minute," Skyler says. "I believe Angel and Peter have shared a recognition. I'm going to go talk with Father and Master Cushing. Jerrin, prepare her as best you can."

The next moment Skyler is gone.

I look at Jerrin. He is sitting with his eyes closed. I'm sure he's trying to figure out how to handle whatever the problem is. My sobbing probably isn't helping him concentrate.

Shiane approaches Jerrin and puts her hand on his shoulder. "Maybe I could help by explaining the basics while you decide how to handle the specifics."

He reaches up and places his hand on top of hers. "You are a jewel beyond price. Yes, please, explain what you can."

Shiane pulls an ottoman over so she can sit in front of me. She takes my hands in hers and warmth flows into me. Gradually my crying settles into a series of sniffles. Then even those stop.

She smiles at me and releases her hold.

"Jerrin told you Friday night that all Auravalians have at least one special magical talent and some people have more than one. Those with multiple abilities are tested at the Magicians Guild to find out exactly what their powers are and how strong.

"When the results have been studied and understood, the person is assigned to one of five different levels: magic-handler, magic-wielder, magician, sorcerer, or mage. Then the strength of each separate skill is assessed. This is done by comparing the individual's power with the power generated by an average magic user at each level.

"You obviously have at least three talents. That means, when your abilities are assessed, you will be assigned to one of the five levels. Regardless of how you're categorized, however, we already know that one of your skills is, or almost is, at the mage level."

"What skills?" I ask. "You mean my ability to light fires when I'm cold or call food when I'm hungry?"

"No," Shiane says. "I mean like instinctively changing the weather pattern over an area of approximately 400 square miles."

"I can't do that!" I start to jump to my feet, but Shiane and the ottoman are in the way, and I flop back into my chair. "No one can do that."

"Apparently you can," Shiane says. "You did it Friday night so your children's choir could perform without being disturbed by a rain storm. Altering the weather is one of the great magics. It's very hard to do, so the echoes it creates are terribly powerful."

I'm vaguely aware when Skyler returns, but I'm too focused on what Shiane is saying to care.

Jerrin referred earlier to the echoes of Bree-Ella's magic, but he didn't explain what he meant.

I decide to ask Shiane. "When you say 'echoes,' you're not referring to sound waves ricocheting back and forth between solid surfaces, are you?"

"No," Shiane says, "but it's a similar phenomenon. Every time magic is used, it creates a ripple through time and space. The stronger the magic is, the bigger the disturbance. Sensitive people on nearby worlds can sometimes feel the ripples, and when they do, we call it 'hearing the echo' of the magic.

"That's why Skyler and Jerrin are so worried about you. You created a gigantic ripple when you translocated that storm. I heard it, myself, even though I was in an isolation chamber trying to transmute metals. Undoubtedly the strongest members of the Darker clan heard it too. Although they don't have farseers or trackers in their family line, it is always possible that they have hired one or two. If they have, it won't take them long to trace the magic back to you."

"Which," Skyler says, "is another reason for us to talk with Peter and Cindy. We need to discuss safety precautions."

"Should Hellie and I go get them now?" Jerrin asks.

"Might as well," Skyler says. "Sounds like Shiane has covered the key points."

"Yes," Jerrin says, giving his little sister a proud smile, "and she did it beautifully."

Shiane turns around and grins at her brothers. "Thanks."

"All right, Hellie," Jerrin says. "Let's go."

"Wait," I call to them.

I turn to Skyler. "Why don't you do this in two stages? Explain things to Peter first and give him a few days to think about it. Then you can bring him and Cindy here together. Since he'll know what's going on, he'll be able to help her understand."

The look on Skyler's face isn't encouraging, but then I get support from an unexpected source.

"Your Highness," Kaden says, "may I offer an opinion?"

"Of course, Kaden," Skyler answers. "That's why you're here."

"Angel is right about Peter and Cindy. Cindy sees things from a unique perspective, and Peter is her link with the world. If you want information from her, or if there are things you want her to understand, you'll need Peter to act as intermediary. Confiding in him first would allow him to consider the best ways to help her."

"Jerrin," Skyler says. "What do you think?"

"I think," Jerrin answers, "we'd be foolish to have a medical finder with us and disregard his expertise."

"All right. Just bring Peter this time, but remember, we'll have to meet with Cindy eventually."

"Acknowledged," Jerrin says. "Ready, Hellie?"

"Wait!" I call again.

"Now what?" Skyler growls with irritation.

"Let me go, too." The words pop out of my mouth without any conscious thought on my part.

"In what way do you think your presence will be helpful?" Jerrin asks superciliously.

His tone of contempt almost intimidates me into silence, but when I think of Peter, I won't let myself back down.

"Although I don't understand what you want from me and I only half believe what I've experienced, I think you mean to help us, not to harm us. I can at least assure Peter of that much. Also, I think he'll accept the rest of it, the magic part, better if it comes from me than if it comes from you."

Jerrin looks over at Skyler.

Skyler stares at me a good long time before he says, "Go ahead. Take her along."

When we reenter Neeve's apartment, nothing feels real.

The people look like mannequins that are all dressed up and ready to be arranged in the window displays of a dozen fancy clothing stores.

My heart just about breaks when I see Peter and Cindy stuck in place like everyone else.

"How do you want to handle this, Angel?" Jerrin asks me.

Fighting tears of frustration and helplessness, I slowly shake my head. I don't know what to do or what to say. I only know it's my responsibility to protect these two people I love.

"Go ahead and release Peter," I tell Hellie. "Then you and Jerrin leave while I talk to him."

"All right," Hellie says. She and Jerrin vanish.

Peter gazes around, confused and disoriented.

Our eyes meet.

"I need to tell you something," I say. "It's incredible, and you'll probably have trouble believing it."

He cups his hands around the back of my neck, pulls my face toward his, and kisses me.

"Does it have to do with the condition of our fellow partygoers?" he asks.

"Yes."

"Are they all right?" He looks at Cindy with concern.

"Yes. You were in the same condition until just a few minutes ago."

"Let's sit," he says, but rather than step around people and head for one of the sofas, he sits on the floor just a few inches from Cindy's feet.

Despite being in my beautiful new dress, I sit down facing him.

"Tell me," he says gently.

"You believe the universe is full of intelligent life forms," I say. "We've talked about it. We've speculated about how they might be similar to us and how they might be different."

115

"Yes." When he looks around the room a second time, his expression is both uneasy and eager. "Have we had an alien encounter?"

"Of sorts," I say, "but they are nothing like we imagined. They don't travel in spaceships, and they look enough like us to pass as human. Also, we're genetically compatible. I know because my family has an ancestor who is one."

Peter blows out a low whistle.

"Have they come to take you back to their planet?" he asks.

"Actually," I say with, what I hope is, a reassuring smile. "I've already been there. They would like to meet you."

"What do you mean you've been there? How long has this—," he waves a hand at the immobilized people, "—been going on?"

"Not long," I answer. "These extraterrestrials have instantaneous travel between worlds."

"Incredible," Peter says. "That's the stuff of science fiction. And they can put people in suspended animation without cryogenics?"

"Something like that."

"All right," Peter says, climbing to his feet. He stretches his hand down to help me stand. "Let's go."

Then he glances at his sister. "What's going to happen to her while we're gone?"

"Nothing," I say. "She and the others will still be like this when we come back. They're in what's called a time bubble."

"A time bubble!" he exclaims. "What's that?"

"It is bit like suspended animation, except they aren't frozen. Time has been slowed down so much for them that when we come back, they won't even realize we've been gone."

"That's bull crap," Peter says disdainfully. "It is impossible to interfere with time. Someone's been messing with your head."

"That's not fair, Peter. You know I'm skeptical about things that can't be proven empirically, but I've been convinced. Come with me and see."

"No, I don't think so. I'm going to take Cindy home." He slips one arm behind her neck and the other behind her knees. He lifts. He can't budge her. "What the h—?" He tries to pick her up again. No luck.

His hands clench into fists.

"Peter," I say, grabbing onto his wrists. "You can't move her because we exist in different moments. Just look around. No one has been hurt. No one is being terrorized. No one has been abducted or experimented on. These beings only want to talk with you. They were perfectly polite to me. They won't harm Cindy while we're gone."

"How do you know?" he snaps at me. "Just because they didn't hurt you—"

I sigh.

Maybe I should have let Jerrin do things his way.

I hate it when Peter and I argue.

Then I remind myself why I felt I needed to do this.

I take a deep breath.

"I know they won't hurt her or us because they're friends of Hellie's. She's in love with one of them."

"Crap!" Peter blurts. "Kaden's an alien?"

I nod. "They're called Auravalians."

He snorts aggressively. "You sensed right from the start that there was something fishy about that guy."

"It's not just Kaden. Neeve and his brothers are too."

Peter becomes completely still, like he does sometimes when he's trying to puzzle out a complex problem with a car or a motorcycle. I can almost see the synapses in his brain firing, searching for answers.

"That cute little girl? Shiane?" Peter says slowly. "She's one too?"

"Yes, she's Neeve's youngest sister."

"Cindy was quite taken with her," Peter says, "and with Kaden, too, if I'm being honest."

His fists relax back into hands, and his voice takes on a thoughtful tone.

"Although Cindy tends to focus on positives and ignore negatives, she's actually a good judge of character. She instinctively knows who's safe and who isn't. So far, I've never known her to be wrong."

"So, you'll come back with me?"

"Yes."

I stroke his cheek. I love touching him.

"Peter, I can't guess what's going to happen when we get to Auravale, but there are three things you probably ought to know first."

He raises one eyebrow, questioningly, like Mr. Spock in *Star Trek*.

He only does that when he wants me to smile at him.

I accommodate him by giving him one of my best.

When he smiles back at me, it's an affirmation. We're in this together.

"I'm ready to listen," he says. "Tell me."

"First, Neeve and his siblings are royals. Their father is the king of Auravale."

Peter nods without saying anything.

"Second, they have wings like butterflies that they can extend or retract at will, and they can fly with them."

His face goes blank, postponing judgment until he gets more information.

"And the third thing?" he asks.

"Magic appears to be a form of their physics."

For a moment, Peter says nothing.

Then he nods his head. "All right, I'll take that on faith. What happens next?"

"Hellie and Jerrin are somewhere around here. They'll transport us."

"Let's go."

I am really impressed with Peter's adaptability.

*Angel.* Hellie's voice sounds inside my head. *Are you ready to leave?*

Since I don't know how this telepathy stuff works, I mentally shout my answer. *I THINK SO!*

*Hey,* Hellie tells me, *I'm not deaf. Just think normally. I'll be able to hear you.*

For just a split second, a patch of air in front of us shimmers like heat waves above the freeway on a hot summer day. Then Neeve's apartment is gone, and we are in the hunting lodge standing beside Hellie and Jerrin.

Peter barely glances out the window at the alien terrain. He spots a beige couch not far from the fireplace. He takes my hand, and we cross the room and sit side by side.

"So, what the hell is going on?" Peter asks.

"It's a long story," Skyler says. "Neeve? Kaden?"

Both guys look surprised, as if they hadn't expected to be asked to do or say anything. I think they had cast themselves in the role of passive observers.

Since Skyler is top dog, I don't think they have the option of not complying with his expectations.

# Chapter Sixteen

Neeve is sitting on a fur rug with his head resting against one of Karissa's knees. She's in a brown wing chair, leaning forward slightly so she can stroke his hair.

Slowly Neeve lifts his eyes and looks at Peter.

"I have been living in Shawon for the past two and a half years," Neeve says. "I was taken there after being tortured by someone who wanted to hurt my father through me. He did unspeakable things to me. To say, during my first months in Colorado, that I was in constant physical and emotional anguish would not be overstating the truth."

Shiane disappears from the couch she was reclining on and reappears next to Neeve on the rug. She has tears in her eyes as she reaches for him.

Neeve gives her a wan smile, lifts their now linked hands, and kisses her fingers. Despite the dispute they had on Friday when Neeve kept changing her snowsuit, it is clear that they are very close. His pain, even though it's two and half years old, hurts her.

Although I notice what is happening between Neeve and his sister, my attention is focused on Peter.

He doesn't react to Shiane's teleportation at all.

Even if Peter believes in extraterrestrial life, which he does, and even if Peter is exceptionally adaptable, which he is, he should have shown some kind of surprise.

My heart skips a beat.

"Usually," Neeve continues, "when our people are away from Auravale, we become increasingly sensitive to the feel of others of our kind. Even though the royal family is generally more sensitive to this phenomenon than the general populace, because of what I was going through, I had lost the ability.

"Last summer, when Kaden was sent to Earth on a mission for the Crown, he asked me who or what was causing the small but infrequent bursts of power that he was feeling around Shawon. I had no idea. He had

119

already identified Hellie as a magic user and, through inference, Angel."

Again, there is no visible reaction from Peter. I'm afraid something is seriously wrong. Either Peter is so stunned that he's unable to comprehend what's going on, or this isn't news to him.

They are equally improbable.

"Although two others of our people reside in Shawon," Neeve says, "their magic is known, and it was not responsible. After Kaden and I reported this information to the king, he gave us the task of identifying the source of the unknown magic. I am embarrassed to admit that we were dismal failures. The surges of power didn't happen regularly enough or strong enough or last long enough to be tracked.

"The situation changed last week."

Neeve motions for Kaden to take over.

"The reason things changed was because I met Angel. Although we didn't get to speak more than a few words in passing, I could tell she was carrying the scent of the unidentified magic."

At this point I expect Peter to glance at me with a question in his eyes. He doesn't. His gaze remains firmly locked on Kaden.

"Is *scent* the right English word?" Kaden asks Neeve. "Did I use it correctly?"

"*Scent* is close," Neeve answers. "*Residue* or *traces* might be closer, but they're still not exact. English doesn't have a word for *denemac*."

"Thanks," Kaden says before he goes on. "Because I recognized traces of the magic on Angel, I asked Hellie if there was a way for me to spend an extended amount of time in her company. Hellie suggested we go on a double date with the two of you. Within minutes of when the girls picked me up, I knew Angel had frequent contact with the source of the magic, and as soon as I met Cindy and you, Peter, it was clear that you two were the answer."

"The answer?" Peter asks, finally reacting, but not dramatically. "You think Cindy and I left magical residue on Angel?"

"Yes," Kaden says, "but I don't mean it in an offensive way."

I am increasing concerned about Peter. Why doesn't he object to being told that he and Cindy are somehow connected with magic? Being adaptive enough to acknowledge that other people might be able to do magic is different from blindly accepting the possibility that you and your developmentally delayed sister can do it.

I make myself go back to listening to Kaden.

"It is like a person's signature," he says. "The reason I used the word *scent* earlier is because the scent of perfume can be transferred from one person to another with a simple hug and without losing its identifying aroma. So can the *denemac* of magic, but it doesn't require physical touch. It can be passed on simply through proximity."

He pauses, and I think he hopes to get another response from Peter.

So do I.

We get none.

"In other words," I say, hoping to make Peter react, "in effect you could smell Peter on me."

Kaden nods. "And Cindy as well. The traces of magic were a combination of the two of them. Before I go on, however, I want to assure you—" he looks at both Peter and me "—that I truly enjoyed sharing an evening with you. I hope the current circumstances won't prevent us from pursuing our friendships in the future."

"Still," Peter says with a hint of hostility, "the only reason you and Hellie went out with Angel and me was so you could track down this magical residue. I suppose it was also the only reason for inviting Cindy and me to Neeve's party."

I feel faint. Of all the things Peter has heard, the only one that upsets him is that Kaden might have sought our company under false pretenses?

"It is true I invited you to Neeve's apartment because the king had given us an assignment, and we had failed. I felt it was essential for Skyler and Jerrin to meet you so they could decide how to handle the situation. But it is also true that I wanted you to meet my friends and I thought Cindy would enjoy attending a party."

Peter looks as if he's struggling with emotions, but if he is, I don't understand what they are or what the timing means.

"The reason this is important," Skyler says, taking charge again, "is that you and Cindy have an Auravalian relative but neither your mother nor your father shows signs of an Auravalian heritage. Kaden said he could clearly identify your magic and Cindy's within the home, but there was a third, possibly a fourth, magical signature that he couldn't place. Therefore, I must ask, are you and Cindy adopted?"

Peter stops breathing.

I watch his chest, hoping to see it rise and fall again, but a minute passes and I haven't seen any movement. I place my hand on his shoulder and squeeze.

He shudders and slowly inhales.

"No, we are not adopted. At least I know that Cindy isn't. I was ten years old during my mother's pregnancy with her. I was in the hospital waiting room with my father when she was born."

"Kaden?" Skyler says, making a quick nod of his head in Peter's direction.

"I've looked," Kaden says. "They are full-blooded brother and sister."

"What do you mean you've looked?" Peter snaps. "You've looked at what?"

Kaden answers Peter's anger with gentleness.

# Sunshine and Shadows: Another Modern Fairytale

"I am in my fourth year of study as a medical finder," Kaden explains. "That means I am learning to assess the mind and the body when medical and/or psychological information is needed. Although I have another year of training ahead of me, I am already quite proficient. I had the opportunity to look into Cindy's eyes while we were discussing painting, and I had the opportunity to look into yours over dinner. The familial markers are undeniable. You and Cindy share the same parents."

"I already knew that," Peter says.

"And," Kaden goes on in that same calm, gentle voice, "neither of your parents exhibits signs of an Auravalian heritage."

"So?" Peter snaps.

"You and Cindy both have magical powers. Of course, you already knew that. It's why you haven't questioned any of the magic you've seen demonstrated since you arrived here."

Peter makes one of those tiny, involuntary, automatic nods that people sometimes make when they agree with what's being said.

*Well, that explains that.* For some reason, I'm on the verge of tears, and I close my eyes tight in an effort to hold them back. Then I realize why I'm so upset. *Peter has secrets.* I wonder what he said or did that tipped me off.

Again, Peter responds to Kaden with a hostile, "So?"

Kaden's voice becomes even milder. "The magic didn't come from your mother or your father. It had to come from somewhere."

Peter's body suddenly jerks with a little spasm.

My eyes fly open.

His hostility turns to rage. "Are you implying that my mother has been disloyal to my father with an alien lover? And she has borne two alien children as a result?"

The room goes deathly quiet.

I clutch at Peter's arm in hopes of preventing him from jumping up and attacking Kaden.

"I'm sorry," Skyler says. "I wish there had been an easier way to tell you, or more accurately, I wish it had been unnecessary to tell you at all. Unfortunately, the situation in Shawon makes it too dangerous to allow you to proceed in ignorance."

"We seldom interfere with human/Auravalian relationships," Jerrin says. "However, sometimes circumstances threaten our father's kingdom, and then we have no choice."

Peter is silent. His fingers dig into his thighs.

I try to think of something to say.

Finally, his entire body shudders, and he takes a deep breath.

He twists on the couch so he can look at me. "You said you have an alien ancestor. Now, it appears that I might have one too. Is it all connected? Has something from the past filtered through to the present?"

"I don't know," I tell him. "They haven't explained it to me yet."

"All right," Peter growls at Skyler, "tell me what the situation is so I can protect Angel and Cindy. We can deal with the issue of parentage later."

"I wish it were that simple," Skyler answers, "but it is possible that the two issues are related. That's why the king wanted you brought to Auravale."

"This lodge," Jerrin adds, "and most of the places we frequent have been shielded against curious, unfriendly, and/or dangerous powers. To implement similar safety precautions on your world would have drawn the attention of the very people we need to shield against."

Skyler stands and stretches. "This is going to take a while. Are you willing to listen to what we need to tell you?"

"I'm not just willing," Peter answers, "I'm insistent."

"Fine, but we'll need more time than we have tonight. Hellie, how long has your time bubble been in effect?"

Hellie glances at her watch. "Going on two hours."

I do a double take.

Hellie doesn't wear a watch. She uses her cellphone to check the time.

I slip my phone from my purse and turn it on.

It doesn't show a date or a time.

Well, duh!

My phone has many great features, but it's not set up for interplanetary readings. No wonder Hellie has to use a watch to track the time on Earth.

"We're reaching the upper limits of how long Hellie can safely control time," Skyler says. "So, let me tell you what our concerns are and why we need to meet with you and Cindy soon, very soon."

I stop watching Peter and stare at the fire.

I don't understand this guy that I've considered to be my boyfriend for over a year.

How much does he know about magic?

When I told him the people at Neeve's party were in a time bubble, he got angry and tried to pick Cindy up so he could take her home. Yet, he didn't blink an eye when Skyler said Hellie was controlling time.

Has he known the truth all along?

Has he only been pretending to be human?

"First," Skyler says, "you and your sister both have magical powers inherited from an Auravalian parent. However, you've lived your entire lives on Earth, and we don't know if your powers have evolved differently there than they would have if you had grown up here. Auravalian magic wielded by humans has surprised us more than once.

"Second, if we don't identify your powers, we can't teach you how to control them. We got involved with Hellie last year because she inadvertently influenced time so she could save a child's life. We're now involved with Angel because she inadvertently altered the weather so her children's choir could perform. Those are two of, what we call, the great magics. The ripples they create can be felt on many other worlds. This could have disastrous consequences for your world if the wrong people traced the magic back to Earth.

"Third, in general, magic is dormant on Earth because its people don't believe in it and don't use it. However, there are a few large pools of untapped power. Depending on what your talents are, it is conceivable that if you accidentally accessed one of these concentrated pools, you could blow up your planet.

"Fourth, we only know of two controlled methods of getting from Auravale to Earth: a member of the royal family can open a passageway for you, or you can get a portal key from the king.

"Although, in the past, natural gateways on our worlds have lined up spontaneously and a few people have fallen through, this happens infrequently. I think there are only a dozen or so documented cases.

"Yet, somehow an Auravalian man has visited Earth at least twice, during which times you and Cindy were conceived. And although we know Bree-Ella, Angel and Hellie's ancestor, was a powerful mage, we don't understand how she got there either. One hypothesis is that she discovered some forgotten spell or bit of magical lore that allowed her to create her own portal key.

"Until our father knows how two individuals, not of our bloodline and without royal keys, transported themselves across space to Earth, he must consider the possibility that if they could do it, others might be able to do it also, which means neither his kingdom nor your world is secure."

"Holy hell," Peter mutters.

"I'll give you a few days to ponder things," Skyler says, "then I'll have Hellie check with you to negotiate a convenient day for our next meeting, and it must include Cindy." He glances around the room at the rest of us. "Now let's all go back to Neeve's apartment and enjoy his party."

# Chapter Seventeen

I don't know how Hellie or Jerrin or Skyler does it, but someone brings us back a second or two before we left. For a moment we're able to see ourselves so we can align our bodies in exactly the right positions.

Hellie restores time, and we're all back where we started.

Skyler has just joined the group gathered around Karissa, but Kaden, Jerrin, and Neeve are still on the other side of the room. Cindy is holding onto Bennett's hand, and they and Jeremy have started to turn so they can go to the TV room.

"Did you need me, Skyler?" Shiane asks as smooth as silk.

"Not really," he says. "You mentioned earlier that all of you young people were going to watch a movie. I wanted to suggest that you make a trip to the buffet before you start gorging yourself at Neeve's soda bar."

Cindy stops and turns around. "What's a soda bar, Peter?"

Peter, who has been scowling ever since we left for the hunting lodge, suddenly smiles. He is never cross in front of Cindy. "Usually, it's a place where there are soft drinks, ice cream, and other treats. In reality, it should probably be called a junk food bar."

Cindy's eyes light up with glee. She tugs on Bennett's hand. "Really?" she asks him.

"Pretty much," Bennett says. "Besides sodas and ice cream, there are cookies and candy bars and popcorn—"

"Just about everything you could want as a treat," Jeremy inserts. He glances across the room at Neeve. "You'd think someone who ate that much junk food would get fat, but Neeve's like me. He doesn't put on weight no matter what he eats."

"I want to go see," Cindy says. She starts to turn again, stops, and looks back. "Peter?"

"You need to eat something healthy first," he tells her. "I'm sure there are things you'll like. Come on, I'll go with you."

Although both of Karissa's brothers are taller than she is, she takes them by the backs of their necks and turns them around. "That's good advice. Let's follow their example." She steers them in the direction of the buffet tables. "Mom will kill me if I take you home on sugar highs. Some real food will buffer the effects of all the treats you're going to eat during the movie."

"You too," Skyler says to Shiane. "Healthy food now, sweets later."

Her eyes dart toward the TV room. "Do I have to?"

"Yes." He offers her his arm. "I saw the size of the chocolate cake Neeve stashed in there for you. I don't want you eating it all in one sitting."

Suddenly, I'm alone.

I'm not sure when Hellie left, but she's across the room with Kaden now.

I spy a couple of chairs at right angles to each other in an isolated corner, and I head for them.

Maybe it's irrational, but I'm hurt to my core.

I thought Peter and I had something special.

I realize now that I've told Peter everything about me—my thoughts, my feelings, my hopes, my fears, my goals, my dreams—and he's told me about his business, his family, his friends, his motorcycle, and the things he's read.

Even the controversial conversations we've had about religion, near death experiences, life on other planets, the supernatural, and a dozen other topics have all consisted of my opinions and beliefs pitted against Peter's information garnered from the Internet and magazines.

I don't know if we've ever really shared anything.

I sit down and stare at my hands.

After a while, someone comes over and sits in the other chair.

I look up and see Peter.

"Why didn't you tell me?" I ask him plaintively.

"Why didn't *you* tell *me*?" he counters.

"I only found out Friday after the church social. We haven't been together since then, not until tonight."

"Well," Peter says, frowning at me, "this isn't the time or the place to discuss it."

"That won't do, Peter." I'm battling tears, but I refuse to start crying in front of him. "We've been going together for over a year. You've had lots of other times and places to choose from."

We stare at each other for several seconds. His frustration shows on his face. I suppose hurt shows on mine.

"Angel," he says, making an effort to be calm, "I realize you're upset. I am too. I got smacked with some heavy-duty information tonight, and I haven't had the chance to process it.

"I'll admit I knew Cindy and I could do a few unusual things, but so what? I've always believed in psychic abilities, and you've told me you conceded the possibility. Learning what the Auravalians can do and being told Cindy and I have inherited similar skills from a man who is not our father is earthshaking. I feel overwhelmed right now."

"How do you think I feel?" I ask. "Even if we disregard the magic, you haven't been open and honest with me. We've discussed psychic powers multiple times, but you obviously didn't trust me enough to tell me you've experienced them."

We do some more silent staring.

Peter stands. "This conversation isn't going to get us anywhere," he says. "I'm hungry. I'm going to check out the buffet."

While I watch him walk away from me, I wonder if we can ever have a future together or if this is the beginning of the end.

I remain in the corner, trying not to cry, while Peter crosses the room, pausing every now and then to chat with someone. He seems to know several of the people here, but that's no surprise. He has probably worked on most of their cars a time or two.

Neeve's apartment has a huge open kitchen with an island bar that separates it from the main room. At present, the bar is covered with an assortment of bottles, various sizes and shapes of glassware, some small opaque bowls, and a bucket of ice. A distinguished looking man with gray hair is behind the bar mixing and serving drinks.

The buffet tables are in front of a long line of windows that form the wall on the east side of the room.

Peter passes the buffet and heads for the bar. I keep an eye on him. Although all of Peter's buddies drink alcohol, Peter says he never has.

He speaks to the bartender, who then picks up a tall glass. He adds a scoop of ice and a slice of lemon and a slice of lime. Then he reaches below the bar. I hold my breath.

He produces a can of Sprite, which he pours.

He hands the glass to Peter without adding anything else.

Peter accepts it and saunters away.

At least I know that stress and anger don't drive him to drink.

I'm hungry, but I don't feel like interacting with the people who are between me and the buffet.

Luckily, I know where I can get something to eat that will be more in tune with my mood and will be more comforting than anything available on those food-laden tables.

I head for the TV room and the soda bar.

The kids pause the DVD and make me feel welcome.

Shiane cuts me a big slice of chocolate cake while I scoop out a pleasantly large serving of cherry cordial ice cream. I sit down with my decadent meal and watch the final scenes of *Beauty and the Beast*.

When the movie ends, Jeremy flips on the overhead lights, and Bennett walks around the couch to a bookcase that's just a few feet away from my chair. Stacked on the shelves are a couple dozen games and puzzles.

"Do you have time to play something before you have to go home?" Bennett asks Cindy. "Neeve's got lots to choose from."

"I'm not very good at games," Cindy says, "but I like puzzles."

"I like doing puzzles too," Bennett says. "Come over and help me find a good one."

They pull boxes off the shelves and spread them out on the floor. Jeremy and Shiane join them, and then all four of them get on their knees with their heads together as they consider the options.

I am happy to see that Shiane and the boys treat Cindy the same ways they treat each other and Cindy fits right in.

Peter and his parents are right. To develop and mature, Cindy needs experiences away from her special-needs program.

"Do you like this one?" Cindy asks the others.

I glance down, expecting to see a puzzle featuring unicorns or kittens, which are two of her particularly favorite items.

Instead, she's holding James C. Christensen's *Superstition*. It's a complex fantasy picture of a house on a lake with a wide variety of characters standing on balconies, climbing stairs, and leaning out of windows, all of them engaged in unrelated activities. The sky is blue. The lake is blue. The house and its occupants are a hodgepodge of colors.

This is no easy puzzle.

"I like it," Shiane says. "It should be a real challenge."

"But," Jeremy points out, "it's got 1,000 pieces."

"So?" Bennett says. "Even if we can't finish it, it'll be fun to see how far we can get." Cindy hands him the box while she gets to her feet, and he carries it over to a circular table that has six chairs around it.

He dumps out the pieces and then stands the box on end so everyone can see the picture and use it as a reference.

"Let's work on the border first," Jeremy suggests.

When I decide I might as well help, Shiane moves to the next chair so I can sit between her and Cindy.

We turn the pieces right-side up while we search for the straight-edged ones that make up the border. As we work two other piles evolve naturally: blue pieces and multicolored ones.

Gradually, bit-by-bit, the border comes together.

I'm feeling pretty smug when I complete the bottom edge before Jeremy finishes the top. Bennett and Shiane are still working on the sides.

I start on the second row of blue lake pieces.

None of us is particularly paying attention to Cindy. She has been reaching across the table and rummaging through the piles just like the rest of us.

Bennett is about to finish up the left-hand border when Cindy says, "Before you close it, may I just slide this in?"

128

We all glance at what is on the table in front of her.

In the time it's taken the rest of us to finish the border, Cindy has put together the entire house, the boats docked below it on the right, the swans swimming below it on the left, and the sky and stars above, plus blue pieces all the way around. When she slides her chunk of puzzle into the middle, she connects it to the upper and lower edges.

"How'd you do that?" Bennett asks with a huge smile. "You must be the fastest puzzle-put-together-er in the world."

Cindy shrugs and grins at the same time. "I just look for pieces that seem to belong to each other. Shall we finish it? Peter isn't coming to get me yet."

I rather expect Jeremy, who undoubtedly has the highest IQ at the table, to be jealous or resentful of Cindy's accomplishment.

However, he's just like the rest of. We all grin and, with renewed vigor, go about filling in the empty spots.

Now, for some reason, every time one of us picks up a piece we seem to know exactly where it goes. It's a few minutes short of 10:00 when Bennett presses the last piece into place.

It's taken us approximately an hour and a half to complete a 1,000-piece puzzle. That's amazing.

My family has been finding a puzzle under the Christmas tree from Santa Claus every year since Hellie and I were old enough not to chew on the pieces. We start on the new puzzle as soon as the kitchen has been cleaned up after dinner. The goal is to finish it by New Year's Day.

We've never completed a 1,000-piece puzzle in much less time than a week, let alone in a single evening. Sometimes, it takes most of January.

Tonight, the five of us are high on our success, and we celebrate with ice cream cones.

At 10:00, Peter comes in and tells us it's time to go. He promised his parents he'd have Cindy home by 10:30.

As we leave the TV room, I'm surprised to find a live band playing music. People, including Hellie and Kaden, are dancing. I suppose this is what you do when you throw a party and have money.

Peter, Cindy, and I take time to thank Neeve for inviting us and to tell his brothers goodbye. We've barely driven out of the parking lot before Cindy cuddles up against me and falls asleep.

When I try to talk to Peter about what happened tonight, he doesn't respond until we get to my house.

He walks me to the door. "I know we need to talk, Angel, but I'm not ready yet. This information about my mother and an Auravalian lover makes some of my childhood memories more believable, but it also makes other ones confusing and unreal. I need time to think."

Then he tells me *good night,* turns around, and walks back to the car.

I go to my room, lie down on my bed, and cry.

I guess I cry myself to sleep.

The next thing I'm aware of is hearing Hellie rummaging around in her room. I glance at my phone to check the time. It's nearly 1:00. I hoist myself off my bed and stumble into the bathroom.

Hellie enters through her door at the same time.

"You're a mess," Hellie exclaims when she sees my wrinkled dress and droopy hair. "I expected you to be sound asleep by now. You guys left so early."

"Peter had to have Cindy home by 10:30," I say.

"I know, but I thought you were coming back. Wasn't that the plan?"

"Things don't always go according to plan," I say. I turn my back, and Hellie automatically unzips my dress for me. I let it fall to the floor.

After I pick it up, I head for my closet. I snatch a nightie from my bureau on the way.

Out of habit, I hang up my dress, put my sandals on the shoe rack, and drop my bra and slip into the clothes hamper. I keep the panties on since the nightie only comes to mid-thigh.

I head back to the bathroom.

Hellie is brushing her hair. "What happened between you and Peter tonight?" she asks me.

"It's complicated," I say.

"Even so, give it a try."

I take my toothpaste, toothbrush, and floss from the shelf and set them on the counter.

"We had a difference of opinion," I say stiffly, trying not to cry anymore. "I thought he should have told me about his and Cindy's abilities—he calls them psychic powers not magic—and he thought it was no big deal. I tried to tell him I felt hurt that he didn't trust me enough to share something that significant, but he walked away. When he brought me home, he told me he needed time to think, and then he left. He didn't even kiss me goodbye."

"I'm sorry."

I don't say anything else. I'm too close to tears. Instead, I do an exceptionally thorough job flossing and brushing my teeth.

Hellie puts her hairbrush away and leans on the vanity. "Are you mad at me? I'm sorry that I didn't understand how stressful it's been for you to be the angel all the time, and I'm sorry I didn't tell you about magic last year when I learned about it."

After I wash away my makeup and moisturize my face, I start taking down the remnants of the hairdo that Jacie created for me. I make a neat pile of the black and white bows. I'll have to find a special container for them in the morning. I want to keep them, even though I'll probably never wear them again.

When I have my emotions a little better under control, I answer Hellie's question.

"No, I'm not mad at you. I don't blame you for not telling me about magic. I wouldn't have believed you anyway." Then I try to make a joke. "I know why you never realized how hard it was for me to be the angel. You were too busy trying to figure out how not to become the hellion."

Hellie laughs ruefully. "That was only half the time. The other half, I was wondering if I shouldn't just let go and show the world how magnificent a hellion I could be."

We go to my room and sit on the bed.

Hellie flops backward and clasps her hands behind her head. "What finally convinced you that magic is real?" she asks me.

Lying down beside her, I stare up at the ceiling,

"It was while we were flying," I answer. "My five senses were in overload. I was sure so many environmental stimuli couldn't be faked, which meant I wasn't being pranked, and I didn't think I could experience so many simultaneous sensations if I had lost touch with reality, which meant I wasn't crazy.

"Besides, there was that whole business between Neeve and Shiane and that awful series of outfits Neeve concocted.

"Then, when Shiane started whining to her older brothers, she sounded exactly like a fourteen-year-old girl who is used to getting her own way all the time, and Skyler and Jerrin responded just like elder brothers who were trying to prevent it from happening again.

"I figured if any part of what occurred was real, then all the rest of it had to be real too. My turn: what convinced you?"

"Do you remember last summer," Hellie says slowly, "when we were at church and Mrs. Baxter's car was hit in the parking lot? And then, right after church, Mr. Thompson dropped a couple of lit matches that set his clothes on fire?"

"How could I forget?" I ask. "No one talked about anything else for days. I got to write the follow-up article for the newspaper."

"I did both of those things," Hellie says.

My mouth falls open.

"I didn't do them on purpose," she adds quickly. "Mrs. Baxter was rushing Tommy and gave him a little shove, which made him drop his backpack. The toys he was taking to play with in the nursery spilled out. When she blamed him and called him clumsy, I wanted her to be reminded of what it felt like to be as helpless as a child. The next thing I knew, the Jenkins boy lost control of his car and sideswiped hers.

"Then, when church was over, Mr. Thompson was hustling Aaron to the car. Aaron tripped and fell off the sidewalk and into the flowerbed. Instead of just helping him up, Mr. Thompson swore at him and reached for a cigarette. I thought, 'I wouldn't spit on that moron if he was on fire.' The next thing I knew, he was.

"After that, Jerrin and Skyler told me I either had to accept training or I had to have my powers bound because it was too dangerous to let me go on unchecked. That's when I finally accepted that I could make things happen magically, and that's when Jerrin began training me."

"Has it been worth the effort?" I ask her.

"Mostly," she answers.

We're silent for a minute or two.

A question that's been bothering me pops into my head. I decide to ask it before I forget. "Did you lie to me when you said graduation night was your first date with Kaden?"

"No, of course not," Hellie answers. "Oh, we tried several times to get together last summer, but Auravalian issues kept getting in the way—like the king telling Kaden and Neeve to track down the bursts of magic that turned out to be caused by Peter and Cindy. In addition, the doctor in charge of Kaden's apprenticeship was pressuring him to get back to his studies and to resume his schedule at the hospital. It was like one big conspiracy to keep us from ever dating. My turn: are you and Peter going to get married?"

I'm caught off guard.

When I catch my breath, I say, "If you'd asked me last week, I would've told you I'd marry him in a heartbeat. But it's really a moot point. He's never asked me. After tonight, maybe he never will. My turn: same question about you and Kaden."

"He's proposed and I've accepted, but he has to complete his medical apprenticeship and pass his professional exams before we can set a date. He'd like me to finish my magic training and take the tests that'll determine my levels before we get married, but he's not insistent about it. At best, it'll be another year or two."

I'd have to be deaf not to hear the longing in her voice.

"I'm sorry," I say.

"Don't be," she says, brightening up. "Kaden is the most remarkable thing that's ever happened to me. I'd wait a century for him. He's worth every minute."

# Chapter Eighteen

"Tell me about magic," I say.

"What do you want to know?" Hellie asks.

I flip over on to my side so I can look at her. "You're a mage like Jerrin, aren't you? And Shiane too."

"Yes and no," Hellie says. "Jerrin is a mage. Shiane and I merely have mage-level potential."

"What's the difference?"

"In order to become a mage, we have to learn how to control our powers so that we never use magic accidentally, or with more force than necessary, or out of fear or jealousy or anger. We have to prove we are calm under pressure and can assess and interpret situations quickly, accurately, and dispassionately.

"We have to be able to identify each of our talents, acknowledge our limitations, and use our skills with proficiency and finesse. We have to recognize the strengths and weaknesses of other magic users. We have to understand a lot about physical and psychological motivations so we can spot anomalies. We have to know the laws of the land so we can recognize if someone is behaving outside of legal parameters."

When Hellie pauses to take a breath, I exclaim, "Good heaven! Do they also expect you to play the flute, dance a jig, and balance a jug of water on your head at the same time!"

Hellie laughs. "Sometimes it feels like that. Anyway, if I can pass all of the requirements—and I understand the testing is hellish—then I will be allowed to become a mage, which involves some kind of confirmatory rituals at the Magicians Guild to make it valid. Does it bother you?"

"Not really," I tell her. "This whole magic business seems like a big nuisance to me. However, I do wonder why Jerrin and Skyler say they need me. I'm not a mage. I'm not powerful. Apparently, all I can do is call things or send them away. So, what do they need me for?"

"Calling and sending are just a tiny part of your talents," Hellie says.

"Don't forget you translocated an entire thunderstorm, which is extremely difficult. In recorded history there have only been a few mages and a couple of weather wizards who could do it. In addition, you have at least one talent that no one else has ever had."

When Hellie doesn't explain, I prod her.

"What? Tell me what it is."

"I'm not sure I should since Jerrin didn't, but I'll make a deal with you. I'll tell you if you promise you'll do something with me next Sunday."

"What," I ask suspiciously.

"Come for a walk with me in the woods. We can have a picnic."

"That's all? Just go for a walk and have a picnic?"

"That's all," Hellie says. "As soon as church is over, we'll pack a lunch and go for a walk among the trees. When we stop to eat, I'll tell you everything I know about your talents."

"It's a deal!"

Even though I dislike sharing space with the bugs, the spiders, the snakes, and the other wildlife in the forest, I can stand it for an hour or two.

When Grandma Powers was alive, she used to take Hellie and me exploring in the woods sometimes. She said our forest was enchanted because it was full of magical little beings that infused nature with their mystical life forces. She always had us take offerings (usually tea and crumbled up cookies or bits of cake) to them. She said it was polite to bring a gift to your hosts when they allowed you access to their home.

I never believed in them (well, actually I did in my preadolescent years, but then I grew up). Now, after my experiences in Auravale, I think almost anything is possible. I wonder if Hellie knows whether the supernatural creatures are real or not? Jerrin has been training her for a year, so she might be able to recognize the feel of magic. I'll ask her when we go for our walk. It would be nice to have some of Grandma's stories confirmed.

Monday morning, I have to pry my eyes open.

I didn't get anywhere near enough sleep, but I hope a shower will revitalize me a little.

It does.

Wearing my bathrobe and with a towel wrapped around my hair, I stand in the doorway of my closet, trying to decide what to wear to work.

I let my mind wander.

A series of events that happened when Hellie and I were in junior high school pops into my mind.

I was just discovering the joys of shoplifting, and I tested the boundaries repeatedly—becoming bolder and more reckless—until I actually believed there was something preternatural going on.

No one ever looked at me suspiciously, not even when I was thirteen years old and picked up a DVD and slipped in under the front of my sweatshirt on Christmas Eve day, one of the busiest times of year at the mall.

The odds were against my having it so easy.

The only explanation I could come up with was that I was doing something to make everyone glance away whenever I took something.

Being scientifically minded, I decided I needed empirical data either to validate or to disprove my theory. My plan was simple. At assemblies, sporting events, church, or anywhere there were large gatherings of people, I would choose one individual and focus on him or her until he or she looked at me.

The results were so astounding I started keeping a record of how often I was successful.

At first it was about 50-50, which I considered amazing.

Let's be honest, why would anyone in a crowd suddenly turn around to look at me?

Even if it occurred once by happenstance, what are the chances that it would ever happen again?

Next to nil.

However, it did happen, again and again and again.

Within four months, I was successful over 80% of the time.

I don't care what anyone says, that's cause and effect.

Then one day I was in the gymnasium waiting to watch Hellie mop up the competition on the basketball court when I saw my favorite teacher sitting almost directly in front of me. I was about halfway up the bleachers and she was on the very first row.

I concentrated on the back of her head for maybe three or four minutes.

All of a sudden, she leapt up, turned around, and glared in my direction. There was absolute fury or hatred in her eyes. My concentration broke, and I don't think she ever realized I was the person responsible for whatever she experienced that upset her so much.

Those must have been my first experiences consciously trying to use my powers. Of course, I didn't call them magic.

If I had known then what I know now, I wonder how my life would've been different. Would I have abused my powers to get more of what I wanted? Or would I have drawn inward to make sure I didn't?

Forcing myself to refocus on today, I decide to wear navy blue slacks with a light blue and white pinstriped shirt to work. I tuck in my shirttail while I head for the bathroom to do my hair and makeup.

Hellie is already in there doing hers.

"I realize," I say, "we talked for a while before we went to bed last night, but I feel wiped out. We weren't up terribly late, were we?" I pick up my hairbrush and go to work on my hair.

"Only until about 2:00," Hellie says, "but we were in Auravale for quite a while. Jerrin had me slow time down in the lodge so we could get a lot done in the limited amount of time I could maintain a time bubble at Neeve's apartment."

"In the light of day," I tell her, "I have trouble believing you can affect the flow of time."

"Well," Hellie says, "whether you believe it or not, it's true."

"I have so many questions," I tell her. "I can hardly wait until Sunday when we'll really have time to talk."

"Even though we'll be walking around in the forest?" she asks teasingly.

"Yes."

"I'll answer what I can," Hellie says, "but remember, when it comes to understanding magic, I'm only a year ahead of you. You should be happy that Jerrin's going to be your teacher. He's one of Auravale's best, most skillful, and most knowledgeable mages. He'll be able to answer everything you want to know."

"He scares me to death," I say with a shudder. "I'll be glad to postpone dealing with him for as long as possible. Right now, I'm thankful that I have you."

Hellie and I are both doing our makeup, and I glance at her refection in the mirror. She smiles at me.

"You'll never know how hard it's been keeping all of this a secret," she says. "It's going to be easier for both of us now that we can talk about it together."

"Angel!" Dad's booming voice yells from downstairs. "We've got to leave in five minutes."

I make a quick swipe of pink blush on each cheek, drop my makeup brush on the counter, and turn my head from side to side to check the overall effect.

It'll have to do.

"See you tonight," I say as I rush to my room to fetch my purse. No time for breakfast. I get to the kitchen just in time to see my dad kiss my mom goodbye. I grab a banana on my way to the car.

I have a terrible day.

Memories of last night and the situation with Peter keep interfering with my concentration.

I get yelled at three times.

Bart yells at me because I take too long finding some background information that he needs for a story.

Mr. Fenton yells at me because I send him a rewrite with two misspelled words in it, which should be impossible with the computer's checks and double checks.

Even, April, the receptionist, yells at me because I don't answer the phone fast enough, and a call returns to her, making her transfer it to me a second time.

By 5:00, I'm about ready to quit—not just for the day but forever.

I wish I could stomp out of the office, jump into my car, and peel rubber out of there. Instead, I have to stand outside, watch everyone else leave, and wait for my dad to pick me up.

Somehow the evening passes.

Tuesday is no better than Monday, nor are Wednesday and Thursday.

Peter and I haven't talked since Neeve's party.

At the beginning of the week, I tried to convince myself that he was just taking Skyler's advice and thinking everything through, dealing with his feelings, and preparing for the next steps.

By Thursday evening, I wonder if he's broken up with me without letting me know. I lie on my bed and try to read, but I end up looking at the clock every couple of minutes.

I refuse to pick up the phone and call him.

Friday morning, when I bump into Hellie in the bathroom, I tell her, "I'm not going to the newspaper office today. I called in sick."

I'm still wearing my baby doll pajamas.

She's fully dressed and fixing her hair.

"Don't you feel well? You look perfectly fine to me."

"I feel okay physically," I say, "but not emotionally. Too much has happened too fast, and I'm in overload. I need time to process all of the weirdness I've experienced lately."

I look at myself in the mirror and see dark semicircles under my eyes.

"Hey, why don't you play hooky with me," I suggest spontaneously.

"I can't," Hellie says. She finishes her hair, puts on some mascara and blush, and then starts stuffing things back into her makeup bag. "I wouldn't feel right lying to Brenlyn and Talitha. They've always been so good to me. Is something wrong at work? I thought you loved your job."

"I do."

"Then why did you call in sick?"

I hesitate a moment, not knowing what to say.

The fact is I have two reasons.

First, I feel burned out. When I told Mr. Fenton that I was too sick to come in, he said he figured I was coming down with something. He said I've been off my game all week.

Second, I don't want to be available to Peter. He nearly always calls me at work on Fridays either to make or to confirm plans for the weekend. I don't want him to be able to reach me today, or tomorrow, or Sunday.

"It's the magic," I finally tell her, which isn't a lie. "It complicates everything. It's messed up my relationship with the only guy I'll ever love. What does it matter if I can do magic, if it makes me miserable? I can't focus, and I can't concentrate. Right now, work is just another stressor in my life."

"Hmm," Hellie says thoughtfully. "Suppose I did stay home. What would you want to do?"

She's hooked.

I want to grin at her, but I don't.

She might misunderstand—or she might understand all too well.

I start reeling her in.

"It's a beautiful day," I say. "We could spend it outside. In fact, why don't we make a lunch and have our picnic in the woods today instead of waiting for Sunday? There's no sense hanging around the house. We could spend the entire day in the forest if you want. It would give us a chance to talk."

Hellie's eyes light up. "You'd do that—spend a whole day with me in the woods?"

"Sure," I say. "Why not?"

"Well, for one thing, you hate the forest."

"No, I don't," I protest, "not really. It's just that I'm afraid of spiders and snakes and dangerous animals. But Jerrin said I have the power to repel as well as to call. Maybe I automatically repel frightening things. Nothing has ever threatened me in the woods. I haven't even gotten a mosquito bite in there."

For a moment Hellie furrows her brow as if she's thinking hard.

Then she smiles.

"All right," she says. "I'll do it. While you make your bed and get dressed, I'll call Quick Fix and tell them I'm not coming in. Then I'll change my clothes and start making our lunches."

# Chapter Nineteen

I put on jeans, t-shirt, socks, and tennis shoes. I'd probably be more comfortable in shorts and a tank top, since it's going to be a warm day, but I like to have my body covered in the forest. It's not just the bugs and the animal life. There are also thistles and prickly flowers and bushes with thorns.

I brush my hair so it hangs in front of my right shoulder and then catch it with an elastic band to make a side ponytail. No sense bothering with makeup. No one will see me except Hellie and the various flora and fauna.

When I get to the kitchen, Hellie is putting two cans of Diet Coke into her backpack. She follows that with a couple of sandwiches, some individual-sized bags of chips, two apples, and a double pack of crème-filled chocolate cupcakes.

"No offering?" I ask.

Hellie picks up a sandwich bag full of smashed Oreo cookies that was on the counter behind her backpack where I couldn't see it. She sets it on top of everything else. Usually that action would have come with a smile, but it doesn't today. Instead, she looks as if she might burst into tears.

Although I know Hellie has packed bottles of water (she never goes into the woods without at least two), I grab one from the fridge.

I twist off the cap and take a long drink.

I go to the pantry and snatch a couple of protein bars from a shelf.

Hellie is putting on her backpack when I return.

After she has it comfortably situated, I hand her one of the bars.

"Thanks," she says as she tears open the wrapper.

"Ready?" I ask.

"Let's go."

I close and lock the backdoor.

Then I stand on the porch for a few seconds. I can see the tops of a few scorched trees above the three-foot-wide, seven-foot-tall hedge that separates our family's forest from the backside of the houses on our street.

"I haven't been out there since the fire," I comment to Hellie.

"Dad told me he and the fire chief roamed around for a few days after the fire, checking to make sure there weren't any hot spots that might reignite. Since then, I don't suppose Dad's gone back either. It's probably just been me."

We munch on our protein bars as we cut across the backyard to where there is a narrow break in the hedge. Grandma Powers called that opening the doorway to fairyland.

Even though I didn't quite believe our forest was enchanted, I always felt something special, something different and exciting, when I stepped out of our yard into the woods.

I sidle through the opening.

When I'm on the other side, I gaze around in a stupor.

The hedge is the only green I see in any direction.

I don't understand.

I was told the fire started near the center of the woods and never got close to the residential area.

I study the nearby trees and the foliage. They don't show any signs of scorching. They appear to have just withered away and died.

"What happened?" I ask.

"It's my fault," Hellie says. She reaches out and plucks a dead leaf from a bush. It crumbles at her touch. She gets tears in her eyes and wipes them away with back of her hand.

She starts walking as she talks.

"The evening of the fire, when I saw the flames, I ran out here to see what was going on. At first, I thought it was just a bunch of kids making a bonfire, and I wanted to give them hell for making such a large one."

"Sorry, sis," I tell her, "you remember it wrong. You weren't even here. You had gone to Seattle with your boss and his wife to attend a large arts and crafts show."

"No, I'm afraid it's you who's wrong," Hellie says, kicking a dried-up weed. "I was here, trying to use magic I didn't understand to put out the fire before it could burn down the entire forest. Although I finally came up with something that worked, I just about killed myself doing it. Jerrin took me to an Auravalian hospital. He gave you, Mom, and Dad false memories to cover for me."

It doesn't even occur to me to doubt her.

"What did you do?" I mean to ask her how one person can put out a forest fire, but I don't think it comes out right. I rephrase the question. "How did you do it?"

Hellie shakes her head, a frown on her face. "I'm not sure you'll believe me even if I tell you. After it was over, I could hardly believe it myself."

"I realize I'm generally a skeptic," I say, "but I'll try to believe."

"All right," Hellie says. She gets a faraway, haunted expression in her eyes. "I pulled water from the streams, spun it around the fire until I made it into a dome, created a small crack at the bottom, and sucked out all of the oxygen. No oxygen, no flames."

I try not to gape.

It sounds fantastical, but as I consider it, I realize it's no stranger than creating walkways that transport you from one world to another in the blink of an eye.

"Holy cow, Hellie," I exclaim, "how could you do that and survive?"

"I almost didn't. I tried to pull Kaden to me in hopes that he could save me, but I passed out. Luckily Jerrin sensed my efforts and was able to intercept Kaden before I dropped him into limbo somewhere. Then the two of them came to check on me. According to Kaden I was curled up in fetal position and was nearly gone. If they hadn't taken me straight to an Auravalian hospital, I would've died. That's when Jerrin decided to give you and the folks the phony memories."

I stare at my sister for a moment and then turn around in a slow circle, waving my hand at the desolation. "You said this was your fault, but it sounds to me like you're a hero. You almost died to save the forest."

We come to an outcrop of ottoman-sized rocks.

Hellie sits down on one, props her elbows on her knees, and cups her chin with her hands. I sit on one of the others.

"Grandma Powers was right when she said our forest was enchanted because magical creatures lived here," Hellie says. "They originated in Auravale but immigrated here to get away from the large predators that hunted them on their own world.

"One day last summer, Kaden told me about them. They're called the stwethil-thage."

She glances up at me, and her eyes twinkle, which is a much better look for her than the saddened frown she wore earlier.

"They're cute little things," she continues. "They're only about five inches tall and basically humanoid—meaning they have a head, a torso, two arms, and two legs. They also have pointed ears and leathery wings. They come in every color of the rainbow and glow with an inner light.

"As a race, they've been on Earth for a long, long time. Grandma Powers said there used to be colonies in every major forest on our world. No one knows when or how the first ones got here, but we know most of them are gone now. Kaden told me that there are only four groups left.

"When Bree-Ella was very young and just learning to use her powers, she made a portal into our forest for a clan of stwethil-thage who wanted to come here and reunite with their families. However, despite being a mage, she wasn't a member of the royal family, and her portal was flawed.

"Although the stwethil-thage could travel back and forth between our worlds, the doorway was a fixed point and so small that only a few could go through at one time.

"When I realized the fire was out of control, I also realized the stwethil-thage's portal was engulfed in flames. Miraculously I managed to protect them anyway, making them into my loyal fans."

"More heroics," I say. "I don't understand why you're so hard on yourself."

"Because the story isn't over. Do you remember when Jerrin mentioned that the king has an illegitimate half-brother named Maldon?"

"I think so." I try to dredge up the memory. It seems as if I heard the story a century ago. "Isn't Maldon the man who seduced and impregnated Bree-Ella?"

"That's right, but he's not just a man. He's a sorcerer. Jerrin also mentioned that Maldon only wants three things: to gain power, to destroy their family, and to find Bree-Ella's child. Because of the stupid magic I accidentally did last summer, Maldon became aware of me. He thinks I'm Bree-Ella's child, and he came looking for me. I don't know if he started the fire to draw me out, but I think it is possible."

She turns her head and looks away. When she starts talking again, she doesn't resume eye contact.

"Anyway, after I regained my strength in the Auravalian hospital, I came back here to the forest and—"

I stop her.

The strain in her voice tells me that she's leaving out something important.

"What aren't you telling me?" I ask.

She doesn't answer for a moment. Then she says, "While I was in the hospital, I realized I had fallen in love with Kaden, so I ran away."

"You ran away?"

"Yeah. I—I can't talk about it now. Maybe someday."

I can accept that. We all have things that are too private to share.

"All right. You regained your strength and came back to the woods. Then what happened?"

"I was heartsick when I saw the destruction the fire left behind. I was wandering around in a daze when three stwethil-thage found me. They literally dragged me through the charred wood and ash to a place between worlds to their leader, who told me the Evil One was after me. Naturally, the Evil One was Maldon Darker.

"The stwethil-thage had intended to protect me from him, as I had protected them from the fire, but that was before they knew he had his hellhounds with him. Maldon had trained them to hunt stwethil-thage even between worlds.

"The little creatures had nowhere to go. The portal Bree-Ella made for them was completely destroyed when the fire changed the landscape. They only have the power to step out of a world. They don't have the strength to travel across space to another world without a portal.

"I was afraid the hellhounds would get them, so I opened a doorway to a safe place in Auravale and sent them through. It seemed like a good idea at the time, and the leader told me they'd come back. But they haven't. That's why the forest is dying. Stwethil-thage have been feeding it energy ever since the first ones got here. When they left, it was as if a supply train that had been bringing the forest its nourishment had suddenly been derailed."

"Why won't they come back?" I ask.

I might not be an outdoorsy person myself, but I have to admit that before the fire burned so much of it down, our forest was extremely beautiful. The flowers here were always larger and brighter than anywhere else, the trees taller, and the wild raspberries and blackberries juicier.

Hellie climbs to her feet, looks around, and stands with her hands on her hips. Her eyes fill up with tears.

"In Auravale the stwethil-thage live in the wild, which is why they are easy prey for larger creatures. I didn't have time to project my thoughts to Auravale to find a natural habitat for them, so I sent them to the only suitable place I'd seen—the gardens at the hospital.

"Unfortunately, the hospital is deep in the heart of Letviat, the capital city, where the stwethil-thage have no predators. Instead, they have flocks of adoring children who take delight in bringing them sweets."

I look at the withered, twisted, shriveled, ugly remnants of our forest, and I want to cry with Hellie.

"Is the entire forest like this?"

"No," Hellie says. "The blight started where the stwethil-thage lived and has gradually worked its way outward. There are still a few patches of green left. The largest is around the pond in the southeastern corner. The fire didn't reach it, and it's far enough away from the former stwethil-thage community that the affliction hasn't reached it either."

"So," I say, "you want me to use the power of attraction to lure the thistle-sage—the pistle-page—the whistle-fage." I mutter a not-so-nice word that I picked up from Peter. "What are they called?"

"Stwethil-thage," Hellie says. She finds a stick that's about 2 feet long, picks it up, and then sits back down across from me.

She scratches sideways in the dirt: S T W E T H I L – T H A G E. "It has a short e, short i, long a, silent e. The hard part is mastering the *stweth* sound. Once you have that, the rest is easy. Stwethil-thage."

I practice a couple of times, and Hellie is right. Once I manage to get that *stweth* right, I have no problem putting the rest of it together.

"Stwethil-thage," I say proudly.

With tears in her eyes again, Hellie nods. "Even if only a couple dozen of them came back, eventually the forest would recover. But if none of them do, by the end of the summer, it'll all be dead."

I get up and scrunch next to her on the same rock. I keep nudging her with my hip until she scoots over and gives me half of the space.

Putting my arm around her, I make her a promise. "If Jerrin can teach me how to use my powers in time to save the forest, I'll do my best to coax a bunch of stwethil-thage back here."

She lays her head on my shoulder. "Thank you, Angel."

I rest my head against hers.

"Now, tell me what the king wants me to do for him."

"The same thing," she says. "He needs the stwethil-thage to come back because Bree-Ella left three magical artifacts in the forest, and he wants the stwethil-thage to give them back."

"Why doesn't he just ask them?"

"Oh, he has—several times. The problem is that the fire changed everything. The stwethil-thage will need to do some hunting to find the items, and they don't want to bother. They're too fat and satisfied now that they're getting sweet treats several times every day."

"What about Kaden?" I ask. "Didn't Jerrin say that Kaden could find anything, whether it is lost, stolen, or hidden?"

"Yes," Hellie answers, "and Kaden isn't just any, regular finder. He is the most powerful finder to be born in several generations. Even so, he hasn't been able to locate the artifacts. Last summer, when the king first told Kaden to come get them, Kaden sensed right away that the stwethil-thage had at least one of them. After a couple of days, he knew they had all three. They're sort of like raccoons. They like to collect shiny things.

"Kaden could have forced the stwethil-thage to give him the artifacts or he could have just made them appear, but Skyler and Jerrin wanted him to find a way to persuade the stwethil-thage to produce them willingly. Apparently the stwethil-thage sometimes perform special services for the crown, and Skyler and Jerrin didn't want anything to damage their loyalty.

"After the stwethil-thage settled in at the hospital gardens, Kaden came back here, fully expecting to make the articles appear. But he couldn't.

"He was puzzled. His first thought was that someone had come and removed them, possibly Maldon Darker. If that were the case, it meant that Kaden had tuned into some residual magic instead of the actual artifacts, but a part of him still sensed them in the forest.

"When he reported to Justus IV, the king himself came to take a look. He has a strong affinity for things that belong to the family. He believes the artifacts are still here, too, but since he's not a finder, he can't just make them appear.

"The king consulted with Jerrin and some of the members from the Council of Mages. They concluded that the effects of the fire combined with the stwethil-thage's withdrawal from the forest have corrupted the magic that conceals the artifacts. They think that's why Kaden, as strong as he is, can't find them. If the stwethil-thage return and infuse the forest with their powers again, the Council believes that'll be enough to allow Kaden to locate and retrieve the desired items.

"When the king heard that, he went personally and spoke with the stwethil-thage chieftain, asking that he send some of his people back until the artifacts were located. He even offered to make the clan a new portal, which the chief could control with his mind."

"And the chieftain turned him down?"

"Flat as a pancake."

"So," I say, "the king wants me to attract the stwethil-thage back to the forest so they'll either conduct a search of their own or prepare the way for Kaden's powers to work again so he can find the artifacts."

"That's about it," Hellie says.

I have a thought. "If I can call things to me, isn't there a way I could simply call the artifacts?"

"Sorry," Hellie says, "but being an influencer is different from being a finder. If you want to call a set of silver candlesticks, you concentrate and they'll appear. But they would be a random set. For you to call something specific, like Mom's big crystal candlestick, you have to know the item well enough to envision it and you have to know where it is."

Yet I called china, crystal, and flatware from the kitchen at the hunting lodge, and I didn't even know I was doing it. Maybe it appeared simply because it was the closest source of what I needed.

Magic is so complicated!

I'm amazed anyone understands it.

I glance around at the charred tree trunks and the shriveled foliage, shake my head, and sigh. "Grandma Powers would be so hurt if she saw the forest like this. Where do you put the offerings now?"

I don't give Hellie the chance to answer.

The absurdity of the situation hits me, and I laugh.

"We brought cookie crumbs to a dying forest with no stwethil-thage in it!" I exclaim.

Hellie shrugs without cracking a smile. "I keep hoping the chief will allow Justus IV to send at least one clan member back, even if it's just to look around and assess the situation. Although they tend to be shy around humans, they're ordinarily curious creatures."

She looks so hopeless that I jump up. "Let's go put out the offering. Who knows? Maybe today will be the day one of them returns." I glance around us. "Can you still find the grotto?"

"Sure," she says, clambering up. "Some of the landmarks haven't changed."

When we start walking, I'm glad Hellie is leading.

I have no idea where we are.

Although I didn't accompany Grandma and Hellie all that often, at least I knew where the grotto was.

But that was then and this is now.

I don't have a clue.

When we reach the right spot, I don't recognize it until we're almost on top of it.

The configuration of stones, albeit a bit scorched, is unchanged. The little cave is a foot and a half high, three feet wide, and two feet deep, but the narrow stream that ran next to it is completely gone. There's not even a trickle of water left.

Looking up and down the dry bed, I ask Hellie, "What happened?"

"I used it," she answers. "When I made the water dome to contain the fire, I emptied every single creek that was anywhere near here. I even had to tap into the river. Then when I released the magic, all the water crashed down at the same time, creating new streams."

She kneels down in front of the stone structure. From inside she removes an old plastic platter left over from a set of doll dishes we had as kids. It's full of dirt and debris blown into the little cavity by the wind.

Hellie gets a tissue from a pocket in her backpack and wipes off as much grit and grime as she can. Her eyes have become dull, and her face is so contorted with pain that she is hardly recognizable.

She's about to dump the cookie crumbs onto the platter.

I snatch it away from her.

"If some stwethil-thage come back," I say, "I don't think they should find their treats on a filthy plate."

I open my bottle of water, pour a bit onto the platter, and scrub the plastic with my fingertips to loosen the remaining soil. I empty the bottle rinsing off the resultant muck. At least now the plate looks clean.

Hellie hands me a napkin, and I use it like a dishtowel. I get the rest of the dirt off while I rub the platter dry.

"Thanks," Hellie says with a choke in her voice.

She puts the plate of cookie crumbs inside the cave, along with a jar of tea and some miniature toy cups that I didn't realize she had with her.

The dullness and the agony in her eyes fade, but the sadness still shows through.

"Let's eat," I suggest. "I'm hungry. That protein bar wasn't enough breakfast."

We sit on some rocks in the empty streambed.

Hellie hands me a sandwich, a bag of corn chips, an apple, and a can of Diet Coke.

"Why did you want to have a picnic out here?" I ask her.

"I thought you should see what the forest looks like without the stwethil-thage, and I knew I couldn't describe it."

"It's awful," I say, feeling oppressed by the devastation. Neither of us speaks while we eat.

When I finish my last corn chip, I crumple up the package and stuff it inside my empty sandwich bag.

Without saying anything, Hellie hands me a chocolate cupcake.

As I accept it, I'm suddenly aware of the absolute stillness.

There are no rustling leaves, no singing birds, no buzzing bees.

"Is controlling magic hard to learn?" I ask in an effort to fill the silence.

# Chapter Twenty

"I don't know if learning how to handle magic is difficult for everyone," Hellie answers. "It was for me."

"Why for you?" I ask.

"The reason was twofold. First, I had trouble believing I could use magic without doing evil. Remember, the first things I was aware of doing were wrecking Mrs. Baxter's car and sending Mr. Thompson to the hospital. Second, I didn't want the responsibility of having so much power if I couldn't use it wisely."

She picks up her can of soda and sips at it.

I want her to continue talking, so I give her a little nudge. "Still, you obviously agreed to let Jerrin train you."

"I didn't know it was going to be Jerrin," she says. "All I knew was that a mage from Auravale would be my mentor. I was scared stiff. If Shiane hadn't offered to take lessons with me, I'm not sure I could have gone through with it. When I found out it was going to be Jerrin, I was so relieved."

"You've got to be kidding!" I exclaim. "He's terrifying."

"He can be," Hellie says with a grin (the only one since we entered the forest, I think). "However, the first time I ever saw Jerrin, he picked up a pinecone and bounced it off of the back of Neeve's head. Knowing he has a playful side makes him seem a little more human to me. Besides, in the beginning, I had no idea he was so powerful."

For a moment, I think she's conquered her low mood, but then her eyes dart around as she looks at the dying forest. "One of the things Jerrin has taught me—and has reiterated again and again—is that our magic has limitations and we can't fix everything."

My heart aches for her.

I realize I'm not as powerful as Hellie, and I don't know if the ability to attract and repel will be significant to me in the long run, but I know one thing for sure: I never want to see my sister look as hopeless and as pain-wracked as she did today when she was ready to pour cookie crumbs onto a dirty plate for stwethil-thage that she didn't believe were ever coming back.

I'll do everything in my power—I'll even learn magic—if I can prevent her from going through that much anguish again.

We finish our Diet Cokes and stash all the refuse in Hellie's backpack.

Without verbalizing a course of action, we start walking down the path created by the missing stream.

After a moment, Hellie stops. "Jerrin is coming. He needs to talk with us."

She barely finishes telling me before he steps out of nothingness.

"I hope you two have enjoyed your day off so far," he says.

"Why?" Hellie and I ask together.

"Because it's over for now. Hellie—"

"Whoa," I say to Jerrin. "How did you know we're taking the day off?"

Jerrin doesn't answer. He merely looks at Hellie.

"My bad," Hellie says. "I wasn't quite honest when I told you I didn't want to tell Brenlyn and Talitha I wasn't coming in today. Actually, I had to clear it with Jerrin first. He mentors me at Quick Fix in the mornings, and I work in the shop in the afternoons."

"Why didn't you tell me the truth?"

"Well, you had just said that all the magic stuff was draining you physically and emotionally. I didn't feel right saying I love it and I didn't want to miss out on a training session."

I'm surprised when I realize I'm happy that Hellie likes doing magic. It gives me hope that I might learn to like it too.

"Are you two finished chatting?" Jerrin asks.

Hellie and I both nod.

"Good. Hellie, I need you to go talk with Peter. Tell him we need to meet with him and Cindy, as well as Angel, right now if at all possible. Then we need to get together again tomorrow for most of the day."

"He's going to ask me why," Hellie says. "What do you want me to tell him?"

"Tell him Skyler will explain."

"I'm not sure that'll be enough," she says. "What do you want me to do if he refuses?"

"He won't," Jerrin says. "He's not a stupid man. He'll realize there's a reason, and he'll want to know what it is."

Hellie disappears.

I close my eyes. It's uncomfortable for me to watch the Auravalians move in and out of reality, but part of my brain insists that it is insupportable that my twin can do it too.

When I open my eyes again, Jerrin is sitting cross-legged on the ground. He points to a spot in front of him.

"Even after Peter decides to come with Hellie," he says, "it'll take him a while to get things ready so he can bring Cindy. That gives us a chance to talk."

I sit down where he pointed. "Talk about what?"

"About what happened between you and Peter at Neeve's party."

Immediately I get defensive. "How do you know anything happened?"

"Angel," Jerrin says gently, "I'm a mage, I'm a telepath, and I'm a man with two eyes. You started reacting emotionally as soon as you realized that Peter wasn't. The more he seemed to control his emotions, the less able you were to control yours. I had to start dampening you while we were still in the hunting lodge. By the time we got back to Neeve's apartment, you were projecting your distress so strongly that if I hadn't intervened, even the humans would have felt it."

As hard as I try to prevent it, tears well up in my eyes.

"He knew," I blurt out, "and he didn't tell me. He didn't call it magic, but he knew he and Cindy have powers, and he didn't tell me."

"How do you interpret that?" Jerrin asks. "What does it mean?"

"It means he didn't trust me to believe him, or he didn't trust me to keep his secret, or both."

I manage to prevent most of my tears from spilling over.

I use a tissue I had in my pocket to wipe away the ones that escape.

"Are those the only explanations you can come up with?" Jerrin asks.

"Why?" I ask belligerently. "Do you know something I don't? Did you read his mind?"

"First off, let me assure you that, yes, I know a great many things that you don't know. Second, no, I did not read his mind. We seldom use telepathy if oral speech will do, but that doesn't make us immune to the strong emotions projected by those around us. I didn't need to read your mind to know how much pain you were in on Sunday, and I didn't need to read Peter's mind to understand what he was going through."

I wait for Jerrin to continue but he doesn't.

I wait some more.

"So," I snap, "are you going to tell me, or do I have to guess?"

Unexpectedly, Jerrin laughs. "Angel, I predict that you and I are going to butt heads a lot when you become my pupil." He pauses a moment. "You are going to let me teach you, aren't you?"

I don't say anything. I'm not sure what the answer should be.

Right now, I'm in the middle of being half angry and half hurt that he's taking my problems with Peter so lightly. My heart has been broken, and he wants to talk about teaching me magic!

"Hmm," Jerrin says, "you're used to bargaining with your family when you want something."

I'm startled he knows that, and I'm indignant when I consider how he must have found out.

"Before you ask," he says, "no, I did not read your mind. You projected a sense of two people weighing one thing against another and questioning the balance or equality. I simply guessed that it meant bargaining. Am I right?"

"Yes," I say grudgingly. "Hellie and I call it negotiating, but I suppose it's the same thing."

"Good. Here's the deal. If you commit to letting me be your teacher, I'll explain why Peter didn't tell you he and Cindy have special abilities."

That would be quite a bargain, I think, but he needs to answer a question before I can decide.

"Why do you want to be my teacher anyway? If you believe we're going to butt heads, why don't you just turn around and forget about me?"

"Because," Jerrin says, "I'm the teacher you need. Although you might not believe it, compared to most mages, I am extremely patient. That's why I volunteered to mentor Hellie. There were several others who wanted the job, but I convinced my father and the Council of Mages that I was the best candidate. The other mages think I was chosen because Neeve was already here and, as my brother, he would be willing to act as my resident expert on humans.

"The real reason was because most mage mentors begin training children as soon as a child demonstrates mage-level powers, which is usually around two or three years old. I didn't think anyone else at my level would be adequately aware of the special treatment a teenage magic-handling human would require. I am."

I give him a wry grin. "I could always tell you I'll let you teach me, but then renege later if I change my mind."

"I wouldn't recommend it," Jerrin says with deathly seriousness. "I might not be the crown prince, and making a deal with me might not be a legal agreement, but if you tell me I'm your teacher and you try to renege, you'll find out that legalities have very little to do with the consequences."

My heart skips a beat.

Did Jerrin just threaten me?

For a moment I'm more than a little frightened.

Jerrin really is an intimidating man.

Still, I tell myself, that might not be a bad thing.

I tend to get lazy when things are easy for me, and I tend to want to quit when they're difficult. Even though I enjoy learning, and I like being proficient, and I strive to reach excellence, it'll probably take someone like Jerrin to push me hard if I'm going to learn how to accomplish anything significant with my powers.

I don't think magic will come naturally to me.

I smile despite myself.

"I haven't had a teacher I couldn't charm my way past since kindergarten. You're probably right, if we do this, we'll frequently butt heads. However, I think it might be worth it. You'll challenge me, and I'll learn faster and better because of it." I can't stop a slightly ironic tone from creeping into my voice when I continue. "Jerrin, if you will be my teacher, I promise I'll do my best to be a worthwhile student."

"Well put," he says. "We now have an agreement. I am officially your teacher." He sticks out his hand. "Shake on it."

When we do, I feel an electrical shock shoot through me.

Suddenly it occurs to me that I've just made a deal with the devil (figuratively speaking) and I might discover this arrangement is harder to break than a legal contract.

"Now, about Peter," Jerrin says, immediately beginning to fulfill his part of the bargain. "Sometimes when we're confused about something, it helps us to discuss it with someone who can facilitate our search for clarity. Other times, talking about it only makes us more confused.

"Peter didn't tell you about him and Cindy because he was trying to figure out what was happening to them and he didn't have the answers yet. How could he explain it to you when he didn't understand it himself? Now that he is aware of Auravale and his connection to it, he'll be able to make sense of his past and his present experiences, which will free him up to make plans for his future."

Jerrin stands and brushes off his backside.

When I get up, I brush off my behind too.

"Cindy just woke up from a nap," Jerrin says, "and is changing her clothes. Hellie is going to take her and Peter straight to Auravale so they don't have to see the burned-out forest. Hellie is afraid it would upset Cindy since Peter has taken so many photographs of it for her. We might as well leave now."

He doesn't wait for me to comment.

We simply appear in the hunting lodge.

Neeve and Karissa are sitting in a loveseat by the fire, and Kaden is in a chair nearby. I go over to say hello.

"I expected you sooner," Skyler says to Jerrin. "Where are Peter and Cindy?"

Before answering, Jerrin chooses a big overstuffed chair and drops into it. "Hellie and Peter had to wait for Cindy to wake up from a nap. They'll be here shortly."

"That explains their absence. What took you so long?"

"I wanted to have a word with Angel," Jerrin says. "She has officially agreed to be my pupil. Where's Shiane?"

"She's in her room finishing her school work," Skyler answers with a slight grin. "Her tutor complained to Alaina Mae that our little sister was getting behind in her non-magic studies. Alaina Mae confined her to her room until she gets caught up. That was yesterday. Shiane has not been a happy girl."

I look questioningly at Karissa and Neeve. "Who is Alaina Mae?"

"My mother," answers Neeve, "and Shiane's."

"The current queen," Karissa says, "is the king's second wife. The children of his first wife all call her *Your Highness* in public and by her given name in private."

"My father has children who are much older than my mother," Neeve says, chuckling, "including both Skyler and Jerrin. It can make our holiday gatherings a bit awkward and stressful sometimes, but they are always interesting."

"Ah," Skyler says, "here comes Shiane now."

As soon as she appears, the first thing he says to her is, "Does your mother know you're here?"

She smiles and bats her eyelashes at him. "Do you need to ask?"

"Yes, I do, and I'd appreciate a straight answer. Did you finish your assignments, and did the queen say you could come?"

Shiane gets a petulant look on her face. "I didn't quite get everything done, but Mother said I could come as long as I promised I'd work very hard to catch up next week and if I'd stay current in the future."

Skyler grins at her. "You know I'll check."

"Yes," Shiane says, "so you know I don't dare lie."

Startled, I turn to Neeve. "Can telepaths lie to each other? Is that even possible?"

"It is," Neeve says. "We're taught how to block our thoughts while we're still very young. In the family we usually don't bother unless we feel strongly about keeping something a secret. Still, lying to each other isn't generally a good idea. It rarely turns out well."

As if he's been pulled by a string, Neeve slowly turns his head and glances over at Skyler.

Skyler is already looking at Neeve.

When their eyes meet, Neeve says softly, "I paid dearly for that."

"I know you did," Skyler says. "I'm sorry. I'd change it if I could."

"So would I." Neeve takes Karissa's hand and kisses her palm. "You said I could find a different way if I tried. I should have listened, but I was impatient."

I glance around the room.

Everyone is suddenly looking subdued and somber.

Karissa and Shiane are near tears.

I assume whatever they're talking about relates to a lie Neeve told his eldest brother and somehow the lie contributed to his kidnapping and subsequent torture.

I don't dare ask anyone to explain, but I'm uncomfortable being on the outside of this group's shared history.

One of these days, maybe I can get Hellie to fill me in.

When Jerrin says, "Hellie and her charges are on the way," he breaks the tension that had settled over everyone.

A moment later, Hellie, Peter, and Cindy appear.

Cindy has her hands over her eyes and is counting.

". . . seven, eight, nine, ten."

She drops her hands and then runs over to the window. Laughing, she throws her arms out and spins around in a circle.

"You brought me to fairyland. I always wanted to come."

# Chapter Twenty-one

Cindy rushes over to Karissa.

"Where are Jeremy and Bennett? Didn't they want to come?"

Karissa puts an arm around Cindy's waist. "I'm afraid this isn't like the party Neeve and I had at his apartment. It's—"

"Oh," Cindy says. "You didn't get to invite them because this isn't Neeve's place. Whose house is it?"

Skyler answers from across the room, "It belongs to our father."

"So," Cindy says, "he got to decide who to invite." She dashes over and gives Shiane a hug. "At least you got to come." Then she looks all around the room. "Where's your dad? He should be here if we're having a party in his house."

"He's at work," Skyler says.

Cindy nods knowingly. "Fathers go to work during the day. That's what fathers do so they can take care of their families. Are you a father, Skyler?"

"Yes."

"Why aren't you at work?"

"Actually I am. I work for my father, and he wanted me to meet with you and Peter and Angel. That's why he said we could use his house."

While Cindy and Skyler chat, I see an elderly man, who is white-haired and wrinkly, unobtrusively slip from an interior room into this one and then sit down. I assume he's not a member of the family since he uses a door like the rest of us mortals.

Then I notice Peter. I've been so focused on Cindy that I overlooked him in those first few minutes. He's standing by the window staring at me. He probably thinks I've been ignoring him on purpose.

Hesitantly, I cross over to him.

"I'm sorry," I say. I reach up and touch his cheek. "I didn't look at it from your perspective. Can we—"

He cups his hands around the back of my neck and pulls my face next to his. He doesn't kiss me—of course not—not in front of the Auravalians, but he presses his cheek against mine. "I'm sorry too. I hate it when things go wrong between us. I love you, Angel. I always have and I always will."

"I love you too," I tell him in a breathless whisper.

He takes my hand and we lace our fingers together.

"Angel," Skyler's voice reminds me that there are other people in the room, "will you and Peter please join the rest of us?"

"Of course," I say, trying to sound casual, but I don't suppose I'm fooling anyone. Peter and I are back together, the way we should be, and I feel like jumping up onto a table and bursting into song as if we were in a 1960s musical.

When we're seated on a couch near the others, Cindy comes over and sits beside Peter.

Skyler address the three of us. "If you were Auravalian citizens, you would be expected to report to the Magicians Guild for testing. You obviously have powers whether you call them psychic abilities or if you call them magic."

"They're magic," Cindy says.

Skyler smiles at her. "I think so too."

He motions to the old man, who stands up.

"This is Master Cushing. He is the head of Evaluation and Classification at the Magicians Guild. The king has asked him to talk with the three of you individually to identify as much as he can about your talents without requiring you to take formal testing. Kaden and Shiane are going to help him."

Skyler nods at Jerrin, and Jerrin takes over.

"If you were being evaluated at the Magicians Guild, after you completed a battery of tests, you'd be interviewed by a mage, a medical finder, and a clairvoyant. Although Kaden and Shiane are still in training, he is a medical finder and she is a clairvoyant, and they are both exceptionally talented. Of course, Master Cushing is a mage.

"At our father's request, I will observe Master Cushing's interviews, Neeve will sit in with Kaden's, and Skyler with Shiane's. Our role is to be observers, but that doesn't mean we won't ask questions if things occur to us. We'll try not to be too disruptive.

"Hellie and Karissa are here as moral support and to act as intermediaries. If you have a question with human connotations that we might not understand, ask one of them to explain. They both know a great deal about Auravalian history, our customs, and the range of our magical powers. Feel free to call on one or both of them at any point during the evaluation process."

"Angel," Skyler says, "we'd like you to meet with Master Cushing first. While she's doing that, Peter we'd like you to meet with Kaden, and Cindy, we'd like you to meet with Shiane." He gives Cindy a reassuring smile.

"After thirty minutes we'll switch. Karissa is going to act as timekeeper. Any questions?"

Peter and I shake our heads.

Skyler leans forward. "Cindy, do you understand what we're going to be doing?"

"Uh huh. It's like at my school when we meet with each of the teachers and talk about what we can do and what we need to work on. Right?"

"That's a very good description," Skyler says.

"Peter has been helping me find words to explain what I think. It's nice when someone tells me I've done it right. Thank you."

"You're welcome." He smiles at her again. He can't help it. Everyone loves Cindy.

"Now," Skyler says, "let's split up into groups. I want us all to stay in this room so Karissa and Hellie are equally available to everyone."

Jerrin gets up and approaches Master Cushing. "Why don't we move over there by the kitchen? Angel?" I follow them.

"Let's go over by the window," Kaden says to Peter and Neeve.

Shiane takes Cindy by the hand. "I get cold easily, so I like to sit by the fire. What about you?"

"I like sitting by the fire even when I'm not cold. It's pretty, and I like the way it smells."

We disperse, and I find myself confronting two mages.

I vaguely remember Master Cushing as the old man I met on graduation night in the room full of books, but he was dressed oddly then. I scrunch up my brow and try to remember exactly what I thought was strange about his clothing. I can't.

Hellie told me Jerrin scrambled my memories of that night, and once again I find myself wanting to smack him.

Today Master Cushing is wearing a silvery gray dress shirt with black trousers. They look good with his white hair and moustache.

"We've met before," I say as we sit across from each other at a small table. "I don't think it was very pleasant."

"Not for either of us," Master Cushing replies. "I hope things will go better this time. Now, I need you to tell me your name and your age. It's just a formality."

"My name is Angelica Prudence Powers, and I'm eighteen years old."

"Thank you, Angelica."

"Please call me Angel. Everyone does."

"All right, Angel." He holds his hands out, palms up. "Place your hands on top of mine."

When I start to comply, he says, "Then look into my eyes."

An image flashes through my mind, and I stare at the tabletop as I envision a mad scientist trying to hypnotize his unwilling victim. *Look into my eyes*, the madman insists in a bad Bela Lugosi's Count Dracula accent.

Before I touch Master Cushing's hands or make eye contact, I attempt to clear my mind so I won't laugh. Somehow, I manage to gain control of myself.

"What are your talents, Angel?" Master Cushing asks me.

I rattle them off without thinking. "I am an excellent writer and photographer. I sing well, both melody and harmony. I have a good sense of rhythm and a sharp eye for color and fashion. I'm a polished public speaker, a fair actress, and a believable liar."

I clamp my lips together in horror.

Where did that last phrase come from?

I'm not saying another word.

"There is nothing wrong with being a believable liar," Master Cushing says. "No one would get along with anyone else in the world if everyone had to tell the truth all the time. Please continue."

I don't seem to have control of my tongue.

As hard as I try, I can't keep silent.

I tell him about lighting the logs in the fireplace and calling hot chocolate, buttered toast, and other things, when I was cold and hungry. I tell him about inadvertently sending a whole storm system away so it wouldn't ruin our church social. Then I repeat everything Jerrin told me about my ability to call what I want and to repel what I don't.

At some point during my recitation, Master Cushing withdraws his hands from mine. Then he pulls his chair closer to the table, leans forward, and peers into my eyes from only a couple of inches away. When I stop talking, he doesn't break eye contact with me, and for some reason, I can't break away from him.

"Jerrin," he says, "take a look."

His paralyzing gaze finally releases me.

I turn to the side and Jerrin locks gazes with me.

After a moment, Jerrin pulls back in surprise.

"Holy stars," he exclaims. "Is that what I think it is?"

"If you read her right, yes," Master Cushing answers. "And she already has the skill at the magician-level. With a little training it's going to reach mage-level. Thank heavens it's buried so deep that she's never tried to use it. You'll have to be very careful when you help her deal with it."

Jerrin turns his attention from me to Master Cushing. "We'll need to discuss this in depth later."

"Not just us," Master Cushing replies. "We'll need to inform the king. The potential for misuse is staggering."

"Did you find something bad?" I can't help but ask.

"Not bad," Jerrin says, "but unique, which shouldn't surprise anyone since all of your talents are unusual."

"Don't worry about it for now," Master Cushing says. "What you need to understand about your abilities is that they all relate to influencing, and there are three major components: attracting and repelling, calling and sending, and inviting and denying.

"The first component, the one you probably use the most often, is attracting and repelling. It refers to your ability to manipulate living things, not just people but also plants and animals. You can influence thoughts, feelings, impulses, instincts, and behaviors, either attracting/promoting or repelling/hindering them.

"The second component, calling and sending, refers to your ability to affect the location and condition of inanimate objects. When you produced the food, the drinks, and the other things you described to me earlier, you called them to you. After you finished eating, you could have sent the leftovers to your refrigerator and the cutlery and china to the dishwasher if you had wanted.

"The third component, inviting and denying, refers to your ability to influence events, happenings, outcomes, procedures, and consequences. Whereas attracting and repelling usually involves influencing a single person or other living thing at a time, inviting and denying can affect large groups all at once. If you drew in enough power and concentrated hard enough, you could control the results of a public election or cause flocks of birds to migrate north instead of south in the fall. You probably haven't used this ability yet—anyway I don't see any signs of it—but if you ever do, I imagine the results will be dramatic."

"Which one did I use to move the rainstorm?" I ask.

"None of them," Master Cushing says. "Manipulating the weather is so complex and so difficult we don't even call it a talent. It is one of the great magics, and very few people can handle them. Most mages live out their entire lives without performing a single act of great magic. The ability seems to pop up suddenly in times of emotional upheaval, and it is completely unrelated to a magic user's rank. We at the Magicians Guild understand very little about them."

"Does that mean I can't learn to control it?" My eyes dart back and forth between Master Cushing and Jerrin. "I don't want to keep accidentally interfering with the weather. I might mess up Colorado's seasons without even knowing it."

It's Jerrin who answers me. "As you learn to recognize and control your other abilities, you'll become aware of what your magic feels like. Once you can do that, you won't use your powers inadvertently again. If you want to learn how to change the weather on command, you'll need to prove to me that you can differentiate between necessity and convenience. Even then, we'd need to have some serious discussions about the possible repercussions and your responsibilities in response."

I'm about to assure Jerrin that I don't ever want to do it again, but Master Cushing begins talking before I can.

"There are subtleties and complexities about your powers that we'll need time to figure out," he says. "Jerrin and I will probably both need to read you a few more times before we understand your full potential. It's possible you'll have to do some formal testing at the Magicians Guild. If we're going to—"

"Time," Karissa calls out.

Jerrin stands up so everyone will pay attention. "Angel will meet with Shiane now. Cindy, you'll meet with Kaden. Peter, you'll meet with Master Cushing."

As I head towards Shiane's table, I wonder if this is what speed dating feels is like. I get just enough information to start asking intelligent questions, and then time is called and I have to move on.

# Chapter Twenty-two

"How was Cindy?" I ask Shiane.

"She was just fine," Shiane answers. "What I do isn't invasive or threatening. That's why Skyler and Jerrin wanted her to start with me. There's none of that staring into each other's eyes."

"That's a relief," I say. "What do you do? Palmistry? Tarot cards? Numerology?"

Shiane giggles. "Nothing that complicated or formal. We just talk about whatever is on your mind."

"Then what?"

"I'll tell you if I see anything. Being a clairvoyant is a passive talent. We don't manipulate or control anything. After years of training and experience, some clairvoyants can make predictions on demand, but they still only see the future with the highest probability of occurring. Because of the number of variables involved in a specific happening, it is difficult for anyone to make a projection that is 100% certain."

This makes more sense to me than most of the magic I've seen or heard demonstrated. Probability, variables, and outcomes are things I can understand. If you give a mathematician enough data, he can develop an algorithm to calculate the most likely result of a specified series of events. When you change or miss a variable, the predicted outcome becomes invalid. If Shiane can do it without a computer, I suppose it must be magic, but it's scientifically based magic.

"What shall we talk about?" Shiane asks.

All of a sudden, my mind goes completely blank.

"I don't know," I answer.

"Hmm," Shiane says. "What's wrong with your forest?"

"Why do you ask that?"

"The forest is on your mind, and you're projecting worried thoughts."

"It's dying," I say. "Hellie sent our stwethil-thage to the hospital gardens in Auravale last summer when the forest was on fire. They said they'd come back, but they haven't. Generations of stwethil-thage have been feeding the forest with their magic. Now that they've gone, the forest is starving to death."

"So," Shiane says, glancing to the side at Skyler, "that's why Father has been so upset about the artifacts Bree-Ella took. With the stwethil-thage gone and the land corrupted by fire, no one can find them."

Skyler's lips purse together and his brow furrows. I think he wants Shiane to change the subject, but she doesn't.

She turns her gaze back on me. "I asked my father why the location of the artifacts had become important after so many years, but he told me it was his problem not mine. He is always accusing me of rushing off and interfering in things that are none of my busi—"

She stops and takes a breath.

Her pale green eyes glaze over.

When speaking resumes, her words come out slower. "I see stwethil-thage living in your forest again. I see the plant life recovering and the birds and animals returning. I see many people enjoying the beauty of the woods, and stwethil-thage are lining the branches of the trees, twinkling with delight because of the work they've accomplished."

Her eyes return to normal.

"Really, Shiane?" I exclaim. "You're not just telling me what I want to hear, are you?"

She sits up straight and stares down her nose at me. "I am not some phony carnival fortune-teller!"

"I'm sorry," I say quickly. "I didn't mean to be offensive. It's just that the forest means so much to Hellie, and its current condition makes her so sad. I want it to go back to the way it was before."

"Oh," Shiane says. "It'll never go back to the way it was."

My eyes get teary. My feelings are awfully close to the surface lately.

Shiane takes my hands and gives them a reassuring squeeze. "It's going to be much better than it was. Hellie will be very happy."

"I hope it's soon," I say.

We chitchat for a while.

Then Shiane suddenly stops, and her eyes glaze over again.

"A time of crisis awaits you. You will have to choose: follow your heart and face death or follow your reasoning and live with self-doubt. If you choose to follow your heart, there are those who will be angry and try to stop you. If you choose to follow your reasoning, there are those who will be angry and blame you. Only you can weigh the risks."

I come halfway out of my chair and grab Shiane's arms. "What do you mean? What crisis? What am I supposed to do?"

Skyler gently disengages my fingers and eases me back into my seat.

"Shiane," he asks, "is there any more?"

"Only this," she answers. "Angel, when the crisis comes, believe in what you know and not what others have told you. You are stronger than you realize. Make the choice, but not out of fear. Fear only makes you weak."

Shiane and I stare at each other as the veiling drains from her eyes.

I want to ask her a dozen questions.

Her expression says she has no more answers for me.

"Time," Karissa calls out.

As I head for Kaden's table, I wish I had brought a video recorder with me. Or I wish it had occurred to me to record everything on my phone. What Shiane told me is already interfering with my ability to remember what Master Cushing said. Now, meeting with Kaden will probably make me forget what Shiane said.

I sit down across from Kaden. Neeve is off to the left.

When Kaden smiles at me with his incredibly white teeth and perfectly shaped lips, I understand how Hellie could have fallen under his spell without ever having had a date with him. He really is a beautiful, almost divine, looking man.

I glance over at Peter, who is draped casually in a chair while he is visiting with Shiane. He is every bit as good looking as Kaden—although in a different way. Kaden is taller, but Peter is more muscular. Kaden is darker, despite his bleached blond hair, and Peter is fairer. Kaden has an otherworldly aura, Peter is a down-to-earth, strong, masculine, passionate man who makes me feel safe and loved and sheltered.

"What happens now?" I ask, pushing aside my impulse to continue comparing Hellie's boyfriend with mine. "Why do I need to see a medical finder?"

"That's a fair question," Kaden answers. "Medical finders have many different functions. One of them is assessing how well the mind and the body work together. It is important for the mind to calm the body when careful thought is necessary during times of physical agitation, just as it is important for the body to overrule the mind when action in required during times of external danger. Does that make sense to you?"

"Yes," I say. "I've never heard it put in those terms before, but it sounds logical."

"Good, now I need to check your organs, muscles, nerves, and vascular system to make sure there is no physical condition that would interfere with your mind/body connection. If you'll—"

"Look into your eyes?"

"Yes," Kaden says, flashing his brilliant smile at me again.

"First," I say, "tell me how this works. How can you learn anything from gazing into my eyes?"

"You have a saying in your world that goes: *The eyes are the windows to the soul.* You've heard that?"

"Of course," I reply. "It's a quote that's often attributed to a sixteenth century English poet and playwright named William Shakespeare, but it's been around in one form or another for much longer than that."

"Your eyes," Kaden says, "are more than the windows to your soul. Without any invasive procedures, I can use your eyes as the entrance to a pathway made of nerves and blood vessels that extends throughout your body. The ability to access this pathway is what differentiates a medical finder from all other types of locaters."

"But you're not limited to medical finding, are you?"

"No, I'm not."

"How do you—?"

"Angel," Neeve interrupts me, "why don't you save your questions for after Kaden completes his exam? We have limited time, and he might need to get information from you. If so, his questions have to take precedence."

"Of course." I'm embarrassed by my lack of focus, but there is so much I don't know about the Auravalians and so much I want to understand.

Tonight, however, we have an agenda.

I rest my arms on the table, lean forward, and open my eyes as large as I can.

"Relax, Angel," Kaden says. "Your eyelids will get tired if you force them to stay opened like that. Just look at me. That's all you have to do."

I don't know how long he gazes into my eyes, but I'm beginning to feel as if we're having a staring contest.

My eyes burn.

"Relax, Angel," he repeats. "You're not blinking. Pretend we're in your living room chatting while Hellie is in the kitchen making snacks."

"But we're not chatting. We're just looking at each other."

"So, let's talk. Tell me what kinds of things you do for relaxation?"

I take a few minutes to think.

"I go out with Peter of course. I also spend time with my family and friends, watch television or movies, and read. Not necessarily in that order. Oh, I also sing. I don't know if singing helps me relax, but it always cheers me up when I feel down."

"Do you engage in any regular physical activity?"

"Regular?" I ask.

He nods.

"Well, every Saturday morning, Hellie and I work in the yard. We alternate tasks—mowing, edging, weeding, and things like that. Does that count as regular."

"Every Saturday morning sounds regular to me. Do you exercise?"

"Not on a fixed schedule. Peter and I take Cindy swimming every now and then. Sometimes Peter and I go for walks. Sometimes we go dancing. We've even gone bowling and jogging and canoeing a few times."

As we talk, Kaden maintains eye contact, so I suppose he's still evaluating me, but I'm not as uncomfortable as I was when we weren't saying anything.

"I have a question," Neeve says. "All the things you've described are positive, healthy activities, but do you ever resort to unhealthy, negative behaviors?"

"I don't smoke or drink or do drugs if that's what you want to know."

"Actually," Neeve says, "I was thinking more like impulsive eating, sleeping too much or maybe not sleeping at all, getting into arguments, or staying up all night playing video games on your computer."

"Oh," I say. "I suppose I do all of those things occasionally, but only when I'm alone and frustrated or depressed. My first choice when I'm stressed out is to be with people I care about, who also care for me."

"You mentioned you like to read," Kaden says. "Hellie has introduced me to science fiction and fantasy, and I am enjoying them very much."

"That's an interesting coincidence," Neeve says, "Karissa has gotten me reading Earth science fiction too."

"What about you, Angel?" Kaden asks. "Are you a science fiction and fantasy enthusiast like your sister?"

"Not really. I've read some sci-fi because Peter likes it, and sometimes he'll ask me to read a specific book or story so we can discuss it. We both have a solid background in science, and we enjoy taking different sides of the scientific theories involved in the plots and then arguing them out."

"What kinds of things do you enjoy reading?" Neeve asks.

"Biographies mostly. Right now, I'm reading about a famous English mystery writer who had quite a mysterious life of her own. One time she took off in her car and disappeared for eleven days. When she was found, she claimed to have amnesia. There are lots of theories about where she was and what she was doing, but no one knows for sure. She never told."

After that, we talk about music and television shows and movies.

Then, out of the blue, Kaden asks, "What kind of magic user do you think you're going to be?"

"I'm not sure that I want to be any kind of magic user. The abilities that Master Cushing says I have are all self-serving. It bothers me that I might have manipulated my way through high school, making people like me, being selected to do things that someone else might have done better, possibly getting awards I didn't earn or deserve. I don't know if anything about my life has been real."

"Kaden," Neeve says, "you don't have much time left."

"Angel, as a medical finder, this is what I've discovered about you. In general, you're in good health, but that's because you're a teenager with a strong metabolism. You need to get more exercise if you want to maintain your health into your middle years, especially since you've chosen to pursue a sedentary career.

"You vacillate between being very critical of yourself and being overly confident. When you begin training with Jerrin, you'll need to work on self-awareness and a more balanced self-image.

"You try to be open and honest in your dealings with people, although I sense there are some questionable things in your past that you haven't told anyone. I didn't push my way into your mind, so I don't know what they are, but you might be more comfortable with yourself if you talked about them with someone.

"You are willing to express your opinions in small gatherings, preferably just two or three people, but you often hesitate in larger groups for fear that someone will tell you you're wrong. Risk being more open, the world won't end if you make a mistake.

"The fact that you think you might have misused your powers in the past and worry about doing it in the future indicates that you will be a cautious magic user. Since you have at least two extremely powerful abilities, being cautious is a good thing, especially while you're learning.

"What all of this means is that there is nothing physically or mentally that should interfere with your ability to reach the highest level of your potential. Do you have any questions?"

"Not right now," I say. "I'm in overload. Maybe—"

"Time's up," Karissa calls out.

I inhale deeply.

I am drained, and when I glance over at Peter, he looks about like I feel. We're both exhausted.

I turn to check on Cindy.

Sometime during the last half hour, someone moved a loveseat across the room so Hellie could sit next to Cindy. I must have been really focused on Kaden to have missed it. Although Cindy looks tired, she is smiling, so I guess her session with Master Cushing wasn't too bad.

Skyler calls us back to order.

Peter immediately goes to get Cindy. She leans on him while they cross the room. The three of us sit on the couch together with Cindy cuddled up next to Peter and his arm around her.

"I want to thank all of you," Skyler says, addressing us as a group, "for participating in this rather unorthodox procedure. It hasn't been an easy experience for any of us, and I appreciate how much effort everyone has extended. I especially want to thank you, Master Cushing, for taking so much time out of your busy schedule. Neeve will take you back to the Magicians Guild now."

Neeve gives Karissa's palm a quick kiss. "I'll be right back."

Neeve and Master Cushing vanish.

Jerrin takes over, turning his attention on Peter, Cindy, and me. "I realize you've been exposed to a large amount of information in a short amount of time. Don't worry about trying to remember it all. Skyler, Neeve, and I have recorded your interviews, and you'll receive a written copy of them when you begin your training, which I hope will be early next week.

"We'll meet again tomorrow. Peter, have you made arrangements to bring Cindy back with you?"

"Our parents left for Denver this morning," Peter answers. "My mother's best friend recently died, and my mother and father are going to the viewing tonight and the funeral tomorrow. They plan on being home around 9:00 tomorrow evening. Until then, I'll be taking care of Cindy. What time do you want us here?"

"Early afternoon, say 2:00, after you've had lunch. Neeve wants to do a barbeque in the evening. That will give us three or four hours to work before dinner and a couple of hours after. Do you think Cindy can handle that much?"

"If she gets tired, she'll tell me she needs to take a nap."

# Chapter Twenty-three

"Hellie," Skyler says, "will you take Peter and Cindy home now, and Neeve, will you take Karissa and Kaden? Shiane, you can see yourself back to your rooms. Angel, Jerrin will take you home in a few minutes. We need a private word with you first."

As the others vanish, I realize I'm left with the two power players. Next to the king, Skyler and Jerrin are probably the two most influential men in Auravale. Suddenly I'm very nervous. I stare at the floor so I don't have to look at them. I'm afraid I'll start trembling.

"This won't take long," Skyler says. I hear him and Jerrin move their chairs closer to me. "We need to discuss your thrill-seeking behaviors?"

My head jerks up, my eyes bulge, and my jaw drops.

"Thrill-seeking behaviors?" I stammer. "I don't know what you mean."

"Angel," Jerrin retorts sharply, "if you are going to learn to use your powers and if I am going to be your teacher, you need to know that you can't hide anything from me. For one thing, I can't teach you effectively if you're not being honest with me. For another, I'm a mage, and I'm a strong one. I'll always know the truth."

I hear the words, but my brain is whirling around inside my skull and I can't think straight.

"Specifically," Jerrin continues, his sky-blue eyes boring into me, "I'm talking about your casual attitude towards the law and other people's property."

I swallow hard.

"You've been lucky so far," Skyler says, "but it won't last. One of the potentially unpleasant properties of magic is that it tunes into what we really want. Your desire to be recognized for who you are, good and bad, is on the verge of overwhelming your desire to get away with the shoplifting."

"Are you a mage too?" I blurt at Skyler, angry because the brothers are ganging up on me.

"No," he answers, unruffled by my rudeness, "I'm a sorcerer, and in the hierarchy of the Magicians Guild that is a step down from a mage. However, don't be fooled into thinking that means I'm not powerful. I've been trained since birth to be a king—a king who will rule over mages."

He smiles, and it is not a nice or a reassuring smile.

"There are advantages to being a king that not even a mage can challenge, that not even the entire Magicians Guild could face if they defied me once I wore the crown. I am a sorcerer, but I am also the next king, and that makes a difference."

Unexpectedly I shiver.

For a moment, I'm struck by how casually I've been conversing with these two formidable men. I wonder if the American belief in "all men [humans] are created equal" makes us lack the appropriate respect and deference that people in positions of great power should be afforded.

Jerrin's voice pulls me back to the original topic of our conversation.

"If you're caught stealing," he says, "you'll certainly be arrested since you are now legally an adult. That could alter many aspects of your life, including how your parents perceive you, how Hellie relates to you, how your friends feel about you, and how you define yourself. It might even damage your relationship with Peter and Cindy. In addition, you would have a permanent police record, and there's no way to predict how that might have an impact on your future."

"You must stop, Angel," Skyler says. "Can you do it on your own? Or do we need to help you?"

I do not miss the implication in Skyler's words.

I stop or they stop me.

My eyes tear up, but it's not because I'm embarrassed or afraid or confused or even sad.

It goes deeper than that.

They expect me to give up something that has become a part of me, something I've used to cheer me up when I'm depressed, to calm me when I'm angry, to support me when I'm fearful, and to comfort me when I'm alone and lonely.

When I've felt weak, it's made me feel strong.

Sometimes when Peter is gone, the only thing that makes me feel real and alive is taking an item right out from underneath the noses of a bunch of sales clerks and security guards.

I don't think I can let it go.

"It won't be so bad," Jerrin says with his voice taking on a milder tone. "You'll find that learning to use your magic correctly will fill some of the empty spots that shoplifting is filling for you now."

"And," Skyler adds, "I promise you, when you can control your powers enough that they become tools for you to use, you'll never feel weak or vulnerable again."

I heave a dramatic sigh, which is only partly put on. "Do I have to worry about you two reading my mind all the time?"

Skyler chuckles. "As fascinating as your thoughts might be, I'm afraid we do have other duties. At least I do. Jerrin's responsibilities right now are almost exclusively centered around teaching and mentoring."

"Which means I have several young minds to monitor," Jerrin says, "not just yours."

I automatically think about my sister taking magic lessons from Jerrin for a year. The fact that they've known each other that long causes me a moment of panic. I'm sure they've formed some kind of bond by now, even if it's only the trust between teacher and pupil.

"Are you going to tell Hellie about the shoplifting?"

"Why?" Jerrin asks. "Do you think I should?"

"No," I beg, "please don't tell her. Don't tell anyone."

"Can we safely assume this mean you're quitting on your own?" Skyler asks me.

"Yes," I answer quickly, although a little voice deep in the back of my mind whispers, *I hope.*

"And," Skyler continues, "you have officially accepted Jerrin as your magic teacher. Is that correct?"

"Yes." Again, I answer quickly. Even though I already told Jerrin I'd study with him, I don't think I committed myself emotionally until this very moment. I'm sure Jerrin will be more likely to keep my secret from Hellie if we are meeting regularly and working together.

"Good," Skyler says with a relieved sigh. "One down and two to go."

"One what?" I ask impulsively.

I don't think Skyler will answer me, but he does.

"One task assigned by our father," Skyler says.

"And two more that you still have to complete?" I ask. "Two more having to do with Peter, Cindy, and me?"

"She's a bright one, Jerrin. You'll have to be careful."

"She and Hellie are alike in that regard."

Jerrin and Skyler stand up, so I do too.

"Good night, Angel," Skyler says to me. "I'll see you tomorrow." He turns to Jerrin. "I'll meet you back at the palace." He disappears.

The next thing I know I'm standing in my bedroom.

I catch a brief glimpse of Jerrin beside me.

Then he's gone.

I collapse onto my bed.

My phone rings just as Hellie sticks her head into my room.

I pull my phone out of my pocket. "It's Peter," I tell her.

"Come talk to me before you go to bed," Hellie says.

"Okay." I tap *accept call.* "Hey, Peter. Have you put Cindy to bed yet?"

"Yes, and she was asleep before I even finished tucking her in. Are you all right? What did the royalty want?"

"Nothing much," I say. "Mostly Skyler wanted to make sure I have agreed to begin training with Jerrin. The first time we met, I was fairly ambivalent about the whole magic thing, and I guess the king has been pressuring him and Jerrin to get a firm commitment."

"This experience feels surreal to me," Peter says. "I've gone from thinking Cindy and I were freaks because of what we could do to acknowledging that we have magic in our blood because of an off-world parent. What did you make of the process we went through tonight?"

"Being honest," I say, "I can hardly remember it. All I know is that I'm physically and emotionally exhausted."

"Me too." Then the tone of his voice changes. "Babe, I really am sorry that we quarreled. We need to talk, but I don't know when we'll have the chance unless we get together Sunday evening. Can I take you out to dinner?"

"I'd like that."

"Me too. Get some sleep, and I'll see you tomorrow afternoon. Hellie said you'd be with her when she comes to get us this time."

"If that's what she said, then I'm sure she's right."

"Good night, Babe."

"Good night, Peter."

I change into some shorty pajamas before I head for Hellie's bedroom via the bathroom.

She meets me half way, so I start washing my face.

Hellie sits on the side of the tub. "Are you all right?"

"Other than being so tired I can hardly stand up, I'm fine. How about you?"

"I'm okay. I didn't do much tonight except sit with Cindy. She called me over when she was about halfway through the interview with Kaden. She asked me if I'd stay with her."

"Thank you for doing that."

"I was happy to. She's a sweetie."

"How did she do? Was she terribly afraid?"

"I don't know if afraid is the right word," Hellie says. "She was apprehensive because she didn't know what to expect, but she handled herself pretty well. In fact, I got the feeling a couple of times that she wanted me to be there more for the evaluators than for herself. I don't think she knows how to lie, and some of her answers caught Kaden and Master Cushing off guard."

"Can you give me a couple of examples?" I switch from cleaning my face to cleaning my teeth.

"Kaden asked her what she was learning in school. She told him she learned that teachers get tired of teaching and it's important to know the right answers to their question so they'll feel okay. She said they can't give good lessons if they feel bad."

"That's quite a profound statement," I say. "How did Kaden react?"

"It wasn't the answer he expected, but he told Cindy it was an excellent observation. Then he asked her to tell him about the lessons the teachers give when they feel good. Again, she surprised him.

"I don't remember the names of her teachers, but she said Mrs. X gave really interesting lessons when she felt well, telling lots of stories and using pictures to explain things. When Miss Y is feeling good, all she wants to do is get them coloring or doing crafts so she can text her boyfriend. Her third teacher, Mr. Z, never feels well, but he tries hard to make his lessons fun. She hopes someday to make him smile."

"Poor Kaden," I say.

"That was my first response too," Hellie says, "but that was before I saw the twinkle in his eyes. I think he was pleased that she told him her observations rather than trying to figure out the *right* answers."

"She's a *tell-it-like-it-is* type of person. How did she do with Master Cushing?"

Hellie starts to giggle. "I never thought I'd feel sorry for a mage, but I felt sorry for Master Cushing. He asked her what her talents are, and she asked him what a talent is. He told her it was something she did very well, and she told him she made her bed, and tied her shoes, and brushed her hair, and cleaned her room, and painted pictures very well. Then he explained a talent was something she could do that other people couldn't, and she said no one could take her bath for her."

"Oh my!" I exclaim. "However, you have to admit her answers fit the parameters he set."

"I agree," Hellie says, "and I think he realized it too. He asked Jerrin to take over. Jerrin simply asked her about magic. She said Peter told her not to talk about it, but Jerrin reminded her that when Skyler said she had powers, she said they were magic, and Peter didn't try to stop her.

"Then Jerrin pointed at a loveseat, floated it over to us, and replaced it for the chairs we were sitting on. He told her being able to move the loveseat was one of his magical talents. Then he asked her about hers.

"After that, it was like someone had opened the flood gates. She talked about seeing things from the inside so she knows who to trust and who to avoid. She talked about looking at the photographs Peter has taken for her and seeing how individual colors blend and combine with others to create images. She talked about feeling and seeing things she can't describe, which is why Peter tries so hard to help her find words to use.

"The last thing she mentioned was knowing things that no one has taught her. She said she has to be very careful when she answers questions or when she volunteers information because she doesn't like being accused of lying, or cheating, or making up stories. Jerrin asked her who accused her of those things, and she said mostly her teachers and classmates at school. But, she said, they don't do it anymore. Now she thinks ahead, and if she can't explain how she knows something, she just keeps quiet.

"I can't remember everything. However, I know that Jerrin and Master Cushing both assured her that she never had to pretend she doesn't know something when she's around any of us.

"Master Cushing asked her if she noticed anything special about her talents as she described them. When she said *no*, he explained that being able to see things from the inside so she could understand people, and being able to see things from the outside so she could understand color, and being able to see things beyond her reality so she knows answers to questions and information she hasn't been taught are all related. He told her she has a special kind of vision that had nothing to do with her eyes. He said it was similar to Shiane's clairvoyance.

"Then Jerrin said they would explore many other aspects of her sight when he starts training her. I can't remember everything they said, but I know it made her feel better."

"I wish I could have heard it," I say. "I'll admit I feel a little jealous, but since I couldn't be with her, I'm glad you were."

"Me too," Hellie says. She shifts position so she can see me in the mirror. "What did Jerrin and Skyler want to talk with you about?"

"Nothing much," I say. "Mostly they wanted to make sure I was going to let Jerrin teach me."

Although the lie was good enough for Peter, it's not for Hellie.

We gaze at each other's reflections.

"All right," Hellie says. "If you ever want to talk to me about what really happened, let me know. I'll be here for you."

"I'll keep that in mind."

Hellie heads for her room.

I turn out the light.

I think I fall asleep before my head hits the pillow.

173

# Chapter Twenty-four

Hellie and I rush through our Saturday morning yard work. We told our parents that Neeve was having a barbeque at his family's cabin in the mountains this afternoon.

"It's nice to see the two of you sharing friends again," Mom tells us.

"Will they have alcohol there?" Dad asks.

"Maybe," Hellie answers. "Neeve's elder brothers are still visiting, and I didn't notice last week if they're drinkers or not."

"But," I insert, "you know that neither Peter nor Kaden drinks, and Hellie and I never have and never will."

"What time will you be home?" Dad asks.

"Do we have a curfew?" Hellie counters.

"No," Mom says. "We just want to know when we should start to worry. With all the switchbacks, driving down the canyon isn't a pleasant experience even during the day. It'll be worse after dark."

"Peter's parents are going to pick Cindy up at his place around 9:00," I say. "After that, if we're not all too tired, Peter has invited Hellie and Kaden to watch a DVD with us."

"We'll probably be home before midnight," Hellie says.

"Why don't you send us a text when you get back to town?" Mom suggests. "That way we won't worry about you on the canyon roads."

After agreeing to Mom's request, assuring her and Dad that we'd be careful, and saying goodbye at least half a dozen times, Hellie and I finally manage to get out of the house.

On the way over to Peter's duplex, we talk about what to do with the car. To make our cover story believable to our parents (although every word we told them was the truth), we either had to drive away or have someone pick us up. Telling them that Hellie was going to open a portal to another world didn't seem like a good option.

We know we can't put the car in Peter's garage. It's full of tools, camping equipment, three bicycles (his, mine, and Cindy's), boxes of Christmas decorations, books, old clothing, some furniture that he got at a garage sale that he intends to refurbish, other odds and ends he doesn't want to throw away, and his treadmill, which he uses 30 minutes every morning without fail (summer, fall, winter, and spring), all of which leaves just enough room for his motorcycle.

We finally decided to simply park the car in Peter's driveway. If the folks happen to drive by and see it (unlikely), we'll tell them we didn't have to drive our car after all, and we left for the mountains from there (true).

When we ring the doorbell, Cindy pulls the door open before the sound has a chance to die away. She must have been standing behind the door with her hand on the knob.

I give her a hug before I go over and give her big brother a kiss. He kisses me back. Seems like a long time since we did that.

"Peter says we're going back to fairyland," Cindy exclaims. "Do I have to close my eyes and count this time?"

"No," Hellie says. "This time you already know we're going there by magic. Are you ready?"

"Yes." Cindy is practically jumping up and down with impatience.

We step out of Peter's living room and into the hunting lodge. Skyler is there with Kaden and Karissa.

The other three royals are missing.

Skyler tells us, "Jerrin, Neeve, and Shiane will be here shortly. The queen's birthday is in a couple of weeks, and the king scheduled them to meet with the chancellor about the parts they'll play in the celebration."

While he talks, Cindy dashes over to the big picture window.

Automatically our eyes follow her.

She presses her hands and her nose against the glass.

When I go stand beside her, she leans against me.

"It's so pretty," Cindy says, "but it's funny to see winter here and summer at home. Hey, Peter, come look." She points up at the sky. "The clouds look like whipped cream, and those birds—" her voice drops low "—aren't birds."

Faster than I can comprehend, Skyler dashes across the room, snatches up Cindy, passes her to Peter, and then grabs Hellie and Kaden by the hands and pulls them over to the window.

Peter, Cindy, and I quickly move out of their way. Karissa leaves her chair and joins us, creating two clusters of people: the magicians at the window and the humans near the fireplace.

Then I realize, if Skyler is correct about Peter and Cindy's parentage and if Hellie's and my ancestor Bree-Ella Dark really came from Auravale, Karissa is the only true human in the room.

In my head I hear Skyler command: *Silence.*

Since no one is speaking, I assume he either wants us not to move a muscle or he wants us not to think.

I hold still and try to clear my mind.

I'm frightened.

My fear is intensified by the fact that Skyler is also frightened. I could hear it in his voice—his mental voice. I can't see it on his face, however, or in his stance. Outwardly he appears completely calm and in control.

Hellie, on the other hand, looks as if she's been cornered on the basketball court. The other team is ahead by one point, she has the ball but is double-teamed, unable to pass or to shoot, and the clock is counting down the last fifteen seconds of the game. Although she looks determined, her forehead is dotted with perspiration.

Kaden is in a similar condition.

"Now," Skyler whispers, barely moving his lips.

I feel a surge of power hit me as if I've been caught in the shock wave of an explosion.

A moment later, Jerrin, Neeve, and Shiane burst through nothingness and into the room.

"What was it?" Jerrin exclaims.

"Soldier scouts from Chankoun," Skyler answers. "We sent them to Father via General Astle."

"How did you spot them?" Neeve asks. "They're usually so well shielded."

"I didn't," Skyler says. "Cindy did."

We all turn to look at Cindy.

She stands with her shoulders hunched and her head down. "Did I do something wrong?" she asks Peter.

"I don't know," Peter says. "What did you do?" He holds out his hand. When she takes it, he leads her over to a couch. I follow them.

Peter and I sit down.

I expect Cindy to climb onto Peter's lap—she often does that when she needs reassurance—but she doesn't.

She stands in front of him, almost like a soldier at attention except her eyes are downcast.

"What did you do?" Peter repeats softly.

Cindy looks up, not exactly defiantly but close enough. It's like she's saying *I did what I did, and I'm ready to accept the consequences.*

"I took away their secrets," she tells Peter.

"What?" Skyler exclaims. He takes a step forward, but Shiane moves to intercept him. She shakes her head, and he stops.

"Why did you take away their secrets?" Peter asks.

Personally, I would've asked *how* before *why,* but when it comes to Cindy, Peter always knows best.

"They were having mean thoughts, Peter, and when they looked down here, they said some bad words about Skyler and his father."

"What did they say?" Skyler asks, stepping around Shiane despite her efforts to block him.

Cindy turns her head and looks at him.

"I don't say bad words, Skyler." She glances back at Peter. "Good girls don't say bad words, do they, Peter?"

"No, they don't," Peter assures her. "Was it the bad words that made you take away their secrets?"

She shakes her head. "I didn't like the bad words, but I took away their secrets because they do mean things."

"What kind of mean things?" Peter asks.

"They hurt people and make them afraid, and sometimes they break things or steal them just because they can. When they do bad things, they think it's funny. I took away their secrets so Skyler could make them stop hurting people."

"Have you always been able to take away people's secrets?" Peter asks Cindy.

"I don't know," she answers. "I never wanted to do it before."

"Have you always been able to tell when people have mean thoughts?" he asks.

She shakes her head. "Not always. Only mostly. I won't play with Marilee at school because her mean thoughts are so loud, they make my head hurt."

Peter nods and gives her a smile.

She takes a step forward and puts her arms around Peter's neck. "I love you, Peter. You always have good thoughts. They're like hugs." Then she includes me in the embrace. "I love you, too, Angel. You bring me good thoughts like bouquets of flowers."

She turns around and stands between Peter and me. Her calves are pressed against the loveseat. Her arms are draped across our shoulders.

"You have lots of questions, Skyler," Cindy says, "and so does everyone else. I don't think I know the answers."

"Maybe you know some of them," Skyler tells her. He crosses the room and sits on the floor in front of the fireplace, maybe eight feet away from us. "Do you mind if I ask anyway? If you don't know the answers, that's all right. This isn't school."

"Okay." She still doesn't sit down.

"When you went over to the window, I looked out at the sky too. I could see clouds and five black birds. I couldn't tell they weren't real birds until you took away their secrets. How did you know they weren't birds?"

"Have you ever listened to birds think?" Cindy asks him.

"No."

"You should," Cindy says. "Then you wouldn't get mixed up about birds

177

and people anymore."

At first, Skyler looks surprised, but then he turns thoughtful. "Thank you for the suggestion," he says.

"You're welcome. Do you have another question?"

"Yes," Skyler says, "I don't know how to listen to birds think. Can you teach me?"

Cindy grins at him and nods.

"First," she says, lifting the index finger on her left hand, "you really have to want to hear them. Second," she holds up two fingers, "you have to believe you can hear them. Third," she holds up three fingers this time, "you have to concentrate on hearing them." Her expression becomes somber. "You have to concentrate very, very hard. If you start thinking about something else, it won't work, and you have to start all over again."

While Cindy talks, Skyler's siblings, one by one, come over and sit on the floor beside him.

I glance at Peter, and he looks as if he's going to be sick. His face is pale, his body is shivering, and I think he's stopped breathing, which he does sometimes when he's startled. I reach behind Cindy and poke him in the ribs.

When his eyes meet mine, they have a haunted look. He gives himself a little shake and takes a deep breath.

"Cindy, may I ask a question too?" Jerrin requests.

"I guess so."

"Did you figure out how to do that? Or did someone teach you?"

Without warning, Cindy plops down on the couch and snuggles up against Peter. He puts his arm around her protectively.

She cups her hand around his ear and does her version of whispering. "Don't let Jerrin make me tell."

"No one is going to make you do anything you don't want to do," Peter says. He turns to Skyler. "I suggest we get on with whatever you have planned for the day. Otherwise, I want to take my sister home."

"Fair enough," Skyler says. "What we had planned to do, as a follow-up to yesterday, was to give the three of you some one-on-one training. Shiane, Neeve, and Hellie agreed to work with you while Jerrin, Kaden, and I wandered around, observing and making suggestions."

I glance over at Karissa. Since she's not a magic user, I wonder why she's here. She is making herself comfortable on a couch, holding a book in one hand and wearing a big wristwatch on the other.

When she catches me looking at her, she whispers, "I'm the official Earth-time tracker."

I flash her a thumbs-up.

Apparently, Skyler doesn't notice our interchange.

He continues talking. "In light of Cindy's experience with the crows, I

178

think we'd better modify our agenda. While you work in pairs, Jerrin and I will consider how best to use the rest of the day. For now, Shiane will work with Cindy, Neeve will work with Angel, and Hellie will work with Peter."

I open my mouth, but Skyler anticipates my question.

"Angel, I'm sure you think it would be more logical for you to work with your sister, but your twin bonding might get in the way, at least in the beginning—"

"What do you know about twin bonding?" I ask. "I thought twin births didn't happen in Auravale."

"They don't," Skyler says. "Neeve and Kaden have been researching twins on the Internet for me. Although some of the information seems to be controversial and contradictory, a large portion of the literature agrees that a number of twins demonstrate a psychic connection. Eventually we'll want to work on strengthening the link between you two, but right now you need to concentrate on learning the basics."

"Let's get you started," Jerrin says. He points at Peter, Cindy, and me. "You three are the trainees, and they," he points at Hellie, Neeve, and Shiane, "are your coaches. Trainees, go choose a mat from the table over there and then join your coach. Coaches, choose a spot with ample space for you and your trainee to work in."

"Kaden," Skyler says, "while Jerrin and I confer, you're in charge. Have them start with deep breathing and relaxation exercises. When you think they've got it, move on to guided imagery. We shouldn't be too long."

"All right, trainees," Kaden says, "spread out your mats and lie down on your backs. The first thing you have to learn is to relax and control your breathing. Nothing will mess up your magic faster than a troubled mind or a tense body."

I choose a yellow mat, and I lie down on it as instructed. I don't know how anyone is supposed to relax under these conditions. In my opinion, lying on the floor, knowing you're going to be monitored by someone who learned these techniques as a youngster (probably while still in diapers), is fairly anxiety provoking.

"Now," Kaden continues, "take in a deep breath from the diaphragm. If you do it right, your abdomen should expand and your chest shouldn't move at all."

I hear Shiane clarifying the instructions for Cindy.

"Now slowly exhale."

He has us repeat it several times.

Neeve is sitting cross-legged on the floor beside me. "As a singer," he says, "I suppose this is second nature to you."

"Sort of," I say.

After we practice breathing, Kaden has us do a progressive relaxation exercise. He has us start at our feet, tightening our muscles and then releasing the tension, gradually working our way up to our heads. He finishes by having us imagine our bodies becoming fluid and heavy until we feel as if we're flowing into the floor.

When I am so relaxed that I'm about ready to fall asleep, Kaden moves on to guided imagery. Talking in a soothing voice, he instructs us to envision a place of complete safety where nothing and no one can trouble us. He has us picture it in as much detail as we can, involving all five senses. He says that any time we are stressed we can go to this place and find inner peace. Then he tells us to let go of our thoughts and allow ourselves to dissolve in a zone of silence.

Just as I'm about to enter a transcendental state, I suddenly wonder what's taking Skyler and Jerrin so long.

They must have been gone for at least a couple of hours.

I guess *We shouldn't be too long* is a relative concept.

I try to release my thoughts and reenter the zone of silence, but I can't quite do it. I'm still trying when Kaden has us reconnect our minds and our bodies and gradually fill ourselves with energy.

Even though I wasn't totally successful with the exercise, I feel surprisingly refreshed and rejuvenated. I roll onto my side so I can tell my coach, but Neeve is gone.

"Whenever you feel ready," Kaden says, "go ahead and sit up. When you are completely recovered, you may stand. Then, please return your mats to the table."

The power duo still isn't back.

A wonderful aroma is filling the air, and I realize I'm hungry.

Before long, Karissa announces dinner is ready.

While Shiane ushers us into the dining room, I notice Neeve, wearing a red and white striped chef's apron, arranging glasses, plates, bowls, silverware, and napkins on a serving counter that's built into the wall.

Then he puts out the food: potato salad, tossed green salad, fruit salad, baked beans, a big basket of rolls, a pitcher of lemonade, and a couple of bottles of wine. He follows all that with a huge platter of barbequed chicken breasts and legs. The last thing he sets out is a lazy Susan holding a variety of condiments.

"Holy cow!" I exclaim. "Who did all the cooking?"

"Neeve," Karissa says. "He did most of the preliminary work last night. He likes to cook. He was disappointed to use caterers for the party at his apartment, but he expected too many people for him to prepare everything by himself."

Nodding, Shiane adds, "All of us have had to learn how to cook, but Neeve is the only one who really enjoys it. Cindy, why don't you go first?"

We line up behind her.

After we've all filled a plate, we sit at a long table and chat.

Skyler and Jerrin show up about the time the rest of us are finishing.

It seems to me that the eight of us have left them slim pickings, but I guess we weren't as gluttonous as I thought.

They manage to fill their plates with plenty. They also each pour themselves a glass of wine.

As soon as they sit down, Skyler nods at Peter, Cindy, and me. "The three of you need to be trained quickly, not just in using your identified talents, but also in magical self-defense and survival techniques. We need to figure out how we're going to fit daily meetings into your schedules."

"Daily?" I squawk. "Some of us have to work for a living."

"We know it won't be easy," Jerrin says, "but if we just meet on the weekends, you'll forget so much between sessions we'll waste half of our time reviewing."

Peter glances over at his sister. "I might be able to squeeze in a couple of hours in the evenings, but our parents will never let Cindy go out that often, even if we could come up with a good excuse."

"But Peter," Cindy says, "I have to learn too."

"I know, sweetie, but I don't see how we can manage it. If Mom and Dad were in town, we couldn't have gotten away yesterday and today."

As Peter talks, I have an awful thought. I wonder if it's occurred to anyone else. I'll have to wait until Peter and I have a little privacy before I can bring up the issue.

We sit at the table discussing our schedules long after Skyler and Jerrin have finished eating. I guess it's a little too boring for Cindy. She scoots sideways in her chair, leans her head against the backrest, and falls asleep.

I nudge Peter.

"She's not used to this much activity on a Saturday," Peter says as he pushes away from the table. "Where can I take her? She'll likely sleep for a couple of hours now."

"There are several bedrooms," Shiane says, "but will she be afraid if she wakes up in a strange place?"

"That's a good question," Peter says. "It hasn't happened before."

"Why don't you just put her on one of the sofas in the living room?" Skyler suggests. "We're not going to be doing anything noisy."

While Peter picks up Cindy, I slip out of the dining room to make things ready. There are a few Afghans and blankets stacked on a rack in the corner. I choose a bright animal-patterned quilt for Cindy. When she wakes up, it'll make her smile. I'm looking at the throw pillows scattered around, hoping to find a suitable one for sleeping, but then Shiane arrives with a regular bed pillow.

She hands it to me then heads back to the dining room.

I decide the sofa closest to the fireplace is probably the best place for a nap. The sun is sinking behind the trees and the room is already feeling cooler. Peter sets Cindy down and I spread the quilt over her.

As we cross the big room to rejoin the others, I speak to Peter in a quiet voice. "We might have a problem."

"What kind?" he asks.

"When you took Cindy home after Neeve's party, did your parents ask her how it went?"

"Of course," Peter says.

We take our places at the table again, and since other people are talking to each other, Peter continues our conversation softly.

"Our parents started asking Cindy questions as soon as we were through the door." Peter smiles warmly. "Apparently the thing that impressed Cindy the most was the aquarium. When she tried to describe it, she ran all over the living room, pointing at things. She said it was as tall as the fireplace, as long as the loveseat, and as thick as the coffee table. She's got a good eye for dimensions. I think she was spot-on."

"What about the movie? Did she tell them she watched *Beauty and the Beast* with the other kids?"

"Yes, and she said you put together a puzzle too. What's up, Babe?" he asks me. "What's bothering you?"

"We didn't consider what's going to happen tonight when your parents take her home."

"Which is?"

"Your folks are bound to ask her what the two of you did while they were gone. What's she going to say? She's too innocent to lie."

# Chapter Twenty-five

"Oh, damn," Peter mumbles. His face develops the haunted look that it had when Cindy counted off the three steps for listening to birds.

His gaze goes straight to Skyler. "You heard?"

"Yes, at least the last part."

"What are the options?"

"You recognize the complications your parentage might present?"

"Yes," Peter says. "I realized it as soon as Cindy started describing how to listen to birds think. I was taught those same three steps when I was little. The man who taught me stopped coming shortly after Cindy was born. I never told her about him, and she never mentioned him to me. I didn't know he had come back and was teaching her too."

"Do you know who he is?"

"By name? No. By description? Maybe. But first, what can we do about Cindy's memories of the past two days? She can't go home and tell our parents we stepped out of my living room and into fairyland twice. Can something be done without harming her?"

"Jerrin?" Skyler says.

"I can give her false memories, but we would need to do some careful planning about what you want me to implant. Since you'll have to corroborate everything she says, we'll need to keep things simple enough that you don't get tangled up."

"It won't hurt her?"

"Not at all," Jerrin says. "Once we decide on the specifics, it'll only take a few seconds to insert the new information."

"All right," Peter tells him. "Let's do it. For last night, you could have her remember Angel coming over to my place to watch a movie and eat pizza. We've done that often enough for it to ring true."

"Before you make that decision," Skyler says, "you need to understand that it is impossible for Jerrin to alter memories totally or permanently without destroying brain cells, which is something he would never do. What that means is, if Cindy's mysterious teacher is an Auravalian magic user, which he must be, he might recognize the false memories. If so, he could conceivably make Cindy remember the real ones. It's unlikely that'll happen unless he visits her within the next couple of days, but you need to know it's a possibility."

"Blast it," Peter growls. "When she asked me not to let Jerrin make her tell, she sounded frightened, as if that man had threatened her."

"As I said," Skyler replies, "unless he visits her soon, it's unlikely he'll notice the implants."

"I assume," Peter says, "she'll be safer if she doesn't go home and start prattling about visiting fairyland, listening to birds think, and seeing people pop in and out of reality, won't she?"

"Probably," Skyler says. "It depends on who the mystery man is and what kind of relationship he has with your mother."

Peter's face goes red. He's showing remarkable control holding in his temper. "We need to save that discussion for a later date. Right now, I want to come up with a reasonable story to account for the time our parents have been gone."

"Wait, Peter," I say, having just had another disturbing insight, "you can't make her forget completely, not if she's going to come back here and have training." I turn to Jerrin. "Isn't there a way to let her remember selectively? When she's here with all of us, or when she practices her skills in private, or when she's with Peter and me at home, she'll remember the truth, but when she's talking with her parents or anyone other than one of us, she'll only be able to repeat the cover story. Couldn't you do something like that?"

Jerrin exhales noisily. "I've never had to deal with that kind of complexity before, but I'm sure it can be done. I'll need to do some quick research."

Without even getting up from the table, Jerrin vanishes.

Hellie is the first one to say anything.

"It isn't just Peter who'll have to keep the stories straight," she says. "We all will. Angel and I told our parents we were going to a barbeque at Neeve's family's cabin in the mountains. It didn't occur to me until just now that Kaden told our parents that he and Neeve are from the same foreign country and their fathers work together. So, in light of that, why would Neeve's family have a cabin in our mountains?"

"Uh oh," I say. "I hope Mom and Dad didn't catch that."

Hellie nods. "It's just one example of how complicated things get when you start fiddling around with the truth."

"Has anyone," Shiane says, "considered just explaining the situation to Cindy, making sure she understands the possible consequences, and then trusting her?"

"It's a good thought," Kaden says, "but the surest way to get a child to mention something is to tell him not to."

Peter gets up and goes over to a window that's almost as big as the one in the living room. I follow him. He puts an arm around my waist and leans his head against mine. The sun has set, the moons haven't risen, and the nearly black sky is full of stars.

"It's beautiful here," Peter murmurs in my ear.

"I know," I say. "It's a shame we can't just lean back and enjoy the view."

"Yeah. What a flippin' mess."

Suddenly his cellphone rings, and we both jump a mile high.

He takes it out of his pocket and stares at it as if it were a snake about to bite him.

"Sorry," Neeve says. "I should have warned you. When the mages figured out how to make Auravalian cellphones work between worlds, we had them rig up the lodge, the palace, and a few other places, so that Earth-produced phones could receive and transmit as well."

Peter swears graphically in an undertone. I'm glad I'm the only one who can hear him.

"Hey, Mom," he says, answering the call on the fifth ring. While he listens, he mouths the word *time* and points to his wrist. I hold up a finger to let him know I'll check.

I go over to Karissa and ask her quietly, "What time is it back home?"

She glances at her watch. "Nearly 6:00."

I hold up six fingers. *Almost 6:00* I mouth silently.

Peter nods. *Thanks.*

After that, his end of the conversation goes like this:

"How was it?"

"I thought you were going to stop and see Aunt Marie on the way home."

"I'm sorry to hear that, but I'm glad you're not bringing back anything contagious."

"We're up in the mountains having a barbeque with some friends."

"It's some of the same people who were at the party last Sunday."

"I think she's had a good time. She certainly enjoyed dinner."

"A barbequed chicken drumstick, potato salad, baked beans, fruit salad, and a dinner roll."

"Of course, I kept her portions small, but she's not a baby anymore, Mom. I told her she could have seconds if she was still hungry when she finished what was on her plate. She decided on her own that she'd had enough."

"She's down for a nap."

"No, I didn't bring her up here on my motorcycle. Angel and Hellie provided the transportation."

"We plan on being home by 9:00."

"I'm sure it will be all right, Mom. We'll see you then. Bye."

When Peter has ended the call, he tells Hellie and me, "We don't have much time left. My parents want to pick Cindy up around 7:30. My mother said to apologize for asking you to bring us back so early, but they're tired and want to get Cindy on their way through town. We'll need to leave here by 7:00 to make sure we beat them home. I don't want to try and explain how we drove up the canyon in your car if it's parked in my driveway before we get back."

He walks over to the serving counter, looks at the lemonade and wine, and then shakes his head. "The next time we come here," he says to me, "please remind me to bring a couple of Dr. Peppers with me."

"Dr. Pepper?" Skyler asks Neeve.

"It's a carbonated soft drink," he answers.

"I don't remember seeing it at your party."

"It didn't occur to me to order any," Neeve tells him. "I don't like the flavor myself."

"Angel," Skyler says, "why don't you call a Dr. Pepper for Peter?"

"Me? I don't know how."

"Of course, you do," Skyler says. "The first time you were here you called a veritable feast. You did it unintentionally, it's true, but there is no reason you can't do it purposefully. Try."

"How?"

"Cindy recited the basic steps. First, want it. Second, believe you can have it. Third, concentrate until you get it. Now, try."

I feel absolutely stupid, but I close my eyes and try.

Nothing happens.

"Try again," Skyler tells me.

Still nothing.

"You have to believe," Skyler says with exasperation. "Remember, you've already done it once. You can do it again. Want it. Believe you can have it. Now concentrate."

Nothing.

"You do know how to concentrate, don't you?"

I glare at him and nod.

"Try it again, and concentrate harder this time."

"All right," I snap. I hate being put on the spot like this, especially by someone so patronizing. I close my eyes. I'd like to call up a dozen cans of pop so I could throw them all at Skyler. I picture doing it in my mind. Nice. Very nice.

All of a sudden there are several thudding sounds.

Peter is laughing when he says, "Hey, Babe, I think that's plenty."

I open my eyes. There's a six-pack of Dr. Pepper on the floor beside Peter's feet, another one on the table, two on the serving counter, and one on the chair Peter used when we ate.

"Five six-packs," Peter says. "Not too bad, Angel. I've got thirty cans and about an hour to drink them. If I can down one every two minutes, I should just make it."

He bends over, picks up the six-pack by his feet, sets it on the counter, pulls a can free, pops the tab on top, and takes a drink.

"Nice and cold, too." He comes over and hugs me. "You're a handy girl to have around. I think I'll keep you."

My heart does flip-flops.

"Would anyone else like a Dr. Pepper?" Peter offers.

"I'll take one," Hellie answers.

"Me, too," Shiane says.

"How about you, Skyler?" Peter asks as he passes the girls their drinks.

"I might as well try one," Skyler says.

He opens the can Peter hands him and takes a sip, licks his lips, and then takes a second sample.

"Neeve," he says, "I think I know why the taste doesn't appeal to you. It's similar to the potion Hayden gives us when we've overtaxed our energy. He had to double dose you that time Rylee bullied you into spending an entire day altering colors and styles of gowns while she tried to decide what her attendants should wear at her wedding."

"You're right," Neeve groans. "What a horrid experience that was!"

Before he can say more, Jerrin steps into the room. Conversation ceases. He glances around. "Did I miss something?"

"A little," Skyler says. "Probably the most important thing is that Peter got a phone call from his mother. His parents will be back in an hour or so, and at that time they expect to pick up Cindy at Peter's house."

"We'd better get right to work then," Jerrin says. "Modifying Cindy's memories so she can recall them selectively is possible, but it'll take a little longer than if I was just imposing new memories over existing ones. Peter, let's start with your suggestion for last night. If Angel came over to your house, what movie would you have watched and what kind of pizza would you have served?"

As soon as Peter answers, Jerrin has another question for him.

There isn't anything the rest of us can contribute.

Even if Cindy weren't asleep in the other room, I doubt we'd leave. I think everyone is as curious as I am about what Jerrin and Peter are doing.

We just sit and observe.

While Peter and Jerrin are going over Cindy's bedtime rituals again and again, trying to make sure Jerrin doesn't implant anything contradictory, Hellie and I start whispering back and forth about doing damage control if our parents ask why Neeve's family has a cabin in our mountains.

We're getting nowhere, but then Neeve makes a suggestion.

"If they ask," he says, "why not simply tell them my brothers rented a place for the summer?"

Perfect.

Problem solved.

Jerrin and Peter spend much more time preparing the false memories for last night than the ones for today. That's because much of what happened today is safe for Cindy to talk about.

She can describe the cabin just as it is. She can list who was here and what we had for dinner. She can talk about seeing blue skies, clouds that looked like whipped cream, and crows. She can even report having a discussion about mean people and wanting them to be punished so they can't hurt others anymore.

However, she'll remember riding in the car instead of stepping through a portal. She'll remember seeing black birds, but not hearing them think. Instead of doing breathing, relaxation, and guided imagery exercises, she'll remember putting together a puzzle that looks exactly like the winter scene outside the big picture window. She'll remember the adults talking about our jobs over dinner, rather than trying to juggle our schedules for future meetings, and she'll remember getting bored enough to doze off at the table.

She is still asleep when Jerrin sits on the edge of the couch and gently places one of his hands at the back of her neck and the other on her forehead.

# Chapter Twenty-six

"Will you come back after your parents pick up your sister?" Skyler asks Peter.

"As long as whoever takes us home is willing to stick around for a while," Peter answers. "Neither of my parents has a very good sense of time, and when my mother says *around 7:30*, she can mean anything from about 7:00 to 8:30."

*Hellie,* I say, trying out the family telepathy, *will you take us back to Peter's house?*

*Sure,* Hellie answers, *but we don't both have to go. You can stay here and visit with the royals. I'll wait for Peter and bring him back.*

*But,* I say, *we've got to figure out what to do with the car. We can't leave it in Peter's driveway, and we can't take it home.*

*Oh,* Hellie says, *I had forgotten about that. Maybe we could just leave it somewhere in the mall parking lot.*

*I hate to be pessimistic,* I say, *but if we do, tonight will be the one night in a blue moon that Mom and Dad decide to go to the movies, and they'll end up parking right next to us.*

Hellie laughs silently. *I'm afraid you're probably right. Things have been going so well with Mom and Dad since we graduated, we're due a little bad luck. However,* she says thoughtfully, *the stwethil-thage showed me how to access the nothingness between worlds. I wonder if I could open a portal and park the car in there.*

*If you do,* Jerrin says, inserting himself smoothly into our conversation, *you'll need to attach it to something in your real world. The nothingness of space has no up or down, no here nor there. If you want to be able to find your car again, you'll need to have a tangible tether.*

*How do I do that?* Hellie asks.

*I'll show you.*

At this point, I disengage from Hellie's mind. The conversation between her and Jerrin becomes incomprehensible.

After a few minutes, Hellie says to Peter, "Whenever you and Cindy are ready, I'll take you back."

"I'll go get her," Peter replies.

He returns with a still groggy Cindy in his arms.

She rallies long enough to tell us goodbye, and then she snuggles against Peter and dozes off again.

After they leave, the rest of us drift into the living room where the overstuffed furniture is more comfortable than the dining room chairs.

I think Peter's parents have a better grasp on time than Peter gives them credit for. According to Karissa's wristwatch, Hellie leaves with Peter and Cindy at 7:05.

It's barely thirty minutes later when Hellie and Peter return.

The expression on Peter's face alarms me.

I'm just about to ask him what's troubling him, but Neeve calls from the kitchen, "I'm setting out dessert. Come and get it."

Peter puts his arm around me as we follow the others back into the dining room.

"Did your folks ask Cindy about—?"

"Yes," Peter says, "and she followed the script, but then she said some things I don't understand. I need to talk to Jerrin."

Neeve has set out three large pies—apple, pecan, and chocolate—as well as a tub of vanilla ice cream, a bowl of whipped cream, and a plate of thinly sliced cheese.

There is also a coffee pot, a pitcher of milk, and more wine.

"Come help yourselves," Neeve says.

Shiane looks disappointed. "No chocolate cake?"

"I made you a chocolate cake last Sunday," Neeve tells her.

"But I already ate it," Shiane whines.

"In that case," Skyler says unsympathetically, "I don't suppose you'll want any dessert tonight."

"I didn't say that." Shiane promptly takes a large slice of chocolate pie, and although it is already topped with whipped cream, she adds several more spoonsful.

Peter waits until everyone has made a selection and is seated at the table before he voices his concerns to Jerrin.

"Besides implanting the memories we talked about, did you say anything else to Cindy?"

"I encouraged her to remember having had an enjoyable time. Why?"

Peter shakes his head. "Maybe I'm reading too much into this. I've had a rough week, and I'm tired. My judgment might be off."

"What happened?" Skyler asks.

"When Cindy told my parents about how good a cook Neeve is, she described him as having eyes like green diamonds. My mother was helping

Cindy gather up her clothing, and she seemed to freeze for a moment."

Peter directs his next comment to Neeve. "Is it well-known in Auravale that you are residing on Earth?"

"I shouldn't think so," Neeve says. "I'm not an important member of the court. I'm simply the fourth child of the king by his second wife."

His brothers start to protest, but Neeve shakes his head and laughs at them. "I'm not important, and you know it. Frankly, I don't want to be. I have my own plans for my life."

"You always have had," Skyler says.

"Still," Peter persists, "I'll bet you are well-known for those green eyes. Neeve isn't a common name in America, but it's not unknown. The most famous Neeve is a female actor, and she spells her name with a single *e* in the middle. However, a boy named Neeve who has bright green eyes, that's going to stand out on both of our worlds."

"What are you getting at?" Jerrin asks.

"I think my mother recognized the name and the description. After that, while she helped Cindy pack up her things, she subtly tried to prompt Cindy into naming Neeve's older brothers and younger sister, as if she wanted to confirm who all of you are.

"If you hadn't told me we probably have an Auravalian father, I wouldn't have paid any attention to it. It sounded casual, but it made me wonder if there are people who might benefit from knowing when members of the royal family are on Earth and not on Panelda."

"There could be," Skyler says. "Did Cindy name us?"

"No. She acted like she couldn't remember. She called you the *tall one*, Jerrin the *taller one*, and Shiane the *little girl*."

"Maybe she honestly couldn't remember our names," Skyler says. "She was barely awake when you took her home."

"I don't believe it," Peter says, "and neither do you. She's called all of you by name half a dozen times today, and that's not counting last night and the party at Neeve's apartment.

"Then my mother asked if the same boys who helped her put together the puzzle on Sunday were here to help her again today. When Cindy answered, she acted as if she couldn't remember their names either, and we know that was phony.

"The first thing she said to Karissa yesterday was *Where are Jeremy and Bennett*? But she referred to Karissa simply as *Neeve's girlfriend*, and she called Jeremy the *skinny brother* and Bennett the *brother with glasses*. It was as if she was trying to prove that her poor memory extended beyond your family."

"What do you think it means?" Jerrin asks.

"If you didn't tell her to respond that way, then I think she recognized that something is wrong at home. I only hope it's not the mysterious man who might or might not be our father."

"Do you think she's in any danger right now?" Skyler asks.

"How the hell should I know?" Peter snarls in frustration. "You've cast my mother in a completely new light, and I don't know what it means. I swear to heaven, though, she loves Cindy and would never hurt her or allow anyone else to hurt her if she could prevent it."

"Without knowing who your father is," Skyler says, "we can't guess how much influence he exerts over your mother. Perhaps Cindy sensed that your mother is being compelled by your father to tell him everything she learns about our world. Having two Auravalian children on Earth, he must realize that one of us would reach out to you eventually."

Peter's hands clench into fists. "Are you implying this man might be forcing my mother to do things against her will?"

"It's possible," Jerrin tells him.

Peter slams his fists down on the table, making dishes, flatware, and people jump.

"If he is," Peter growls, "I'll rip his heart out."

"Take it easy," Jerrin says. "We're talking in suppositions here. It is completely possible that your mother is in love with the man and is willingly cooperating with him."

"Not if it means—"

Skyler cuts him off.

"We're also making assumptions about why Cindy didn't reveal our names," Skyler says. "For all we know, she could have been playing a little game of her own. Her mind and how she uses it are unique. We need to be cautious when assigning meaning to her behaviors."

"That's well and good for you to say, but she's not your sister. What if it was Shiane in these questionable circumstances? Could you just ignore them? What if that man is there right now? What if Cindy wasn't keeping your names from our mother but from this mystery man?"

"Again," Skyler says, "not knowing who he is cripples us."

"Let me go see," Shiane offers.

She and I are sitting at the end of the table directly across from each other, and I can tell she's worried.

"No!" Skyler says loudly and unequivocally.

"Yes!" Shiane responds just as ferociously. "Peter has just described a series of events that don't make any sense. It's not as if we haven't had the opportunity to observe how honest and forthright Cindy is by nature. Now that she's done something so completely out of character, one of us needs to go check on her, and I'm the only one who can do it."

"Humph!" Skyler snorts sarcastically.

Skyler and Jerrin are at the other end of the table, and Skyler and Shiane are sitting diagonally across from each other.

I don't know if everyone else is rubbernecking back and forth to watch the conflict, but I sure am.

"Skyler," Shiane continues, "you and Jerrin are too powerful. If the mystery man is at the house, even if he is the lowest ranking magic-handler, he'd sense your approach long before you arrived. You would never catch a glimpse of him because he would take off as soon as he felt you coming. Neeve could go, but if the mysterious man turned out to be a mage, he would sense Neeve before Neeve could open a portal to get out of there. Hellie has the power but not the experience or the subtlety. It has to be me."

"Shiane," Skyler says tenderly with none of the previous rancor, "as always, you are brave and kind and caring, but if anything happened to you through my negligence, I wouldn't even have to wait for Father to pronounce my punishment. If I was responsible for your loss, I wouldn't be able to live with myself. I'd fly straight into eternal darkness."

Shiane gives him a sweet smile. "I love you too, Skyler, but we have an obligation to Peter and Cindy. If the man's not there, what's the harm? I can leave the tiniest recognition spell, and the next time he shows up, we'll know who he is."

"And if he is there?" Skyler asks.

"I can go in on a moonbeam or a speck of dust, and if he's there, I'll take a quick peek at him and come straight back here, I promise." Her expression darkens as she continues, "Unless he's harming Cindy in some way."

"Then what would you do?"

"I'd hurt him, Skyler," gentle little Shiane says in a voice that is truly menacing. "I don't care who he is or how powerful. He wouldn't know I was there until it was too late for him to get away. If he tried to harm Cindy, I'd hit him with a spell so strong he'd never recover."

I don't know about anyone else, but I believe her.

Skyler exhales an enormous breath. "Jerrin?"

"She has the power," Jerrin says.

Skyler glowers across the table at his brother. "That's not what I'm asking."

"I know," Jerrin says. "I'm sorry, but it was the first thought that flashed through my mind. About allowing her to go, I'll admit I'm torn. It would be a risk, but Shiane is right, it's her or no one. I also agree with her that we have an obligation to Peter and Cindy, especially since if there is danger in that home right now it's because we set it up."

"What do you mean by that?" Skyler asks.

"No matter who the male visitor is, if he shows up tonight or within the next few days and if he's ever been at court, he'd recognize our *denemac* all over Cindy. We have no way of knowing how he would react to that, but I doubt it would be good. We have an obligation to protect Cindy and Peter until we can teach them how to do it for themselves."

Everyone is focused on the two brothers.

"I can't condone this," Skyler says, standing up, "but I'm willing to present it to our father."

He vanishes.

I've been watching Shiane out of the corner of my eye, so I'm probably the only person who notices that she disappears at exactly the same time.

I don't make a sound.

She is a courageous girl.

Jerrin and the others will notice she's gone soon enough.

I'm not going to betray her.

"What will your father say?" Peter asks Jerrin.

"It's hard to predict," Jerrin answers. "Our father is very old by earthly standards." He barks out a hollow laugh. "He's fairly old by Auravalian standards too. He's seen over two centuries' worth of history being created, written, and rewritten. It gives him a unique perspective.

"Sometimes he seems capricious, but he's not. He simply knows more than the rest of us, and he doesn't generally bother to explain his reasoning when he makes decisions. Shiane is his youngest daughter, and he dotes on her. It's hard to know if he will insist on keeping her safe or if he will decide to let her have her way."

"I'm confused," Karissa says. "Since there are only two reliable ways of getting from Panelda to Earth—first, a member of the Auravalian royal family can open a doorway between worlds or, second, the king can loan out a magical key and teach the borrower the activation spell—how is this mystery man traveling back and forth?"

"That question has been foremost on our minds," Jerrin says.

"Is it possible," I ask, "that he fell through over twenty years ago and has been living on Earth fulltime since then?"

"No," Neeve says. "I've regained my ability to sense our people, and my father has officially appointed me as his Earth liaison. Last summer, when Kaden and I were searching for the unknown magical signature, we systematically checked out—"

Suddenly there is a change in the air pressure, like abruptly dropping from 30,000 to 5,000 feet in an airplane.

My ears pop.

Everyone jumps up, shoving chairs back with so much force that they make loud screeches as they scrape across the hard tile floor.

Peter and I are a little slower than the rest, but we leap to our feet as well.

It doesn't take a genius to realize some sort of calamity has occurred.

When I turn around to face the front of the lodge, I expect to discover that half of it has been destroyed by some kind of magical super-bomb.

Instead, in the doorway, I see a tall, broad man, who has gray-streaked brown hair and a pointed beard. He is standing with his feet apart, his fists on his hips, and a scowl on his face.

As he stands there glaring around the room, he seems to be producing heat waves.

He is undoubtedly this clan's alpha male, aka King Justus IV.

And he is angry.

# Chapter Twenty-seven

"I knew the little minx wouldn't wait," the king says.

Standing at his right hand is Skyler.

That's when everyone else seems to realize that Shiane is gone.

"I'll go get her," Jerrin says. His face is red, but I can't tell if the color is caused by embarrassment or by fury.

"No need," the king responds.

He makes a simple gesture with his hand and points to the floor in front of him. Shiane appears. She is leaning forward at the waist as if she was in the process of peering through a keyhole when she was plucked out of wherever and brought back here.

When she stands up and spots her father, she goes deathly pale.

"Father," she gasps. Then, dropping to her knees with her eyes downcast, she says in a quivery voice, "Your Majesty, before you banish me or impose whatever punishment you devise, please at least let me tell you what I found out."

The king says nothing.

After a few seconds of total silence, Shiane's shoulders slump and her head droops farther down. I can see her tears splash on the floor. She looks totally defeated, and it breaks my heart.

I want to give her father a good hard slap.

Then I want to go take Shiane in my arms and tell her everything will be all right. But I'm not sure it will be.

The alpha male rules his pack with absolute authority.

Still, a king should be wiser than a wolf.

Shouldn't he?

A king values the qualities of caring and empathy and kindness.

A king recognizes the bravery it takes for a person to follow his or her conscience.

A king appreciates the necessity of the strong protecting the weak and the innocent.

A king uses intelligence to evaluate all available information before he reaches a decision that could make or break a life.

A king exhibits understanding and forgiveness when confronted with the impulsivity of youth.

A king is—

"All right, Angel," Justus IV rumbles, startling me senseless, "I'll listen to what she has to say. Stand up, Shiane."

While Shiane wipes her eyes and gets to her feet, the king turns to Jerrin. "Does Angel know she does that?"

"I doubt it," Jerrin answers, "even though she does it constantly. Usually she's more subtle about it, though."

"Angel," the king says to me, "are you aware that you've been projecting your thoughts directly into my head?"

He frightens me so much I can hardly breathe.

"M-m-my thoughts?" I stammer.

"Yes," the king says. "Beginning with 'The alpha male rules his pack with absolute authority,' I have had a continuous litany of an ideal king's characteristics flowing from your mind straight into mine."

"I'm-m-m sorry, Your M-m-majesty." I am so intimidated I can't seem to get this sudden stammer under control. "I d-d-didn't know. I'll t-t-try to m-m-make it stop, but I d-d-don't know how I'm d-d-doing it, so I'm-m-m not sure I can f-f-figure out how t-t-to quit."

"She's agreed to study with you, correct?" the king asks Jerrin.

"Yes."

"Teach her to control her thoughts as quickly as you can. It'll be hard for telepaths to be in the same room with her unless you do. I can tell you've dampened her, but she's so worked up right now that it's not enough."

Jerrin nods. "I'll take care of it."

For just a moment I feel as if my head isn't balanced properly on my neck. Then the feeling is gone.

"Also," the king says, "see if you can break her of the habit of stuttering when she's frightened." Then he turns his attention on his daughter. "All right, Shiane, start talking."

Shiane tries twice to speak, but nothing comes out.

I'm not exactly sure how the family telepathy works, but I was able to speak to Hellie earlier and the king said I projected my thoughts into his head, so I figure I can communicate with Shiane if I try.

*Courage, Shiane,* I think at her. *Be brave. You can do it.*

Her eyes dart in my direction.

I give her a nod and a quick, encouraging smile.

She takes a deep breath and tries again.

"First of all," Shiane says in a squeaky timid voice, "the mystery man wasn't there, so I was able to speak directly with Cindy. She felt guilty for not telling Skyler and Jerrin what they wanted to know. She said I'm not as scary as they are so she'd answer their questions for me. She said there are two different otherworldly men involved.

"The man who taught her about thinking, believing, and concentrating has been visiting her off and on for all of her life. He is kind to her, and she likes him. However, he hasn't come to see her for a while. Her concept of time is sketchy so I don't know if she meant it's been weeks or months.

"The second man started coming shortly after the first man stopped. He comes more frequently than the first man did, sometimes two or three days in a row. Every time he shows up, he makes her mother cry. Cindy was going to try thinking, believing, and concentrating to make him disappear, but a voice inside her told her that was a bad thing, so she never tried it."

"A voice?" Peter and Jerrin exclaim at the same time.

"I'm just telling you what she said."

Shiane glances at her father, so I do too.

He seems impatient.

She begins talking faster.

"The reason she pretended not to know our names was because the second man came recently, and sometimes he leaves something behind so other people can listen. Usually, she finds it fairly quickly and wishes it away, but with all the new experiences she's had lately, she keeps forgetting. She wasn't sure it was safe to talk so she didn't."

The king looks as if he's about to comment. Shiane keeps going.

"Today, when Cindy said she took away the crows' secrets because they did mean things, she was only telling half the story. It's true she could hear them thinking hateful thoughts and she didn't like their bad words, but the main reason she wanted Skyler to lock them up was that she recognized one of the birds as the man who comes to the house and makes her mother cry."

Shiane sighs as if she's grateful to have that ordeal over.

"A soldier from Chankoun has opened a doorway to Earth?" Skyler exclaims incredulously.

"Repeatedly," Shiane says. "Cindy thought he had been there at least a couple dozen times."

Skyler turns to the king. "How is that possible?"

"It shouldn't be," Justus IV replies. "We need to go get General Astle and make a trip to the dungeons." He turns to his daughter. "Well done, Shiane. You've brought us information that could prove valuable in the defense of two worlds."

She gazes up at him hopefully.

He gives her a stern look in return. "But it doesn't get you off the hook for disobeying Skyler." He waves his hand, and she's gone.

"What did you do to her?" I cry out before I can stop myself.

The king locks eyes with me, and I take a step backward.

He really is the alpha male, and I'm just a visitor to his pack. He could easily rip out my throat, figuratively and physically.

His expression softens. "I really am not a tyrant, Angel. I sent Shiane to her mother, who will find ways of keeping her out of mischief for at least the next two weeks."

"How?" A vision of Shiane chained to the wall of a tower flashes though my mind. "Doing what?"

For some reason, the king is in an indulgent mood now.

He answers my impudent questions instead of shipping me off to an oubliette somewhere.

"Performing odious tasks like assisting the cooks in the kitchen, putting things away in the pantries, doing embroidery, mending her own clothing, shining her own shoes, cleaning up her rooms, which are always a mess, and taking dancing lessons." The king gets a diabolical smile on his face. "Shiane hates dancing lessons. I'll have to suggest that Alaina Mae schedule them at least a couple of hours every day."

The king returns his attention to his sons.

"Jerrin, since Shiane won't be available for a couple of weeks, that'll free up some of your time. I hope you can begin working with Angel and Peter right away—and Cindy, too, if you can figure out how to arrange it."

"I've been thinking about having Hellie put us in an external time bubble," Jerrin says.

"I'll leave it up to you. For now, though, I suggest you send them all home. I've never heard so many suppressed yawns at one time before. They need to get some sleep."

The king clasps Skyler on the shoulder.

"All except for you. We need to check out this Chankoun-Earth traveler. Let's go."

The two men vanish.

This has been one heck of a day, which unfortunately followed on the heels of another one heck of a day yesterday.

I feel as if I've gone a week without sleep. Hellie said time flows differently on Panelda and on Earth, so maybe I have.

"With your leave," Neeve says to Jerrin, "I'll take Karissa home."

"Go," Jerrin says. They disappear.

"Before you ship off the rest of us," Hellie says, "you need to tell me how to retrieve our car."

"Let me send the others back," Jerrin says, "then I'll go with you and show you."

The next moment, Kaden is gone.

Peter and I gaze at each other.

This is where we would ordinarily share a kiss good night.

However, because of the Auravalian prejudice against unmarried lip kissing, Peter and I agreed not to kiss on the mouth in the presence of anyone from this world.

It was a nice, noble gesture at the time, but right now I resent the idea of saying goodbye without a proper show of affection.

I presume Peter is feeling the same way.

But then he grins at me, takes my hand, turns it over, and kisses my palm.

Tingles shoot all through my body.

"Good night, Gorgeous," he says.

Then he's gone, too.

I expect to materialize in my bedroom, but Jerrin, Hellie, and I end up in front of Peter's duplex, standing at the end of his driveway.

Facing the garage, Jerrin draws a line in the air about two feet from the ground and approximately as long as our car is wide. Our little blue Mazda appears out of a gray mist.

"If you ever do this," Jerrin says, "remember to cast a concealment spell so there are no witnesses. I did it this time, but if I'm not here, it'll be up to you."

Then he's gone.

I climb into the car on the passenger's side.

We get home around 11:30 p.m. Earth-time.

After I go through my nighttime rituals, I sit on my bed and stare at my hand as if I've never seen it before. I can still feel Peter's lips pressed against my skin.

Hellie comes into my room and sits down beside me.

"He kissed your palm while I wasn't looking, didn't he?" she asks.

"Yes," I answer. "It's terribly sensuous. I can still feel it."

"As I've said before, welcome to my world."

# Chapter Twenty-eight

I sleep so soundly that I barely tumble out of bed by 10:00.

On Sundays our family usually only has two meals: brunch around this time of the morning, since church services start at 11:00, and *linner* (which is what our family calls a meal that's a combination of lunch and dinner) around 4:00. If we get hungry after that, we're on our own.

Yawning and rubbing my eyes, I stumble down the stairs expecting to find my parents working together to prepare pancakes, scrambled eggs, and bacon—or something similar.

There's no one in the kitchen.

There's nothing cooking on the stove.

Instead, on the bar between the kitchen and dining room, there are three boxes of cereal, a bunch of bananas, and a pint container of strawberries.

There's also a note.

I'm just picking it up when Hellie staggers into the room.

I motion her over, and we read the note together.

*Dear girls,*

*We just got a call from the couple who were the maid of honor and best man at our wedding. They were on a flight from California to New York last night when their plane developed some kind of mechanical difficulties. They were laid over in Denver and have decided to delay the rest of their trip long enough for us to get together. We're going to drive up and spend the day with them. We might stay overnight. We'll let you know our plans as soon as they're finalized.*

*Have a good day. Take care of each other. We love you.*

*Mom and Dad*
*Sunday, 6:15 a.m.*

Hellie and I sit down at the bar and stare at each other.

"Church?" I ask.

201

"Not enough time to get ready," Hellie says. "Do you feel like having cold cereal for breakfast?"

"Not really," I answer, "but I don't feel like cooking either."

"Why don't we pack a lunch and go wandering through the woods again?" Hellie suggests. "I wanted to show you the green area around the pond on Friday, but Jerrin interrupted us and we ended up going to Auravale instead."

"All right," I say. "If I have to eat a cold breakfast, I'd rather have a sandwich and some chips anyway. But I have a dinner date with Peter at 6:00."

"I'm sure we'll be back before then."

We hastily put the cereal back in the pantry and the strawberries in the refrigerator.

"First one dressed gets to decide what we have for lunch!" Hellie yells as she dashes for the stairs.

I'm only a couple of feet behind her.

Hellie wins, but only because I take time to make my bed before I head back downstairs. I hate getting into an unmade bed at night.

When I reach the kitchen, I stop in the doorway and look at everything Hellie has spread out on the counter: peanut butter and jelly, tuna fish, sliced ham, sliced cheese, lettuce, tomatoes, onions, celery, carrots, and pickles.

"I couldn't decide," Hellie says, "so I opted to make a little bit of everything. We can share the sandwiches, half each. What do you think?"

"I think you're a genius. I'll go get the chips." As I head for the pantry, I call over my shoulder, "Do you want crème filled cupcakes or cookies?"

"Why not both?" Hellie says. "Anything we don't eat we can bring back home."

Working side by side, it doesn't take us long to pull lunch together.

While Hellie arranges it carefully in her backpack so nothing will get crushed, I crumble up a chocolate cupcake for the stwethil-thage just in case they've returned. If they haven't, the field mice will enjoy it.

Once we're through the hedge, I stop and look around to see if the forest is as devastated and depressing as I remember.

It is.

I glance over at Hellie. Once again, she is fighting off tears.

"Let's take our offering over to the grotto," I say, "and then head straight for the pond. I need to see some green."

Hellie sniffles. "Right. Let's focus on what's left, not what's been destroyed."

When we reach the grotto, it's evident that the wild life took care of our last offering. The plastic platter has been dragged out of the little cave and is covered with scratch marks. We wash it with bottled water and dry it with a napkin before we pile the cupcake crumbs on it and set it back in the cave.

With that ritual completed, we start walking down the dried-up creek bed. Suddenly, I have an idea.

"Hellie," I say, almost slurring my words with excitement, "why don't we go to the wilds of Auravale and entice some new stwethil-thage to come to our forest. You said predators hunt them there. We can offer them safety here. They could settle in the area around the pond."

Hellie's mouth drops open, and she stops short.

"What a brilliant idea!" she exclaims. She does a little dance right then and there. "It doesn't solve the king's problem of getting Bree-Ella's artifacts back, but really that's a separate issue."

"When can we go?" I ask. "You don't need to make any kind of preparation, do you?"

Hellie stops her impromptu dance.

"Actually, I do. I'll need to find a clan of stwethil-thage in the wilds, make contact with the chief to see if he'll talk with us instead of hiding, and then get the location firmly in mind before I create an entrance into Auravale. It sounds complicated but actually it shouldn't take too long."

"Can you do it now?" I pull my cellphone from my pocket. "It's just a little past noon."

"I can at least do the preliminaries." Hellie sits on the charred stump of a tree and closes her eyes. Having nothing better to do, I use my phone's stopwatch to time her.

Three minutes and sixteen seconds later, she says, "I've found a clan that was just raided by a couple of *boftkaz* two days ago. *Boftkaz* are sort of like hyenas. They're hunters and scavengers. The stwethil-thage chief has been looking for a new home." She positively glows. "I offered him one, and he's going to talk it over with the other leaders in the clan. Let's go take a look at the pond."

I guess Hellie is too excited to walk.

She opens a portal, and we step through.

The area isn't as beautiful as it was when I brought Peter here to take photos for Cindy, but compared to the rest of the forest, it is positively lush. In the distance I can see the skeletal branches of dying trees, but the sight isn't as overwhelming as it was when we were right in the middle of it.

Whether or not the stwethil-thage like it here, I suppose, will depend partly on how unsafe they feel in their own world.

I try to view the area with a critical eye, not that I know how the stwethil-thage evaluate an environment or how they'll decide if this is a suitable place for them to live.

From my perspective, however, I am suddenly aware of the amount of rubbish that's scattered around. Hellie seems to notice it at exactly the same time.

Even though the entire forest is fenced off with three rows of barbed wire (except for the residential area, and it's bordered by our gigantic hedge), teenagers and college kids sneak into the woods to party where they can have some privacy. Usually, they don't get this near to the neighborhood, preferring to stay on the other side of the forest and closer to the highway since they don't want anyone to call the police if they get drunk, disorderly, and deafeningly loud.

Since the interlopers habitually leave a mess, Hellie always comes prepared. She carries disposable latex gloves and trash bags in her purse, her lunch tote, and her backpack.

She hands me a pair of gloves.

Some plastic grocery sacks are floating in the pond, and we fish them out with a couple of sticks.

"We might as well use these and save the trash bags if we can," Hellie says. She nods at the pond. "Meet you on the other side."

"Okay."

I go left and Hellie goes right.

Within minutes, I find four empty beer cans and two of those 32-ounce soft drink cups that you can get at the all-night convenience store. I stack the cups inside each other and shove them, the lids, the straws, and half a dozen wadded up napkins into the bag. I stomp on the cans to flatten them and then shove them into the cups. A few feet away, I find two empty cigarette packs and a mound of cigarette butts.

This mess was probably created by some of the neighborhood boys, those around junior high school age. They're always finding ways to breach the hedge so they come back here to smoke (obviously), to drink beer (and soda, it appears), and to goof off. I suppose they read comic books and look at girly magazines too, but I can't prove it.

If Dad smells cigarette smoke blowing from this direction, he bolts through the opening in the hedge and chases the kids out of here with threats of telling their parents what they're doing. Usually that'll scare them away for a day or two. But really, does anyone seriously believe the parents don't know? The same wind that blows smoke into our backyard blows it into theirs.

I pick up a few bits of unidentifiable paper. Then I spy a mildewed cardboard box stuffed under a bush. When I open it, I find a dozen comic books, two graphic novels, and three *Playboy* magazines—all of them crinkly and faded from the weather.

This garbage won't fit inside a plastic grocery sack.

"Hey, Hellie," I call, "I need a garbage bag."

"I'll find one for you," Hellie calls back, "but come over here first." She is about half way around the pond at the point that is closest to the hedge. She looks as if she's kneeling in the grass.

"Coming." I start walking in her direction, but she is impatient.

She motions with her hand for me to speed up.

Obligingly, I break into a jog.

I find her crouched beside a jumble of white bricks that were probably chucked over the hedge years ago when the neighborhood was just being built. There are a couple of houses nearby that are constructed of white bricks and a couple more that use it as contrast with a darker color.

"What do you think?" she says.

"I think it'll be a lot of work to haul them out of here," I say. "And if we do, where are we going to put them? Dad will have a fit if we stack them in the yard or in the shed."

"No," Hellie says. "You're missing the point. I don't want to haul them away. I want to use them."

"For what?"

"To make a place to put the offerings for our new stwethil-thage. Look around. There aren't any rock formations like there are where the grotto is. I don't want to just set the treats on the ground. That would be too much like feeding a pet. The stwethil-thage are sentient beings. They're people. They need to be treated as such."

"Hmm," I say as I crouch down beside her, "what do you have in mind?"

"I think we should find a nice sheltered spot and lay down a foundation of bricks that'll keep our offering up out of the dirt. Then we could make walls by standing the bricks on end. We could use the shelves from that old broken bookcase in the garage for a roof. What do you think?"

"I like the idea," I say, "but I don't think it would be very sturdy. The neighborhood boys would probably just kick it apart. Speaking of which, I really need a garbage bag. I found a box full of someone's intellectual reading material: comics, graphic novels, and *Playboys*."

Hellie laughs and starts digging through the pocket on the front of her backpack.

"If we can't build something out of the bricks," she says, "where can we place our offerings? I really hate the idea of setting them on the bare ground." She produces a big lawn-n-leaf bag "I knew I had to have one."

"Thanks," I say. Then I sit on the grass, pull my knees up, and wrap my arms around them. "If we did enough research, I suppose we could learn how to make a structurally sound little building with bricks, one that the kids couldn't just knock over. But surely there are other things we could do that would be just as functional and less work."

"Like what?" Hellie asks.

"I can think of two possibilities," I say, "but neither of them would be convenient for both us and the stwethil-thage."

"Like what?" Hellie repeats.

"My first thought was that we could get out our old dollhouse and nail or wire it to a high branch in a tree. The stwethil-thage can fly, so it would be no problem for them. But you or I would have to climb the tree every single time we came out here with an offering, and that wouldn't be so great for us.

"Another option would be to continue using the grotto. That would be the easiest solution for us, but the stwethil-thage would never know when an offering was there. If we had to come here to tell them, then why use the grotto in the first place?"

Hellie sighs and clambers to her feet. "I guess we'll just have to think about it some more."

"There has to be a solution," I say as I get up too.

"Do you believe every problem has a solution?" Hellie asks me.

"I don't know," I answer. "I read once that if you can't find a solution to a problem it's because you've asked the wrong questions."

I head back toward the mess I left behind.

"What other questions are there?" Hellie asks, picking up her grocery sacks of garbage and then trotting along behind me.

"I don't know." I pause and think. "Instead of wondering what kind of structure we could make to hold our offerings, maybe we ought to wait until the stwethil-thage get here and ask them what they want."

Hellie grins at me. "*Simplest is always best*," she says, quoting Grandma Powers.

When we reach the adolescent outdoor library, Hellie holds the plastic bag open while I chuck in the moldy magazines and the cardboard box. Then we stuff in the rest of the trash we've gathered. Before we remove our latex gloves, we take a few more minutes to canvas the area. We find and clean up another pile of beer cans, soft drink cups, fast food wrappers, and cigarette butts.

"I think we've gotten the worst of it," I say.

"I suppose we could do some cosmetic cleaning, like digging up the weeds," Hellie says, "but who knows, maybe the stwethil-thage prefer the natural look. I say let's call it good."

She pulls off her latex gloves and drops them on top of the trash in the large garbage bag. I do the same.

"I'll get rid of this," Hellie says while she ties the top closed.

She vanishes.

I don't know if I'll ever get used to seeing that.

Just standing around and waiting for Hellie to return doesn't appeal to me, so I mosey back toward the pond, trying to view the scenery the way a visiting stwethil-thage might see it.

A breeze rustles the leaves on the trees, creating a sparkling dance of light across the water as the branches shift.

A couple of butterflies flit past on my right side. A dragonfly zips by on my left.

A happy trilling erupts from somewhere in the shadows.

The scent of blooming flowers and moist dirt drifts on the air and tickles my nose.

Everywhere I look I see brilliant colors and fanciful shapes—from the bright white clouds and azure sky overhead to the green grass and yellow buttercups at my feet.

*It really is lovely here*, I tell myself.

A place like this deserves to be filled with magical creatures.

I don't know why I had to wait until the forest was so badly damaged before I could appreciate its beauty.

# Chapter Twenty-nine

When Hellie returns, we sit in the shade and eat our lunch.

We brainstorm about things we could do to make our new stwethil-thage happy here.

We've finished eating and are sipping on our Diet Cokes when I decide to change the subject.

"Is there a secret to working with Jerrin?" I ask. "He scares me. I'll probably turn into a blathering idiot the first time he tries to give me a lesson."

Hellie gathers up our trash and stuffs it into her backpack while she answers. "There is only one thing you need to remember when you work with Jerrin. Do whatever he tells you to do. Do it immediately and as precisely as you can. Jerrin will never ask anything of you without a good reason. And he isn't trying to catch you doing something wrong. He's trying to catch you doing it right. His number one goal will always be your success."

"Hellie," a voice says from behind us, "that's quite a compliment."

I twirl around on my butt, jump to my feet, and come face-to-face with Jerrin.

"Do you do things like that on purpose?" I shriek. "You almost gave me a heart attack."

"Sorry," he says with nonchalance and total unbelievability. "I was looking for you, and there are no doorbells out here."

I guess my body is full of adrenalin, because I feel like I'm about to explode. I express it through sarcasm.

"You're a mage," I say. "Are you telling me your magic isn't strong enough for you to create the sound of a bell?"

"The sound of a bell?" Jerrin repeats.

"Yes," I say. "Bells ring when a clapper that's on the inside strikes the metal casing that's on the outside, causing the metal to vibrate. This creates sound waves that travel through the air until they reach our ears and make our eardrums vibrate, which is what enables us to hear the sound. I should think a mage could flick his fingers and create a wave that would make our eardrums vibrate like the sound waves of a bell. That would be more polite than just appearing out of nowhere."

"I'll consider it," Jerrin says before turning away from me and focusing on Hellie. "Skyler and I need to meet with Angel and Peter and Cindy, right now if possible. I want you to put us in a bubble outside of time."

"But—" Hellie starts to say something, but I talk right over her.

"I thought you were the super mage," I say, still riled up. "Why don't you just do it yourself?"

Jerrin doesn't react to my rudeness. He simply answers me.

"Mages are like everyone else. Some have skills that others don't. Manipulating time is one of Hellie's talents. Manipulating memories is one of mine."

"You make it sound as if mages can't teach each other how to do things," I say.

"When I was in training," Jerrin says, still refusing to argue with me, "the pedagogues at the Magicians Guild believed that everyone was born with all the magical talent they would ever have. Training focused exclusively on natural abilities.

"Things are changing now, in large part because of the way Hellie and Kaden work together. He helps her with control. She helps him with power. They have both gotten stronger and have increased their range of skills since they began assisting each other. In the past, that was thought to be impossible. The Magicians Guild is conducting a series of research projects right now to see if other bonded couples can do the same thing. Regretfully, requests to conduct research to see if unaffiliated subjects can learn to enhance each other's magical skills have been denied."

"Why?" I ask with curiosity.

"Some people fear that the closeness required for sharing talents and powers might interfere with our inborn ability to recognize a soul bond. In our world there is nothing more important or more sacred than a couple sharing a soul bond."

"Yet you have arranged marriages," I say.

"It's complicated."

I start to make another comment, but Jerrin cuts me off.

"I would be happy to discuss this with you in depth another time, Angel," he says, "but not today. We need to figure out how we're going to manage your training, as well as Peter and Cindy's. You and Peter both have jobs that fill the bulk of your waking hours during the week, but meeting only on the weekends just won't give us enough time."

"Sunday is Peter's one day off," I tell Jerrin. "He opens his shop at 7:30 in the morning on weekdays, and he doesn't close until 6:00 in the evening.

# Sunshine and Shadows: Another Modern Fairytale

On Saturdays he's open from noon until 5:00. He closed his shop this Friday and Saturday so he could take care of Cindy, which means he'll probably have to work extra-long hours this coming week. I don't see how he can fit anything else in."

"That's why I'd like Hellie to put us in an external time bubble. We would leave and return at exactly the same moment."

Immediately I see the flaw in the plan. "Except," I say, "we will have lived an extra hour or two or three—however long we're gone—won't we? We'll still feel the effects of those extra hours."

"You are quick," Jerrin says. "We'll have to pace ourselves. There are a few things we can do to mitigate the effects of the additional time, but the most important will be staying self-aware and admitting when we're tired, hungry, or burned out."

"We?" I ask.

"Skyler and I are not immune to the needs and the limitations of the body," Jerrin says, "and we'll be adding those hours to our lives too."

"Jerrin," Hellie says impatiently, "you're forgetting one thing."

She pauses.

He gives her a questioningly look, but doesn't say anything.

She waits another minute before continuing.

"I haven't mastered the technique of stabilizing bubbles outside of time yet," she says, clearly exasperated. "That last one I tried collapsed in less than an hour. If you hadn't been watching so carefully, who knows when we might have ended up?"

"True enough," Jerrin says. "That's why Skyler has arranged to have Kaden and Shiane help you. It'll be a good training experience for the three of you, and I'll be there to back you up if necessary."

"But you'll be working with Angel, Peter, and Cindy," Hellie says.

"If you need me," Jerrin says, "I'll be there. Skyler is completely capable of handling the others without my assistance. He and I are setting this up together because, even though I am officially the teacher, there will be times when Skyler needs to take charge. Since he's not a mage and neither are Angel, Peter, or Cindy, there will be things he can deal with better than I can. He has skills and experiences to draw on that I don't have."

"But," I say, jumping into the conversation, "Skyler said that as a mage mentor you've been trained to teach and you're better at it than he is."

Jerrin laughs heartily. "I probably shouldn't tell you this, but I will anyway. Skyler is thirty-seven years older than I am, and he's spent his entire life training to be a king. He's the eldest son and I'm the second, but we have several sisters in between us. There is absolutely nothing I can do better than Skyler can. When he defers to me, he has a reason. However, like our father, he doesn't always explain what it is."

I can't help but stare at Jerrin.

Thirty-seven years between him and Skyler?

They don't look more than five or six years apart, and Skyler doesn't look older than his mid-thirties. He must be significantly older than that, though, because Jerrin is certainly not a child. If Jerrin is in his late-twenties, then Skyler would be over sixty, but that doesn't seem possible.

Neeve said he was the fourth child by the king's second wife, so there have to be at least three children between Neeve and Jerrin, and Neeve is probably nineteen, having graduated from high school and finished his first year of college. Surely Jerrin is more than six or seven years older than Neeve if there are three siblings between them, unless the king married very quickly after the death of his first wife and then fathered the children in rapid succession.

But just a minute, didn't Jerrin say his father was over 200 years old? Skyler has to be older than sixty unless the king waited until he was around 140 before he started having kids.

The king looks as if he's in his sixties. Skyler appears to be in his thirties, and Jerrin in his twenties. Neeve and Shiane, however, look their ages. So, at what point do Auravalians stop aging—or at least begin aging so slowly that it's negligible.

I wonder if Hellie knows enough about the king, his wives, and his children to draw me a timeline.

As my attention returns to my companions, it is obvious that I've missed part of their conversation.

"All right," Hellie is saying to Jerrin. "If we're doing a bubble outside of time, I guess it doesn't really matter when. Did you want to do it now, or do you have other things to arrange first?"

"I wanted to see you and Angel before I spoke to anyone else," Jerrin says. "Now I'll go talk with Peter. He said last night that he'd had a rough week and was exhausted. If he still is, there are a few things Kaden can do to help revitalize him if he's willing. If so, I'd like to do this as soon as Peter feels up to it. Will you two still be here in half an hour?"

Hellie and I look at each other.

"Our parents aren't home right now," Hellie says. "I'm not in any hurry to go back, are you, Angel?"

"No," I answer. "Peter and I have a dinner date, but since he'll be with us, I guess we'll be fine until we start to get hungry."

Hellie turns to Jerrin. "We'll be here in the forest, maybe not exactly in this spot, but we won't go home until we hear from you."

A moment later, Hellie and I are alone.

"What do you suppose the urgency is?" I ask Hellie. "This'll be the third day in a row the royals have insisted on meeting with us."

"I don't know, but if I had to guess I'd say it has something to do with Peter and Cindy. Their parentage seems really important."

# Sunshine and Shadows: Another Modern Fairytale

"I guess so."

We wander around for a few minutes, and then Hellie stops. "I'm not going to haul this stuff all the way to Auravale and back," she says, shrugging the straps of her backpack off of her shoulders. "I'm going to pop home and drop this off. Do you want anything while I'm there?"

I shake my head. Then I change my mind. "Take me with you. I have to go to the bathroom."

"Me too."

We finish our business and Hellie takes us back to the pond just seconds before Jerrin arrives with Peter, Cindy, Kaden, and Shiane.

Cindy runs to me and throws her arms around my waist.

"Angel," she says, "this is your enchanted forest." Then her eyes mist over. "But something is wrong here, something bad."

"I know," I tell her, "but Hellie and I are going to fix it."

"Really?" she exclaims. "You know how?"

"We think so. Anyway, we're going to try."

She brightens up. "Good. Then everything will be okay—"

Jerrin's voice overrides the last of Cindy's sentence. He is obviously speaking to Hellie.

"Skyler is waiting for us at the hunting lodge," Jerrin says. Then he looks over at Shiane. "Remember you're here by special dispensation. Behave yourself. Try not to make Skyler regret having convinced Father to let you come."

A much-subdued Shiane leaves Jerrin's side and stands beside Hellie.

"I'm going to open a doorway," Jerrin continues. "As soon as we're on the other side, Hellie, I want you to suspend the entire lodge in a bubble outside of time."

"Not the whole lodge!" Hellie exclaims. "I can't."

Jerrin frowns at her and spits out four words like a slap in the face. "I beg your pardon!"

Hellie drops her head. When she raises it again, she says, "I apologize. May I have a moment to confer with Kaden and Shiane?"

"Of course," Jerrin says in a normal tone of voice, just as if he hadn't verbally backhanded her a moment earlier.

Suddenly I'm not so sure I want to work with him.

If he snapped at me like that, I'd probably burst into tears, run away, and hide in a closet somewhere.

Kaden and Shiane flank Hellie. She takes their hands.

"Shiane," Hellie says, "you know the lodge, don't you?" Shiane nods. "Will you help me shape the bubble so I don't miss any sections and so I don't stop time on the outside too?"

Shiane nods again. "I can do that."

"Thanks." Then Hellie looks over at Kaden. "Please don't let me blow

212

us all up."

He turns her hand over and kisses her palm. "Take some deep breaths and relax. You've got this. Have faith in your talent."

While Hellie closes her eyes and breathes in deeply and then exhales slowly, I can actually see the stress leave her body.

Opening her eyes, she tells Jerrin, "I'm ready."

He creates the doorway between worlds, and we're pulled through.

I don't feel any difference when Hellie moves us outside of time, but I know when she does it because the view of the mountains and sky disappears from the window, replaced by a grayish fog.

Still holding onto Kaden and Shiane, Hellie leads them over to the nearest sofa and sits down. Her eyes appear a little out of focus.

They don't speak.

Skyler motions for Peter, Cindy, and me to join him over on the other side of the room where he has five chairs arranged in a rough circle. Jerrin is already there.

Peter and I scoot three of the chairs closer together and put Cindy in between us. I don't know what to expect, but even if I'd had an idea, I would have been wrong.

Skyler starts by addressing Cindy.

"I'm glad you could come, Cindy. I wanted to tell you in person that the man who has been making your mother cry won't be visiting your house anymore. He is a very evil man. He is in prison now."

"Thank you," Cindy says.

"Do you know what he said to your mother to make her cry?"

Cindy nods.

"Have you ever told Peter?"

She shakes her head.

"Don't you want him to know?"

Cindy looks down and shrugs.

"Peter and I need to talk about some things, and it might be easier if he knows. If you don't want to tell him, may I?"

Cindy slumps down in her chair. "How do you know what he said?"

"The bad man told me."

Cindy jerks upright and stares at Skyler.

"He didn't want to tell me," Skyler says, "but I made him."

"Can you fix it now?" Cindy asks.

"I don't know. That's why I need to talk to your brother."

Cindy reaches over and touches Peter's hand. "It's about the man who taught me how to listen to birds think. He taught me other things to, but listening to birds was first, so I call him Birdman. It always makes him laugh. I like to hear him laugh."

She gets tears in her eyes.

"The bad man wants Mama to tell him something and she won't do it, so the bad man said he's going to hurt Birdman until she does. Every time he comes, he tells Mama about the horrible things he's done to Birdman, and Mama cries. She doesn't want Birdman to be hurt, but if she tells the bad man what he wants to know then he'll do all those terrible things to someone else. Mama says—I think I remember it right—she says: *Birdman won't thank me if I pay for his freedom with someone else's pain.* She cries whenever she says it."

"Thank you, Cindy," Skyler says. "Now I need to talk with Peter. Why don't you go over and sit beside Shiane for a while? Will you do that for me please?"

"Okay, if you really want me to go, but I already know what you want to ask Peter, and I might be able to help."

Skyler leans forward in his chair. "What do you think I want to ask your brother?"

When Cindy looks at Skyler, her expression is mildly amused, maybe even a little smug. "You want him to help you figure out who Birdman really is."

"You're right," Skyler says. "That's exactly what I want."

"Couldn't you make the bad man tell you?" Cindy asks.

"No," Skyler answers. "He said he doesn't know the Birdman's real name, and I believe him. Under the circumstances, I'm fairly certain he'd have told me if he could. He said he was paid by someone else to go to your house and say those mean things to your mother."

"Then that person's a bad man too."

"I agree," Skyler says, "and when we find him, I'll make sure he's punished. Now, what can you tell me about Birdman?"

# Chapter Thirty

"I shouldn't have said I could help." Cindy scrunches way back in her chair. "Birdman told me not to talk about him to anyone except my mother and Peter."

Peter takes her hand. "He said you could talk to me about him?"

"Uh huh," Cindy says.

Peter smiles at her. "So, come over here and tell me about him."

"But they'll hear," she says, pointing at Skyler and Jerrin.

She doesn't point at me, so I guess it's all right for me to listen.

Peter cocks his head to the side and pinches his eyebrows together, as if he's puzzled. "Did Birdman say you could only talk to me about him if no one else was around?"

Cindy shakes her head.

"So, let's pretend they're not here. Okay? It'll just be you and me talking about Birdman."

"Okay. I guess that's all right." Cindy leaves her chair, goes over to Peter, and sits on his lap. "Do you remember Birdman at all, Peter? He said he used to go see you sometimes when you were lots younger, but when you got older, you didn't like him anymore, so he stopped. Is that true?"

"I suppose it is," Peter says. "I remember thinking he was making fun of me by telling me make-believe stories and pretending they were real. I didn't believe in magic back then, and I got mad at him." He looks around the room. "I think now that he was trying to tell me about Auravale, but I didn't understand."

"You hurt his feelings," Cindy tells Peter solemnly. "If Skyler and Jerrin can find him, you need to say you're sorry."

"I will," Peter assures her, "I promise."

"Good. What do you want me to tell you?"

"Do you know his name?" Peter asks.

"No," Cindy answers, "but he said I could call him *paithaer*."

"But *paithaer* isn't his name?"

"No. I usually just call him Birdman, but sometimes he asks me to call him *paithaer*, so I do."

Cindy reaches up and touches Peter's face.

"Whenever I call him *paithaer*, he is happy for a while, but then he gets sad. The last time he came, while Mama was making lunch, I asked him how one word could make him feel good and bad both. He said it was because he never thought he would hear a child call him that. Then I knew what the word meant."

"What does it mean?" Peter asks.

"You won't tell Mama and Daddy?"

"Of course not."

Cupping her hand around her mouth, she speaks into Peter's ear. "Because *paithaer* means father. I patted his hand and told him I could love two fathers. It made him cry. He hugged me for a long time."

Cindy leans back so she can see Peter's face. "It's all right if I love two fathers, isn't it, Peter? He needs someone to love him. He's so lonely. The girl he loves can't marry him."

"Holy stars!" Skyler exclaims, his eyes on Jerrin. "Could it be him?"

"I don't see how," Jerrin answers. "How could he get there? His family never had a key."

"But she might have," Skyler counters. "We know she experimented with portals."

"It would certainly explain a few things."

"I'll go—"

"Wait," Jerrin exclaims. "You can't leave until Hellie returns us to real time. We might as well continue."

"Of course," Skyler says, sounding disgruntled. I don't think he is used to postponing what he wants.

"Do you know who Birdman is?" Cindy asks, directing her question at both Skyler and Jerrin.

"We might," Skyler says. "If we do, then we can guess who has him. We'll do everything we can to find out if we're right, and if we are, we'll do everything we can to get him back."

Cindy scoots off Peter's lap and goes over to Skyler.

"Thank you," she says. "He's a good man. He's been hurt deep in here." She puts her hand on Skyler's chest over his heart. "It was a long time ago, but the pain won't go away. It's a little bit better when he's with Mama and me, but we're not enough. Before, he was big and strong, but he's getting thinner and sicker and weaker all the time.

"His hair used to be brown, and his face was smooth and handsome. Now his hair is almost all white, and he has wrinkles here and here and here." She traces lines on Skyler's forehead, around his eyes, and by his mouth. Briefly her lips turn upwards into a soft, sweet smile. "To me he's still handsome."

Jerrin turns to Skyler. "He'd be about the right age for this to happen."

"And," Skyler adds, "I've heard he's gone into seclusion. I know he hasn't been at court for quite a while."

Cindy's expression becomes somber again, and she pokes Skyler on the arm to get his attention. "He's not very strong anymore. If the bad people keep hurting him, he's going to die."

Skyler takes Cindy's hand and kisses it.

"We'll try hard not to let that happen, Cindy." He turns to Peter. "Does any of this sound familiar to you?"

"All of it," Peter says. "I must have been really messed up as a kid. I interpreted everything about him negatively. When he asked me to call him *paithaer,* I thought he made up the word because it sounded a little like Peter. I thought he was making fun of my name."

Peter shakes his head ruefully while he breathes out a loud sigh.

"He was so tall, one time I asked my mother if he was a giant, and he heard me. He smiled and said, *No, but I can introduce you to some.* I ran from the room because I thought he was mocking me."

Peter glances from Jerrin to Skyler. "Could he? Could he have introduced me to giants?"

"If he's who we think he is," Skyler answers, "then, yes, he could have."

"If you know who he is," Cindy says, "you need to go get him right now before the bad men hurt him anymore."

"When I take you back home," Jerrin tells her, "it'll be like we haven't been gone at all. No time will have passed."

"And," Skyler says, "I'll go straight to the king and see what we can do and how fast we can do it. I promise—"

"Oh, crap," Peter says, smacking the arm of the chair with his hand. "I know his name. I heard it once. I was about eight years old. He wanted to take me someplace, but Mom said *no.* He insisted that I had a right to see for myself.

"After that, he and my mother argued. She finally yelled at him: *Stop it, Stace. This isn't what we agreed on.* He yelled back at her: *And neither was that!* Then he left. I always wondered about that last sentence. It makes sense now. They must have agreed never to use his real name, but Mom did that one time when she was angry. Stace, that's his name. Is he who you thought he was?"

"I'm afraid so," Skyler says. "Stace Jory Merek is his full name, but how he got to your world and to your mother is a mystery, especially since he apparently has gone multiple times over multiple years."

Cindy tugs on Skyler's shirtsleeve. "You said if you knew who he is, you could guess who has him. Can you go get him now?"

"Even if we're right about who has taken him, and we might even have a clue as to where, going to get him won't be easy. We'll do our best, but it will take some careful planning."

Jerrin nods and adds, "The man who almost certainly has Stace Merek is Maldon Darker. Maldon wants Hellie. He must have learned that Stace is your biological father and that your mother knows how to find Hellie through your link to Angel."

"What do you want us to do?" Peter asks.

This is one of the things I love about Peter. He's a problem solver, a doer, an achiever. He never shirks or squirms or procrastinates when something has to be done.

"Arrange an hour a day that the three of you can get together with Hellie so she can put you in an external time bubble with us. Since no time will pass while you're gone, you shouldn't have to make complicated arrangements. See if you can manage it for tomorrow. We can't take any more time today."

Jerrin gestures toward the sofa where Hellie, Kaden, and Shiane are sitting. We all turn to look.

Hellie is pale, and she's quivering.

"She's not going to be able to hold on much longer," Jerrin says. "We've got to wrap this up."

Jerrin goes over to where Hellie is on the sofa. He opens a doorway. In one big swoosh we're all swept through except for Skyler. He vanishes a second before we do.

We're back in the forest beside the pond.

"Angel," Jerrin says, "they need something sweet to drink and something light to eat. Call it for them."

My heart thumps erratically.

"I—"

I start to say *I can't*, but I remember how he snapped at Hellie when she said it. I don't ever want him to give me that kind of verbal slap.

I've done this before. Twice. Once instinctively. Once on purpose.

I can do it again.

I close my eyes. What were the three steps?

I want it, I believe I can have it, and I concentrate until I get it.

I want, I believe, I concentrate.

Silently I chant it to myself like a mantra, all the while visualizing juices and snacks.

Suddenly, I hear clanking and rustling and plopping all around me.

I open my eyes.

On the ground are about a dozen small bottles of fruit juice, two quart-cartons of chocolate milk, two large bags of corn chips, a box of crackers, a jar of peanut butter, one of raspberry jam, one of nacho cheese, one of bean dip, a cellophane bag of carrots, three apples, a bunch of bananas, and three bags of cookies. In the middle of the jumble are a package of napkins, a stack of paper plates, and a box of plastic spoons.

Cindy busily passes out juice to everyone, not just to Hellie, Kaden, and Shiane. When she notices me watching her, she runs over, hands me a bottle, and throws her arms around my waist.

"You're magic," she says. "I always knew you were."

Even though Hellie and I had just barely finished eating lunch when Jerrin came for us, Hellie grabs an apple, takes a bite, and then chews while she opens the jar of nacho cheese. She takes another bite before she rips open a bag of corn chips. She doesn't bother with a paper plate but scoops cheese right out of the jar.

In the meantime, Kaden is spreading peanut butter onto crackers and then dropping a blob of jam on top. Two small empty orange juice bottles lie on the ground beside him.

Shiane is eating cookies from all three bags, alternating them with swigs of chocolate milk.

It's a gorge-fest.

"What's wrong with them?" I ask Jerrin.

"When Hellie started to run out of energy, she drew it from Shiane and Kaden. As she took more and more from them, they grew weaker, and she began to lose control of the time bubble. Right now, they're trying to rebuild their strength. After they've finished eating, they'll need to nap for a while. Until their stamina increases, we'll have to keep our sessions short while we're outside of time. I'd better make arrangements for all of you to get home. The three of them won't be up to doing much for a while."

Within minutes, Neeve appears. Kaden snatches up the box of crackers and the jars of peanut butter and jelly.

"I have plenty of food at the apartment," Neeve says.

"I know," Kaden replies, but he doesn't set his loot back down.

Neeve's laughter stops abruptly when they disappear.

Skyler shows up a few seconds later. When Shiane sees him, she tries to shove a whole handful of cookies into her mouth at one time.

"You don't have to eat them all at once," he says to her. "You can take them with you."

Quickly Shiane gulps down the last few swallows of chocolate milk and drops the carton. Clutching the bags of cookies to her chest, she lets Skyler take her away.

"I'll escort Peter and Cindy home," Jerrin says to me, "and then I'll come back for you and Hellie."

"Okay."

I look at the clutter on the ground.

We have a family rule: we don't leave litter—not ours or anyone else's—in the forest.

Feeling fairly confident now with at least one of my talents, I concentrate and call my backpack and a trash bag to me. When they've popped into existence, I start picking up the mess.

I don't remember seeing anyone use a napkin, but there are several crumpled ones on the ground, plus two apple cores and a banana skin. They go into the trash bag along with all the empty containers. The unopened items go into my backpack.

"I wonder what's keeping Jerrin," I say, sitting down next to my twin. Hellie doesn't stop eating long enough to say anything. She just shrugs.

"Sorry you had to wait," Jerrin says. "I needed to speak with Peter for a moment."

Like Kaden and Shiane, Hellie won't give up what she's munching on. Her family-sized bag of corn chips is only half-gone, so when she ran out of nacho cheese, apparently, she switched to bean dip.

I'm in the process of standing up when I suddenly appear in the living room of our house. I almost stumble, but Jerrin catches my arm and helps stabilize me. My backpack and the bag of trash appear at my feet.

Hellie is still eating in the same position as before. The only difference is while in the meadow she was sitting in the grass and now she's sitting on the carpet.

"She'll stop soon," Jerrin says. "Make sure she goes to bed."

"I will."

"Before I leave, can we step into another room for a minute?"

"Sure." I lead Jerrin into the family room.

"I need to meet alone with you and Peter," Jerrin says. "He suggested that I bring you to his garage tomorrow at noon. He said to tell you he'll have lunch ready."

"Why do you need to see us?"

"I'd prefer to explain it to you both at the same time."

"All right," I say. "How are you going to pick me up? You can't just open a portal to the newspaper office."

"I'll have Neeve drive me over. When you get in the car, I'll open a portal from there to Peter's lunchroom. When we're finished, I'll take you back the same way."

"Fine. I'll see you tomorrow."

Jerrin nods and disappears.

When I go back to the living room, Hellie has stopped eating and is yawning. I wonder how I'm supposed to maneuver her upstairs by myself. The least Jerrin could have down was open a portal straight into her bedroom.

Luckily, Hellie gets up and stumbles for the stairs on her own. I follow along behind her, ready to catch her if she falls.

Since Peter is taking me out to dinner at 6:00, as soon as I get Hellie settled, I gather up some clean clothes and head for the bathroom to take a shower.

As usual I set my cellphone on the vanity. I'm undressing when I get a text from Mom.

> Spending the night in Denver.
> Should be home around 4:00
> tomorrow afternoon. Love you.

When I've showered, dressed, and finished with my hair and makeup, I check on Hellie. She's still asleep. Just in case she wakes up and wonders where I am, I leave a note on the bathroom counter to remind her. I add the information from Mom's text even though I'm sure she sent the same message to Hellie's phone.

Peter takes me to the Sunset Diner.

We find a corner booth, sit side by side, and order the fried chicken dinner. It's the best in town, and it's the diner's specialty.

"Cindy seemed fine today," I say. "I guess Jerrin didn't scramble her brains or anything when he fiddled with her memories."

"No. I talked with her about it for a few minutes this morning. She remembers Friday and Saturday at the cabin better than I do, and she is completely aware of the cover story and the need for using it."

"I guess Jerrin knows his business." I sigh ruefully. "I keep looking for some sign of imperfection. No one should be that powerful and that infallible at the same time."

"Oh, Babe, I disagree," Peter says, shaking his head. "If someone is going to be that powerful, he'd damned well better be infallible. I'd hate to be around if Jerrin ever makes a mistake."

I shiver. "You're right. I didn't think it through."

The waitress brings us our drinks, Dr. Pepper for Peter and Diet Coke for me, and I wait until she's gone before I ask the question that's been on my mind all day.

"How are you doing? Are things okay between you and your mom?"

"You mean because of what Skyler told me about my parentage?"

"Yes."

"There's nothing I can do about the past," Peter says, "and there's nothing that can make me stop loving my parents. But, Angel, I watched them interact last night, and they are totally devoted to each other. It's impossible that my mother snuck around behind my father's back to have an affair."

"So, you think Skyler and Jerrin are wrong?" I ask.

"No, I believe they're right. My parents were married six years before I was born, and there's nearly eleven years between Cindy and me. If my parents could have children, I don't think they'd have waited so long to have us. Since they've said they always wanted to have a family, I imagine they saw at least a couple of different doctors to find out why my mother wasn't getting pregnant. I assume they were told that my dad is infertile.

"After learning they'd never have a family together, they must have decided to try an alternative. I don't know how an Auravalian man got involved, but I'll bet my parents made a joint decision to let him father their children."

"If they did," I say, "that must have been rough—especially for your dad. I don't think many men would have agreed to it."

"My father has always been a remarkable man."

When the waitress approaches with our dinners, we stop talking.

After she leaves, Peter asks me, "Have you had a chance to look through the scrapbook I gave you for graduation?"

I feel my face burn with embarrassment. "I've gone through the first little bit," I say, "but there's been so much going on, I haven't felt like I had the time to do it justice."

Peter takes my hand, turns it over, and kisses my palm.

I can hardly breathe.

"Don't worry about it," he says. "I've been hoping that some evening we could sit down and go through it together."

"I'd like that. It would be fun to look at the pages and relive the special moments we've shared. And," I say, poking his arm with my finger, "you can explain to me how you got some of those pictures of us together. You must have had spies hiding in the bushes."

"I'll tell you all about it," he says with a laugh. "We'll find the time as soon as things settle down a bit."

# Chapter Thirty-one

Neeve and Jerrin pick me up at noon, and Jerrin teleports us from the car directly into a long room at the back of Peter's garage.

Peter calls it his lunchroom.

I call it his office.

It's where he pays the bills, orders his supplies, and meets with the people who are worth changing out of his overalls and cleaning up for.

But it's also where he eats lunch. At one end of the room, he has a refrigerator, a microwave oven, a coffee maker, and a hot plate, as well as a small table with two chairs so he doesn't have to eat at his desk.

"Are you sure you won't join us?" Peter asks Jerrin after he seats me at the table. He pulls an extra chair from over by his desk for Jerrin to use.

"Our times are out of synch right now," Jerrin says. "I had dinner a couple of hours ago."

"A cup of coffee or a soft drink?" Peter suggests.

"If you have one of those Dr. Peppers," Jerrin says, "that would be nice. Skyler said he really enjoyed the one you gave him."

Peter takes a Dr. Pepper out of the refrigerator for Jerrin and one for himself at the same time. He gets a Diet Coke for me.

In the middle of the table is a crockpot of homemade soup and to the side a basket of dinner rolls. After Peter sits down, he ladles soup into two bowls. He hands me the first and then takes the second.

I taste a spoonful and give him a thumbs-up. Peter makes great soups. Today it's turkey and vegetables.

Jerrin gives us time to butter our rolls and begin eating before he starts talking. "Has Hellie ever explained to you what a soul recognition is?"

"No," we answer together.

"But," I say, "you mentioned a soul bond yesterday."

"In our world," Jerrin says, "we believe we are born with only half a soul. In order to become a complete person, we must find our other half. When we do, the recognition and the bond of love we feel is instantaneous and lasts forever. Hopefully both parties feel it at the same time."

"Hellie and Kaden have that bond, don't they?" I ask.

"Yes, although Kaden felt it for quite a while before Hellie did. It's been argued that humans can't experience it, but we know now that's not true, because Neeve and Karissa are also bonded. So are you two."

No one needed to tell me that.

I was in love with Peter the first day we met.

Peter reaches across the table and takes my hand. "I knew as soon as I saw Angel that I'd never love anyone else."

With a nod of acknowledgement, Jerrin goes on. "We also believe that it is the first kiss on the lips that merges the two souls into one." His eyes meet mine. "That's why we can risk arranged marriages. Even if a man and a woman are not exactly soulmates, if their souls are compatible, they will still combine with that first kiss, making both parties whole."

"So that's why you don't kiss on the lips before marriage," I say with sudden comprehension. "Casual kissing could result in all kinds of unsuitable or incompatible pairings."

"Correct," Jerrin says.

"But," I persist, "what if one of the parties of an arranged marriage has a soul recognition with someone other than the intended partner?"

"If that happened," Jerrin answers, "naturally the arranged marriage would be cancelled, but it's not allowed to happen."

"How can you prevent it? Do you put magic spells on people to make sure they fall in love the right person?"

"No," Jerrin answers. "No magic user, not even a mage, is strong enough to make one person love another. Most Auravalians are allowed to grow up, fall in love, and marry whomever they please. The lucky ones find and marry their soulmates. The others do the best they can, knowing that their souls will unite with their chosen partners as soon as they are married and share their first kiss.

"Members of the royal family and of the court are in a different position. We cannot marry without the king's consent. In the past, a few monarchs have forced courtiers into politically desirable unions by telling them they could never marry anyone unless they married the king's choice.

"Some children, however, are expected from the moment of birth to marry for the betterment of the kingdom. To prevent them from having premature soul recognitions, they are not allowed to have contact with unmarried members of the opposite sex unless they are members of the immediate family.

"The sequestering lasts until a betrothal has been arranged, the legal documents have been signed, and both parties have reached an appropriate age. The couple meets for the first time at the altar on their wedding day.

"I think Skyler's isolation lasted nearly three years after he reached maturity while he waited for his intended bride to become of age. Our sister, Natallia, was betrothed while still a baby. She never saw a man outside of our family until she was eighteen years old and married."

"What about you?" I ask brazenly.

"I was lucky," Jerrin says with a smile. "My father had a difficult time deciding which of two potential alliances would benefit the most from my marriage. I had just turned eighteen when he decided to visit both kingdoms and to take me along with him. Since I had nearly finished my mage training, he hoped I'd have a precognition that would show him which alliance to favor.

"Of course, I wasn't allowed to extend my wings and fly for fear I'd glance down at the countryside, see a lovely maiden, and form a bond. We traveled overland, and I had to ride in a completely enclosed carriage. When we sailed across the Eastern Sea, I was confined to my cabin, and only bonded servants were allowed to approach me.

"After we reached the kingdom of Badden, my father would not let me out of his sight. Pages preceded us everywhere, making sure hallways were free of unattached females of all ages. While my father and King Hanar were negotiating, I was given a book and told to sit in a corner and read.

"Somehow, my future wife, who was fifteen at the time, managed to escape from her governess' supervision. She wanted to sneak a peek at me, and I just happened to glance up when she opened the door a crack and peered into the room. Our souls called out to each other in recognition. After that, since neither of us would ever love anyone else, we no longer needed to remain in isolation. We were allowed to get acquainted and—"

Jerrin clears this throat. "I'm sorry. I've gotten off the subject."

I start to ask a question, but he shakes his head at me. "Later. Right now, I need to talk to you two about your relationship."

"*Our* relationship?" Peter says incredulously. He frowns at Jerrin and then turns his questioning eyes on me.

I shrug.

I don't have a clue what's going on.

"I apologize for being intrusive," Jerrin says, "but your incessant longing for each other is blatantly evident. When you're in the same room, I have to dampen you both. As you are trained to use your talents, it will become necessary for you to interact with other Auravalians, and I won't always be available to intercede. Your physical desire will be apparent to everyone who has even a tiny bit of telepathic skill.

"I realize your customs are different from those of my world and I don't know what circumstances prevent your marriage in Colorado, but you've shared your first kiss, your souls have merged, and your bond is permanent. I don't think you should wait much longer before you have your union officially sanctioned, at least on Panelda. When you've consummated your marriage, you'll stop broadcasting the frustrations you're having because of your growing and unfulfilled passions.

"If you're worried about the possible complication of an unplanned pregnancy, I assure you Auravalian doctors have perfected several types of contraception."

I don't know if my mind has ever gone so completely blank before.

How do you respond to a relative stranger who tells you that the sexual tension between you and your boyfriend is so apparent that you ought to go ahead and get married? Oh, and by the way, for your convenience the pesky unplanned parenthood problems have been solved.

My mind is in a whirl.

"I'm sorry," Jerrin says. "I have made you both uncomfortable. I wouldn't have brought up the subject so early in our acquaintance except that it has become problematic."

"With whom?" I ask.

"In what way?" Peter asks at the same time.

"It's Shiane," Jerrin answers. "She's been obsessed with everything earthly ever since the first time she came here. It was my fault actually. When Hellie had only known Kaden for a day or two, she innocently or capriciously, I've never been sure which, performed a type of binding ritual with him."

My mouth falls open and I gawk.

"It was not nearly as meaningful or as powerful as a soul bond," Jerrin is quick to add, "but it draws the couple together and can play havoc with their feelings. I needed Neeve and Kaden to teach Hellie about Auravale in preparation for her learning to use her powers. However, the binding ritual was so fresh I felt they needed a chaperone, and I sent for Shiane.

"She had been begging our father to let her go visit Neeve, and I hoped I could solve two problems at one time.

"Even though I knew Shiane was fascinated by Neeve and Karissa's love story, I foolishly exposed her to another one—the one developing between Hellie and Kaden."

With a shake of his head, he mumbles to himself, "At my age, I should have known better." Then he continues.

"The problem now is that Shiane has expanded her romantic notions about Hellie and Kaden to include you two. Twin sisters in love. One sister promised, the other not. The sexual tensions growing daily.

"The queen asked me to talk with you because Shiane is spending an inordinate amount of time daydreaming about your relationship. One of the queen's strongest talents is empathy, and she is nearly always in tune with her children. She wasn't worried at first, when Shiane was just titillated by the complexities of male-female relationships in your world. But now, according to the queen, Shiane is actively fantasizing about you nearly every day, and it's interfering with her studies.

"If for some reason marriage isn't in the near future for you, then I need to schedule times to meet with you individually so I can teach you how to dampen your physical and emotional desires."

I close my eyes to think.

How am I supposed to react?

Peter has never asked me to marry him.

I can't very well propose to him.

Since I don't know what to say, I wait for Peter to comment.

"The timing isn't right," he finally says to Jerrin.

I open my eyes and stare.

Peter looks at me with an almost anguished expression on his face. "You know I love you, Angel. I always will, but—"

That simple three-letter word is like a knife in my heart.

When I took psychology in high school, the teacher told us that when a person uses the word "but" it actually means: *Don't pay any attention to what I just said in the first part of this sentence because whatever comes next is what is actually important.*

I want to burst into tears.

I won't let myself.

"It's all right, Peter," I say. "Even though I'll always love you, I don't want you to make commitments you're uncomfortable with. When the time is right, you can let me know. Now, I have to hurry and get back to work."

I stand up as quickly as I can.

I need to get out of there while I have any control and any dignity left.

"Angel," Peter calls after me.

"Don't," I hear Jerrin say. "Let me take her back, then you and I can talk."

# Chapter Thirty-two

Somehow, I make it through the rest of the day.

I do my job at work, I eat dinner with the family, and then I go to my room, sit at my desk, and wonder how I'll ever get any sleep with this terrible pain in my chest.

How can Peter say he loves me and yet not want to marry me?

Hellie knocks on my door from the bathroom.

When I look up, she comes in and sits on my bed.

"What's wrong?" she asks me.

"Nothing," I answer dully.

"Sure," Hellie says, "that's why you can hardly speak without getting tears in your eyes. Did you and Peter argue again?"

I cover my face with my hands, and tears pour down my cheeks.

"Oh, Hellie," I blubber.

Before I know it, Hellie is standing beside me at the desk, and I throw my arms around her waist, lean against her, and start to sob.

She strokes my hair and lets me cry.

When I reach the sniffling, hiccupping stage, she takes my hands and gently pulls me off of my chair. She leads me over to the bed.

We sit together on the edge.

"Angel, what's happened?"

"He doesn't want to marry me!" I cry. The tears had almost stopped, but now they're gushing again. "After over a year together, he doesn't want to marry me."

Hellie puts her arm around me. "Angel," she says softly, "have you and Peter been—I mean, you don't need to get married, do you?"

"What?" It takes me a moment to understand what she's asking. I reach across her and grab a tissue from the box on my bedside table. "Of course not! You and I promised each other when Mom and Dad explained the facts of life to us that we'd wait until after we were married."

"Then what's all the crying about?"

I tell her.

I relate everything Jerrin said in as much detail as I can, and then I repeat how Peter responded.

"Oh, you idiot!" Hellie exclaims. "*The time isn't right* is not the same as *I don't want to marry you.* The time isn't right for Kaden and me either. He has another year before he finishes his medical training and then he has to take his professional exams. It's actually in his apprenticeship contract that he can't get married until he has received his medical license."

"But," I say defensively, "at least you know Kaden wants to marry you. He's proposed, and you've accepted. You're engaged even if you haven't announced it and don't have a ring. Peter has never asked me. He's never even mentioned the subject."

"Still, he loves you," Hellie says. "Anyone can see that."

"Yeah," I mumble, "but *I love you* isn't the same as *Will you marry me?*"

Hellie passes me the tissue box and then waits patiently while I finish crying for the second time.

"So," she asks, "do you just want to sit here and be depressed?"

"Do you have a better idea?" I ask, sniffling and wiping my nose.

"I don't know. We made a deal and you kept your end of the bargain, but I haven't had the chance to keep mine."

"What deal?" I ask.

"I said if you'd go on a picnic with me in the woods, I'd tell you what I know about your powers. We've gone twice, and Jerrin has interrupted us both times. Of course, you've had Master Cushing, Kaden, and Shiane tell you all sorts of stuff, so maybe that's enough."

"Not if you know something they didn't tell me. Do you?" I ask.

"I probably do, but you'll need to understand the information is incomplete."

"I'll take whatever you have to offer."

"I didn't get to hear what Master Cushing told you on Saturday. Did he explain that influencing is your strength?"

"Yes. He said it had three parts: attracting and repelling, calling and sending, and inviting and denying."

"Did he tell you how rare it is for one person to have access to all three of those?"

"No," I answer.

"Well," Hellie says, "let me assure you it is exceedingly rare. Did he mention anything else?"

"He told me that manipulating the weather isn't a talent. It's a great magic."

"But he didn't tell you anything particularly unusual about your influencing abilities?"

"No." I'm getting nervous. The tone of Hellie's voice implies something bad is coming.

Hellie shakes her head. "If Master Cushing and Jerrin didn't tell you the rest of it, maybe I shouldn't. I'm not sure they're even aware that I overheard them. But I think you have the right to know."

She chews on her thumbnail for a moment and then takes a big breath.

"Remember when Skyler told Peter that Jerrin can't alter memories completely or permanently without killing brain cells?"

"Yes."

"It's the same thing with all of the thought processes, not just memories. A mage can force you to eat broccoli, but he can't make you enjoy it. Likewise, a mage could force you to marry a particular man, but he couldn't make you fall in love with him—not before or after. A mage can't make you believe in purple dragons, or make you think black is white, or make you want to become a doctor, a lawyer, or a priest. If you see an assault, a mage can't make you reinterpret it as a church picnic. There are dark practitioners who try, and sometimes they can almost carry it off, but they do irreparable damage in the process."

I wait for her to go on, but she just looks blankly at me for a moment.

"So?" I ask pointedly.

She purses her lips and shakes her head.

I realize this isn't easy for her. I decide to be patient.

"Somehow," Hellie tells me, "you're able to do it without inflicting harm."

"Do what?"

"You can influence how people think and behave. You can alter their memories, change their feelings, manipulate their wants and their needs, and direct their actions and their reactions. It's all part of the power of influencing. Master Cushing said you have the power to induce people into wanting to remake themselves according to your desires.

"That's why there is no brain damage. You don't impose anything. You don't inflict anything. You don't erase anything. Somehow you convey your wishes, and people respond accordingly. If you want someone to believe black is white, that's what he'll think. If you want broccoli to become his favorite food, it will. But it's not because you force them to comply. You simply convince them that it's true."

I feel sick to my stomach.

I flop onto my back and stare at the shadows being cast on the walls by the moonlight coming in through my window.

"You know, Hellie," I say, "I consider myself to be fairly bright and reasonably moral, but what you've just described alarms me almost to the point of panic. It's much worse than being told I can change the weather.

"Jerrin said I've used small magics to influence people to like me and to gain a few advantages. I can live with that. People who study the art of persuasion, or who dress for success, or who have life coaches are trying to do the same thing. The major difference is that I've done it unconsciously and they've worked hard at it.

"But being able to convince people that something is true when it isn't, or being able to make them want something or do something or say something against their will, that's not only dangerous, it's just plain evil. No one should have that kind of control over someone else's mind. There are a thousand ways it could be abused, even by a saint who is committed only to doing good."

I start shivering, and I have to clamp my jaws together to prevent my teeth from chattering as I consider the horrible possibilities.

"I'm not a saint," I mutter. "You've only just now told me I have this ability, and already I've come up with a dozen self-serving things I could accomplish if I nudged people's thoughts in new directions, and no one would ever know. I wish I hadn't asked you to tell me."

My mind is racing a million miles a minute as I try to consider all the possibilities and all the potential consequences.

"I'm sure there are all kinds of maniacs out there who would just love to kidnap me and lock me away forever if they could force me to use this power for them. Luckily, no one knows about it except for you and me."

"And the Auravalians," Hellie says. "At least Master Cushing, Skyler, and Jerrin know. I didn't mean to eavesdrop, but I heard them discussing it on graduation night shortly after Master Cushing met with you. I was tired after dancing all evening and I wanted to know if Jerrin was going to take you home, or if he wanted me to hang around so I could take you with me. Apparently, Master Cushing was able to do a partial reading before you started screaming for help."

"If they know," I say with a sense of despair, "then the king knows. He's probably been sitting in his throne room chortling over the political implications. He could make me turn his enemies into allies. Or if he prefers more extreme measures, he might make me convince his enemies to kill each other off. Then he could wait until it was over, pick up the pieces, and rule the world."

I shudder violently. "If the king turned the full force of his gaze on me, like he did on Shiane, I'd never be able to stand up to him, to defy him, to tell him no. I'd crumble and let myself be used as a pawn on an alien world."

"Angel," Hellie says, taking hold of both of my hands, "I know it's scary, but the king would never put you in that position. He is a sorcerer in his own right, and he has a whole kingdom full of subjects who have some kind of magical abilities. He knows the ethics and the morality required of a sovereign. He's intimidating—it's true—but he's a good man."

"I don't believe any person at his level could be good enough to resist that kind of temptation. Do you remember studying the historian, Lord

# Sunshine and Shadows: Another Modern Fairytale

Acton? He's the one who said: *Power tends to corrupt, and absolute power corrupts absolutely.*"

"Angel, you're reacting this way because you don't have enough information and you haven't had any training. All of us could misuse our abilities if we wanted to. After you've had a few sessions with Jerrin, you'll begin to see how everything works together."

"Uh huh," I say skeptically. After a brief pause, I go on. "All right, let's disregard my ability to rewrite people's brains without damaging them, since that's a skill I'm never ever going to use. Tell me about attracting and repelling. I've been thinking about it, and I can't come up with a single scenario that wouldn't be self-serving for me and intrusive for others. It's as if all of my talents are designed to fashion me into a selfish, manipulative person."

Hellie is silent for several minutes.

"All right," Hellie says. "Pretend that Mrs. Kendall is out walking her dog when they're hit by a car. She and her terrier, Tristan, are both injured. As the medics load her into the ambulance, she hears a police officer calling Animal Control Services to come get Tristan. Mrs. Kendall sees us and begs us not to let them take her dog. Instead, she asks us to transport him to the vet and get his injuries treated.

"Poor Tristan is hurting while he watches his beloved master being driven away by strangers. We need to get him into our car so we can take him to the veterinarian hospital, but he yips, and barks, and snaps at us. What can we do?

"I could use my kinetic powers to pick Tristan up and put him in our car, but he'd fight the whole way because he wants to go with Mrs. Kendall. If I'm not careful, I could damage him worse than the car did.

"You, on the other hand, could use your powers of attraction to get Tristan to come with us voluntarily, possibly happily, and you wouldn't have to touch him or sweet-talk him or anything."

"That's no kind of example," I say. "If all I ever had to do was help dogs, I wouldn't be worried."

"Well, you didn't give me much time to think," Hellie responds. "But that same basic situation could be played out a hundred different ways. You could comfort a lonely and frightened child. You could guide depressed people toward a more positive lifestyle. You could help soldiers with Post Traumatic Stress Disorder to redefine their disturbing past experiences."

"A good psychotherapist can do those things too," I say.

"Possibly after years of therapy sessions and thousands of dollars," Hellie says. "However, once you've had training in psychology, physiology, and pathology, you'll be able to do it with a thought."

My mouth drops open. "I have to study all of that?"

"Of course," Hellie says. "There is a lot that goes into learning how to

232

use our powers properly. Did you think Jerrin would turn you loose on the world with unchecked capabilities like yours? The first thing he did with me was bind my powers so I couldn't accidentally harm anyone while I was learning control. Since you've officially agreed to let him be your teacher, I imagine he's put limitations on you too by now."

"What?"

"Part of his job as your teacher is to guarantee that you aren't a danger to yourself or to others, and as you pointed out, your talents have a great potential for being abused.

"But you also have a great potential for doing good because of the type of person you are. Your abilities all have to do with influencing others, and you're not limited to people. You've already caused an entire storm system to move for you, and you sent it to an area that desperately needed the water. Even though manipulating the weather is considered a great magic, it falls under the general heading of influencing, rather than directing or commanding or constraining."

I don't want to talk about my abilities anymore.

I change the subject. "Jerrin once said that you've used two great magics. One was stopping time so you could save the little girl who fell off the slippery slide. What was the other?"

"It happened when I was so upset about accidentally ruining Mrs. Baxter's car and sending Mr. Thompson to the hospital," Hellie says. "I opened a portal and pulled Kaden from Auravale to me. Being able to reach across space for someone and then translocate him, with or without his permission or cooperation, is a great magic. That's the only time I've ever used it, and I don't know if I could do it again. The great magics tend to manifest in times of emotional upheaval."

I sigh. "The ability to move people from one world to another has as much potential for abuse as my powers do."

"I suppose that's why Auravale has so many rules, and regulations, and laws. Having magical abilities is a little like toting a couple of loaded machineguns around with you—except you can't just set them down and leave them behind when you want to."

So, I wonder, why does the king need me?

I assume, when Skyler and Jerrin say they need me, what they are really saying is that the king needs me to do something for him, and simply coaxing the stwethil-thage back into our forest to get Bree-Ella's artifacts, doesn't seem worth all the hoopla.

Although the three components of influencing might not be the most common talents, they aren't unknown. I'm sure the king could find someone with more skill, more training, and more experience than I have who could persuade the stwethil-thage to cooperate with him.

As for altering memories, Jerrin's ability and mine are nearly identical.

233

# Sunshine and Shadows: Another Modern Fairytale

He might not be able to manipulate a person's thoughts permanently without causing damage, but what's the real difference? Unless some outside stimulus forces recall, the result is essentially the same: a mind has been altered and the person doesn't even know.

Then it hits me.

I understand what Skyler and Jerrin are preparing me for.

I present my theory to Hellie.

"The king wants me to attract someone into doing something that he can't simply order anyone to do, and then he wants me to alter that person's thinking so that person will never be able to remember having done it or remember that the king had any connection with having had it done, doesn't he?"

"I must be tired," Hellie tells me. "That sentence was completely incomprehensible to me."

I take a good look at my sister.

Her eyes are droopy, and she appears half asleep already.

Suddenly she sneezes, one, two, three times. She reaches across me to grab a tissue from the box she handed me earlier. After she blows her nose, she falls back on the bed.

"I hope I'm not coming down with a cold," she says. "We can talk about this some more tomorrow after work. I've got to get some sleep. I'm so tired I don't even know if I've got the energy to get up and go to bed."

She yawns, making me yawn.

"All right," I say. "Toss me a pillow and you can stay."

Lying on my side, I stretch out my arm so far that I just about pull it out of the socket, but I manage to snag the lightweight quilt I keep on my rocking chair.

While I toss the quilt over us, Hellie stuffs a pillow under my head.

We fall asleep curled up on my bed, facing each other, with our hands barely touching, just like we used to when we were kids.

# Chapter Thirty-three

"Angel, wake up."

I roll over and prop myself on my elbow. The time on my phone reads 6:30, which means the alarm would go off in fifteen minutes anyway.

I guess I won't bite Hellie's head off for waking me.

"What?"

"Jerrin wants us to meet with him today. Since you, Peter, and I didn't get together and figure out how to arrange it, as we were instructed, he did it for us. At 12:00 noon, Peter will go into his office. I will meet him there and open a doorway for him. At the same time, you need to step into the ladies' room at work so I can open a doorway for you.

"Jerrin decided we don't need to bring Cindy this time. We'll be in a bubble outside of time, so I should be able to take you back within seconds of when you left."

"Okay," I grumble, wondering if Jerrin plans on taking control of my time for the rest of my life.

When noon approaches, I'm hungry so I snack on a protein bar.

Exactly at noon, I head for the ladies' room.

Hellie is already in there.

The next thing I know, we're in the hunting lodge. Master Cushing is present. Neeve, Karissa, and Skyler aren't.

"Skyler isn't coming," Jerrin answers when I ask about his elder brother. "He and our father are working on plans to get Stace Merek back home."

He switches his attention to Hellie.

"You can draw on Kaden and Shiane's help all this week, but by next week I expect you to be able to do this on your own. If you need me to walk you through it again, just tell me."

"If I don't have to keep changing locations," Hellie says. "I'm sure I can get the hang of it. Are we going to continue meeting here for a while?"

"At least for the next few weeks," Jerrin says. "In order to fine-tune your abilities, we'll need to get out in the field eventually."

"All right," Hellie says. "I'll keep that in mind."

Hellie, Kaden, and Shiane place three chairs in a triangle. Hellie has Kaden on her right and Shiane on the left. They all clasp hands, creating an enclosed circle.

"We're ready whenever you are," Hellie says.

Jerrin puts a timer on a nearby table.

"Fifty minutes," he tells her. "Now."

The three in the chairs close their eyes and do whatever it is they do.

"Angel," Jerrin says, "Master Cushing will be working with you today. Peter, I'll be working with you."

Master Cushing and I go over to a small table in front of the picture window. Even though the room is comfortably warm, I shiver.

There is something about the gray fog outside that is chilling.

I don't know if I'm having a physiological or a psychological reaction to it, but I shiver again.

"When we met to do your evaluation," Cushing says, "I couldn't help but notice your preoccupation with your family's forest. Tell me about it?"

"I guess it was on my mind," I say, "because Hellie and I had just been there. Last summer, a fire burned over half of the forest down. Hellie sent our stwethil-thage to safety and they promised to come back, but they haven't.

"Apparently stwethil-thage have been living in our woods for generations, and they have been feeding the forest with their magic. Between the loss of the stwethil-thage and the devastation of the fire, the forest is pretty much dying now. Hellie says it won't last more than a few months unless we can do something to revitalize it."

"You have come up with a plan now, haven't you?"

"Sort of," I say. "Hellie thinks she's found a clan of wild stwethil-thage here in Auravale that might be willing to relocate. If they do, we hope they'll help the forest recover. Right now, the chief is consulting with the other clan leaders. When they come to check it out, I'll be doing my best to *invite* them to stay. This is a chance for me to use that part of my influencing ability, right?"

"Yes. When you meet with them, let Hellie do the talking while you focus mentally on all the positive aspects of your property. The stwethil-thage will sense the damage caused by the fire and the withdrawal of the other clan. From the image you're projecting, I can tell the devastation is widespread. The stwethil-thage might feel overwhelmed by such a large task."

I feel a twinge of conscience for my plans to manipulate the little creatures. "Our forest really was a lovely place," I say defensively. "It's not like I'm trying to sell them worthless swampland in Florida."

When I see confusion on Master Cushing's face, I realize he doesn't understand the Florida reference, but then I see him smile with comprehension.

I've got to get used to dealing with telepaths.

I will NOT be offended that he looked inside my mind to find out what *worthless swampland in Florida* meant.

"You realize, I hope," Master Cushing continues, "that you'll have the opportunity to *invite* new growth to the forest as well. Let the stwethil-thage know that you look forward to helping them heal the land."

"I can do that?"

"Yes. Let me show you how."

In a pot in the corner is a tall plant that looks like it's having a rough time. The leaves are limp and brown at the tips. Master Cushing goes and gets it then sets it on the table close to me.

Automatically, I poke a finger into the soil to see if it's moist. It is. I wonder who waters it here in the lodge, but I wouldn't be surprised if there is a special plant-watering spell in every modern Auravalian home.

As I glance around, I realize there are several other potted plants scattered around the room. I never noticed them before.

Well, actually I did.

I just assumed they were fakes.

Now that I look closer, though, I can tell they're all real. I wonder why they don't freeze solid when the lodge isn't in use, but if there is a watering spell, there is probably a warming one too.

"Close your eyes and focus your thoughts on the plant," Master Cushing instructs. "Let it know it has everything it needs for health: sunlight, water, nutrients, and love. Open your heart to the wonders and beauty of nature. Visualize a world full of sunshine and gentle rains, beautiful tall trees, brightly blooming flowers, lush grass, and velvety moss. Make the picture in your mind as real and detailed as you possibly can. Now, surround the plant with your vision and feed it energy."

I do my best.

"Well done," Master Cushing exclaims. "Now open your eyes."

The leaves in the pot are a bright purplish-green. The stem appears to have eight or nine inches of new growth, and the new growth is covered with dozens of pale blue blossoms.

"I did that?" I ask. This unfamiliar plant is so beautiful my eyes fill with tears that start leaking down my face.

Master Cushing pats my hand. Then he pulls a white linen handkerchief out of the air and hands it to me.

I blot my cheeks with it.

"You can help your forest in the same way, by concentrating on its beauty when it's healthy. Now, I'm going to have to hurry through the rest of this. You can attract, call, and invite in many different ways. Focusing your thoughts should be effective in most situations, but you can also sing, laugh, and recite poetry to activate your powers. You might find that the forest responds particularly well if you sing to it, especially if you choose bright, cheerful songs that you can infuse with love. Jerrin will teach you how to modify your skills to suit specific circumstances. Other than—"

Suddenly I hear Hellie sneeze, one, two, three times.

The room around us goes all wobbly.

Vivid colors flash like lightning through the gray fog outside the windows.

Jerrin knocks his chair over as he springs to his feet and dashes across the room to where Hellie and her helpers are sitting. He drops to his knees and slides on the tile for the last few yards, breaking the triangle for a split second while he grabs Kaden and Shiane's hands.

After that, I'm not aware of any sound except Jerrin's labored breathing.

The timer goes off, and I jump about ten feet in the air.

More minutes pass.

Gradually, the world around us stabilizes.

"Angel," Jerrin calls with a strain in his voice, "you'll have to open the doorway back to real time."

"Me?" I yelp. "Why me?"

"As a descendant of the royal family, you have the power to open portals between worlds. When Hellie sneezed, her concentration was broken and she has almost depleted her energy, and Kaden and Shiane's as well, trying to reestablish it. Right now, I'm using all of my strength to support theirs. You're the only one left with the ability. I'll talk you through it."

"I'll help sustain her," Master Cushing says. "Peter can assist as well."

Peter nods his agreement even though he can't possibly have any idea what he's agreeing to. Neither do I.

"Angel, are you right-handed or left?" Jerrin asks.

"Right."

"Fine. Hold Master Cushing's hand in your right and take Peter's with your left."

I do as I am told.

"Now," Jerrin says, "I'm going to have you restore us to real time by taking us back to your world. Hellie's not going to be able to manipulate time for quite a while, and this will be the easiest way for you to return us. How well do you remember the meadow where we met on Sunday?"

"Very well," I say. "I took particular notice while we were there."

"Perfect. Close your eyes and think about the meadow. Picture it in as much detail as you can: the pond, the hedge on one side, the surrounding trees, the flowers, the insects, the burned forest in the distance. Include sights, sounds, smells, textures, and anything else you can remember, but make the time reference today at noon instead of on Sunday. Do you have that clear in your mind?"

"I think so."

"That's not good enough. You have to know so. Concentrate. Fill your mind with the meadow: the sky above, the ground below, and the forest all around. You know this place. It's essence today is the same as before. Experience it. Pull it into your mind. Do you have it?"

As he talks, I do as he says. Suddenly, the images are so clear and powerful that I feel as if I'm actually there.

"I have it," I say.

"Insert all of us into the picture: first yourself, then Peter and Master Cushing. Add Hellie, Shiane, Kaden, and me."

His voice rises in volume and pitch. "See it, want it, believe it—MAKE IT HAPPEN!"

With the force of the last phrase, I feel something magnificent, something electrifying, something wonderful building inside of my body. Then, it shoots out through my fingers and my toes.

When reality shifts, I experience it deep inside my body's core.

I open my eyes. We're in the meadow not far from the pond.

Hellie collapses to the ground. Shiane and Kaden fall beside her.

Seeing my twin lying in the grass, no color in her face and no movement in her chest, causes me a momentary panic.

Saturday, Jerrin had me call up things for them to eat and drink.

I focus and pull as hard as I can. Immediately, food—a lot of food—appears all around us: scattered across the ground, floating on the pond, and dangling from the trees.

Sitting behind Hellie, I grab her under the arms and pull her up until she's leaning against me.

I snatch the first bottle I see. It's pineapple juice. I glare at the cap and it flies off.

"Here, Hellie." She doesn't respond.

I wave the bottle below her nose, hoping the aroma will rouse her. She loves pineapple juice.

"Hellie, drink," I tell her.

Her lips part slightly, and I tip the bottle so juice dribbles into her mouth. She swallows.

I give her another sip.

The bottle is half empty when Hellie starts to groan and to twitch a little. I look around for something nourishing she can eat.

I spot a prepackaged microwaveable bowl of teriyaki chicken on rice about six feet away. I reach out and call it to me. When it arrives in my hand, the bowl is out of the box, the plastic film is gone, the food is hot, and there is a plastic fork lying across the top. I set the bowl on the ground at my side and start feeding my sister.

After a dozen tiny bites, she manages to sit up on her own. For safety's sake, I remain where I am so she can lean back on me if she needs to.

I hand her the bowl. She begins wolfing down the contents as if she hasn't eaten in a year.

Only then do I glance around to check on everyone else.

On the right, Kaden is sitting up, drinking chocolate milk directly out of a half-gallon jug. He has an opened box of graham crackers on his lap and a bag of string cheese at his side. Several string cheese wrappers are on the ground.

On the left, Shiane is squirting whipped cream from a can onto a frozen waffle and then shaking sprinkles on top. She has dabs of whipped cream and sprinkles around her mouth, so I assume she's on her second or third helping. A deli bag that contained sliced ham is lying empty in her lap.

Peter is sitting on the ground looking slightly dazed. Master Cushing is crouched next to him.

Even Jerrin looks almost wiped out. He is off to the side eating some kind of sandwich.

I let my eyes wander.

What a mess!

Jars, bottles, cans, bags, and boxes of food are everywhere.

There is so much and such a variety I wonder where I pulled it all from.

Skyler and Jerrin told me I have to stop shoplifting, but I think calling stuff to me is tantamount to the same thing.

The big difference is that now I can't control what I take, how much, or from where.

I was much more conservative as a shoplifter.

Not too far from where I'm sitting, I spy a sandwich box from a popular hamburger joint. Printed on top are the words: *bacon cheeseburger*. I call it and lift the lid. Inside, untouched in its original wrapper, is a luscious smelling burger. I hope I didn't snatch it right off of someone's lunch tray. But, even if I did, I have no way of returning it, so I peel back the paper and start munching away.

Suddenly, Skyler and a short, middle-aged man appear next to Jerrin.

Skyler quickly hops to the side to avoid stepping on top of a three-layer chocolate cake. The other man barely misses landing in a tray of frozen lasagna.

Making a show of looking over the foodstuffs that are spread everywhere, Skyler says dryly, "You've got to admit our Angel doesn't do things by halves."

Hearing Skyler use the possessive "our" makes my heart flutter.

Until this moment, I hadn't realized how jealous I was of Hellie's connection to Skyler, Jerrin, and the rest of the royal family. Now that I recognize the feeling, I also understand that I'm connected to them too. It makes me want to jump up and start hugging people.

While the man with Skyler carefully works his way through the edible obstacle course, Kaden tries to clamber to his feet.

"Master Mertley," he says.

The man points his finger at Kaden, "Stay down. I'll tend to you and Shiane as soon as I find out how serious Hellie's condition is."

When the man reaches us, he looks right at me and says, "Hello, Angel, my name is Mertley. I'm Hellie's Auravalian doctor."

He kneels down between Hellie and Kaden.

"All right, Hellie," he tells her, "let me see how bad it is."

She looks at him.

He stares into her eyes for two or three minutes.

"Well, at least this time you stopped short of disaster."

He reaches up with his hand, closes his fingers as if he's grasping something, and pulls a vial containing a greenish liquid out of nowhere.

He picks up Hellie's bottle of pineapple juice, dumps the green liquid into it, swishes the bottle around for a few seconds to mix the contents, and then hands it to her.

He tells her, "Drink it, all of it, without stopping."

Obediently, she guzzles it down, after which, her entire body quivers.

"Water," she gasps.

I call a bottle to me, twist off the cap, and hand it to her.

She takes a couple of big swallows, shivers again, and then she takes a couple more.

"Thanks," she tells me. "Auravalian medicines taste awful."

"Only to humans," Mertley says. Then he pivots on one knee so he's facing Kaden.

After a quick look into Kaden's eyes, Mertley gets up and steps over Hellie's legs so he can check on Shiane. He pulls two more vials from the air and gives one to each.

I watch to see if they'll react the same way Hellie did.

Nope. They both drink their dosages straight down, not diluting them with water, juice, or soda.

After taking care of the trio, Mertley returns to Jerrin.

"Let me take a look," Mertley says.

"Don't worry about me," Jerrin says. "I'm fine."

"Let me take a look," Mertley repeats.

"I'm fine," Jerrin insists.

Mertley folds his arms and waits.

I wonder who will win the standoff.

Both men appear to be stubborn and used to getting their way.

I'm betting on Mertley simply because he is older and has had more time to practice being obstinate.

I turn out to be correct.

"All right, Mertley, you win," Jerrin says. "Let's get it over with. I need to help Angel clean up this mess before she goes back to work."

I had completely forgotten about having to return to the newspaper office. I pull my cellphone from my pocket and check the time. Hellie opened the doorway out of the restroom at 12:03. It's now almost 12:30. If we arrived in the meadow at exactly the same time that we left the restroom, we've spent nearly half an hour just trying to recuperate.

When Mertley bullies Jerrin into taking a dose of the greenish liquid, Skyler bursts out laughing. Jerrin gives him a dark look, and they glare at each other for a few minutes. I'll wager they're having a lively silent conversation.

Suddenly Skyler laughs again.

"Are you ready to go, Mertley?" he asks.

"I need just another minute." He pulls Jerrin aside. The expression on his face is so serious that I strain to hear what he says.

"This experience has taken its toll on Hellie's mind and her body," Mertley says. "Even though manipulating time is one of her talents, she needs a while to build up the necessary stamina. I'd like you to take it slower—much slower."

"I'll discuss it with the king," Jerrin says, speaking barely above a whisper, "but Maldon Darker has escaped from prison again. When he is recaptured, the king wants Hellie to suspend him outside of time until his trial date."

"Holy stars!" Mertley exclaims. "There hasn't been a mage strong enough to do that kind of suspension since Larauch died."

"I know, but Hellie has the power. All she needs is to develop the finesse and, as you said, the stamina."

"I can't recommend that you go against the king's wishes, but perhaps you should explain the situation to him. If he's adamant about your pushing Hellie forward, let me know. For safety's sake, I'll start working on a potion to increase her endurance as soon as I get back to the hospital, but a slower pace would be the better course of treatment."

"I'll talk with the king."

"Thank you," Mertley says. "I'm ready now, Skyler."

The two men disappear.

Jerrin calls out to the rest of us. "I'm going to return all of you to where you belong," he pauses, "everyone except for you, Angel."

A moment later, we're the only two left in the field.

I hope no one at work remembers that I went into the restroom half an hour ago. If they do and if they realize I've been gone quite a while, I hope they'll assume I slipped away to get something to eat.

"Clearing up this mess will be good practice for you," Jerrin says.

"Although you need to be trained to control what you take, you have obviously figured out how to call things to you. Now let's see how well you do when sending them away."

"Sending them where?"

"Neeve said your town has something he called a *food bank*. Do you know where that is?"

Automatically, I look for Neeve, but then I remember he wasn't with us at the hunting lodge. Obviously, he and Jerrin have been using the family telepathy.

"Sure," I say, answering Jerrin's question, "but there's a lot of this stuff that they won't take, like the frozen foods."

"In that case, the first thing we'll have to do is sort it," Jerrin says.

I turn in a slow circle, trying to calculate how much time this is going to take. My guesstimate is between three and six hours.

I check the time on my cellphone again.

Then I tap the number of the newspaper office.

When April, the receptionist answers, I ask for Bart.

I turn on the speaker so Jerrin can hear without having to read my mind.

"Hi, Bart, this is Angel. Is Mr. Fenton back from lunch yet?"

"Not yet, but you know how he is. He gives himself a thirty-minute window on both sides of the hour."

"Right," I say. "How are things looking for the afternoon?"

"About as slow as they were this morning. When Leonard gets back from lunch, if he shows me one more picture from his cruise, we might have our first real story of the day. How's this for a headline: *News Reporter Shoots Coworker then Phone*."

"Oh no," I exclaim, "you can't shoot his phone. The jury would need to see all those pictures of his meals, his shirts, his sandals, and his daily agendas—as well as all those cheesy selfies—in order to hand in a verdict of justifiable homicide."

"You're right. I'll let the phone live if it agrees to testify."

We share a laugh.

"Listen, Bart, I've had a bit of an accident and—"

"Are you hurt?"

"No, it wasn't that kind of accident. It's the kind where you've made an unholy mess and it's your responsibility to clean it up. I think it'll take all afternoon. Will you tell Mr. Fenton? If things start going crazy and you need me, call, and I'll see if I can get away."

"Is this something we can publish, even for the humor?"

"Sorry. There's no story here. *Clumsy Girl Causes Chaos* isn't a headline that'll sell newspapers."

"But the alliteration's not bad," Bart says.

"Hmm." I laugh. "If what you want is alliteration how about *Maladroit*

*Miss Makes Majestic Mess?*"

"Even better! You've got talent, girl."

"Thanks. I'd really better go now before the mess gets any messier."

"Okay, Angel, I'll explain to Mr. Fenton. Good luck."

"Thanks, Bart. I'll see you tomorrow."

I tap the end-call button.

Then I phone my Dad to let him know I've taken the afternoon off and he doesn't need to pick me up on his way home.

# Chapter Thirty-four

"All right, Jerrin," I say. "How do I start?"

"Actually, we have a couple of choices. We can walk around and you can sort it by hand—"

"By hand?"

"Figuratively speaking," Jerrin says. "What I mean is you can look at each item separately and make a decision about whether it is something for the food bank, something you want to keep, something you'd like your pastor to pass on to the needy in your church, or something that needs to go to the dump. That's one way.

"Another way would be to decide on categories and let the food sort itself out. You could categorize by breakfast foods, entrees, snacks, and desserts or by fresh, precooked, instant, ready to cook, and random ingredients. In the end, you'll still have to make decisions about where everything is to go.

"Whichever way you do it, you will not touch anything physically. This is as good a time as any to teach you levitation, which you would use to do the first method, or spell casting, which is how you would do the second."

Hmm, I think.

Levitation or spells?

Watching Hellie and Shiane move coffee pots, cups, saucers, napkins, and food around the hunting lodge was certainly entertaining. Still, even though they both knew how to do it, Shiane's trouble with the liquids made it clear that it wasn't as easy as it looked.

The only time I've heard anyone mention anything about spells was when Shiane said if the mystery man who sometimes visited the Bradley home threatened Cindy, she'd hit him with a spell so strong he'd never recover. It made me curious about how and when the Auravalians use incantations.

"I think sorting by categories makes the most sense," I tell Jerrin. "If I start by sorting out the canned, boxed, bagged, and bottled items, probably most of it can go straight to the food bank. I'm afraid the frozen foods will most likely need to go to the dump. In the end, I think I'll only have to sort the fresh foods by hand."

"Perfectly logical," Jerrin says. "Let's sit down in the shade, so we can get started."

When I turn toward the shadows of the trees, I discover Jerrin has produced a couple of camp chairs for us with a little table in between.

I grin at him. "You're a thoughtful teacher."

"Don't get used to it," he says. "When you've had a little more practice, I'll expect you to conjure up the amenities. Let's go sit down."

When we're seated, I decide to provide us with some comfort of my own. I call a pitcher of iced tea and two tall glasses. They land on the little table, and I pour.

I hand a glass to Jerrin, and he lifts it in a silent toast. "Thank you."

I lift my glass and toast him back. "You're welcome."

We both take a sip.

Jerrin sets his glass on the table and starts teaching.

"When Cindy talked about the way to listen to birds think, she listed three steps. First was to want it, second was to believe you can have it, and third was to concentrate on getting it. In effect, she was describing the steps to casting a spell.

"In the fantasy movies and books of your world, people write verses or use special words to design their spells, and they flick wands or wave their hands through the air to cast them. In reality, none of that is necessary. In Cindy's three-step process, *wanting* is the spell. *Believing* and *concentrating* are how you cast it.

"The most difficult part of any spell is its creation. The trick is to identify what you want and then to make it specific and to set limitations. You can't just say *Sort out the canned goods*. If you put enough force behind that kind of spell, you could cause the canned goods in every house and every store in your immediate vicinity to sort themselves out. Also, since there is no stipulation about how they should be sorted, it might be done alphabetically, or by expiration date, or by color, or by size.

"The best spells are visualized not verbalized. When you opened the doorway between the hunting lodge and the meadow, you actually cast a spell, and you did it completely without words. That's what I want you to do now.

"Look out over the meadow. Visualize everything that canned foods have in common. The cans are cylindrical and made of metal. The cans have labels on them. Whatever is inside the can is edible. You don't need to visualize individual cans. It's like when you visualized the meadow. You didn't try to remember every tree or flower or blade of grass. You pictured the essence, not the particulars.

"This should be easier than imagining the meadow because all cans are

246

similar. Before you start formulating your spell, however, you need to identify what you want the end result to be. When you opened the doorway, the goal was to move the people from the hunting lodge to here. The goal now is to gather all the cans together in one location, perhaps in front of that stack of bricks. How does that sound?"

"Okay," I say. But I don't feel okay. I am really uncomfortable with the concept of *want* being a magical spell. I might *want* to spend a whole night eating Baskin-Robbins chocolate chip ice cream, but I know I'd better not if I want to stay slender and if I don't want to get sick.

"It doesn't work like that," Jerrin says, responding to my nonverbal notion. "Remember *want* is only the first part of a three-step process."

Since he warned me that he would be monitoring my thoughts, I clamp down on my inclination to be irritated. Actually, I'm kind of glad he was listening because I would never have had the nerve to say what I was thinking.

"We'll need to spend some time working on your self-doubts," Jerrin says. "A timid magic user is going to make mistakes, and mistakes at your capacity level could be disastrous. Hopefully your confidence will grow as you identify your skills, recognize your strengths, and increase your powers. If not, I'll structure some exercises to help you. Now let's start cleaning up this mess.

"Visualize the essence of canned food. See the cans and the labels. Sense the contents: meats, vegetables, fruits, soups, and such. Don't focus on one food. Imagine a montage of flavors and textures and consistencies. Do you have it?"

"Not quite," I say.

I try to figure out what kinds of canned foods I'd have called here, and I can't think of any. It doesn't make sense that I'd have called canned fruits and vegetables when fresh ones are tastier and more convenient. And who eats canned meat anymore? Except for tuna fish and oysters and a few things like that, canned meat is a thing of the past.

My thoughts start getting heavy.

I have trouble thinking.

What was I trying to do?

I can't remember.

"Whenever you're ready," Jerrin says, "let me know, and I'll talk you through it again."

I don't say anything for a minute or two while I struggle to figure out what's happening to my brain.

"I'm sorry," I say. "I got distracted by the particulars, didn't I? And you stopped me by making my thoughts go fuzzy."

"Yes. I'm pleased that you reasoned that out so quickly. Perhaps it would be easier for you if we do the cleanup one item at a time. It'll take longer, but it'll require less abstract thought. You've hardly had time to adjust to the fact that you have magical powers, and I could be pushing you too hard too soon."

"Let me try one more time," I say. "If I can't manage the macro thinking, then we can switch to the micro."

"All right," Jerrin says. "Why don't you close your eyes? Sometimes that helps. Visualize the essence of canned goods. The can. The label. The contents. Many varieties of foods, all enclosed within a metal cylinder. Feel it. Experience it. Do you have it?"

Quite unbelievably, I do.

I know what it feels like to be a can of food.

"I have it."

"You want all the cans in this meadow to move, to collect in one spot. Want it. Believe you can do it. Concentrate on where you want them to be. Want. Believe. Concentrate. Now make it happen!"

Like when I opened the doorway between worlds, I feel an exquisite force flow through me like an electrical current and then burst forth. I don't know why I didn't get this feeling when I called the food here. Maybe it has something to do with specificity. I called randomly to provide the food. Now I'm moving particular items. Maybe that takes a different kind of energy.

I don't need to open my eyes to know I've succeeded.

I open them anyway.

There, in front of the white bricks, are the canned goods. They are arranged in a pyramid, the large cans on the bottom, medium in the middle, and small ones on top.

"That," Jerrin says, "is a reflection of how tidy your mind is. Let's move on to the boxes."

It takes most of the afternoon. As I practice, I get better at thinking in generalized terms within a specific category.

When I'm finished, there are six basic divisions of food: cans, boxes, bags, bottles, fresh, and frozen. Surprisingly, when I called the frozen foods, I somehow arranged for them to maintain their temperatures. None of them have thawed, not even the ice cream.

As I walk among the piles of food, I realize I know five families in our church who are having rough times right now. Some extra provisions could make a real difference in their lives.

With Jerrin's approval, I conjure up five cardboard boxes and start dividing the food.

Inside each box I include cereal, soup, crackers, canned chili and/or spaghetti, bottled juices, peanut butter, tuna fish, both fresh and canned fruits and vegetables, bread, dinner rolls, chips, cookies, and a variety of microwaveable dinners. One family has six children, and I give them the large, family-sized tray of lasagna that Mertley, the doctor, almost stepped in and the two containers of ice cream. I conjure a gallon jug of milk, two pounds of hamburger, and a whole chicken for each family too, except I make it three pounds of hamburger and two chickens for the extra-large family.

That gives all of them fresh and frozen foods for their refrigerators and boxed, bagged, and canned goods for their cupboards.

Everything that's left, all except for one special item, can go straight to the food bank.

I could keep dividing things among the five families until all of the food is gone, but I don't want to go too far.

Whereas one box of groceries will, hopefully, feel like a gift and be appreciated, I'm afraid two or three boxes of groceries might feel like charity and be resented.

I write a note to go on top of each box: *Always remember there are people who love you.*

Before I propel the boxes on their way, Jerrin teaches me how to enhance my vision so I can observe each house and watch what I'm doing.

I wait until no one is around to see the packages arrive.

I push with my powers.

A box is here, and then it's there.

I use an invisible finger to ring the doorbells.

Because of my enhanced vision, I have the fun of watching the reactions.

At each house, a family member answers the door, sees the box, looks up and down the street, and drags the box inside.

Everyone who is at home gathers around to examine the contents.

Their faces look like I've given them Christmas in the summer. I've never felt so warm inside.

Sending the rest of the goods to the food bank isn't nearly as much fun. When no one is in the immediate vicinity, I deposit my contribution just inside the door of the warehouse with a note saying *Anonymous Donation* on top.

That takes care of everything except the trash from the most recent gorge-fest, which I quickly gather and send to the dump, plus one special item.

"How do I send this to Shiane?" I ask.

"We'll have to go back to Auravale," Jerrin says with a grin, "but then it is exactly the same as you did with the other packages. First, I'd like you to open the doorway between worlds. You need the practice."

"All right."

He walks me through the process of opening a portal, and I'm disappointed that it's no easier the second time around.

In fact, I think it is actually harder.

Last time, I had Master Cushing and Peter supporting me.

When I'm about to give up, I feel Jerrin enter my mind.

*Let's open this one together,* he says.

One step and we're back in the hunting lodge.

Jerrin shows me how to use my enhanced vision to find Shiane's suite within the palace.

She is sitting beside a deep window hemming a skirt by hand. She looks absolutely, totally, and completely dejected.

I send her a gift to cheer her up.

When it materializes on the windowsill, she is so startled she jumps up and drops her sewing onto the floor.

Then she sees my note. It says *Thanks for checking on Cindy after the barbeque. I'm sorry you had to settle for pie that night.*

Of course, she knows it's from me even though I didn't sign it.

She mouths the words, "Thank you, Angel."

Then grinning broadly, she picks up the box.

Inside is the three-layered chocolate cake.

# Chapter Thirty-five

Hellie's time-shifting ability is out of commission for the most of the next two weeks. Even though, otherwise, she is completely unscathed, she is grumpy in the extreme.

Finding a time and place to meet with Jerrin and Skyler, however, turns out to be no big deal. Peter says if we're going to keep our training sessions short and if it's only going to be the four of us (five if he can arrange with his parents to have Cindy come over), we might as well use his duplex after work.

When Peter approaches his parents about allowing Cindy to spend a couple of hours with him two or three times a week for the rest of the summer, they are delighted. Besides giving them the opportunity to run their errands after the outside temperatures have cooled down in the evenings, it also lets them rejoin their Bridge club.

"Keep your eyes closed," Jerrin says to Peter, Cindy, and me, "and try to visualize where Skyler is while he moves around the room. Try seeing with your third eye."

Although the concept of the third eye is not new to me, treating it as if it is real and trying to use it is. Peter and Cindy both have an easier time than I do.

It is so frustrating.

I'm not accustomed to being at the backend of the class.

According to Jerrin, however, learning to access the third eye is the first step in mastering the use of magical defenses.

I grit my teeth and keep striving.

I can hardly wait for the upcoming weekend, and when I go to bed Friday night, I fall asleep, blissfully looking forward to a change of pace.

Saturday morning, I wake up to the sound of the weed whacker buzzing under my bedroom window. Last night before we said *good night*, Hellie and I realized that we'd lost track of whose turn it was to mow the lawn and whose turn it was to do the trimming.

251

## Sunshine and Shadows: Another Modern Fairytale

We agreed that whoever got out to the yard first could choose which task to do. Apparently Hellie decided to do the edging. I'm slower at it than she is, and I'm touched that she took the harder job.

I toss on some shorts and a tank top and gallop down the stairs.

I plan to just grab a bottle of water and skip breakfast, but my parents are sipping coffee at the bar between the kitchen and the dining room.

"Whoa," Dad says. "What's the hurry?"

"You and Hellie have been so busy lately," Mom says, "it seems like we've hardly seen you. We made Hellie sit down and have some breakfast with us. You can spare us a few minutes too."

Uh oh. This is not a good sign.

I appreciate it that our parents love us, but they generally have a *live and let live* attitude toward our lives. When they start insisting that we spend time together—especially on a Saturday morning when there is yard work to be done—something is not right.

Casual nonchalance is the only response to their opening gambit.

"Sure," I say. "I was just trying to beat the heat, but ten or fifteen minutes isn't going to make much difference one way or another. Are you cooking, or can I just grab what I want?"

"Either way," Mom says. "Do you want me to fry you some eggs?"

"Not really," I say. "When I opened the fridge, I thought the cantaloupe looked good. I'll have some of that and a couple of pieces of toast."

I turn around and pop two slices of whole wheat bread into the toaster and then get out the cantaloupe.

Every time Mom buys melons, as soon as she has a free moment, she cleans out the seeds (if needed), cuts the fleshy parts into bite-sized portions (removing the rind as she goes along), and then stores the pieces in clear plastic containers in the refrigerator. She discovered long ago that we are more likely to snack on healthy foods like watermelon, cantaloupe, and honeydews if they are visible and convenient. She cuts up fresh pineapple the same way.

All other fruits we have to manage on our own.

I fill a cereal bowl with chunks of cantaloupe.

When my toast pops up, I butter it.

Then I sit down at the end of the bar and look at my parents.

"What's up," I ask while I spear a piece of cantaloupe with a fork. I chew while I wait for them to answer.

"Does something have to be 'up' for us to want to spend a little time with our girls?" Dad asks.

"Well, yeah, pretty much," I say. "Especially when you go to this much trouble to corral us one at a time."

My parents give each other one of those *Well-she's-YOUR-daughter* looks. They drive me crazy.

Why not go straight to the point and get it over with?

"It's actually no big deal," Dad says.

"It's Grandma Dark," Mom says at the same time.

My heart stops. "Is she okay?"

"Ooooh yesssss," Dad says, drawing the words out dramatically.

"You don't need to worry," Mom says. "She's fine. In fact, she is so fine that she'd like to spend an entire month with us."

"A whole month? That's great!"

Grandma Dark is an unorthodox combination of a gypsy, mystic, fortune-telling hippy and a very cool, up-to-date, modern grandmother.

Hellie and I love having her around, but she's never stayed longer than a week with us before except once when mom was sick and again when mom had surgery. Even then, it was only a couple of weeks each time.

"So, what's the problem?" I ask.

"Well," Mom says, "we can adjust to having her camping out in the family room for a week, even two weeks in a pinch, but an entire month?"

"That's easy," I say. "Hellie and I can double up in one room for a month. We can flip a coin to see who gives Grandma her room. Ask Hellie. I'll bet she tells you the same thing."

"We already did," Dad says, "and she already did."

"Super. Has Grandma bought her plane ticket yet? Do we know when she's coming?"

"No," Mom says. "She insisted that we talk with you girls before finalizing her plans. She said she didn't want to force her way into our home for such a long visit if it was going to put a stress on anyone."

"Tell her I vote for her coming and staying as long as she wants—or as long as she can stand us."

When I finish eating, I give Mom and Dad each a quick kiss on the cheek and then go out to mow the grass.

Since I had to take time to eat and chat with the folks, Hellie has already edged the front yard and has started on the back. I mow the front yard first. When I come around the side of the house so I can begin on the back, Hellie is hanging the weed whacker on its hook in the shed.

"I'll start deadheading," she says.

By the time I finish mowing, she's almost done with the petunias. We do the last of it together.

Both of us are hot, sticky, and covered with dirt and bits of plant debris.

"Why don't you go shower while I finish out here?" I suggest. "Then you can make our lunches while I get cleaned up."

"Excellent idea," Hellie says.

After dumping the bucket of wilted petunias into the garbage can, I put our gardening gloves and buckets in the shed and pull out the leaf blower. I clear away the grass trimmings from the driveway and the sidewalks in front and then continue with the sidewalk as it winds around the house to the back porch. I end with the patio. I put the blower away and lock the shed. Then I turn on the hose and water the flowers in the decorative pots.

Finished!

When I enter the kitchen, Hellie has bathed and is pulling things out of the refrigerator.

"By the time you've showered," she says, "I'll have lunch packed and ready to go."

When I get back down to the kitchen, all showered and dressed, Mom and Dad are leaning on the bar talking with Hellie. Mom has a purse dangling from her shoulder.

"We were just telling your sister," Dad says, "that we're going to drive over to Silver Mine City to have lunch and then to do some shopping. We'll plan on being home by dinnertime."

"Hellie has her house key with her," Mom adds," but I think you should both take your cellphones if you're going into the woods."

I laugh as I pull my phone from my pocket. Hellie does the same. "You automatically put on shoes when you're going out. We automatically pick up our phones. It's a generational thing."

While we are talking, Hellie finishes preparing our lunches. She puts four bottles of water, two small bags of chips, two sandwiches, two bananas, and two individual bottles of orange juice into her backpack. She slips her arms through the straps.

"I'm ready," she says.

As she steps away from the counter, I notice a plastic sandwich bag full of crushed chocolate chip cookies nearly hidden behind the toaster. She must have gotten distracted by the folks and forgot about the offering. I give her a quick nod of the head in that direction. She picks up the bag and stuffs it into her pocket.

"I'm ready to go too," I tell her.

"Have fun," Mom says, "and be back here no later than 5:30. We'll probably pick up dinner on the way home."

"5:30," I say.

Within minutes, Hellie and I have crossed the yard, scooted through the hedge, and turned south toward the pond.

"I'm nervous," Hellie says. "What if the stwethil-thage have changed their minds over the past couple of weeks? I thought we'd be able to get back to them quicker than this, but with everything that's happened—"

"Then you'll just have to find another clan," I tell her. "Say, what do you think about Grandma Dark coming here for a month?"

"I'm delighted, of course," Hellie says, "but the timing seems strange. We're eighteen years old, and except for a couple of emergencies, she's never come to visit us for longer than a week before. Now, here we are with all of this complicated magic stuff going on, and this is the time she decides to come for a long holiday? Why now? Why not for our graduation? Or why not in the fall when we're ready to start college?"

"Do you think that she senses something's wrong? She comes from Bree-Ella's direct line, just as we do."

"I don't know," Hellie says. "Unless things level out soon, I imagine we're going to be too busy to worry about it."

"At least until she gets here," I say. "If things don't settle down, Grandma could become another complication."

When we get to the meadow, we do a quick reconnaissance to make sure none of the neighborhood kids are hiding in the bushes and to make sure there are no new messes.

Everything looks fine. Hellie reaches out to the chief that she talked to earlier. He is still interested in our forest.

Hellie opens a doorway.

Whereas the portals Jerrin opens have sort of a "heat wave" appearance and mine are just a reddish splotch, Hellie's are beautifully opalescent.

Usually no one bothers to look through a doorway. It opens, and the next second you're on the other side. But it doesn't have to work that way. If you want, you can take your time and look around before you go through. That's what Hellie and I do today.

Beyond the milky-white haze of Hellie's portal, I see ginormous trees with dark brown bark and bluish green leaves. On the ground below the branches are spikey patches of grass between mounds of brilliant yellow flowers that seem to have crepe paper petals. Strange, multi-colored birds flit through the air, and a beetle the size of a teacup plods through the foliage.

Half a dozen balls of bright light drift toward the doorway on the Auravalian side.

Hellie and I step through.

Inside each ball of light is a tiny little creature. They're about five or six inches tall, and Hellie was right—they are amazingly cute.

Their pointy ears are a little too large for their humanesque faces, which have two round eyes, tiny little noses, and mouths without visible lips. Although their heads are mostly bald, they have a narrow strip of hair that starts just a little higher than their eyebrows and goes down the middle of their scalps and stops at the base of their skulls, like a long Mohawk haircut or possibly a horse's mane. Their hands and feet have three digits instead of five. Their leathery wings look way too small to support their weight—but then so do the wings of the Auravalians.

And the colors! Holy cow! I've never seen such vivid shades of pink and green and blue and purple and—

A fiery orange stwethil-thage flies right up to Hellie, almost nose to nose. "You are Hellie," it says in a chirping voice. "I am Valadoric, chief of this clan. You may address me as Val."

"I am happy to meet you, Val. This is my sister, Angel."

He gets right in my face too. "You and your sister look alike."

"Yes," Hellie and I answer together.

"How odd," Valadoric replies. "You say you have a forest with no stwethil-thage and none of the beasts that hunt us."

"That's right," Hellie says.

"That is also odd," the tiny chief muses.

To me he sounds skeptical.

When he starts to fly away, I remember what Master Cushing told me to do. I visualize our meadow with its lovely little pond, its ring of towering pines, and the diverse clusters of flowers. I include a gentle breeze and the sweet scent of life.

At the same time, Hellie takes the bag of crushed cookies from her pocket. "We brought you a little treat."

Val pauses and turns around, smiling.

I wish I knew if it was my visualization or Hellie's offered goodies that made the difference in his attitude.

Probably the food! But I like to think I contributed.

Val flies over to examine the bag.

Hellie opens it and dumps a tablespoon or so of crumbs onto her palm. "We do hope that you'll like this."

Val lands on Hellie's hand, picks up a chocolate chip, and nibbles on it. I continue to concentrate on the beauty of our forest before it burned.

"Oh, yes," Val says. He tries a chunk of plain cookie next. "This is very nice." He motions with his hand, and the other stwethil-thage alight beside him.

I wonder what their three-toed feet feel like on Hellie's hand. I wish I had a palm full of cookie crumbs too so I could find out, but I don't want to reach for the bag and risk disturbing the current scene.

The rest of the stwethil-thage start nibbling on bits of cookies.

"Oh, yes," they say in unison, sounding like a delayed echo of their chief. The crumbs disappear from Hellie's hand.

"Would you like to come through the portal now and look around our forest?" Hellie asks.

"We will look," Val says.

Hellie leads the way.

As soon as the stwethil-thage enter our world, they flutter around and check things out.

They sample the water in the pond.

They smell some flowers and taste the petals of others.

They fly up into the trees and crawl along the branches. Then they swoop down so they can shuffle through the grass.

Val picks up a few spherical objects that might be seeds, smells them, and passes them on to his deep purple comrade, who pops them into his mouth and chews them up.

"Not bad," he says.

Val rubs his hands in the dirt and then licks it off his fingers. He chases a butterfly, pets a ladybug, and chirps at a passing bluebird.

Then Val and his friends huddle together and talk.

When their consultation is complete, they position themselves in an arrowhead formation: Val in front, two stwethil-thage behind him, and three in a line behind them. Maintaining the configuration, they fly up to confront Hellie and me. They hover at our eye level.

"There is much sickness here," Val says. "The plants, the soil, the creatures, and the water all yearn for the loving care that your other stwethil-thage took away with them. We will provide it if we can."

"You'll stay?" Hellie exclaims.

"Yes, for now," Val says. "We will gather our best healers to see what can be done. If we can return health to the land, we will bring our families through and settle here."

"I'm a mage," Hellie says, "and a member of the royal family. I can make a portal for you so you can come and go as you please. It will only allow you and your people to pass. None of those who hunt you will be able to follow."

"I am not a mage," I tell them, "but I have the power to attract strength and wellbeing to living things. I love this forest, and I would be honored to help your healers as much as I can."

Val flies right up to my face again. "Hmm. You have not always loved this place, but now you do. That is remarkable."

Val eyes the bag in Hellie's hand.

"While we try to heal the land," he says, "it would be nice if you brought us things to eat. We will carry food with us, and there are many nutritious things living and growing here, but none are quite as nice as the gift you brought us today."

"We'll leave this entire bag of treats with you," Hellie says.

"We don't want to just put goodies on the ground," I add. "While you were looking at things, did you notice anywhere that would be a suitable place for us to leave food for you?"

The stwethil-thage crowd together in a huddle again.

"No," Val says, "but Lendorin is our head builder, and he said he felt a potential construction over there." He points to the white bricks that Hellie wanted to use to create a pavilion. "He said you had a plan but discarded it. He can help you make it work."

A lime green stwethil-thage joins Val. "Your building materials are nice and can be made sturdy, but what are the *smoking neighborhood boys* that you fear will try to destroy a new structure?"

"They are willful and rebellious adolescents," Hellie says with rancor, "who sneak back here to hide from their parents and to engage in forbidden activities."

The resultant stwethil-thage laughter is like wind chimes in a tornado—musical but terrifying. It is not a pleasant sound.

"We have had to deal with Auravalian youngsters," a florescent pink stwethil-thage says. "We are not without powers. We know how to handle adolescent troublemakers."

"Did these adolescents bother your previous stwethil-thage?" Val asks.

"I don't think so," Hellie answers, "but the others lived farther away from human homes." She points to the burned-out forest in the north. "Also, the stwethil-thage usually stayed hidden when humans were close."

"Did the smoking boys start the fire?" Val chirps ominously.

"We don't know who or what started the fire," I say, not liking Val's tone of voice, "but we believe it was an accident."

"Well," Lendorin says to Hellie, "why don't you show me what you had in mind for us. Then I will see about assisting you."

"Angel," Hellie says, "help me carry some bricks over to the other side of the pond."

I shake my head. "Jerrin told me to practice my skills every chance I get. Let's just make a stack of bricks. Then you tell me where you want them, and I'll send them there."

"That's even better," Hellie says with a grin.

We make six stacks of six bricks each. Three dozen seems like a lot to me, but I don't know what Hellie has in mind.

She points to a shady spot. "How about over there by the wild rose bush?"

"Okay."

The bricks feel heavier than the canned, bottled, and boxed goods that I sent to the food bank, but they have the advantage of being arranged in a more compact bundle.

I focus my attention: I want. I believe. I concentrate. I make it happen.

The bricks appear right where Hellie pointed.

In the shadow of the wild rose, Hellie uses a stick to inscribe a rectangle in the dirt. She uses three bricks end to end to establish the length, and six bricks side by side to establish the width.

The stwethil-thage stand in a line and watch.

Hellie loosens the dirt with the stick and starts to scoop out soil with her hands. I call a garden trowel to me and give it to her.

She smiles. "You're becoming handy to have around."

She digs down about an inch and a half, levels the ground with the side of the trowel, and then pats the dirt down to make it smooth. Inside the depression she lays bricks as tightly as she can, making a foundation that looks about two feet long and a little over a foot and a half wide. She plugs the holes in the bricks with mud. At each corner of the rectangle, she sets a brick on end like a pillar. On the shorter sides, she stands up a single brick in the middle, and on the longer sides she divides the space into thirds.

When she's finished, she's created a cute miniature picnic pavilion. All it needs now is something to cover the top.

"We have some boards at home that I thought I could cut to size and use as a roof," Hellie says.

"You have created the basic structure," Lendorin says. "Perhaps you will allow us to finish it."

"By all means," Hellie tells him. "Go ahead."

Grinning with his no-lips mouth, Lendorin steps onto the brick floor.

He glides across it as if he is ice-skating. While he skims over the rough surface, it alters and becomes as smooth and glistening as polished marble. When he comes to the pillars at the corners and on the sides, he skates around the bases and then takes flight, going around and around and around each brick, trailing his hand along the surfaces until they soften and reform into round columns that match the glossy floor.

When Lendorin has finished, he lands beside Val and strikes a "ta-dah" pose. The other stwethil-thage give him a round of applause. Hellie and I join them.

"My turn," says a lemon yellow stwethil-thage, whom Val introduces as Alavic. (I think she's female. She is slightly smaller than the others and has softer features. I'm only guessing. I have no idea how to determine gender).

The yellow stwethil-thage flies up and grabs a leafy twig on the wild rose bush. She pulls on it gently, and it grows. Starting level with the floor, she weaves the tendril in and out among the columns on two sides of the pavilion: the sides that face north and east.

As she works her way up the columns, the tendrils grow new shoots that sprout new leaves, filling in the blank spots. When she reaches the top, she flies from north to south above the structure, then from east to west, weaving over and under, back and forth until she has created a rooftop of foliage. Tendrils sprout at each column on the western and southern sides and twine their way down to the floor, attaching the roof to the open sides of the building.

She flies under the roof, pops up through the center, and pulls on the twig so it trails after her. The gap she made in the middle of the roof quickly fills in. Then Alavic twists the end of the twig around the original branch. When she lets go, the branch pulls the roof up, making the top look like a tent.

Lendorin tells us, "This will fool your smoking neighborhood boys. They will see nothing except the rose bush if they look in this direction."

"But it's not completed," says the florescent pink stwethil-thage. I think this one is female, too. She's the one who said they could handle adolescent troublemakers, and she sounded just like a mother.

She flies around the structure. Every now and then she flicks two of her fingers, and each time she does, a rosebud develops. By the time she lands again, the bush is covered with blossoming pale pink flowers.

"It's beautiful," I say under my breath, "like a temple or a cathedral."

"Yes," Val says. "Stwethil-thage do not build places of worship, but if we did, this is what they would look like."

Hellie opens her backpack, takes out a pretty patterned plastic saucer, dumps the remaining cookie crumbs onto it, and sets it inside the pavilion.

"We'll bring you something every time we come to the forest," she tells Val. "I'm afraid it won't be every day, but we'll come as often as we can."

"We will receive your gifts with most gracious gratitude," he says solemnly.

"Perhaps you'd also like something special to drink," I suggest.

"Good idea," Hellie says. She pulls a bottle of orange juice from her pack, opens it, and pours some into the lid. "Is this something you would enjoy?"

Val tears himself away from the cookies to sample the juice. He has to wrap his arms around the bottle cap to lift it. Still, he manages to drink without spilling anything.

"Oh, yes," he says, "this is very nice, too."

I reach for Hellie's backpack, thinking I'll pull out the water bottles. If we use the caps off them plus the one from the other bottle of juice, we'll have five more cups, one for each of the other stwethil-thage.

I look at Hellie and try the family telepathy. I project the image of my plan and ask her, *What do you think?*

*If we take the lids off of all our bottles, we won't be able to carry the liquids without making a mess. Why don't you try calling my miniatures to you? I could open a portal, but I hate to leave even for a minute.*

I answer with a nod.

I know where she keeps her miniature dishes. The box they're in appears on my outstretched palm. I hand it to her.

She removes the lid and takes out six tiny cups and two matching teapots.

She fills the cups and both teapots with orange juice and sets them in front of the cookie crumbs. The five other stwethil-thage are quick to give the new drink a try. Val finishes the juice in the bottle cap before reaching for one of the cups, which turns out to be the perfect size for his hands.

The stwethil-thage respond with a series of *Oh, yeses,* just as they did before. They drain their cups and use the teapots to refill them.

Then they settle down, alternating cookies with orange juice.

"I'll make your portal now," Hellie says, handing me the bottle of juice so I can refill the teapots as needed. "Then my sister and I will leave you."

It only takes Hellie a few minutes.

When she's finished, she provides instructions. "To activate the portal from this side, say 'Home to Auravale.' To activate it from the other side, say 'To the forest.' If for any reason you need to move the portal to a new location on either side, simply go where you want it to be, and say 'Portal, come to me,' and it will move. Do you have any questions?"

"No," Val says. "I think we will be happy here. We will bring our healers tomorrow and begin to work."

Leaving their treats behind, the stwethil-thage fly up and take their arrowhead formation.

Val says, "Home to Auravale." They fly through the portal.

The floor of the pavilion is a mess, covered with scattered cookie crumbs and puddles of juice. I wonder if we should clean up before we go so the place doesn't fill with ants.

I don't get to ask Hellie for her opinion because the stwethil-thage, still in their arrowhead formation, are back in an eyeblink.

"It works very well," Val says. "Thank you, Hellie and Angel."

"You're welcome," we say in unison.

Like the arrow they resemble, the stwethil-thage shoot through the air and swoop back into the pavilion. They gather around the plate of cookie crumbs, fill their cups with orange juice, and begin eating and drinking in earnest.

# Chapter Thirty-six

When Hellie and I walk away, we have no particular destination in mind. We simply go where our feet take us.

We end up at the grotto and sit down in the dry creek bed to eat our lunch. As Hellie is divvying it up, I pose a question.

"Do you suppose we could do something so special for the new stwethil-thage that it would make the old ones jealous enough to come back. Surely our forest is big enough to house two clans."

"What a deliciously devilish idea," Hellie says. "There is one other fairly large patch of green left. It's in the northwestern corner and borders the highway. It's below a rise and has a nice little stream that's fed by the foothills. They could use it as a temporary base while they helped regrow the forest, and then they could choose any spot they liked."

"But," I say, "if they're getting treats daily from the Auravalian children, what can we bribe them with? Do they like anything more than they like eating?"

"I don't think so," Hellie answers. "They like telling jokes, solving riddles, flying, singing, and dancing, but not more than they like eating."

"What about—"

"Blackberry pie!" Hellie suddenly exclaims. "They LOVE blackberry pie more than any other food, and Auravale has no blackberries."

We glance at our burned-up forest.

"It'll be a long time before blackberries grow anywhere around here again," Hellie says sadly.

"Maybe," I say, "or maybe not. Master Cushing showed me how I can use my attracting ability on plants as well as on people and animals."

"How do you attract a plant to do something? They're stationary."

"They can grow," I tell her. "While you were keeping us in a bubble outside of time, Master Cushing talked me through the process of helping a sickly plant become healthy. It leafed out, grew nine new inches of stem, and blossomed in a matter of seconds. Maybe he could help me reestablish the blackberry bushes."

"I'd love to see them flourish again," Hellie says, "but remember when we wanted to transplant some closer to the house? Dad talked to the man at the Garden Shop. He said it takes two years after being planted for blackberries to produce fruit. I think the canes grow one year, lie dormant the next year, and then blossom and create berries the third year."

"Maybe there's a way to make them go through the cycle super-fast," I suggest hopefully. "Maybe Cushing and I could manipulate the plants so just a couple of days equal a year."

"Too risky," Hellie says. "If we had blackberry bushes blooming among the charred tree stumps, someone would be bound to notice."

"Not the people in the neighborhood," I say. "No one but the junior high school kids sneak through the hedge, and I don't think they pay enough attention to the environment to see the forest for the trees."

"Ha, ha," Hellie says with a grin, "but you're right. The real risk would be from the air: the hospital's life-flight helicopter or planes from the private airfield on the outskirts of town. Still, if someone noticed, he'd tell others, and we might end up in a mess we couldn't explain."

I sigh. "They're too expensive to buy enough for a bunch of pies."

We eat while we consider the problem.

As Hellie opens her backpack so we can stuff the trash inside, she suddenly stops. "We've ignored one important factor."

I quit gathering rubbish and stare.

"The king of Auravale wants the stwethil-thage to come back here as much as we do. I'll bet he'd be willing to pay for the blackberries if it would help persuade the stwethil-thage to retrieve Bree-Ella's artifacts for him."

I finish stowing our garbage inside Hellie's backpack before I climb to my feet and brush dust and leaves off of my fanny.

I say, "We'd have to figure out the best way to approach the stwethil-thage before we presented the idea to His Majesty. We might be able to bribe them back for a while with a few pies, but they'd probably leave as soon as the pies were gone. We'd need to create a situation that made them want to return and to stay."

"Well," Hellie responds, "we have time to consider possibilities. The berries in our forest always bloomed and ripened earlier than those grown in the mundane world. We'll probably have to wait at least a month before we can buy fresh blackberries anywhere around here."

"True," I say, "and we'll need the time to develop a plan. It'll have to be spectacular to pry our old stwethil-thage away from their adoring and generous fans."

As we amble homeward, we toss ideas back and forth.

"I've got it!" Hellie exclaims. "How about a *welcome to our forest* celebration for the new clan? We could have it in the clearing by the pond.

The old stwethil-thage are more child-like than this new group. They're almost like little kids. I don't think they'd like another clan getting all of the attention."

"Not to mention," I add, "getting all of the pies. Of course, they'd probably expect a *welcome back to the forest* party of their own."

"Two parties would be fine with me," Hellie says with a little laugh.

"We could invite the king and queen, Skyler and Jerrin and their wives, Neeve and Karissa and Karissa's brothers if she's told them about Auravale, Shiane, Peter and Cindy, your friends at the Quick Fix Repairs shop, that doctor what's-his-name—"

"Mertley," Hellie says, "and don't forget Kaden."

"Kaden, of course," I agree, "and our former stwethil-thage residents."

"We could make it a real big deal," Hellie says. "I think Brenlyn, my boss at Quick Fix, would let us borrow his portable generator so we could have twinkle lights in the trees."

"And big crepe paper flowers," I suggest.

"We'd need some kind of entertainment," Hellie says, "at least music."

We're both getting caught up in the excitement.

"We'll have to provide a variety of finger foods and soft drinks," I say.

"And lots and lots of blackberry pies!" Hellie exclaims.

Then I have a new thought. "What about our human neighbors? How do we keep them from noticing the commotion and trying to crash the party?"

"I don't know," Hellie answers, "but don't worry, Jerrin will."

"Let's see if we can get everything planned out so that when the blackberries are in season we can go ahead and schedule the event."

"If our old stwethil-thage agree to come back," Hellie says, "and if the new ones agree to stay, maybe the forest will recover fast enough that we can see new greenery before winter."

My enthusiasm dies a little when I remember a comment Hellie has made several times. "You've mentioned before that our old stwethil-thage are very timid. Do you think they'll come to a party hosted by humans?"

"Maybe," Hellie says, "if we present it right. First of all, they're not shy around Auravalians, and if we have more Auravalians than humans, that might help them feel safe. Second, I saved them from the fire, so they're my devoted fans, and since you're my sister and we look alike, that might intrigue them. Third, they might actually enjoy having another clan of stwethil-thage as neighbors."

"Even if we can't lure the old clan back," I say, "I really like the idea of a *welcome to our forest* party for the new one."

Hellie and I spend much of the weekend planning and making lists of things that will need to be done to have the kind of party we envision. It'll take time, preparation, and money.

The money could present a problem since we're both saving as much as possible for college. We discuss asking the king to foot the entire bill, but we agree something that drastic would require a lot of thought before we considered it seriously.

As soon as Jerrin decides Hellie has recuperated enough from her experience with the bubble outside of time, he has us go back to meeting at the hunting lodge.

Peter brings Cindy on Monday, Wednesday, and Friday evenings with the understanding that those meetings never go over an hour.

Then one night while Peter and I are enjoying a cool breeze in Centennial Park, Jerrin and Skyler unexpectedly join us. They suggest we sit at one of the picnic tables away from other people so we can talk.

"We're sorry to interrupt your evening," Skyler says, "but we want to share some information with you."

He seems to be talking directly to Peter.

"Through some clever and dangerous reconnaissance, we have learned that Stace Merek is being held prisoner in Chankoun. As we suspected, he was kidnapped by Maldon Darker, who escaped from prison for the second time a few months ago. We also learned that Maldon has been opening a doorway between our worlds and sending through the man who was harassing your mother.

"In the beginning, we planned to discover the exact location of Maldon's hideout and then solicit King Voeton's aid in recapturing him and recovering Stace.

"Unfortunately, we've learned that Maldon has made a pact with Voeton. We don't know what Maldon has agreed to do for Chankoun's king, but we know the king has vowed to protect Maldon from us. That means officially our hands are tied unless we want to plunge our country into war."

I feel Peter tense up.

His voice trembles when he asks, "Does that mean you're just going to let them torture Stace to death?"

"No," Skyler answers. "Just because we can't do anything overtly, that doesn't mean we're willing to tolerate this kind of cruelty. We know Maldon is holding Stace on the outskirts of Eloviev, which is the Chankoun capital city. One of King Voeton's minions has given Maldon the use of his manor, but we're not sure which one.

"Our father's most trusted advisors are currently working on several different plans. One group is trying to come up with the safest and most effective route into and out of Chankoun, another group is considering the best means of travel, and another group is reviewing personnel to find the best-trained, most qualified men to handle Stace's extraction. In the meantime, our foreign operatives are still working to identify the exact site of his imprisonment."

"How long do you suppose all of that will take?" Peter asks.

To Skyler I suppose it sounds like a reasonable and polite question, but I know Peter.

He is struggling not to explode.

We both know the best way to make sure an issue is never decided is to turn it over to a committee—or, worse yet, to several committees.

Perhaps Jerrin senses Peter's mood, because he answers for his brother. "The problem, Peter, is that we can't just open a doorway into Chankoun. The country is heavily shielded against Auravalian magic. Nor can we fly there since their border guards have weapons that not only can knock us out of the sky but can also destroy our wings in the process. We have to find a way to sneak across the border at night and go cross-country on foot without being caught. Chankoun is a large country. It won't be easy."

I feel the rage seep out of Peter to be replaced by hopelessness.

Jerrin places his hand on Peter's arm. "Based on our knowledge of Maldon, we're certain he won't kill your father until he gets the information that he wants either from him or from your mother. Maldon's most logical course of action right now is to find another messenger, which hopefully will buy us the time we need to devise a doable plan."

Peter doesn't say anything. He merely nods.

"Excuse me, Jerrin," I say, "would you answer a question for me?"

"Of course," he says. "Go ahead."

"You and Skyler seem more than a little put out that Maldon Darker has escaped from prison again. But if Maldon is your father's half-brother and if he is capable of opening doorways between worlds, how can anyone hope to keep him inside a prison cell? If you lock him up somewhere, can't he just open a portal to get out?"

"Yes," Jerrin answers, "if he has access to his powers, but when a magic user of any level is arrested, a special metal band is placed around each wrist and each ankle to block his magic. How Maldon is getting out of them is a mystery yet to be solved."

"Obviously," Skyler says, "he has been getting help from someone within the palace guards. Extensive inquiries are being made."

"Why doesn't the king just bind Maldon's powers?" I continue. "Hellie said you threatened to bind her powers if she didn't agree to training."

"Maldon is too old and too powerful for a binding to be effective," Jerrin says. "His mind would have to be completely destroyed, which is the same thing as a death sentence. Until he has been tried and convicted of the murders he is accused of committing, he cannot be executed under the law."

"Right now," Skyler explains, "none of the offenses Maldon has been convicted of carries the death penalty. We have evidence that he killed four merfolk when he escaped prison the first time. If convicted of those murders, he will be hanged. In the meantime, the best we can do is track him down, arrest him, and confine him in a more secure location until his trial."

I carefully don't let it show on my face that I know what that *more secure location* is supposed to be. I wonder if Hellie knows the king intends to use her powers to suspend Maldon Darker in a bubble outside of time. Probably not. I think she would have told me.

Now that I think about it, though, it doesn't make any sense.

What good will it do to put him in a time bubble if he comes out at exactly the same moment he went in? If his trial date is six months from now, even if he's inside the bubble for a year or two (or a decade or two), when he is released, his trial will still be six months away.

Unless?

I wonder if it's possible to turn Hellie's magic inside out. When we're inside the bubble, time proceeds for us but seemingly not for the rest of the world. What if it's possible for time to stand still inside the bubble and continue for those of us on the outside?

If they could do that, they could put Maldon away and never have to deal with him again. If he's suspended inside a bubble where time never changes, technically he isn't dead. He's not even aging. He's just waiting to be let out.

I shudder. I don't think anyone should have the power to do that to another person—not even to Maldon Darker.

# Chapter Thirty-seven

For the next few days, Peter vacillates between being angry and being depressed. Cindy senses the news the very next time we pick her up.

As always when I drive, Peter sits in the back seat with his sister. He helps get her seatbelt fastened and then he does his own.

"They aren't going to go get him, are they?" Cindy asks, beginning to cry.

I pull out of the driveway, hoping Mr. and Mrs. Bradley won't look out the window and see their daughter in tears.

"Skyler said they're working on a plan," Peter tells her. "If they don't want to start a war, they have to be careful."

"But, Peter," she says, "he's our other father and bad men are hurting him. Can't you do something? I'll help."

"Maybe they'll have good news tonight," Peter says.

We meet Hellie and Kaden at Neeve's apartment. Karissa is there too. Neeve opens the pathway to the hunting lodge for us since Hellie is still conserving her strength.

Cindy runs straight over to Skyler.

"Why haven't you gone to get him?" she demands, clutching onto his shirtsleeve.

"We're still not exactly sure where he is," Skyler answers. "But we haven't given up. We're going to try something different tonight. Kaden is a very powerful finder, but Chankoun is shielded against Auravalian magic. We hope, if we all join hands and support him, he might be able to make a crack in their defenses long enough to identify the location. Are you willing to help us try, Cindy?"

"Of course," she says. "I want Birdman to come home."

"Why are you having us do this?" Peter asks. "Surely you have access to magic users who are stronger than we are."

"We do," Jerrin answers, "but we don't want Maldon's spies to realize that we know he's in Chankoun and that he has Stace."

"What makes you think Maldon has spies?" I ask.

"Because they've been lurking around the palace ever since our father's coronation," Skyler answers. "There is still a faction that would like to see Maldon on the throne. We're not sure who all of his supporters are, and we don't want Maldon tipped off that we're coming. We plan to arrest him at the same time that we retrieve Stace."

"Chankoun is a large country," Jerrin says. "If Maldon has even a few hours warning, he could take Stace and disappear inside one of the massive urban areas, or he could hide Stace somewhere in the vast agricultural countryside. We don't want to give him the chance."

"Kaden," Skyler says, "are you still willing to do this? As the focal point, if there is a backlash of power from Chankoun's defenses, it will hit you first."

"I'm aware of that," Kaden says. "I believe it's worth the risk."

Skyler waves his hand and a large continental map appears in the air. The countries are outlined and labeled in red. Water masses are blue.

He has Kaden stand in front of the map with Jerrin holding his right hand and Hellie holding his left. Then he arranges the back row in this order: himself, me, Peter, Cindy, Neeve, and Shiane. He has us join hands, then he puts his left hand on Hellie's shoulder and has Shiane put her right hand on Jerrin's shoulder.

"Kaden," Skyler says, "we're in position. Are you ready?"

"Yes," Kaden answers.

"All right, people," Jerrin says, "we need to focus our attention on Kaden and surrender control of our powers to him. With us joined together this way, he should be able to syphon off what he needs fairly evenly so no one person ends up depleted. Also, we should be able to experience, on some level, what he does. Everyone, focus NOW."

I twitch when I first feel Kaden's essence touch me. Knowing that he is accessing and using a portion of my energy, a portion of my life force, gives me a weird feeling. My impulse is to close myself off, but I don't. I want to know what's happening.

Our conjoined minds hit resistance right away.

Kaden does something I don't understand, but I feel us slide right through a barrier.

Hooray, I think. We've made it past Chankoun's border defenses!

My feeling of triumph lasts about half a second.

Wham!

I feel as if we've hit a steel wall.

Kaden concentrates our powers like a blowtorch, aiming it at a single point and exerting a steady pressure.

More energy is pulled from me.

When we slid through the first barrier, it was no more difficult than punching a hole in tissue paper.

When we pass through the second one, it's more like swimming under water. The resistance isn't awful, but it takes effort to travel forward.

Suddenly, it feels as if rapid-fire projectiles are hitting us from every direction. Kaden continues pressing forward with the same slow, steady force. It's as if we're struggling through chest-high mud.

When we emerge from this obstacle, it's so sudden, I feel as if I'm going to pitch forward. The firmness of Skyler and Peter's grips keeps me upright.

A spot on the map begins to glow.

"Now, Karissa!" Jerrin says.

The shutter of a camera goes clickety-click, clickety-click as Karissa snaps photos in rapid succession.

Like on Google Maps, the image expands and becomes more distinct as we move closer and closer to the glowing dot.

Eloviev, the capital of Chankoun, is an enormous city. Zooming in on it must be like zooming in on Manhattan. There is a blindingly bright center, the downtown commercial area I presume. Scattered around it, in clusters of lesser brightness, are the bedroom communities, the suburbs.

Karissa continues taking pictures.

Skyler's grip on my hand loosens, so I loosen my hold on Peter.

Gently Peter pulls his hand from mine and puts Cindy's in its place, breaking the chain of power for only a split second.

From the corner of my eye, I see Peter take his phone out of his pocket.

Not wanting to give Skyler a reason to look in our direction, I stare straight ahead.

The images on the map continue enlarging. Now we can identify separate communities. Within a few more seconds, we can see streets and individual houses.

Even though the clacking from Karissa's camera is still going strong, I hear a soft tick-tick-tick coming from Peter's phone.

He's taking pictures too.

One house, the target, glows brighter than its neighbors.

We move in close enough to count the windows and the doors.

We view the structure from every angle.

"I've got all of it," Karissa says.

The map disappears.

Peter slips his phone back into his pocket.

The chain breaks apart.

We all head for the couches and the chairs.

Peter, Cindy, and I sit together.

Karissa hands Skyler the camera before she joins Neeve in one of the loveseats.

"Well done, Kaden," Skyler says. "Well done, everyone. I wasn't sure we could do it, but we did. As soon as the king and his advisers show the photographs to their informants, they'll learn who owns the property where Stace is being held. Barring unforeseen circumstances, they should have a rescue party ready to go within a few days."

In an aside, Skyler tells Jerrin, "I think this should count as tonight's training session."

"I agree." Jerrin turns to their younger brother. "Neeve, will you take everyone from Colorado back home?"

"Of course."

Jerrin raises his voice slightly. "We're going to call it a day. When you get home, I suggest you all eat something and get some rest. You can take the next few days off. Hellie or Neeve will call you and let you know when and where we'll get together again."

"Kaden," Skyler says, "are you going back with Neeve?"

"Yes," Kaden answers, "unless you prefer I do otherwise."

"I'm sure the king will want to ask you about Chankoun's defenses and the barriers you encountered," Skyler says, "but I doubt it will be right away. I'll let you know when."

We disperse.

And we wait.

After five days without word from Skyler or Jerrin, Peter calls me on the phone, sounding really agitated.

"Do you know how to reach them?" he asks. "This waiting is driving me crazy."

"I suppose you could call Neeve or ride your motorcycle over to his apartment. I'm sure he could put you in contact with his brothers. But if you're actually just looking for something distracting to do, why don't you come over and help me sort through some material on paranormal activities in our forest. I've got to write an article for the Founder's Day issue of the newspaper, and that's the topic Mr. Fenton gave me."

"Are you working with hard copies?"

"Yes. I printed out everything interesting so I could look at it all together. I need to come up with an angle."

"Why don't you bring it over here? I'll set up those collapsible tables I have and we can really spread things out."

"I'll be right there."

I dash upstairs long enough to brush my hair and my teeth. I grab my purse, my keys, and a box stuffed with papers from work.

Mom and Dad are watching television in the family room. I pop in long enough to tell them where I'm going. Luckily Hellie isn't using the car tonight. Kaden picked her up in Neeve's car about an hour ago.

"Holy crap," Peter exclaims when he starts pawing through the material I brought over. "Where did you get all of this?"

"Vanessa collected it before she started having trouble with her pregnancy. This was originally supposed to be her story."

"Listen to this," Peter says. He reads from an old, Xeroxed article, *"Dancing naked under a full moon is one of the ways to cast a complicated spell."* He drops the paper and it flutters down to the table. "Do people really believe this garbage?"

"Maybe not that particular quote," I tell him. "Nevertheless, some of these pieces are pretty compelling, especially the ones where three or four witnesses all tell the same story."

"I thought you were basically a skeptic," Peter says. "Aren't you the Angelica Prudence Powers who loves quoting Carl Sagan's *Extraordinary claims require extraordinary evidence?"*

"I don't know how many Angelica Prudence Powers you know," I respond teasingly, "but you must have me confused with one of the others. My motto is *Keep an open mind."*

"Well," Peter says, "you know what they say about open minds—just make sure your brains don't fall out."

I laugh. "I'll never become gullible, but right now I have so much extraordinary evidence that extraordinary things are possible that I'm willing to accept that as my starting point."

"Good for you," Peter says. "I think more things are possible than the average person wants to believe. Let's see what else you have in here."

He pulls out a stack of photocopied newspaper articles that are paper clipped together.

He flips through them.

"Some of these stories," he says, "go back almost to the Civil War, and they all report that there is a witch in the woods. Of course, they can't be referring to the same person. The first story was published in 1868 and the most recent one is dated 2015. That's over 140 years of articles that were current and considered newsworthy at the time, all about a witch in Powers Forest."

He puts the articles on the table and rummages around in the box some more. He pulls out the copies I made of *Witch's Wisdom,* the website by Miss Ellie. I suppose it's the spookiness of the banner that catches his attention.

I read through some interviews Vanessa did with a bunch of teenagers who reported having supernatural experiences in our forest just last year. Since the kids went into the woods to make out, to drink beer, to smoke pot, and to summon up demons, not necessarily in that order, they don't have much credibility with me.

I dump the interviews and pick up the stack of news clippings that Peter mentioned about the witch in the woods.

We spend a quiet ten or fifteen minutes, just reading.

"Hey," Peter says, "have you looked at this stuff by Miss Ellie?"

"I've glanced through it. Why?"

"On her home page she gives a history of witches and witchcraft that reads more like an article prepared for a scientific journal than fluff for the Internet. She says throughout history most of the people who were condemned as witches were accused and executed for the political, personal, or religious reasons of the accusers and had little or nothing to do with the lifestyles of the condemned.

"She goes on to say that self-proclaimed witches, the ones who provided services to communities before there were doctors or social workers available, were probably just observant and insightful people who were in tune with their minds, their bodies, and their environments and who looked for creative solutions to daily living problems by watching and understanding nature."

"Sounds logical," I say.

"But listen to this postscript: *All of that having been said, I cannot discount the possibility that some 'witches' were actually individuals who had developed physical and/or mental capabilities that were so far beyond those of their contemporaries that their skills seemed supernatural. Since the average human being is so limited in his or her belief system, viewing even a fractional increase in the innate intelligence of other people could produce dramatic and frightening results. Out of the billions of men and women who have lived on the earth, there must have been several who exceeded what was considered natural or normal. Depending on the eras in which they lived, these extraordinary people might have been called prophets, soothsayers, geniuses, demigods, or even witches.*"

"Seems to me like she wants to have it both ways," I comment. "First she says most witches were innocents who were falsely accused or they were self-styled naturalists. But then she turns around and says, based on statistical probabilities, there had to have been a few real witches who had supernatural-type abilities. I think she should have chosen a single point of view and stuck with it."

"Don't criticize what she says until you've read it all," Peter says. "Her website is full of well-written, instructive, informative articles. Under the heading *Homemade Health,* she includes grassroots remedies that even my mother uses: Aloe Vera and turmeric for burns, rice water for diarrhea, honey for cuts and scrapes, warm milk for sleep, and hot peppers and onions for stuffy noses and head colds. She also makes suggestions about how to turn everyday activities into aerobic exercise sessions and how to plan and make simple, nutritious meals.

"Under *Invaluable Intuition* she writes about the importance of learning how to appreciate silence. She discusses how to recognize messages from your body, how to identify dreams that are communications between your unconscious and conscious minds, how to let go of negative feelings, and how to focus on positives. She offers a lot of sound psychological advice.

"I think Miss Ellie is probably a well-educated woman who chose a catchy webpage title so she could pass on some useful, common-sense material to the masses."

I put down the papers I've been looking through. "You haven't addressed the one thing that I'm the most interested in: *Power in Powers Forest.*"

"That's her blog. She has a paragraph of explanation at the top. I'll read it to you: *I live in Colorado where there is a privately owned timberland called Powers Forest. It is beautiful and magical, as are all wooded areas. In places like these, fairytales were born. Here unicorns can run free, dragons can hide their treasures, and princesses can find poor, but honest, working men to marry. Here anything is possible. In this blog I'll tell you stories that have been inspired by this forest. Some are daydreams, some are retellings of old tales, and some are true. It is up to the reader to decide which are which.*

"After that there are numbered entries describing experiences or fantasies that occurred in your family's forest. There are no dates, so there's no way of knowing if she posts daily, weekly, monthly, or simply when the mood hits her. The top entry is #1137."

"Choose one at random and read it to me."

"All right," Peter tells me. "Pick a number between one and 1,137."

"Okay. I choose #1070."

Peter flips pages for a moment. "Got it: *Today while I was walking through the forest, I saw a beautiful girl who was nervously darting from one tree to another. Every now and then she stopped, looked around her, and trembled. I feared she was lost.*

"*As everyone who has ever read a fairytale knows, it is dangerous to ignore an opportunity to do a good deed, especially in the woods. One never knows what spirits might be watching, waiting to bestow a reward or to pronounce a punishment.*

"*What was I supposed to do?*

"*I was a trespasser and did not know if the girl would welcome my help or report my encroachment to the authorities.*

"*I had just decided that I must speak to her to make sure she was safe when a male voice called out, 'Darling, where are you?'*

"*She called back to him, 'Here I am.'*

"*Within minutes they were in each other's arms.*

"*Not wanting to intrude on their privacy, I blended back into the shadows. Powers Forest had worked its magic once again, for they had a love-bond that could never be broken.*"

Peter and I stare at each other.

"Did that have an awfully familiar ring to you?" he asks.

I laugh, but it sounds forced even to me. "So? Maybe this woman stumbled across a young couple who met in the woods. That doesn't mean it was us."

"It doesn't mean it wasn't," Peter counters.

"All right," I concede, "but it doesn't matter. Everyone knows we met in the woods a few times—"

"A few?"

"All right, so I didn't tell my parents how often. But what can anyone do about it now? It's in the past. We're together. Nothing can change that."

"How many people do you know that talk about a *love-bond that can't be broken?* Americans don't. We'd simply end the story with *They lived happily ever after,* or if we wanted to be fancy, we might say *Knowing they'd found true love, they lived happily ever after.* We don't talk about romantic bonds."

"Oh, come on," I say. "You don't think we have an Auravalian wandering through the family forest and then blogging about it, do you?"

"I don't know," Peter says. "I think I'd like to find Miss Ellie and ask her a few questions." He looks up at the clock on the wall. "On the other hand, I've had a long day. Maybe I'm just tired."

I glance over my shoulder. The clock reads 12:15.

"Holy cow," I exclaim. "How did it get so late? We've both got to work tomorrow."

I start gathering up papers, but Peter stops me.

"We can spend some more time on them over the weekend. Might as well leave them where they are."

He kisses me good night, and I head for home.

That was Wednesday.

The next morning, he calls me at work.

"Hey, Babe, I feel like I'm coming down with something. I don't have anything pressing to do at the garage, so I'm going home and back to bed."

"Do you want me to come over after work and cook dinner for you? Maybe I could keep you company for a little while?"

"You know I love having you here, but I really feel rotten. I would be terrible company. Besides, I don't want to make you sick too."

"Okay, but if you need anything, call me."

"I will. I love you, Gorgeous."

"I love you too, Peter."

275

# Chapter Thirty-eight

Thursday evening, there's no word from Peter.

I assume he's still sick in bed. If he's asleep, I don't want to wake him up, so I don't call.

Friday, still no word. Peter doesn't get sick very often, which is good, because he makes a very grumpy patient. I decide I'll give him one more day before I check on him.

Saturday, as soon as I finish my share of the yard work, I dash up to my room and ring Peter. I get his voice mail. I shower, and then I call a second time. Voice mail again.

On Saturdays, he opens his garage at noon.

I'm there and waiting.

He doesn't show up.

I drive over to his duplex.

I ring the doorbell, no answer.

I knock on the door, no answer.

I pound on the door with my fists, no answer.

The guy who owns the other half of the duplex comes outside.

"I haven't seen him for a couple of days," Buddy responds when I ask if he's seen Peter around.

"He told me he was sick," I say.

"Might be. I saw him around noon on Wednesday—no, I think it was Thursday. He was putting stuff in the saddlebags on his motorcycle. I thought maybe he was going out of town with his folks again. But if he was sick, maybe he was just going home so his mom could take care of him. I do that sometimes."

"Thanks, Buddy. I'll go check with his mother."

"Good to see you again, Angel." Buddy turns around and heads back inside.

I'm thoroughly frightened now.

Peter doesn't go home to his mother when he's sick. Having people around when he's not feeling well makes him cranky. The sicker he is, the more he just wants peace and quiet until it passes.

When I ring the bell, Mrs. Bradley answers. As soon as she sees me, she says, "You haven't heard from him either?"

Unable to speak, I just shake my head.

"Come on in."

As Mrs. Bradley offers me a seat, Mr. Bradley joins us in the living room.

"You don't know where he is?" Mr. Bradley asks.

Again, all I can do is shake my head.

"He called on Thursday," Mr. Bradley says, "and told us he wasn't feeling well. He said he was closing the garage so he could take a long weekend and rest up."

"I went over yesterday to take him some homemade chicken noodle soup," Mrs. Bradley tells me. "When he didn't answer the door, I figured he was asleep so I used my key to let myself in. He wasn't there. His bed was made, his kitchen was clean, and his motorcycle was gone."

"Where could he be?" I ask, finally finding my voice. "Why would he leave and not tell anyone where he was going?"

"I think he told Cindy," Mrs. Bradley says. "But she won't say a word about it to us."

"They've always kept each other's secrets," Mr. Bradley adds.

"May I talk with Cindy?" I ask. "Maybe she'll tell me something. I'd be grateful just for a hint that he's okay."

"She's in her room painting," Mrs. Bradley says.

I knock on Cindy's door, and when she doesn't answer, my first thought is maybe she's gone to join Peter.

Then I hear her voice. "Is that you, Angel?"

"Yes."

"You can come in."

I close the door behind me.

Cindy has her easel set up and there is color on the canvas, but she doesn't exhibit her usual enthusiasm when painting.

"Do you know where Peter's gone?" I ask her.

She nods.

"Is he all right?"

She starts to sniffle. "I don't think so."

She sets down her palette, rinses out a couple of paintbrushes, wipes her hands on a paper towel, then comes over and throws her arms around my waist. I lead her over to the window seat, and we sit down together.

"Where is he?"

She puts her hand around her mouth and talks into my ear, "He's gone to get our other father."

"How? He can't open doorways between worlds."

"He said someone was going to help him. He met a witch in the woods who knew all about Auravale and Chankoun and him and me. She told him his magic lets him see patterns and how things fit together. She said that's why he's so good with cars and motorcycles. She said that's why he's so good with me too.

"She gave him something to help him find our father. She said it would take him part of the way, and after that, he had to follow the patterns to where he needs to go. I wanted to see what she gave him, but he wouldn't let me. He told me he'd be back real soon and he'd have our father with him. Then he took something from his pocket, cupped it in his hands, said something, took one step, and he was gone."

She begins crying. "Now I need someone to go find my father and my brother."

"Have you told any of this to your parents?"

She shakes her head and sniffles. "You know I can't talk to them about magic or Auravale or Skyler or Jerrin or Neeve or Shiane or anything we've done together."

I put my arms around her.

"I'll talk to Skyler and Jerrin. If someone is helping Peter, they'll be able to figure out who it is."

"It's the witch in the woods," Cindy says.

"Then that's what they'll find out. Don't worry, Cindy, we're going to get them both back."

"Promise?"

"I promise."

We hug each other tight.

"Now," I say, "even if you can't talk to you parents about magical things, I think you should tell them that Peter said he had to go help someone in trouble and he'd be back as soon as he could. Do you think you can do that?"

"Uh huh. What about the witch in the woods?"

"If she knows about Auravale, then I'm afraid she falls in the magical category."

"Okay," Cindy says. I give her another hug.

"I'll call or come see you as soon as I learn anything."

When I return to the living room, Mr. and Mrs. Bradley are waiting for me. "Did she say anything?" they ask at the same time.

"Yes. I think she was worried about being disloyal to Peter if she repeated what he told her, which wasn't much."

"What did he say?" Mrs. Bradley asks.

"I think you ought to let her tell you. She's willing now."

Peter's parents rush to Cindy's room.

I let myself out.

As soon as I'm in the car, I start shouting mentally for Hellie.

*For heaven's sake,* Hellie's voice comes into my head, *what's the matter? You just about fractured my skull with all that noise.*

*Did you open a portal for Peter to go to Auravale?*

*Of course not! Why do you ask?*

*Because he's gone, and he told Cindy he was going to get their Auravalian father.*

*How did he intend to get there?*

*Cindy said someone agreed to help him. She saw him go, and her description sure sounded like he went through a portal.*

*Kaden and I are at Neeve's apartment. Let me ask Neeve if he knows anything.*

Since we're psychically connected, I expect to hear her conversation with Neeve, but I don't.

*Neeve doesn't know anything about it, and he's concerned. He's going to talk with Skyler and Jerrin. He suggests that you come over to his place.*

*I'll be there in twenty minutes.*

When I get to Neeve's apartment, Skyler, Jerrin, and Shiane are already there—Karissa too. I expected that. But Master Cushing is also present, which I didn't expect.

"What can you tell us?" Skyler asks.

"Not much," I say. "Cindy said—"

"Go back further," Skyler says.

"I don't know what you mean," I tell him. "Go back further where?"

"Go back to the last time you saw Peter," Jerrin says. "Something that happened recently must have prompted his decision to leave. Otherwise, why go now?"

"To me," I say, "the big question isn't why but how?"

"Once we understand the why," Jerrin says, "it might give us a clue as to the how."

"The why is obvious," I respond. "He got impatient because he hadn't heard from you."

"Is that a fact or an assumption?" Jerrin asks.

"What?" I feel like he's trolling for a specific answer to a question that only he knows.

"What you need to do," Jerrin says, "is start at the beginning of the story. That he's gone is the end of the story. His conversation with Cindy might be the climax. Is Peter's impatience the beginning? If it is, what happened next?"

I take a minute to shake off my journalistic bent (which is to start a story with the most important information and work backward to the details, of which *why* is often the least newsworthy) and try to think in literary terms (which is to start at the beginning and proceed through subsequent events, which should expose motivation, until everything builds up to a climax that produces an ending.)

The switch isn't easy.

I have to take a few minutes to organize my thoughts. Then I start talking.

"Wednesday evening Peter called me. He was frustrated because he hadn't heard from anyone about going to get his Auravalian father. He asked if I had the means of communicating with you two." I indicate Skyler and Jerrin with a quick nod at each. "I told him *no* and said that going through Neeve would probably be the easiest way of reaching you. Then I suggested that, if he was actually just looking for a way to distract himself, he could help me sort through some background information for an article I've been assigned to write at work.

"He seemed to like the idea and invited me to take the material to his house. He has two six-foot-long folding tables, and he offered to set them up in his living room so we had ample space for spreading out the papers. We spent Wednesday evening going through old fact sheets, dozens of newspaper clippings, and pages and pages of handwritten notes.

"Then Thursday morning he called me at work and said he was coming down with something so he was going to close the garage and go back to bed. When I didn't hear from him yesterday, I figured he was still feeling sick. I decided to wait until today to call him.

"This morning I tried his cellphone, but he didn't answer. I drove to the garage. He wasn't there. I went to his duplex, and he wasn't there either. So, I went to his parents' house. His parents didn't know where he was, but they thought Cindy might. I talked to Cindy, and she told me Peter was going to get their Auravalian father. She said he met a witch in the woods—"

"A witch?" Skyler asks. "In your family's forest?"

"Yes."

"I think we're still missing part of the story," Jerrin says. "Did the paperwork that you took to Peter's house have anything to do with witches?"

"Some of it. The article I have to write is about paranormal activity in Powers Forest. A coworker of mine named Vanessa did the research. It was originally her story, but she's had some complications with her pregnancy, so Mr. Fenton told me to write the story using her research."

"Tell us about the witch."

"Local mythology claims that a witch moved into our woods sometime in the early 1860s to get away from the Civil War. Back then, *The Shawon Gazette* was just a two-page newssheet established by one of our great-great-great-grandfather's cousins, Claud Barlow.

"In 1868, Claud printed a short article called 'The Witch in the Woods,' describing how a mysterious woman came out of Powers Forest, mixed a potion for a little girl who was dying of a fever, and saved her life.

"Going through the newspaper's morgue, Vanessa found a couple dozen similar stories covering a period of 140 years. Interestingly, all of the articles were positive, giving the witch credit for helping maidens find husbands, for healing the sick, for mending broken bones, for driving away bad luck, for helping barren women have babies, and even for curing one alcoholic, carousing husband of his bad habits so his wife wouldn't leave him.

"There were also a dozen or so stories about women who claimed to be the witch, but I think they were printed for comedic effect. Peter told me he read one that said a person has to dance naked under a full moon to cast complicated spells."

Jerrin murmurs, "I'd like to see that."

"Right," Skyler says, "as long as the practitioner is beautiful, young, shapely, and female."

"Of course," Jerrin responds with a grin. "That goes without saying."

"It's interesting," Master Cushing says, "but I don't see how that could make Peter take off on a dangerous journey by himself. Is there more?"

"Yes," I say. "There is a website on the Internet called *Witch's Wisdom,* written by someone who calls herself Miss Ellie. I printed out the whole thing because it is current and most of the other stuff Vanessa collected was old and outdated. Peter was fascinated by it.

"There's a tab called *Witch's Brews: Homemade Health* that's full of do-it-yourself healthy living tips. Another tab is called *Witch's Strengths: Invaluable Intuition,* and it lists steps a person can take to get in touch with his or her inner wisdom. But the section Peter and I were both the most interested in is called *Witch's Magic: Power in Powers Forest*, and it's her blog.

"In the introduction, Miss Ellie begins by stating that woodlands are magical and anything can happen in them. Then she says she's going to write about the experiences she's had while wandering through our forest. She says some of the stories are daydreams, some are old tales, and some are true. The entries are numbered, and Peter asked me to choose a number at random. When I did, he read the corresponding story to me.

"It sounded very familiar. Before I told my parents that Peter and I were seeing each other, we used to meet in the forest. The story Peter read could easily have been about us. She ended with something like this: *the forest worked its magic, and now the young couple's love-bond can never be broken.*

"Peter thought the wording sounded like she was talking about a soul bond, which he interpreted to mean that Miss Ellie was either Auravalian or knew someone who was."

"Did he make plans to go see her?" Jerrin asks.

"No. He said he'd like to meet her and ask her a few questions, but it sounded like a casual comment to me. Besides, her website doesn't show her real name or where she lives."

Skyler turns to Neeve. "How hard would it be for someone who is good with computers to find out who Miss Ellie really is and where she lives?"

"I've never tried anything like that myself," Neeve answers, "but there are hackers who can find out just about anything. Peter is really good at identifying patterns and figuring out how things work. I imagine he is quite computer-savvy, in which case it might not have taken him very long at all."

"All right," Jerrin says to me. "It's time to hear what Peter told Cindy. Try to remember it exactly if you can."

In my high school journalism class, the teacher said many people wouldn't talk to a reporter if the reporter insisted on taking notes or making a recording, so she had us practice interviewing each other and then writing down everything we could remember that was said.

I was pretty good at it.

The conversation with Cindy was short.

When I repeat it for Jerrin, I think I have it verbatim.

"She didn't say who was going to help him?" Skyler asks needlessly.

"No," I reply.

"Obviously what she gave him was a portal key," Jerrin says, "but where would she have gotten one?"

"She made it," Shiane says. "Miss Ellie has to be Bree-Ella Dark."

"No," Neeve tells her. "We age at the rate that is normal for wherever we're living. If Bree-Ella came here in the 1800s, she would have died nearly two centuries ago."

"Does that include mages?" I ask. "Before Bree-Ella came here, was there ever a mage who settled on Earth?"

"I don't know," Neeve says.

We all turn to look at Jerrin.

"I don't know either," he says. "Mages tend to live longer than the average person on Panelda, but I don't know if that's true on Earth."

"Regardless," Skyler says, "if Bree-Ella made a key and was growing old, she might have bequeathed it to someone she trusted."

"The newspaper articles cover 140 years," I say. "Maybe being the witch in the woods is like a family business, passed from generation to generation. If Bree-Ella made the key, she might have given it to one of her children. We know she had a child by Maldon Darker." I turn to Hellie. "You know more family history than I do. Did Bree-Ella have other children as well?"

"No, and her daughter, Edith, only had one child too. Neither Bree-Ella nor Edith ever married, but Edith's daughter, Marleena, got married and had several children. Our great-grandmother, Aura, wasn't the only daughter. But even if Aura gave a portal key to one of her children, it wouldn't explain the witch in the newspaper articles or how Peter got the key. Aura and her husband moved to Pullman, Washington, and that's where they raised their family. Our grandmother Dark still lives there."

"If Bree-Ella didn't make it," I ask, "who else might have?"

"I suppose Maldon could have," Skyler says, "but why would he bother since he can open portals?"

"Who makes the keys for the king?" I persist. "I don't suppose His Majesty has time to make them himself."

"Now, that's a thought," Jerrin says.

"But," Master Cushing says, "it presents the same problem that Hellie identified with Bree-Ella's passing a key to her descendants. It doesn't explain the witchy articles or how a portal key got into Peter's hands."

"I'm afraid this hasn't been as productive as I'd hoped it would be," Skyler says. "We need to move on to plan B."

"Angel," Jerrin says, "the next step is to ask you to focus on your bond with Peter to see if you can sense him. If he hasn't passed into Chankoun, I'll open a portal and go get him."

"Wouldn't it be easier if Kaden located him," I ask, "the same way he located Stace?"

"Generally," Skyler answers, "it would be, but Kaden assisted in a difficult and complicated healing yesterday, and Mertley doesn't want him to do anything today but rest."

"Regardless," Kaden says, "I'm willing to try."

Skyler shakes his head. "Even if you're not afraid of crossing Mertley, I am. I'm not going to risk having him take his anger out on me if you're unfit to return to work tomorrow."

I think Skyler is making a joke—I don't believe anyone is capable of intimidating him—but no one is laughing so I can't be sure.

"Angel," Jerrin says, "it's up to you. You and Peter are bonded. You should be able to sense him if you try."

"Just tell me what to do," I say.

# Chapter Thirty-nine

"Focus on Peter," Jerrin tells me, "the same way you focused on the meadow when you returned us to real time. However, you are not—I repeat—you are NOT to open a gateway. If anyone is going through a portal to get Peter, it will be me. Is that understood?"

"You don't have to worry about it," I answer. "You know I've never been able to open a portal without someone helping me. I just don't have the knack."

"All right. Focus on Peter. Think about how he looks, how he feels, how he smells. Let all of the complex emotions he inspires in you rise to the surface. Picture him in as much detail as you can, just as you did with the meadow. Now, I'm going to join my mind with yours to see if I can identify his location from the images you get back. Skyler and the others will join their minds with mine in case I need their help."

Part of me is embarrassed that so many people are going to see Peter and our relationship through my eyes, but the rest of me is grateful that they are willing to help me try to find him.

I close my eyes and envision Peter. I don't have to concentrate on him the way I did on the meadow. I had to struggle to remember details of the area around the pond.

All I have to do is think of Peter and images flood my mind.

I see his reddish-brown hair blowing in the wind, his changeable eyes going from green to blue to gray, his muscles putting a strain on the seams of a t-shirt, his body glistening with perspiration when he's shirtless on a hot day, his cocky expression when he's cooking me a special meal.

I can smell the spiciness of his aftershave, his musky aroma when he's been working hard, the lingering scent of grease, oil, and gasoline on his hands, and the smell of popcorn when we watch a movie.

I remember the taste of his mouth when we kiss. Even though I am vaguely aware of the Auravalian discomfort with that memory, I'm too intent on locating Peter to waste time or energy censoring what pops into my mind.

The physical images give way to emotional ones: Peter's volatile temper, his bad language when he's angry, his gentle patience with his sister, his devotion to his parents, his loving kindness and understanding with me, and his confusion and curiosity about his Auravalian father.

It's this last image that pulls Peter into focus in the here and now.

His arms are in the tight grasp of two men in strange uniforms.

A third man stands in front of Peter and scrutinizes him with disdain.

He looks a lot like His Royal Majesty, King Justus IV. He has the same brown hair streaked with white. His chin sports a similarly pointed beard. He is tall and broad, and his facial features are enough like the king's that there is no mistaking the family resemblance.

He also radiates an air of power and authority.

But this man would never be able to say, as Justus IV said to me, *I really am not a tyrant.* Or, if he tried, he would never be believed.

This man's power comes from dominance, from inflicting pain, from provoking terror, from arousing despair, and from debasing, humiliating, and brutalizing others.

I've never seen him before, but I know who he is.

He is Maldon Darker.

"Who are you?" Maldon demands.

"My name is Peter Bradley."

"You're human, aren't you?"

"Yes."

Peter is standing ramrod straight without any hint of anxiety or nervousness. I'm sure his heart is pounding like a blacksmith's hammer but it doesn't show. I'm so proud of him I could burst.

"Why are you here?"

"I've come for Stace Jory Merek."

"Why? What's he to you?"

"He is my father."

For a moment, Maldon looks stunned.

Then he doubles over with laughter.

"So that's it! That's why he won't break and neither will she. Stace managed to procreate. He had to mate with a human to do it, but then Bree-Ella was in no position to honor their bond after I forcibly broke it.

"I thought they were hiding Bree-Ella, but it must have been you and your sister they were protecting—you two, plus Angel and Hellie.

"If I can't have Bree-Ella, I'll settle for the twins. Of course, I'll have to break your soul bonds first. I haven't had the pleasure of breaking a soul bond in decades. I'll enjoy breaking yours in the same way I broke Stace's."

Sometimes I'm a bit slow. It doesn't occur to me what Maldon did to destroy Bree-Ella and Stace's bond until I hear Peter's reaction. He's always been smarter than I am. That's not modesty or self-criticism. It's just a fact.

"If you lay a hand on Angel," Peter yells, straining against the men who are holding him, "I'll kill you. I'll rip out your guts and shove them down your throat. I'll—"

"You'll do nothing to me," Maldon sneers. He looks at the guards. "I have no use for him. Take him to the Wastelands and give him to the sun."

I feel Jerrin pull at my mind.

"Let go, Angel," Jerrin says. "You don't need to watch this. Let go so Skyler and I can report to the king. None of the other kingdoms claim the Wastelands. We should be able to go there and get Peter."

The last I see of the man I love more than life itself is when four guards change into huge birds, clasp Peter's arms and legs in their talons, lift him, and carry him away.

I collapse sobbing onto the floor.

Through my tears I see Skyler, Jerrin, and Master Cushing disappear.

Hellie and Karissa help me up and onto a sofa.

"Neeve," I cry, "what are they going to do to him?"

Neeve's face gets that faraway look that means he's communicating via the family telepathy. When his eyes meet mine, his lips tighten into a straight line, and he shakes his head at me.

I turn to Shiane. "Please, tell me."

Shiane and Neeve stare at each other. Neeve shakes his head again.

Shiane gives me a grief-stricken glance before she vanishes.

I turn to the only other Auravalian in the room.

"Kaden?"

"Tell her," Hellie says. "If you know what it means, tell her. No matter how bad the truth is, it's better than letting her imagination run wild."

"I can't," Kaden says. "I am a subject of the king. If Neeve and Shiane can't tell her, neither can I."

I drop my head onto the arm of the sofa and cry.

I don't know how I'll ever stop.

Whatever they are doing to Peter, it's so bad that the king won't let anyone tell me.

Hellie kneels beside the couch and strokes my hair. "I'm so sorry. Try to have faith. Peter is tough. He loves you, and he wants to get back to you. He'll hang on."

I know she means well, but it's not comforting to know he's got to suffer and hang on so he can come home.

I want him safe now!

A thought tickles the back of my mind.

I sit up and wipe my face with my hands.

Neeve hands me a box of tissues.

"I'm sorry," he says. "Sometimes our father's decisions seem arbitrary,

Connie A. Walker

but I can assure you of one thing. He's angry as hell, and he has both councils meeting right now. He won't let them drag their feet for long."

"What's changed?" I ask as I sop tears from my face.

"Maldon bragged about forcibly breaking Bree-Ella and Stace's soul bond, and he threatened to do the same thing to you and Peter."

"Why is that significant?"

"In many ways," Neeve says, "breaking a soul bond is more serious than murder. If you murder someone, you merely kill the body and release the soul to join the Light. If you break a soul bond, you doom two people to the horror of half-lives in this world and the next. That's unforgivable. There will be no clemency for Maldon when he is recaptured. If he isn't executed, he will spend the rest of his life incarcerated in a maximum-security prison, and ours are nowhere near as nice as your American ones."

I use about a dozen tissues on my face and nose before I'm able to contain the waterworks.

"Where's a bathroom?" I ask Hellie.

She points me in the right direction. "Are you okay?"

"No," I say, "but I will be."

I hug her before I head for the privacy of the bathroom.

While Neeve was talking, the thought that was tickling my mind came into crystal clarity.

I have to make a choice.

When Shiane saw my future the night Peter, Cindy, and I were evaluated, she said a time of crisis was ahead of me.

This is it.

She said if I follow my heart, I face death, and people will be angry and try to stop me. If I follow my reason, I'll live with self-doubt, and people will be angry and blame me.

Now I understand what she meant.

There's a part of my magic that I haven't touched yet.

Master Cushing told me I could influence people, animals, plants, inanimate objects, and large groups. Hellie said I could influence human thought processes without causing harm. She also told me I influenced the position of the rainstorm.

When Jerrin was explaining magic to me, he had me toss him a pillow. After I did it, he said I influenced the position of the pillow through a series of unconscious, instantaneous decisions.

When I add it all together, I know what Master Cushing and Jerrin saw in my eyes that startled them, what they were glad I hadn't experimented with yet.

I have the power to influence myself, to allow myself to do all of the things I can influence other people and objects to do.

I can go get Peter.

I clamp down on the thought as hard as I can.

I don't want the telepaths to hear.

Hopefully they're all preoccupied with other concerns right now, having no reason to focus on me.

If I try this, since I don't actually know how to do it, I'll face death, as Shiane predicted, and if Jerrin senses my intention, he'll be angry and will try to stop me.

Even so, I have to make the attempt. If I don't, I'll live the rest of my life with self-doubt. Cindy will be hurt and I'll be angry, and we'll both blame me if Peter doesn't come back.

So many things make sense now.

I have trouble opening doorways between worlds because I don't need to use them. I can influence my location by myself.

I focus on Peter. I concentrate on how much I love him and how much I want to be with him.

His image fills me.

For the first time, I am absolutely certain of what I can do. The magic builds and builds, making my powers swell.

I can see the Wastelands.

I can see Peter.

I know what Maldon meant when he told the guards to give him to the sun. They stripped him down to his boxer shorts, tied ropes around his wrists and ankles, and then tied the ropes to spikes pounded into the ground so he is face up and spread-eagle under the blazing hot sun.

I am here.

I want to be there.

I know I can be.

I concentrate.

I make it happen!

Just as I feel the spell take hold, Jerrin bursts through the bathroom door. I hear his angry voice yelling at me. Luckily, I don't understand the language, but I think I just got cussed out in Auravalian.

I materialize next to Peter.

I don't know how long he's been out here, but more time has passed on Panelda than on Earth. Peter looks as if he's been out here for at least a day or two.

What the Auravalians call the Wastelands is really one huge, flat, glaring slab of salt mixed with a little sand. The dusty top layer is stirred by frequent gusts of wind and whirling little dust devils. It's difficult to imagine a harsher, more dehydrating environment than this.

Besides being red and blistered with sunburn, Peter's skin is scratched and abraded from the constant swirling grit. His lips are swollen and cracked. There are white crusty deposits in the corners of his mouth and around his eyes where saliva and tears have mixed with the salty air and then evaporated.

I call a bottle of water to me. I don't know where it comes from—Earth or Panelda—and I don't care. I dampen the hem of my shirt so I can moisten Peter's mouth and remove the salty residue. His lips part, and I lift his head so I can give him a small drink.

His eyes flicker.

He opens his mouth as if he wants to speak, but no words come out.

I give him another sip of water.

"You came," he croaks. "How?"

"First things first. Let's get you untied and out of the sun."

I try pulling up the pegs. I can't.

No problem.

I call a knife to me so I can slice through the ropes.

I help Peter sit.

He reaches for the water bottle and I let him take it.

His skin is so hot I can hardly bear to touch him.

Now that he has water, the next thing he needs is shade. I call a canvas pavilion that's open on three sides. It arrives fully assembled. I call for two matching camp chairs.

I help Peter move from his spot on the ground to one of the chairs.

Next, his skin needs to be cooled and cleaned so the burn can be treated. I call for a stack of washcloths and two pans of tepid water. As an afterthought, I call a camp table, so I have a place to work from.

Peter has been slowly sipping from the water bottle and watching me.

I dampen a cloth, wipe the salt from Peter's face, and then rinse the cloth in one of the pans.

I get a fresh cloth, wet it in the clean water, and fold it into a pad for his forehead. He holds in place with one hand.

I fold and drape another cool, moist washcloth on the back of his neck since I've heard that's where the body's thermostat is.

He leans forward so the cloth will stay put.

Gently I wash sand and salt from his shoulders and his back.

He sets the bottle on the table, rewets the washcloth that was on his forehead and uses it to wipe down his neck, chest, arms, and legs.

While he does that, I call for a can of Aloe Vera mist like the ones that Mom has always used on us girls when we've been sunburned. I spray it all over Peter's body. It'll take away the sting and re-moisturize his skin. For his face, I call a small jar of Aloe Vera cream and carefully smooth it on his forehead, cheeks, chin, and nose. For his mouth I call a lip balm that contains cocoa butter. It tastes better than aloe and works just as well.

With him shaded, cleaned, treated, and in the process of rehydrating, I figure it's time to get him dressed.

# Sunshine and Shadows: Another Modern Fairytale

I call a lightweight, button-front, long-sleeved, over-sized cotton shirt to protect his skin from further sun damage. It's not his style, but I don't think he could get a t-shirt on. Even if he could stand the pain of bending his arms and sliding them into the sleeves, unless the shirt was gigantic, pulling it down over his chest and shoulders would exacerbate his already inflamed and sensitive skin.

The cotton button-front is a better choice.

He lets me help him into the shirt. His hands are so swollen from the ropes and the heat that he has to let me do the buttoning. He doesn't even scowl at me, but I suppose that's because it would make his face hurt.

Adding insult to injury, I won't get him a pair of jeans even though that's what he wants. Instead, I call some loose, baggy, just-below-the-knees cotton shorts. The shirt and shorts are the same creamy white color. This time he does scowl as I button the waistband and zip up the front.

His feet are as sunburned as the rest of him. I don't think there's a prayer that he can tolerate shoes and socks. I call for a pair of flip-flops.

Dressed in the baggy white clothing, he hardly looks like himself. In fact, all he needs is the right kind of hat and some hiking books instead of the flip-flops to make him look like he's ready for his first African safari.

I'm so glad that we're together, even in this awful place, that I can't help but smile at him.

I guess he's glad to see me too. He cups his hands around the back of my neck, pulls me to him, and kisses me, and kisses me, and kisses me.

In the strange clothing, he might not resemble the Peter I adore, but there is no mistaking his kisses. I want to press against him for a full body hug, but I know his sunburned skin is too tender for that kind of pressure.

"Let's go home," I say.

"My father?" Peter asks. "He's why I came."

I am still brimming with magic.

I can almost hear my powers crackling like lightning bolts through my entire body.

"Do you know where he is?"

Peter crouches down. Using the knife I called earlier, he scratches a map in the salt.

"We're here," he says, marking the spot with an X. "The manor is here." He starts to draw another X, but instead he angrily plunges the knife into the ground. "It's quite a distance as the crow flies."

"I don't think I can get there by following a map," I tell him. "But I'm getting better at the family telepathy. If you visualize the building clearly, I should be able to take us there based on the image in your mind. But how will we find where they're keeping him once we get there?"

"According to Miss Ellie, people's minds are like car engines. Even though many appear to be the same make and model, each one is different.

My talents are all related to identifying patterns, designs, and configurations. Miss Ellie said that's why I chose to be a mechanic and why I can work with Cindy more effectively than anyone else can."

Peter gives his head a little shake.

"I'll explain it all when we get home," he says. "The important thing is that if you can get us to the manor, I can find Stace. I know where Maldon would hold a prisoner."

I stroke his face with my fingertips. "Are you sure you're strong enough to go right now? You look awful. Can I get you something to eat first? Or something else to drink?"

In spite of the thick coating of lip balm, Peter's lips are still swollen and cracked. Nevertheless, he managed to kiss me multiple times, so I'm not too surprised to see him grin.

"I'll admit I'm hungry. How about a couple of corn dogs and a Dr. Pepper? And another bottle of water?"

While he eats, I sit in the other chair, enhance my vision the way Jerrin taught me, and follow Peter's map the best I can. Even though I watched Kaden zoom in on the community and then on the neighborhood, increasing details until individual streets were defined and the house itself was identified, I'm not that good.

I search up one street and down the next, again and again.

When I finally spy the right house, I involuntarily utter one of Peter's pet swear words.

He looks over at me startled. "What's up, Babe?"

"They know we're coming."

"How?" Peter asks. "They think I'm out here roasting to death. They have no reason to believe anyone would come to rescue me. No one has ever come for Stace."

"Nevertheless, they're expecting some kind of trouble. Guards are patrolling the grounds, other men are crouched behind the windows, lying on the rooftops, and hiding in the bushes."

"Damn it," Peter growls. "I promised Cindy I'd have our father with me when I came home!"

"Personally," I say, jumping to my feet, "now that I think about it, I'm rather glad the guards have the place surrounded."

"Why?"

"Because if they're guarding the outside, they're not patrolling the inside."

# Chapter Forty

"Those guys might not be patrolling the inside," Peter says, "but someone will be."

"Maybe you're right," I say, "but the fewer people there are, the fewer we'll have to go through to get to Stace."

"Angel," Peter takes my hand and pulls me back into my chair, "what is going on with you? You seem almost gleeful at the prospect of taking out some bad guys. You're not thinking this through. Even through Maldon was born illegitimate, he is still a sorcerer and a member of the royal family. If you try opening a portal from here to somewhere inside the house, I think he'll be able to tell. We'll be overrun by guards or put down by magic before we can take half a dozen steps."

"Then," I say with a grin, "it's probably a good thing that I'm rotten at opening portals."

Peter gives me one of his Mr. Spock impressions, raising one eyebrow and looking skeptical. "Then how'd you get here? Did someone send you through?"

"My powers have to do with influencing. I can influence people, animals, plants, and inanimate objects. When I call things to me, I'm influencing the location of those items. Today, when I wanted to get to you, it occurred to me that if I can relocate objects, I should be able to relocate myself. I didn't open a portal to get here. I teleported, and when we have your father, I'll take us back the same way. No one will sense my magic when I teleport us into the house."

"What makes you say that?"

"Because it's what I'll wish."

"Angel—"

"We have a lot to talk about when we get home. Right now, just trust me when I say I can keep people from noticing our arrival. After that, we'll have to improvise." I smile at him and caress his cheek with my hand. "Let's go do what we have to do, so we can get out of here."

Holding his hand, I get to my feet and pull him up too.

We spend a few seconds just gazing at each other.

Then Peter becomes brisk. "I'll tell you what I know about the house so you can decide where to teleport us." He closes his eyes. "When I was captured, I was taken into the house through the back door. We immediately turned right and went down a steep flight of stairs.

"At the bottom to the left, is a large room filled with couches and tables and bookcases. While I was there, some guards were sitting around playing a game involving colored tiles and dice. Other guards were reading. Some were eating.

"On the right is a long hallway. There are doors about every twelve feet. I could see inside the nearest one, and it looked like a small bedroom to me. It's probably where the guards sleep.

"Straight ahead, about six feet from the bottom of the stairs, is a barred doorway. Maldon came through that door to confront me."

"Could you see through the bars?"

"Yes."

"What's on the other side?"

"A hallway that's about thirty feet long. At the far end there's a metal door. I'm sure that's where Stace is. Unfortunately, about two-thirds of the way between the barred entry and the metal door, there's a corridor that branches off to the left and to the right. I don't know what's down there."

"It seems to me that we should arrive fairly close to the metal door. It's too bad you didn't get to see what was on the other side, or I could take us straight there."

"Before we go, you probably ought to call me a baseball bat and a crowbar."

"I'd rather call you a couple of machineguns."

"I'd prefer that myself," Peter agrees with a nod, "however, I asked Jerrin about Auravalian firearms, and he said there aren't any. Gunpowder doesn't work here. They fight their wars with magic or with things straight out of our middle ages—bows and arrows, knives, swords, axes, and catapults."

"Why a baseball bat and a crowbar?"

"Well, I don't know swordplay, but I'm a heavy hitter with a baseball bat. The crowbar is in case I have to pry the metal door open."

Having watched Peter play baseball with his buddies, I know he prefers the Rawlings Quatro Pro bat, which is fairly pricey to buy, but I'm not paying for it, so I figure I might as well get him the best.

Since I know absolutely nothing about crowbars, I merely call him a sturdy, good quality one and let the magic fill in the blanks.

When Peter sees the bat, his eyes light up and he takes a couple of practice swings even though they make him grimace with pain.

"Nice, Babe," he murmurs.

Then he hefts the crowbar and glances down at his clothes.

"You could have at least gotten me shorts with belt loops. How the hell am I supposed to carry this thing?"

Being a natural born problem solver, he doesn't wait for me to make a suggestion. He picks up the knife and makes a slit below the waistband on the left side of the shorts. He slips the crowbar behind the waistband and out through the slit so it's riding on his left hip like a sword.

He finishes his Dr. Pepper and sets the can on the camp table. "What are you going to do with all this stuff?" he asks, waving his hand at the clutter, the pavilion, the chairs, and the table.

"Just leave it?"

"You wouldn't leave this kind of a mess in your forest. I don't think you should leave it on an alien world."

"Do you have a better idea?"

"Send the small stuff to my kitchen table, and I'll dispose of it when I get home. I guess the table and chairs can go in my living room for now, but I have no idea what to do with the pavilion. It would fit in my backyard, but the neighbors might talk if it just suddenly appeared out of nowhere."

"I suppose I could send it to the forest. There are some burned-out places where it would fit. No one's likely to notice it except for Hellie, and I'm sure she won't be wandering through the woods for a while. Jerrin is probably taking his anger with me out on her."

"Why would Jerrin—? Did he tell you not to come here?"

"Not technically," I answer. "He just told me I couldn't open a portal to you, which I didn't."

Peter takes my hand and kisses my palm.

I tingle all over.

"I think you're in for a bit of trouble when we go back," Peter says. "Jerrin doesn't strike me as the kind of guy who goes in for technicalities." He kisses my palm again. "There's nothing we can do about Jerrin right now. Let's go find my father."

Quickly I dispose of everything the way Peter and I discussed.

With Peter holding onto the bat with his right hand, I take hold of his left. "Ready?"

"Ready."

"Envision the area in front of the metal door."

I look into his mind and teleport us.

I should have used my enhanced vision to check it out first.

Just as we're materializing, half a dozen guards come down the stairs and see us through the bars. When I formulated the spell in my mind, I stipulated that no one would be able to sense our arrival, but I didn't cover the possibility of being spotted physically.

The guards start shouting, and a man elbows his way to the front of the

294

group while he tries to unhook a key ring from his belt.

Peter pushes me behind him.

At the same time, we hear foot beats running toward our position from the intersecting corridor on our side of the metal gate.

Peter raises the bat.

I'm so startled that my brain hiccups for a few seconds.

The man with the keys finally gets the ring off of his belt and is fumbling with the lock on the barred door.

I react in a state of panic.

I send his keys to limbo.

The pounding of feet gets closer.

Peter steps forward to meet it, and I hear a thunk as his bat catches the first man across the back. When the man hits the ground, Peter whacks him in the head.

Another man rounds the corner, and Peter takes him out with a jab to the pit of the stomach and then an uppercut with the tip of the bat.

In the meantime, I'm trying to do something with the men on the other side of the bars so they can't reinforce the ones that Peter is fighting.

It's hard for me to concentrate in all of the commotion.

The third man to come around the corner draws a sword, but Peter has the bat ready. He smashes the man's wrist, probably breaking it, and then bashes the man in the head with one of his heavy hitter swings.

These three will not be getting up any time soon.

The man whose keys I sent away yells that he's going to get the master key. Without really meaning to, I wipe that idea from his mind. He leans blankly against the wall, and I realize I need to replace the thought with something else.

I have him tell the other men that they all ought to go check on the security of the grounds. I feed him the notion that no military leader would send one guy and one girl inside a building except as a diversion while the main force attacks from the outside.

I influence all the other men to believe him, and they pelt up the stairs.

I turn my attention to Peter.

Although three men are sprawled on the floor, Peter didn't win his victory without effort. He leans against the wall and breaths in uneven gasps. Two corn dogs, a Dr. Pepper, and some water weren't enough to make up for the effects of being staked out in the hot sun. Peter needs a couple of days of bed rest.

"What happened to the other men?" he asks.

"I sent them to reinforce the guards outside in preparation for a major assault. I don't know how long it'll be before someone in authority asks them what they're doing out there and then sends them back down here."

"I'd better get to work on the door then," Peter says.

He heaves himself forward.

He pulls the crowbar from his waistband and starts to jam in between the door and the frame, but then he stops.

On impulse he tries the knob.

It turns. He pushes gently. The door moves.

We look at the door and then at each other.

"I don't like it that it's unlocked," Peter whispers. "Feels like a trap."

"Or maybe a bored, careless guard," I whisper back. "Either way, if your dad's in there, we have to go in too."

"Stay behind me," he says softly.

He eases the door open, revealing a large square room.

There are only two guards visible, and it's clear the door and walls are soundproofed. The men show no signs that they're aware that anything was going on in the hallway.

They're playing cards, munching on garlic bread balls, and drinking beer (I'm guessing from the odors).

Centered in the middle of the room is a small square cell made completely of glass.

Inside it are a bed, a table, a chair, and a commode.

No books. No writing materials. No personal grooming items. No sink. No pictures. No nothing.

Lying on the bed is a man with matted hair and a wild beard. He looks as if he's gone months without a shower and a shave. His is wearing rags that do nothing to hide the bruises and cuts and clotted blood that cover his body. His eyes are closed, and there is only a faint movement in the chest to indicate that he's even alive.

After the confrontation in the hall, Peter looked as if a stiff breeze might knock him down. Now, his face is red and his hands, clutching the bat, are white knuckled. He looks as if he's been taken over by a rage that's pouring adrenaline into his body by the gallon.

He doesn't make a sound.

He glances behind him and sees that the door has a steel bar. He slides it into place, bolting the door closed.

With five long strides he crosses the floor to the guards and lays them out with one swing of the bat each.

They were so intent on their game they never saw him coming.

Then Peter takes aim at the nearest cell wall and swings again.

The glass shatters in a hailstorm of splinters.

The man on the bed rouses and gazes in our direction.

Despite his disheveled condition, it takes only a glance to see where Peter and Cindy got the red highlights in their hair and the changeable colors in their eyes. He's taller than Peter and much thinner, but there is no doubt as to their relationship.

"Peter?" Stace Merek asks in a rough voice. With effort, he swings his legs over the side of the bed and sits up.

"Yes," Peter says.

"Are you actually here? I've hallucinated you so many times."

"I'm here, and I—"

"You shouldn't have come. Leave, quickly. Maldon would take great pleasure in torturing you in front of me and your lady friend in front of you. Please leave before it's too late."

"I can't," Peter said. "I've only just found you. I'm not willing to let you go again."

Stace stretches out his hand, and Peter takes it.

"You've grown up," Stace says. "I'm sorry I've missed so many years of your life. I wanted to reach out a hundred times, but I was afraid you didn't want to see me. Cindy told me she could love two fathers. Could you possibly—"

"I already do," Peter says gently. "Now, let's get you out of here."

Suddenly there is a loud boom and the metal door flies off its hinges. Maldon bursts into the room.

I feel ferocious energies pulsating all around him.

I grab Peter's hand.

"Hold onto your father," I cry.

I wish us out of there.

Maldon throws his magic at us a split second before we vanish.

Peter covers his father and me with his body.

I smell charred flesh as the three of us hit the carpet in Neeve's living room.

# Chapter Forty-one

"Holy stars!" Kaden exclaims. He is the first to react.

He goes straight to Peter and rolls him onto his stomach.

That's when I notice the plate-sized, steaming wound in the middle of Peter's back.

Kaden lays his hands on either side of the lesion and seems to glare at it for a moment. The wisps of smoke fade.

Peter groans.

At least I know he's alive.

"We need to get them both to the hospital," Kaden says.

"I'll take you," Jerrin responds.

"May I—?" I start to ask.

"No," Jerrin and Kaden say at the same time.

Jerrin is clearly furious.

Kaden's tone is gentler.

"May I?" Hellie asks.

"No," Kaden answers. "There's nothing either of you can do. Go home. I'll call you when there's anything to tell."

Jerrin glares at me. "We'll discuss this later."

Then the four men disappear.

I'm still sitting on the floor.

I'm stunned.

I went to Panelda to save Peter. If it turns out that I traded his life for his father's, I'll never get over it.

Hellie comes and sits beside me on the floor. "How did you do it? I didn't feel a portal open."

I sigh and look around the room.

Only Neeve, Karissa, Hellie, and I are left.

"How long was I gone?" I ask.

"I'm not sure," Hellie answers. "It's almost 5:00 on Sunday evening. It was yesterday afternoon around 2:30 when Jerrin showed up and blew a hole through the door to Neeve's bathroom. I think he saw you leave, but I'm only guessing. He's hasn't talked about it. We've all asked him questions, but he's just been too angry to answer. He did tell you not to go get Peter, and you agreed."

"Wrong on both counts," I say. "He told me not to open a portal, and I told him not to worry because I don't have the knack. So, technically he didn't tell me I couldn't go get Peter, and I didn't tell him I wouldn't. I obeyed him precisely. I didn't open a portal. I translocated."

"You what?" Hellie asks.

"I teleported."

"You'll have a tough time selling that reasoning to Jerrin," Neeve says. "He was so mad and he was swearing so colorfully, I was glad Karissa and Hellie couldn't understand our language."

"I'm sorry if I made Jerrin angry," I say, "but he's never going to make me feel sorry that I went to get Peter."

"Angel," Neeve says seriously, "let me give you a little advice. Don't say that to Jerrin. As your teacher, he's responsible for making sure that you survive long enough to learn how to use your talents.

"The reason he was enraged enough yesterday to practically destroy my guest bathroom was because he was scared to death for you. He's going to come down on you hard to make sure it never happens again. I suggest you do your best just to take it without excuses, without explanations, and certainly without saying you're not sorry."

"I can try," I say to Neeve, "but I don't know if I can pull it off."

I turn to my sister.

"What *giving Peter to the sun* meant," I tell her, "was that they stripped him down to his undershorts, tied him spread-eagle to pegs pounded into the ground, and left him to die under a blazing sun on a big salt plain. When I got there, his skin was already blistered with sunburn, he had salt caked around his eyes and mouth, and he was dehydrated inside and out."

I look back at Neeve. "Nothing and no one will ever make me regret having saved Peter from dying like that. Do you really think Jerrin won't understand?"

Neeve starts to answer, but Karissa puts her hand on his arm and stops him.

"Of course, he understands," Karissa says. "It's just that in order to work with you, he's got to know that you accept his authority. If you want him to continue being your teacher, you'll have to convince him that you're not going to defy him and take off to do whatever you want whenever the impulse hits you."

"Oh," I say. After taking a moment to process what Karissa just said, I glance at Neeve and then at her. "You're telling me that now, because of what I did, Jerrin doesn't know if I trust him enough to be guided by him, and therefore he doesn't know if he dares trust me to learn and to use appropriately what he needs to teach me."

"Well put," Neeve says. "Trust between teacher and student is the key to learning to control magic."

"All right," I acknowledge. "I owe Jerrin an apology, not for saving Peter, but for not showing him the respect and appreciation that I feel toward him and for all that he has taught me."

"I don't want to sound dense," Hellie says to me, "but since Jerrin isn't here to explain, will you please tell me the difference between opening a portal and teleporting? Specifically, tell me why Auravalians can't open a portal into Chankoun but you could translocate there."

"I'll try," I say, "but once Jerrin calms down, you probably ought to ask him. He'll be able to offer you a technical explanation, which I can't. All I can give you is my opinion based on what I've experienced."

"That's good enough," Hellie says.

"Okay, this is the way I envision it. Opening a portal is like folding a piece of paper in half so that you can punch one hole simultaneously through two places. When you step through, you go from one material plane to another, like walking through a tunnel even though it is infinitesimally small in width.

"Chankoun's defensive barrier is like a metal strip placed between the two halves of the paper. A hole-punch designed to go through two sheets of paper isn't strong enough to punch through the metal. That's how they keep Auravalian magic out.

"Teleporting is like making a jump. I'm here. I jump. I land there. Even though I leave one physical plane for another, I don't go through a tunnel. I arrive without having traveled through anything but empty space.

"Chankoun's magicians couldn't build a barrier that would keep me out. I'm not limited to a portal with a specific endpoint. They can't erect a wall against nothing. I don't know if that makes any sense to you. Even though I can feel the difference, I realize I don't have the vocabulary or the experience with magic to express it."

"My heavens, Angel," Hellie says. She looks at me as if I've sprouted a second head or something. "How did you conceptualize that clearly enough to try it?"

"Do you remember anything Jerrin said when he was first trying to explain magic to me?" I ask.

"Not much," Hellie admits.

"I remember it all," I say. "I could probably recite it word for word. Its impact on me was that profound. But in the interest of time, I'll summarize. First, he told me that magic doesn't create or destroy anything. It manipulates. Second, he told me that no one knows if magic is a form of energy or a psychic power, and it doesn't matter. Third, he said that magic users can reshape mechanics, functioning, and physical properties of various things in their environment. Fourth, he said if a person has the ability and focuses properly, he can make his desires become realities.

"When I still didn't understand, he had me toss him a pillow. He used that as an analogy, saying that magic was like my throwing the pillow to him. Through a series of unconscious and split-second decisions, I influenced the pillow to go from one place to another without using a portal.

"The pillow left me and arrived at Jerrin, traveling through nothing but empty space. Although the room was full of air and the exchange wasn't instantaneous, it was that image that pulled everything together for me. Suddenly, I knew intuitively what I could do.

"The one consistent thing everyone's told me about my magic is that it's all about influence. So, it occurred to me that if I could influence the location of inanimate objects, I should be able to influence my location as well. Maybe I wouldn't have had the courage to try it without discussing it with Jerrin first if I hadn't been so worried about Peter. But I'll be honest, I'd rather have died trying to get to Peter yesterday than spend one more minute feeling as terrified and as helpless as I did."

My eyes tear up.

"Now, it might all have been in vain," I say with my lips quivering. "He still might die on foreign soil." I clamber to my feet. "I'm going home. I'm sorry about the damage to your bathroom, Neeve."

"Don't worry about it," Neeve tells me. "You didn't do it. Jerrin has already made arrangements for the repair work."

"Do you want to ride home with me, Hellie?" I ask.

"I guess I should. Mertley probably won't let Kaden come back until tomorrow."

We tell Karissa and Neeve goodbye.

As we walk to the car, I ask Hellie, "How did you explain my absence last night to Mom and Dad?"

"I told them that Peter's family didn't know where he was and that you were staying over to help with Cindy."

"How'd they react?"

"They were worried. What are you going to tell them?"

"That Peter was injured while helping out a friend and is currently in the hospital."

"And if they want to go visit him or send flowers?"

"I'll tell them the hospital is out of town, which it is, and Peter has already requested no visitors and no gifts, which is totally in character for him. He hates to be fussed over when he's not well."

"Are you going to tell his family the same thing?"

"Yes," I answer, "as soon as Kaden gives me enough information that sharing it with Peter's family will help them feel better not worse."

When we get home, we exchange a few words with our folks.

I guess I look fairly bad. Mom and Dad tell me to go to bed. They say I can tell them all about it in the morning.

Although I get ready for bed, I know I won't be able to sleep.

I want to be with Peter.

I want to hold his hand and tell him I love him.

I want to know he's going to be all right.

I sit down at my desk, turn on the lamp, and reach for the scrapbook Peter made for me. If I can't have him, I can at least relive some of the happy moments we've shared together.

I start at the beginning.

Centered on page one is an 8 x 10 copy of the first picture Peter ever took of me. The caption below it says: *Today I met an angel and found heaven on earth.*

It was early spring, over a year ago, and he had been looking for wildflowers to photograph for Cindy, who wanted something new to paint.

I've never spent much time in the woods, but that day Mom sent me to look for Hellie since she'd forgotten to take her cellphone with her when she left the house to prune back the wild raspberry bushes.

I found Peter instead.

The next few pages are all pictures taken in the forest: pictures of me pointing out my favorite flowers, pictures of me wading in a stream, a couple of selfies of Peter and me together.

Then there's a photograph of Cindy standing beside her easel, proudly gesturing toward the first painting she did of flowers from our forest: a cluster of delicate white mountain lilies.

When I come to a series of pictures taken on the day Peter gave me my first ride on his motorcycle, I can hardly believe it. He must have had his friends strategically positioned all along our route. There are half a dozen shots of us together: the two of us standing beside his bike, me climbing up behind him, us on the bike while it's actually moving (one shot shows me with my arms around his waist, my head against his back, and my eyes tightly closed), us sitting on a bench outside of a gas station in a little, no-name town where we stopped to buy soft drinks.

Then there's a picture that was taken a few weeks later when Peter presented me with my own bright pink princess helmet. When I thanked him, I kissed him on the lips. I'd forgotten that. But someone managed to get a picture of it.

Technically, I don't suppose it counts as our first real kiss. Peter was so stunned he didn't kiss me back.

Even though I knew I fell in love with Peter the day we met, and he's told me that he felt the same way, I've always harbored secret doubts that anyone could fall for me that fast. As I look through this amazing book tonight and recognize the planning and the loving attention that's gone into its creation, I have to believe him now.

I savor each memory.

When I'm nearing the end of the completed section, my worry about Peter's condition hits me hard. What if Peter doesn't recover? What if we never have the opportunity to add new photos and souvenirs to this book? What if its end is our end?

The thought hurts so much, I almost slam the book closed, but I don't. Peter made this for me.

His love permeates every sheet, every picture, and every written word.

I turn the page.

It's Easter Sunday this year.

Peter's mother made matching dresses for Cindy and me. They were white with tiny clusters of pink roses and had wide pink cummerbunds. I bought us matching white hats. In honor of the day, Peter wore a pink dress shirt with new black jeans.

Before we left for church, Mr. Bradley took a picture of us: Peter in the middle with Cindy holding his hand on one side and me holding his hand on the other.

Mom and Dad invited the Bradleys to have Easter dinner with us, and Peter filled two full pages with pictures of us hunting Easter eggs in the backyard and then eating dinner together. He even got a shot of us watching a DVD of *The Robe,* starring Richard Burton, and eating coconut cake for dessert (which are two of my favorite family traditions).

When I turn the next page, however, I'm puzzled.

The printed program from my high school graduation is on the left side, and a picture of me receiving my (fake) diploma is on the right side. I turn the page, and Hellie and I are helping each other put on the lockets our parents just gave us, followed by pictures taken at Peter's parents' house while I open presents (which includes a shot of me opening the box this scrapbook was in), while I blow out graduation candles, and while I eat cake and ice cream with his family.

This is not possible.

Peter must have completed the scrapbook, wrapped it, and dropped it off at his parents' house prior to riding his motorcycle over to the high school. He certainly didn't do it after the ceremony. I was with him the entire time.

For about half a second, I consider the possibility that Peter might have used magic to insert the extra pictures into the book, but I'm fairly certain his powers don't include translocation.

Grandma Powers used to say, *Simplest is best. Always look for a simple solution first.*

I get up and go through the bathroom to Hellie's room.

There's a light showing under her door, so I knock.

"Come in, Angel," Hellie calls.

She's lying on her bed watching a movie on her computer. She pauses it, and I sit down beside her.

"Do you know when and how Peter got ahold of the scrapbook he gave me for graduation?"

Hellie sits up and grins. "Sure. A week or two after graduation, he asked me if I'd sneak it out for him. He said he wanted to update it and then add something special. He said he wanted it to be a surprise. He was so excited I couldn't tell him *no*. Did you just find it?"

"I just found something," I say. "Apparently he added a bunch of pictures from graduation night."

"That's rather anticlimactic," Hellie says with disappointment. "Are you sure that's all?"

"I don't know. There might be a page or two left."

Hellie swings her legs around, forcing me off the bed, so she can get up. "Do you mind if I watch while you check the final pages? I'm really curious now."

"Come on, then."

I sit back down at my desk, and Hellie pulls over my rocking chair so she can see.

"Hey," Hellie says, "that's a great picture of us with our lockets. I'd like a copy of that."

"I'll scan it for you." I flip over the page.

On the left are some more graduation shots, but on the right is a great big red cutout of a heart. In the middle is an envelope that sort of bulges.

I open the envelope and pull out a hand printed card.

It reads: *I love you, Angel. Will you marry me?*

Tied with a pink bow below the message is a ring.

# Chapter Forty-two

I can hardly see through my tears as I slip the ring onto my finger.

"It's beautiful," Hellie says.

I have to dry my eyes with a tissue before I get a clear look at it.

She's right. It has a large center diamond surrounded by six diamond chips. I don't know enough about precious stones to guess the carats, but it doesn't matter. It is the perfect size and shape for my hand.

I give it a kiss before I take it off.

"Aren't you going to wear it?" Hellie asks.

"Not until Peter gets home. We should announce our engagement together."

Still, I'm not willing to put the ring back in the scrapbook. Instead, I get a gold chain from my jewelry box and hang the ring from it like a pendant. I put the chain around my neck.

"That'll have to do for now," I say.

Hellie gives me a hug. "I'm happy for you. Do you have any idea when you'd like to get married?"

I laugh. "Let me get used to being engaged first. I'll worry about a wedding later."

I'm still sitting at my desk, wondering what I did to deserve someone as marvelous as Peter, when Shiane calls me on my cellphone and asks if she can come over and see me.

I say *sure*, assuming she has news for me about Peter.

She rings the doorbell a few seconds later.

I slip the ring under the neck of my t-shirt as I sprint down the stairs to answer the door. I meet Mom in the hall.

"I'll get it," I say. "It's Shiane, Neeve's little sister." My parents have met her a time or two and have heard Hellie and me talking about her a lot, so Mom knows who she is.

Mom heads back to the family room.

Shiane and I go up to my room. She sits in my rocking chair and I swivel my desk chair around so we're facing each other.

"Peter's injuries from Maldon's magic were so severe," Shiane says, "and he was so weakened by what he experienced on the desert and while fighting to save his father, Mertley decided to do a complete healing, which is a rather rare occurrence.

"It took Mertley, Kaden, two additional apprentices, and one other doctor about three hours to complete the complicated ritual. When they were finished, however, Peter's body was covered with fresh new skin, eliminating the sunburn, the abrasions, the bruises, and the enormous raw wound in the middle of his back.

"He's resting peacefully now, and Mertley said he can come home tomorrow."

"When can I go get him?" I ask eagerly.

"That's why I wanted to talk with you face to face," she says. "Skyler recommends that you let Hellie go get Peter."

"Why?" I ask, puzzled.

"Skyler doesn't want to risk you and Jerrin bumping into each other at the hospital and possibly causing a scene. Jerrin hasn't decided yet if he's going to forgive you for going to Chankoun against his wishes."

I almost laugh. *Forgive me?* That sounds so junior high school.

Then Shiane continues. "Jerrin is considering asking the Magicians Guild to find you a different teacher."

Suddenly it's not so funny.

"Was what I did so awful?" I ask plaintively. "I saved two lives."

"I know you did," Shiane says, "and so does Jerrin. While Mertley worked on Peter, our family doctor, Haden, took care of Stace. If you had waited for the king to authorize a rescue party to the Wastelands, Peter might not have survived the sun, and Haden said Stace was mere hours away from death when he arrived at the hospital.

"Now Peter has been healed, and although Stace is still weak from hunger, thirst, blood loss, and pain, Haden thinks he'll make a full recovery in time."

"I'm glad," I say, sniffling a little. "I hope someone has told Peter and Cindy."

"I did." Shiane reaches over and gives my hand a squeeze. "You did a good thing, Angel."

"So why is Jerrin mad at me?"

"It's just that he's had other students who have defied him and achieved remarkable things, but then afterward they got so cocky that when failure eventually came it was cataclysmic. All that was left for Jerrin to do was pick up the pieces. I think he's trying to decide if he's up to facing that possibility again."

My lips start to quiver.

Shine gently pats me on the back. "Regardless of what happens between you and Jerrin in the future, don't ever forget what you accomplished."

"Thanks."

"Uh oh," she says, "I'm being summoned. Will anyone notice if I don't go downstairs and leave by the front door?"

"No."

"Good. I've got to go."

She vanishes.

I get ready for bed, but I know I won't be able to sleep.

I put on a nightgown, a shorty robe, and the matching slippers and then go downstairs. I stop by the family room, where my folks are watching the ten o'clock news.

"I'm going to go sit on the patio and watch the stars for a while. Don't lock me out."

"Shiane's already left?" Mom asks.

"Yes. She was in the neighborhood and just stopped by to say *hi*."

"Don't stay out there stargazing too long," Dad says. "Remember tomorrow's a workday."

"As if I could forget."

I get a Diet Coke from the fridge.

Before I open the backdoor, I turn off the yard lights.

I pull a lawn chair out from under the eaves so I have an unobstructed view of the sky. I look at the stars, thinking that somewhere in that vast, endless universe is the planet Panelda and on it is Peter.

Will I be allowed to go back there, even for a visit, if Jerrin decides not to be my teacher anymore? Will he keep tutoring Peter and Cindy while fobbing me off onto someone new?

I don't want to study with anyone else.

I realize that now.

*Jerrin,* I call out with my mind, *I know you can hear me if you want to. I'm sorry. I can't say my decision to go get Peter was wrong, but I'll admit that not telling you what I was going to do was.*

*Please don't dump me.*

*Neeve said you would come down on me hard because I frightened you. He recommended that I take whatever you dished out without offering you any excuses or explanations. I can do that.*

*I want to point out, though, that you've taught me everything I know about magic. It was how you explained the similarity between tossing you a pillow and performing an act of magic that let me know—not guess, not hope, not pray, but absolutely KNOW—I could teleport myself to Peter and bring him and his father home the same way. That's remarkable! Not only that I could do it, but also that you instilled in me enough confidence in my powers for me to undertake it.*

*You told me that you're the teacher I need. You're right. You've taught me so much in so short a time. Thank you.*

*I don't suppose I'm the student you need or want, but maybe I could grow into being that person. I'll try if you'll let me. If you choose not to work with me, I'll understand. I know you'll do whatever you think is best for both of us. Thank you for caring enough about me to become angry when you thought I was putting myself in danger.*

*I decided to talk to you tonight instead of to God. I figured He'd always be there, but you might not be. Good night, Jerrin.*

From out of nowhere, I hear the tinkling of an invisible doorbell.

The next thing I know, Jerrin is sitting in a lawn chair next to me.

"I knew we'd butt heads," Jerrin says, "but I had no idea that you could frighten me the way you did yesterday when you teleported out of Neeve's bathroom." He pauses. When he speaks again, his voice is harsh, as if he's barely keeping his anger under control. "If you try anything like that again without my permission, Angel, I'll bind your powers so tight you won't even be able to make a wish on the evening star. Is that clear?"

"Yes, Jerrin," I answer meekly.

"Do you have ANY idea how risky it was for you to teleport halfway across the universe?"

"No."

"Do you want to know?"

"If it's something I need to understand, then yes, I want to know."

"It is so difficult to do that, even after extensive training, almost a third of the magic users who have the talent for teleportation either kill or seriously injure themselves on their first off-planet attempt. When Cushing and I saw that potential in your eyes, we were relieved that it was buried so deep that you hadn't had the chance to experiment with it.

"As soon as I heard Maldon order his men to give Peter to the sun, I should have realized that the emotional upheaval you experienced would propel that ability right up to the surface. The realization hit me about two minutes too late for me to stop you."

"Could you have stopped me?" I ask. "If you had arrived a little earlier, could you have forcibly prevented me from going?"

"I don't know," Jerrin admits, "but I sure as hell would have tried."

I nod. "In which case, we'd have argued yesterday, and I probably would've threatened to quit instead of you threatening to drop me."

"It almost seems inevitable that we'd end up having this conversation, doesn't it?"

"Yes," I say, "but, Jerrin, I don't care if we get mad at each other and argue. Hellie and I do it all the time. The question is can we do it without quitting on each other?"

Jerrin doesn't say anything.

I'm afraid he's already found someone to take over my training.

I won't cry, I tell myself. No matter what he says, I won't cry.

"If we both commit ourselves," Jerrin finally says, "I think we could make it work."

I'm so relieved that all I can think to do is nod my head again.

We sit and silently watch the stars for a few minutes.

"Angel," Jerrin says, "the way you worked your teleportation spell was an excellent bit of magic, I want you to know that. But it was so dangerous, I can hardly believe you did it three times in close succession without losing control. Before attempting it again, you must have formal testing at the Magician's Guild. Until that's done, you are not to experiment, or to practice, or to do anything else with your powers that you think you can get away with as a technicality. You are to stay strictly within the parameters of your training. With great power comes great responsibility."

"All right," I say.

He gives me a stern look. "I need something more than *all right.* I won't have this conversation with you a second time."

I pull myself together and meet him eye to eye.

"Jerrin, I promise I won't teleport off-planet again until you tell me I can. I also promise I'll stick to my training and won't attempt anything new without consulting you first."

"In that case, I'm still your teacher."

When Jerrin leaves, I'm way too stirred up to go to bed.

Instead, I go to my room and get dressed.

I told Jerrin I wouldn't teleport off-planet, but I didn't say I wouldn't practice opening portals. A portal across town shouldn't take too much energy, certainly not as much as going between Earth and Panelda.

Closing my eyes, I picture Peter's living room. I envision myself stepping through a doorway and arriving there.

I want it.

I believe I can have it.

I concentrate.

I make it happen.

I open my eyes.

I'm there.

Jerrin is sitting in Peter's recliner, glancing through the material about the witch in the woods. He looks over at me and shakes his head.

"Did you not want me to practice relocating anywhere?" I ask.

"It didn't occur to me that you'd try until I felt you gathering power. I'm curious, though, why was it so easy for you to open a portal to get here when you have so much difficulty with them otherwise?"

I shrug. "I guess it's because this was such a short distance."

"It takes the same amount of desire, belief, and concentration to open a portal to cross a room as it does to cross the universe."

"It doesn't feel that way."

"Then that will be our next lesson."

Jerrin vanishes.

As soon as Jerrin leaves, I start cleaning up the mess in Peter's living room. I shove my papers back into the box and set it on the floor beside Peter's recliner in case he wants to read through any of them while he is convalescing—or maybe he doesn't need to convalesce after a healing. I should have asked Shiane.

Next, I fold up the tables, all three of them—the two tables Peter set up and the camp table I shipped from the Wastelands. They aren't particularly heavy, but they're awkward. I carry them down to the basement one at a time to put them away. I fold up the camp chairs and take them down too.

Then I move on to his kitchen. I put the Aloe Vera products in the medicine cabinet in Peter's bathroom and the washcloths in the clothes hamper. I toss away the trash. All that leaves are the two pans that had cold water in them. His dishwasher is full, the contents clean, but I don't take the time to empty it. I wash the pans by hand, dry them, and put them on a shelf with similar pots.

I wipe down the counters and the table.

Peter is a good housekeeper, so I don't have to do anything else to make the place presentable. I'm about ready to open a portal to go home when I decide to add a final touch.

Since daffodils are Peter's favorite flower, I call a large bouquet of them. I have no idea where they come from. They haven't been in bloom around here since early spring.

I look through his cupboards for an appropriate vase, but I can't find one. Mom has a nice ceramic vase that's just the right size, so I call it.

I put the flowers in the middle of the kitchen table. Then I get a piece of paper and a red marker from Peter's desk. I draw a heart on the paper and write *yes* in the middle. I put the note in front of the vase and then open a portal to my bedroom. I take off my shoes, socks, and jeans and collapse into bed.

Work the next day is a nightmare. Every time a phone rings anywhere in the office, I stop what I'm doing, hoping that it's Peter calling to say he's home.

Hellie didn't know when she was supposed to go get him. She said Kaden would let her know.

I'm clearing off my desk at the end of the day when my cellphone rings. It's Hellie.

"I've got Peter with me, and I'm coming to pick you up. I've already called Dad and told him he doesn't need to stop by and get you."

All day I've worn the engagement ring from Peter on a chain around my neck. Now, I slip it onto my finger.

When Peter opens the car door, he spots it right away.

"Yes?" he asks me.

"Yes," I answer.

Being in Colorado, not Auravale, we're able to cement the deal with a kiss. That night we announce the news to our families.

No one seems particularly surprised.

Cindy's response is, "Do I get to be a bridesmaid or the flower girl?"

# Chapter Forty-three

"You didn't," Hellie exclaims. "Tell me you didn't call Grandma Dark and ask her that!"

"I did," I say. "She told me Mom and Dad have known about magic, Auravale, the enchanted forest, and Bree-Ella for a long time. She wasn't sure when they exchanged information about it, but she figures it was at least by the time we were born."

Hellie and I are on our way to take down the pavilion that I deposited in the forest. I suggested the outing so we'd have a private place to have this conversation. I wasn't sure but what Hellie would rip my head off when I told her what I'd done.

"When you think about it," I continue, "it makes perfect sense that Dad knew. For five generations, his family has owned an enchanted forest, which Great-great-great-granddad Eugene recognized, purchased, and protected.

"Eugene must have been one of those humans who is sensitive to magic and who can hear its echoes, and his son Michael must have been one too. What that suggests to me is that there is probably a genetic component involved with the ability.

"Grandpa Powers grew up with an enchanted forest in his backyard, and he married a woman who was sensitive enough to magic to recognize the forest for what it was. Our dad must have gotten a double dose of sensitivity to magic, and what did he do?

"He went out of state to get his doctoral degree and just happened to meet, fall in love with, and marry a woman who is the descendent of a powerful magic user from another world.

"Grandma Dark said she explained about Bree-Ella, her flight from Auravale, and her magical powers to her daughters the same way her mother explained them to her. And what did our mother do? She fell in love with and married a man whose family owns an enchanted forest.

"If you believe all of that was a series of unrelated coincidences, I'd like to sell you some valuable swampland in Florida."

"Then why have our folks been playing dumb all these years?" Hellie asks.

"I don't know. Maybe they were afraid we'd ridicule them for believing."

"That doesn't make sense," Hellie asserts. "They knew we believed Grandma Powers, so why didn't they reinforce what she told us?"

I answer her slowly, having just had a new thought. "Maybe they were trying to discourage us from talking about it freely in public. They might have been afraid that if we had confirmation from them, we'd be more apt to try to convince other people it was true."

"So?" Hellie says. "No one I ever told believed me."

"But if we were really adamant, people might have started asking Mom and Dad questions or making jokes about it. Think of the position that would have put our folks in. They wouldn't have dared admit the truth to their friends, coworkers, or employers. Yet if they said it was all our imaginations and if we heard them, we might never trust them again. Maybe they thought denying the truth from the get-go was the easiest way to avoid complications in the future. What do you think?"

"I think it's enough to make me crazy," Hellie grumbles.

We reach the pavilion, look at each other, and burst into laughter.

Neither of us has any idea how to take it apart.

We sit on the ground in its shade.

"Now that you know they know," Hellie asks, "what do you plan to do about it?"

"Tell them it doesn't need to be a secret anymore. Peter's parents, too. He and I discussed it. We don't want to have a wedding here that excludes Stace and all our Auravalian friends, and we don't want to have a wedding there that would exclude our families and our human friends."

"But Angel," Hellie says, "most people wouldn't recognize the Auravalians as nonhuman, and it's no great stretch for them to pretend to be earthlings. Neeve's been doing it for years."

"I know. We considered that, and it's good enough for our friends but not for our parents. Aren't you sick and tired of leading a double life? I am. Peter is. And poor little Cindy is having a terrible time. We need to stop the pretenses, at least at home. We'd love to have you and Kaden with us when we make the confrontations."

"Let me think about it."

"Grandma Dark said she'd be happy to back us up if we want to wait until she gets here."

"When's she coming?"

"In a week, maybe two. She's checking round trip dates and prices. She'll let us know as soon as she's booked her flight."

I glance up and notice there are Velcro tabs connecting the canvas top to the pavilion's frame. The panel that makes up the one wall is attached the same way.

I get up and start unfastening Velcro.

After a moment, Hellie joins me. "Have you and Peter set a date yet?"

"We're still discussing it. He wants to get married right away so we can have a nice honeymoon and get settled before I start college next month. I've told him that planning a wedding is a complicated process, but he insists that it doesn't have to be."

"Who's winning?"

"I have to admit I'm leaning his way, but it's only because you and I have been planning a big celebration for the stwethil-thage. I don't see why Peter and I shouldn't get married at their party. I'd even be willing to have blackberry pie instead of a wedding cake."

As soon as the side panel comes loose, we fold it up and then go back to work on the top.

"When are you going to talk to the folks?" Hellie asks.

"Sunday. We've invited Mom and Dad over to Peter's place for brunch before church and Peter's parents and Cindy over for dinner that evening. You and Kaden are invited to one or both if you'd like to come."

"I'll talk with Kaden about it."

After we get the top off and folded, Hellie and I glare at the frame.

"What would happen," I ask, "if we tried to take it down with magic. Jerrin says magic can fill in the blanks sometimes."

"I think we'd end up with a metal pretzel, in which case we might as well ship it straight to the dump."

"Ooh, I hate to do this," I mumble as I pull my cellphone from my pocket. "What?"

"Call Peter and ask him to come take care of it. He never says it, but he gets this *you-poor-little-helpless-female* look, sometimes. If I ever turn to murder, that'll be the reason."

When Peter agrees to come, Hellie opens a portal for him. It takes him about two minutes to fold up the frame. He gets the look.

"I see what you mean," Hellie says.

We burst out laughing.

"What?" Peter asks. "There's something funny about taking down a pavilion?"

"No, of course not." I take his face in my hands and kiss him. "Thank you." I pick up the side panel and the top and hand them to him. He's still holding the collapsed frame. "They're all yours," I say.

On Sunday, Hellie and Kaden join us for brunch. They politely decline our invitation to return for dinner.

Peter and I decide that I'll take the lead with my family and he'll take the lead with his, so when brunch is ready and we're all sitting around the table eating, I start by saying, "We'd like to talk with you about Auravale."

Mom and Dad automatically look at Kaden.

"We've been curious, of course," Dad says.

Mom nods. "You were going to point it out for us on a map, weren't you?"

"No, Mom," I say. "We want to talk about the real Auravale, not an imaginary country in Europe but a magical kingdom on another world. It's where Bree-Ella Dark was born and raised before she ended up pregnant and having her baby in Colorado. It's where the magical little creatures come from that turned a simple woodland area into an enchanted forest. It's where Peter's birth father was born and where Kaden is from."

# Chapter Forty-four

Mom and Dad give me the zombie stare, as if their brains have been fried and they can no longer think.

Allowing them time to process, I take a bite of breakfast pie, one of Peter's specialties. He might not be as versatile a cook as Neeve, and he doesn't ever do desserts, but the things he cooks are always excellent.

No one says anything for several minutes.

Then Dad says very quietly to Mom, "Bethany, we agreed that when they were older, if they ever brought up the subject, we'd be straightforward and honest with them."

"I know, Nathan," she says, "but where do we start?"

Dad glances around the table. "How do you want to do this? Do you want to ask us questions? Do you want us to ask you questions? Do you want—"

"I have a suggestion," Hellie says. "Why don't we do something similar to counting our blessings on Thanksgiving?"

"I like it," I say. I turn to Peter and Kaden to explain. "At Thanksgiving dinner, we take turns naming one special thing that's happened in the past year that we're thankful for. Each comment has to be original with no repeats."

"So," Hellie says, "let's go around the table and we'll all tell one specific thing that we know about Auravale. We can keep going around and around until no one has anything else to add. How does that sound?"

Dad smiles. "It's as good a way as any. I'll start. When my great-great-grandfather Eugene Powers rode into our forest for the first time, he sensed right away that there was something paranormal about it. As he rode deeper and deeper into the woods, he became obsessed with the feeling that he should purchase and protect the land.

"He knew people would eventually be drawn to the lumber, and he felt instinctively that if they began cutting down the trees, they would destroy whatever magic was involved. He didn't know about the mystical creatures that lived here until years after he bought the land.

"He never discussed his belief in the supernatural with anyone except his son Michael, who also had the ability to sense the forest's enchantment."

Dad turns to Mom, "You're up, Bethany."

"When my sisters and I were little, our mother told us bedtime stories about Bree-Ella Dark. It wasn't until we were all teenagers that she told us that some of the stories were true.

"She said while Bree-Ella was being trained to use her magical powers, she befriended a clan of little people who told her about an enchanted forest where members of their family had immigrated decades earlier, and they begged her to help them get there too.

"So, Bree-Ella opened a way for them to cross between worlds. When she found out she was pregnant, she came here to have her baby because the little people told her if she ever needed anything from them all she had to do was ask. She asked them to help bring her baby into the world, which they did. Her daughter Edith was born in the little glade that Grandmother Powers loved so much."

Kaden is sitting next to Mom. She says, "It's your turn."

"I came to your forest originally," Kaden says, "because the king of Auravale wanted me to retrieve three magical artifacts that Bree-Ella Dark borrowed from the palace when she left. No one knows exactly what she took or why, but the king wants the items returned."

"I thought you were in medical school," Mom says, "studying to become a doctor."

"Technically I am training to be a medical finder," Kaden explains. "I suppose in your world you would label my specialty as a doctor who diagnoses and treats physiological and psychological anomalies. I am already a powerful locator, which is why the king chose me to find the lost artifacts." He turns to Hellie. "You're next."

She smiles at him before she turns toward Mom and Dad.

"People from Auravale have two sets of wings like butterflies," Hellie says. "They are absolutely beautiful and can be extended and retracted at will. Their wings are perfectly functional and can support more than double an individual's own weight."

Hellie turns the stage over to Peter with a glance.

Peter accepts it with a nod. "My birth father is named Stace Jory Merek and he is from Auravale. He was betrothed to Bree-Ella Dark before a man named Maldon Darker raped her, getting her pregnant and causing her to flee from Auravale and to hide on Earth. People from Auravale are born with only half a soul. They must find and join with their soulmates in order to become whole. When Maldon Darker forced himself onto Bree-Ella, he not only shattered her soul but also the soul of my father. Now, neither one will ever find true completion."

"There is hope," Kaden says to Peter. "When Maldon Darker dies, the hold he has on the souls of Bree-Ella and Stace will be broken. If Bree-Ella and Stace are both alive when that happens and if they are both still unbonded, they can marry, and their souls can be united."

"Those are big *ifs*," Peter says.

"I know," Kaden responds, "but hope is always better than despair. Besides, seeing you and Cindy is already strengthening Stace. It is possible, even without Bree-Ella, that you and Cindy will be enough to help him choose to live during this critical stage of his life cycle."

"I hope you're right," Peter says.

"As do I." Kaden looks at me apologetically. "I've interrupted the proceedings long enough. I believe it's your turn, Angel."

"Right." I look at my parents. "The little creatures that you both mentioned are called stwethil-thage. Their presence is what has imbued Powers Forest with magic, and there are three other colonies on our planet. A new clan of stwethil-thage is moving into our forest, and Hellie and I have been planning a big celebration to welcome them. I want to get married at their party."

As quick as lightning, the conversation switches from talking about Auravale to planning a wedding. What began as a nervous confrontation about family secrets has developed into an exciting discussion about an upcoming event.

Getting Peter's folks to acknowledge their connection with Auravale is much more difficult because of the parentage issue. Mr. and Mrs. Bradley have trouble believing that we aren't judging them and that all we want is to stop pretending.

Of course, Cindy finds the key to opening up her parents.

She goes over to her father and puts her arms around his neck. "I can love Stace Merek because he's my first father. He likes to come see me, and he's nice.

"But you're the father I live with. You taught me how to tie my shoelaces. You picked me up when I fell off my bicycle, and you cleaned up the blood and put Neosporin and Band-Aids on my knees. You taught me knock-knock jokes. You still read me stories sometimes, and give me hugs, and tuck me in bed at night.

"You're the father who tells me when I make mistakes. You make me say *sorry* when I've been rude. You tell me not to talk with my mouth full. You remind me not to track mud in on the carpet. You take care of me and play with me and teach me how to grow up properly.

"Stace is a good man, and I like him, but he's only a part-time father. You're my fulltime for-real father. I love you, Daddy."

After Peter's parents finish crying and hugging Cindy, they agree to discuss Auravale with us.

However, they stun me when they start by saying it was Grandma Dark

318

who first suggested that, instead of adopting, they might consider having a male donor so Mr. and Mrs. Bradley could share the joy of seeing their children being born.

It happened while Grandma Dark was in Shawon because Grandma Powers was having an engagement party for Mom and Dad. Grandma Dark went to the beauty salon to have her hair done at the same time Mrs. Bradley did. They got chatting about children, pregnancy, and infertility while they waited. (Mrs. Bradley pauses in the middle of the story to admit that sometimes she still finds it is easier to explain her problems to a stranger.)

When Grandma suggested having a male donor, Mrs. Bradley said she would be too embarrassed to talk about such a thing with her doctor, but how else would she find an honorable man who was willing to father another man's child. So, Grandma Dark told her about the witch in the woods.

She said she had been researching Shawon ever since Mom told her this was where she and Dad were going to live. Grandma told Mrs. Bradley she'd read that this witch had helped other infertile couples have babies.

Mrs. Bradley found Miss Ellie, and Miss Ellie introduced her to Stace. In turn, Mrs. Bradley introduced Miss Ellie and Stace to her husband. Then the four of them had a meeting to discuss the situation.

At first, when Stace told them he was from Auravale, had wings, and could do magic, they thought he was crazy, but it was easy enough for him to prove. Then they were concerned about the possibility of having a child with wings, but Miss Ellie assured them that the wings would only come in if the child was born in Auravale. She said they would not develop if the child was born on Earth.

After some negotiating back and forth, they reached an agreement, which included allowing Stace to visit the child once a month with the stipulation that none of the parties would reveal Stace's name, his origin, or his true relationship.

When Mr. and Mrs. Bradley finish telling us their story, they don't offer to explain the process they went through for conception to take place.

We don't ask.

We do ask if inviting Stace to the wedding would make either of them uncomfortable. They both smile and say *not at all.*

Grandma Dark arrives the next week.

Hellie and I rush outside as Dad pulls into the driveway.

"Grandma," we squeal together.

Never ruffled, Grandma takes her time getting out of the car.

We pounce on her, practically smothering her with hugs.

Looking at her, you'd never believe she's almost sixty-five years old. Her straight, chin-length hair is light brown, like mine and Hellie's, and what little white she has hardly shows. Except for a few laugh lines around her blue eyes, she has absolutely no wrinkles.

She's taller than Mom, but not as tall as Hellie and me, and most women would probably say she's about ten pounds overweight. I disagree. I think she looks great. She is wearing blue jeans, a white PBS *Masterpiece Mysteries* t-shirt, and pink tennis shoes.

Hellie grabs one suitcase, and I grab the other.

As we start up the stairs, Grandma asks, "Who am I displacing?"

"Hellie and I tossed a coin," I say, "and I won."

"Does that mean I'm taking over Hellie's room?"

"Of course not," I say. "I won. You get to have my room. I've already moved my stuff into Hellie's."

"When is the wedding?" Grandma asks.

"Two weeks from Friday," I tell her.

"Sounds like I got here just in time," she says. While we set her bags on my desk, she pulls a notebook from her purse.

"Now, who's doing what?" she asks.

Just like that, Grandma takes over the task of making sure everyone follows through with what they've agreed to do.

It's amazing how fast a wedding can be pulled together when there are a dozen or so people working on it.

Mom and I concentrate on finding the perfect wedding gown for me and the right wedding band for Peter. While we shop, Mom keeps an eye out for a nice mother-of-the-bride dress for herself.

Peter decides to wear his black slacks and shirt with the white sports coat that he wore to Neeve's party. For this occasion, however, he agrees to wear a white bowtie with it. His best man will be dressed similarly.

Peter arranges with Pastor Keating to perform the ceremony.

I decide I'll only have two attendants: Hellie and Cindy. I tell them they can select their own gowns as long as they are the same shade of pink. Mrs. Bradley offers to help them coordinate.

Dad arranges with a friend of his who owns a printing business to do the invitations. We keep the guest list short because we're going to be married in the stwethil-thage meadow in our forest.

Shiane persuades the king to purchase all of the blackberries they can find and to have the palace pastry chef bake the pies. When the chef finds out they are for a wedding and I'm not going to have a cake because the blackberries are so expensive, the chef complains to the king, and the king tells him to go ahead a make a wedding cake too.

Neeve takes over the responsibility of planning a buffet for the reception, and Karissa agrees to help him cook. They will also provide all of the necessary china, crystal, cutlery, tablecloths, and napkins.

Kaden offers to take care of the entertainment, as well as incidentals like a guest book and a photographer. He also volunteers to hand carry our invitation to the chief of our old stwethil-thage clan. He promises to mention blackberry pie at least half a dozen times while they visit.

Hellie's boss, Brenlyn, will set up the chairs, tables, and sound system. Since we're getting married at 7:00 in the evening, he will also make sure we have adequate lighting.

His wife, Talitha, who is a horticulturist, cuts a four-foot-wide section out of the hedge in our backyard so the guests will have easy access to the forest. She brings the top of the sides together to form an arch. She suggests constructing a solid pathway that goes from the arch, through the woods, and to the meadow. She says she can do it without damaging the environment.

After the wedding, Mom and Dad can decide if they want to keep the opening and the path. If not, Talitha will regrow everything. She also insists on providing the flowers, including the bridal bouquet, nosegays for the attendants, and corsages and boutonnieres for the rest of the wedding party.

Jerrin is going to handle crowd control, making sure the nosy neighbors have nothing to see or hear and arranging for any overflow of vehicles to be parked in the nothingness between worlds.

Hellie meets with the new stwethil-thage clan almost daily, helping them tidy up the meadow. She tells me they are extraordinarily excited about the wedding. (We never got around to suggesting a *welcome to our forest* party). All of their healers and growers and builders are working overtime to get the clearing ready. Hellie says I'm going to love it.

Val, the chief of the new clan, asks Hellie to take him to Auravale and introduce him the chief of our former tenants. Apparently, Val has big plans and wants to solicit some assistance. The two chiefs hit it off right away. After a few days of working together, the old chief decides to move his clan back. He had forgotten how good it felt to nurture the forest, and he likes the idea of having some stwethil-thage neighbors.

Both clans intend to have their families moved in and settled before the great day, so they can all enjoy the party. Heaven only knows how we'll explain them to Pastor Keating and our earthling friends.

(Actually, Jerrin solves the problem by casting what he calls *a tiny mind control spell.* People who don't already know about magic will simply not notice anything magical that they see.)

Auravalians are better at RSVP-ing than humans. Maybe in this case it's to give us time to adjust our thinking and get over the shock. The king and queen graciously accept our invitation, as do Skyler and his wife, Jerrin and his wife, Master Cushing, and the doctors Mertley and Haden.

# Chapter Forty-five

When the morning of the wedding finally arrives, I hardly know what to do with myself. It doesn't seem fitting for me to engage in mundane tasks such as eating breakfast and helping clean up the kitchen.

Hellie solves the problem.

She calls me up to her bedroom and gives me her wedding gift. She has brought Jacie all the way from Auravale to get me ready.

Jacie takes me in hand.

She supervises my bath, conditions my hair, and makes sure I'm soft and smooth everywhere. She shapes and polishes my fingernails and toenails. (When Jacie shapes nails, she does it right. She encourages them to grow to an attractive length first.)

She studies my wedding gown and veil before she styles my hair.

Sometime in the middle of all this activity we have lunch, but I don't remember when.

My gown is white floor-length lace, smooth and sleek across the front, but gathered and full in the back with a 6-foot-long train. It has a scooped neckline and no sleeves. At first glance it might seem a little plain, but when it catches the light, you can see the patterns in the lace are outlined with seed pearls.

My veil is fingertip length and flows down my back from a headpiece that is basically a white comb with five small white velvet flowers across the top.

Jacie does my hair with the back part in a high bun so the comb has an anchor, then she curls the top and sides. She does my makeup with care, keeping the colors subtle, giving me a dreamy, feminine aura.

Suddenly it is 6:30, and everyone is clamoring to know when I'll be ready. Jacie helps me get dressed. At 6:45 she opens the bedroom door so everyone in the wedding party (except Peter) can see how I look.

At 7:00, exactly, Cindy and Hellie start down the path through the forest in their matching pink gowns.

My Dad has tears in his eyes as I hook my arm in his, and we follow.

I feel like a princess in a fairytale.

The faint music I hear isn't the traditional *Wedding March* by Mendelssohn nor *The Bridal Chorus* by Wagner. I don't know what it is except that it is soft and romantic and beautifully played by—by—I don't know what. A violin? Two violins? Briefly, I wonder if Hellie's favorite violinist has an album of wedding music.

When we reach the meadow, I discover it isn't prerecorded music at all. Neeve is playing the violin and Kaden is playing the panpipes in a heavenly Auravalian duet.

The grass is deep green and as thick as a carpet without even the hint of weeds anywhere.

Outlining the meadow are clusters of white, pink, and purple petunias, with daisies, delphiniums, and foxgloves growing behind them.

A fountain in the middle of the pond is bubbling over and sprinkling the surface with the pitter-pattering of water droplets.

Our trees are full of bright, living twinkle lights—the stwethil-thage, both clans of them—lined up on the branches.

Bushes of white roses stand like sentinels at the end of the path.

Across the clearing from them, two intertwined dark pink climbing roses fill a metal trellis, creating an effect that looks amazingly like a stained-glass window. Standing in front is Pastor Keating.

On his left are Peter, handsome and smiling, and the best man.

After Hellie and Cindy take their places, my father places my hand in Peter's before he goes and sits down beside my mother.

Pastor Keating performs a beautiful, simple ceremony.

When he gives Peter permission to kiss the bride, and Peter does, we are enveloped in a brilliant light that feels as if it's fusing us together, truly joining our souls into one.

After that, there is a lot of cheering and hugging and kissing.

My mother leans against my father, crying (happy tears, I hope), and he has an arm around her shoulders.

In contrast, Peter's mother positively beams, and so does his dad.

Hellie and Shiane help Neeve and Karissa lay out the buffet. I suspect they're using a little magic so the hot foods remain hot and the cold foods stay cold.

Peter's friends pitch in and give Brenlyn a hand shifting chairs around and setting up tables so people can sit down to eat.

In the background, soft violin music plays continuously, and I suspect Hellie has created a disc of her favorite pieces by David Garrett and has convinced Kaden to use it.

As people finish eating, the best man leads the first toast, basically saying Peter was a lost soul before I came into his life and he doesn't know what

# Sunshine and Shadows: Another Modern Fairytale

Peter did to deserve me. It's very flattering, and I appreciate it that there are no raunchy jokes or put downs like I've heard at other weddings.

No one seems surprised or disappointed that we serve nonalcoholic bubbly cider instead of champagne.

While Peter and I cut the cake, Hellie and Shiane cut the pies.

Since everyone, I hope, is watching Peter and me, either Hellie or Shiane, or probably the two of them working together, levitate a dozen pies and set them down in the trees. Soon each one is surrounded by stwethil-thage, whose delight deepens their already brilliant colors.

Then the tables are taken down and the chairs are rearranged to encircle the meadow. A live band arrives, probably through a portal from Auravale, and plays dance music.

When Peter and I share our first dance as husband and wife—with his arms around my waist and my head on his shoulder—I'm the happiest I've ever been in my life.

Next, I dance with my father and Peter with his mother, and then we switch, and I dance with Peter's father and Peter dances with my mother.

That done, we feel as if our obligatory partnerships have been fulfilled and we are free to wander around talking with people.

The king introduces us to his gorgeous golden-haired wife, Queen Alaina Mae. I certainly understand why Neeve said their family gatherings could sometimes be stressful. I don't think the queen looks much older than I do. It's hard to believe she's had six children, three of whom are older than Neeve.

Skyler's wife is a statuesque beauty who is almost as tall as he is, and Jerrin's wife is a pretty, round-faced woman who looks as if she has the disposition of a saint. If she is soul-bonded to Jerrin, I'm sure she needs it.

We see Peter's mother and Grandma Dark getting reacquainted.

We watch Karissa's brothers, Jeremy and Bennett, take turns dancing with Cindy, who glows with delight.

Hellie and Kaden are holding hands and telling Karissa and Neeve about their wedding plans, which they'll implement as soon as Kaden has taken his professional exams and is free of his apprenticeship.

Love is definitely in the air.

The only sad note is that Stace is not here. Haden, the royal physician, decided he wasn't strong enough. We got a nice note from him, though, telling us he hoped to be discharged from the hospital in time to welcome us home from our honeymoon.

Overhead the crescent moon and the stars shine brightly.

In the trees the stwethil-thage, high on blackberry pie, dance and twirl and hop, creating a twinkling effect that rivals the stars.

The scent of roses combines with all the other sweet aromas in the air—ladies' perfume, men's cologne, blackberry pie, wedding cake, and bubbly apple cider—making the atmosphere smell good enough to eat.

As the evening winds down, we start saying our goodbyes.

According to tradition, people pepper us with rice when we start back towards the house. As soon as we're out of sight, I open a portal to Peter's duplex where we'll spend our wedding night.

Tomorrow we fly west, first to San Francisco for a couple of days and then on to Hawaii.

Peter and I, together forever, just like we're supposed to be.

Connie A. Walker has been an insatiable reader and a compulsive writer since childhood. She is the author of the prize-winning plays *The Light Still Burns* and *Nearly a Woman,* as well as the prize-winning children's book *Timmy and the K'nick K'nocker Ring.*

Her novels include the Wolkarean Inscription Trilogy (*The Spire of Kylet, The Eyes of Landor, Triumph at Serpent's Head*), the Wolkarean Enigma Trilogy (*Revelation of Riddles, Sorcerers in Shokareen, Temple of Rulianthabah*), and the Modern Fairytale Series (*Echoes, Dark in the Forest, and Sunshine and Shadows*).

Ms. Walker was born in Idaho, attended elementary school in Kansas, and graduated high school in Alaska. She has a B.A. in theatre/playwriting from Brigham Young University, plus a B.S. in psychology and a Master's degree in social work from the University of Utah.

She has worked as a graphic artist, a technical writer, a foster care caseworker, a psychotherapist, and a mental health program manager.

www.ingramcontent.com/pod-product-compliance
Lightning Source LLC
Chambersburg PA
CBHW070539260626
47161CB00002B/448